A tough-but-tender-hearted man

Bounty hunter Chad Delaney is always on the move, for heartless women have turned him into a hard man with no use for emotional ties. But then he rides into the life of single mother Sarah Temple, and an unexpected prick of conscience leads him to take the side of a fiercely independent woman and her little boy. And suddenly, the thought of moving on is no longer his burning passion.

A proud and beautiful woman

The last thing Sarah wants from this rugged drifter, or from any man, is his help. But while his wild arrogance raises a passionate fury in her blood, she sees a different man deep within him: one who might learn to trust again—and to love for a lifetime. Can she summon the power to gentle this rough-riding renegade, and give herself over to the splendor of heaven in his arms?

Avon Romantic Treasures by
Connie Mason

TO LOVE A STRANGER

If You've Enjoyed This Book,
Be Sure to Read These Other
AVON ROMANTIC TREASURES

THE LAST HELLION *by Loretta Chase*
PERFECT IN MY SIGHT *by Tanya Anne Crosby*
SLEEPING BEAUTY *by Judith Ivory*
TO CATCH AN HEIRESS *by Julia Quinn*
WHEN DREAMS COME TRUE *by Cathy Maxwell*

Coming Soon

A RAKE'S VOW *by Stephanie Laurens*

CONNIE MASON

TO TAME RENEGADE

An Avon Romantic Treasure

AVON BOOKS NEW YORK

This is a work of fiction. Names, characters, places, and incidents either are the product of the author's imagination or are used fictitiously. Any resemblance to actual events, locales, organizations, or persons, living or dead, is entirely coincidental and beyond the intent of either the author or the publisher.

AVON BOOKS, INC.
1350 Avenue of the Americas
New York, New York 10019

Inside cover author photo by Jerry Mason
Published by arrangement with the author
Visit our website at **http://www.AvonBooks.com**
Library of Congress Catalog Card Number: 98-92454
ISBN: 0-380-79341-5

First Avon Books Printing: September 1998

AVON TRADEMARK REG. U.S. PAT. OFF. AND IN OTHER COUNTRIES, MARCA REGISTRADA, HECHO EN U.S.A.

Printed in the U.S.A.

WCD 10 9 8 7 6 5 4 3 2 1

Prologue

Dry Gulch, Montana
1880

"Don't go!" Pierce pleaded as Chad packed his belongings into his saddlebags. "Things will look better tomorrow."

Chad gave a bitter laugh. "How can you say that after what we just witnessed? My God, Pierce! Four deaths! Hal deserved what he got but old man Doolittle didn't."

"Ed Doolittle was a sick old man who hadn't long to live. You can't blame yourself for the chain of events that led to his death. I'm more to blame than anyone."

Chad continued as if Pierce hadn't spoken. "I know Cora Lee was a liar and completely without morals or conscience, but I understand that she was duped and intimidated by her brother. She can't be held solely responsible for her actions in this mess. God knows she shouldn't have died in childbirth. And the child was innocent in all this."

"Chad, listen to me. All that aside, Ryan needs you here on the ranch."

"He can manage without me. Don't you see? I have to get away from Dry Gulch, away from the tragedy. I never wanted to marry. I only did it to save your skin. And look what came of it. My life is a shambles. I can't even trust myself anymore. Don't try to stop me, Pierce. Neither you nor Ryan would like living with me if I stayed here."

"When will you come back?"

Chad glanced off into the distance, his expression hard and determined, his eyes bleak. "I don't know."

Chapter 1

Carbon, Wyoming
1882

"Yer mama's a whore and yer a bastard!" A group of ragtag boys shot out into the dusty street ahead of Chad, their cruel words aimed at the small boy they were chasing.

Chad Delaney had lost count of the number of towns like Carbon he'd passed through during the past two years. You've seen one, you've seen them all. The one distinction between Carbon and any other Wyoming town was that Carbon was the coal production center on the Union Pacific Railroad line. Chad reined his spirited black stallion down the rutted road, noting the vast number of saloons on the main drag. A general store, bank, barber shop, feed store, hardware store, and dressmaker's shop stretched along either side of the street, interspersed with saloons and dance halls.

Clusters of houses were scattered in haphazard fashion down the side streets, with a church rising against the horizon. On the other side of the tracks running through the north edge of town, Chad saw rows of ramshackle shanties that he assumed housed the coal miners and their families. Coal dust permeated the air and rested upon the buildings and houses like a dirty blanket. It collected in Chad's eyes and he dashed it away.

"Yer mama's a whore! Yer mama's a whore!"

Chad was almost upon the boys now. They had caught up with the hapless lad they were chasing and brought him to the dusty ground. Chad watched dispassionately as the larger boys began pummeling him with their fists.

"Where's yer pa? Why ain't ya got no last name?"

The boys were getting vicious now and Chad could no longer ignore them. The little fellow taking the beating hadn't uttered a cry and Chad was impressed with his valiant but futile effort to defend himself. The mother's sins weren't the child's fault, Chad thought. Chad may have grown callous, and lost the spark of compassion he'd once possessed in abundance, but he wasn't completely heartless when it came to children.

Bringing his horse to a halt, Chad leaped from the saddle and one by one began to pull boys off the small lad.

"What do ya think yer doin', mister?" one of the bigger boys asked. "This ain't none of yer business."

"It is now," Chad said, facing the assortment of boys squarely. "Go on home where you belong. You ought to be ashamed of yourselves, picking on someone too young to defend himself."

"He's a bastard. He don't even know who his pa is," the bigger boy said defensively. "His ma's a whore."

"Go on! Get!" Chad said, making as if to reach for his guns.

The outspoken boy's eyes widened in fear as he glimpsed the pair of walnut-handled single-action Colt .45 Peacemakers riding low on Chad's hips. Combined with Chad's forbidding expression, the guns were enough to frighten most grown men.

"Come on," the boy shouted, motioning to his friends, "I ain't tangling with no gunman."

One corner of Chad's generous mouth angled up into a crooked grin as he watched the boys skedaddle away. Then he turned his attention to the lad sitting on the ground, who appeared dazed and somewhat bruised from the beating he had received. Chad squatted down beside him and lifted him to his feet.

"Are you all right, son?"

Huge blue eyes shiny with tears stared back at Chad. "I'm okay, mister." He wiped the moisture from his cheeks with a grubby fist, the gesture belying his words. "Most times I run faster than they do."

"Has this happened before?"

The boy nodded solemnly. "It's okay, mister, I'm used to it."

Chad studied the bruises on the boy's face and arms, deciding they weren't as bad as they looked. He'd received worse just scrapping with his brothers. He, Pierce, and Ryan had gotten into numerous scrapes during their youth, and their reputation as hellraisers was well earned. But all that was behind him now. His life had taken a turn he hadn't expected.

"How old are you, son?"

"Five."

Chad stifled a smile. "That old, are you? What's your name?"

"Abner."

"Come on, Abner, I'll take you home."

Abner balked, giving his head a vigorous shake. "Mama said I wasn't to go off with strangers."

At least his mother did one thing right, Chad thought, wondering who cared for the boy while his mother plied her trade as a whore. He held out his hand. "I'm Chad Delaney. Now we're no longer strangers."

Abner stared at Chad's large hand, and after giving it considerable thought placed his smaller one in it. As Chad's hand closed around Abner's tiny one, he felt a twinge in the vicinity of his heart. Chad didn't know much about small children, had never been around them, in fact, but this brave little boy made him feel things he thought he'd lost that tragic day two years ago when he'd watched an innocent babe die.

"Where do you live, Abner?"

Abner pointed toward the rows of shanties squatting at the edge of town. Whores must not earn much in this town if that's the best Abner's mother could afford, Chad thought disparagingly as he eyed the rundown shanties critically.

Chad lifted Abner onto his horse and climbed up behind him. He felt the boy stiffen and guessed at the cause of his fear. "Do you like to ride?" Chad asked conversationally as he aimed his horse toward the poor section of town.

"This is the first time I've been on a horse," Abner said in a shaky voice. "He's awfully big, mister. What's his name?"

Chad patted the big gray gelding, his favorite of

all the horses bred and raised on the Delaney ranch. "I call him Flint."

"I never saw you before. What are you doing in town?"

"I'm a bounty hunter," Chad explained. Abner gave him a puzzled look. "Do you know what that is?"

"No. Tell me."

Chad laughed. "You sure are inquisitive. It means I hunt bad men for money."

"What do you do with them when you catch them?"

"Take them to jail."

By the time Abner sorted through Chad's explanation, they had crossed the tracks into shantytown.

"Which house is yours?" Chad asked. All the shacks looked alike to him. All were in desperate need of fresh paint and overdue repair.

"Put me down here and I'll walk the rest of the way," Abner said. "If I sneak into the house and clean up before Mama sees me, maybe she won't find out what happened. She worries about me."

"I'll bet," Chad said with a hint of sarcasm. The boy's mother was probably sleeping after a hard night of entertaining men, letting her child fend for himself. He could feel anger building up inside him on Abner's behalf. From what he knew of women, they were greedy, wanton creatures and he wanted nothing to do with them. His own father hadn't been worth a damn after his mother ran off.

"Point out your house, son. I think I'll have a word with your mother about taking better care of you."

Suddenly a woman came flying out of one of the shanties, calling Abner's name.

"Mama!" Abner tried to slide from Flint's back but Chad held him securely in the saddle.

Seeing her son restrained by a stranger brought the woman rushing toward Chad like a virago, ready to snatch her son from the devil on horseback. Her black hair swirled behind her like a dark cloud and her face was like a thundercloud.

"Put my son down, you—you child molester! Look at him! What have you done to him?" She reached for Abner, tearing him from Chad's grasp and hugging him to her breast.

"Aw, Mama, I'm all right," Abner said, shying away from his mother's overprotective arms. "Put me down."

Sarah Temple reluctantly set Abner down on the ground, but she clutched his hand tightly, refusing to let him run off as she glared up at Chad.

"I'm Sarah Temple, Abner's mother. Who are you? What are you doing with my son?"

Chad shoved his hat to the back of his head and returned Sarah's glare. He couldn't recall seeing eyes that particular shade of violet before. Like huge pansies. Sarah Temple was a shapely little thing with the face of an angel. Why would a beautiful woman like that choose such a degrading occupation?

"The name's Chad Delaney. I pulled Abner out from beneath a pile of older boys. I'm afraid they were getting the best of him." His face hardened. "You should take better care of him."

Red dots of rage exploded behind Sarah's eyes. "How dare you criticize me!" She eyed his guns, her disdain evident. "I rarely take advice from a gunslinger."

"Mr. Delaney is a bounty hunter, Mama," Abner said in a rush. "He gets money for catching bad men."

"Why don't you go into the house and clean up, honey," Sarah said to Abner. "I'll be there in a few minutes." She eyed his bruises with misgiving. "Are you sure you're not hurt?"

"He's fine, Mrs. Temple," Chad assured her. "I chased the boys off before they could do him real harm."

"Thank you," Sarah said stiffly as she watched Abner run off. "And it's Miss Temple. I'm not married."

It wasn't necessary for Sarah to enlighten Chad concerning her single state but she didn't want him to have any misconceptions about her. She'd never tried to hide from the truth and never would. Carbon's respectable citizens had been quick to condemn her for bearing a child without benefit of marriage. They had labeled her a whore though she'd done nothing to earn the name. Even her own parents considered her a fallen woman. They had listened to her explanation, called her a liar, and promptly disowned her.

Chad gave Sarah a hard look. "Abner's a fine boy. You really should take better care of him. A woman of your—er—calling must know how the townspeople feel and take measures to protect innocents like Abner from their vicious gossip and cruel acts."

Sarah bristled defensively. Chad Delaney was a stranger in town yet he had judged her on rumors alone. "You men are all alike. You're self-indulgent, conscienceless creatures who take what they want and to hell with the consequences." Unfortunately Sarah was all too aware of the consequences. Abner was the result of a domineering man's lust and she wasn't going to let her child suffer because of it.

"You have a harsh opinion of men," Chad taunted. "Experience has taught me it's women who can't be trusted."

"Experience taught me just the opposite. What right have you to jump to conclusions?" Sarah blasted. "You shouldn't believe everything you hear. As for Abner, have you ever tried to keep tabs on an active five-year-old?"

"Does the boy know what you do for a living?" Chad asked harshly.

A brief flare of anger lit the centers of Sarah's violet eyes. "He most certainly does. He often helps me empty the tubs."

Her words utterly baffled Chad. What had tubs to do with anything? "I beg your pardon."

"I take in laundry for a living. Not a glamorous occupation but at least it's an honest one."

Chad gave a shout of laughter. "Take in laundry? You? Now I've heard everything. Those boys hounding your son referred to another occupation, one much less respectable."

A flush of bright red crawled up Sarah's neck. "Do you always believe everything you hear, Mr. Delaney? Children aren't terribly reliable sources of information. Thank you for helping Abner." Whirling on her heel, she stomped away.

Chad watched her through narrowed lids, admiring the slender curve of her back and the way her black hair tumbled around her shoulders in a mass of springy curls. The frayed hem of her skirt swished enticingly about shapely ankles and vaguely Chad wondered if her legs were as enticing as the rest of her. He reckoned he wasn't the only man to wonder, nor would he be the last.

Chad saw her disappear behind her shanty and suddenly realized there was much more he wanted to say to the woman. Abner's sad plight had made a small crack in the wall Chad had erected around his heart, and he wanted to make sure Sarah Temple knew that her son was being mistreated by other children. Most mothers would do everything in their power to keep their children safe.

Chad dismounted and prepared to follow Sarah, cursing Freddie Jackson, the outlaw who had brought him to Carbon. Since leaving Dry Gulch he'd not used a cent of the profit from the Delaney ranch. He hadn't earned it and refused to accept it. Instead, he'd earned his keep by collecting bounties on outlaws. Currently he was tracking a man named Freddie Jackson, a notorious bank robber wanted by the law. The reward for his capture was a hefty one.

Jackson was an elusive bastard. Chad had been ready to give up on the man when he learned that Jackson hailed from Carbon, Wyoming, and was reported to have relatives in town. Since Chad was in the vicinity, he'd decided to look over the town and question Jackson's relatives. He hated to give up on the outlaw. He hadn't counted on encountering a small lad named Abner to distract him from his job and wondered what it was about him that inspired Chad's protective instincts.

Chad caught up with Sarah in her backyard. He stopped short when he saw a tub filled with steaming water, piles of dirty clothes, and clotheslines stretched across the backyard. His mouth fell open as he watched Sarah stir soft lye soap into the washtub filled with boiling water.

"Good God, she wasn't lying," he muttered to himself. Or was she? Nothing made sense. He'd never known a woman who didn't stretch the truth when it suited her.

Sarah heard Chad behind her and spun around to face him. "What are you doing here? Have you brought your laundry for me?"

"You really do take in laundry."

She gave an inelegant snort and held out her hands for his inspection. "Look at my hands and judge for yourself."

Chad stared at Sarah's hands. They were red, raw, and roughened. Certainly not the hands of a whore. He noticed other things, too. Like her scrupulously clean but neatly mended dress. And her shoes. They were scuffed and worn beyond repair. He couldn't see the soles but he'd bet his last dollar he'd find holes in them. What he'd observed just didn't jibe with his perception of a whore. She had freely admitted to being unmarried. She didn't even try to hide her sinful past by claiming to be a widow as some women might have done.

Suddenly, seeming embarrassed by her red, chapped hands, Sarah pulled them away and hid them in the folds of her skirt. "I don't have time to stand around talking, Mr. Delaney. There's laundry to be done and little time in which to do it."

Turning abruptly, she marched to the firepit and lifted a heavy kettle from the tripod. Chad watched a moment as she struggled with the heavy kettle, then sprang to her aid.

"Here, let me take that," he said, grasping the handle of the kettle.

"I don't need your help. I've managed by myself quite adequately these past five years and will continue to do so long after you ride out of town."

Sarah had no idea why she declined Chad's help. Perhaps it was because she recognized something dangerous in the handsome man. She knew nothing about him. He looked like a gunslinger, and for all she knew he was of the same ilk as Freddie Jackson, a man she loathed above all others. There was a hardness about Chad's strong features that didn't bode well for his enemies. Rigid, unpredictable, dangerous. Intuition told Sarah that the calm readiness of his body was more lethal than the weapons he wore.

He was tall and wide-shouldered, with a lean, dark face shadowed by the slant of his dusty, flat-crowned hat. His buckskin trousers and jacket were stained with sweat and trail dust, and permanent squint lines fanned out from the corners of his hazel eyes, giving mute testimony to his vigorous outdoor life. There was a raw, uncompromising strength about him, but the hank of dark brown hair that fell across his forehead softened his appearance.

"Most women would welcome help," Chad said, trying again to wrest the kettle from her hands.

"I'm not most women. Let go and leave me alone."

Chad had about all he could take from Sarah Temple. She was obstinate and unappreciative. He didn't know why he was hanging around, offering to help when his help was spurned. Hadn't he learned his lesson? Helping people could lead to tragic complications. He was living proof of that.

Disgusted, Chad let go of the kettle and spun on his heel, completely unaware of Sarah's plight as he walked away. Unprepared for his abrupt release, Sarah tripped over her skirts and stumbled forward. The kettle flew from her hands. Momentum carried her toward the tub of steaming water.

Sarah's first instinct was to fling out her arms to brace herself. Unfortunately there was nothing to stop her fall except the vat of scalding water. She let out a piercing scream as her arms plunged into the water.

Chad heard the scream and automatically went for his guns, turning into a low crouch. What he saw made his hair stand up on edge. Sarah was on her knees beside the washtub, cradling her arms against her. She was deathly pale, her face contorted in pain. Slapping his gun back into his holster, Chad raced to her side, appalled to think that he was to blame for Sarah's injuries.

Chad's expression turned grim when he saw how badly she had been scalded. The skin on her hands and arms was red, raw, and already blistering. Chad scooped her up into his arms, noting that she was barely conscious. She needed a doctor, and quickly.

Just then Abner came bouncing out of the house. He saw his mother in Chad's arms and flew at him. "What happened to Mama? What did you do to her?"

"Your mother fell into the tub of hot water, Abner. She needs a doctor. Is there one in town?"

Abner thought a moment then gave his head a vigorous nod. "There's Doctor Clayter. He keeps an office above the One-Eyed Jack saloon. Mama took me there once when I broke my arm."

"Do you think you can find him, Abner? I don't want to leave your mama alone."

Chad knew he was placing a big responsibility on the boy but felt he had no choice. The responsibility would be even greater if he left the child alone with his injured mother.

"I'll bring him back, mister," Abner promised as he scampered off.

"Tell him your mother's been scalded," Chad called after the boy. "And tell him to hurry."

Chad heard Sarah moan and glanced down at her. Her eyes looked like huge violet smudges in her pale face and her full lips had thinned into a grimace of pain.

"Abner has gone for the doctor," Chad said, unable to tell whether or not she understood. Her soft moans continued as he carried her into the house. He found himself in the kitchen and paused a moment to get his bearings.

"No . . . doctor," Sarah gasped. "Can't . . . pay him."

"Don't worry about paying the doctor," Chad said. "The accident was my fault, I'll take care of it. Where's the bedroom?"

"There," Sarah said, trying to indicate a direction with one of her injured hands. It was a futile attempt; her hand fell away uselessly.

"I'll find it," Chad said, moving from the kitchen to the tiny parlor. He found the bedroom immediately and carefully placed Sarah on the bed. Then he stared down at her, feeling helpless.

"You don't have to . . . stick around," Sarah said. She was in such excruciating pain she could barely think beyond the fact that there was a strange man in her bedroom, and that she didn't trust men any farther than she could throw them.

"I may be a callous bastard but I'm not inhuman," Chad said through gritted teeth. "I'll wait around until the doctor arrives. Is there anything I can do for you?"

Sarah started to shake her head no but changed her mind. "There's some lard on a shelf in the kitchen. I've always found it helpful in treating burns."

Chad left wordlessly and returned a few minutes later with a container of lard. "I'll do it," he said when Sarah failed in her attempt to scoop lard from the container.

Chad dug out a large dollop and smeared it over both of Sarah's hands and arms. When he finished, he placed her arms gently down on the bed beside her, not surprised that the quilt beneath her was threadbare and faded.

Faded bedclothing, threadbare dresses, taking in wash; he found the situation confusing. Most whores he knew weren't rich but they lived better than this, unless they were old and ugly. And Sarah Temple was neither old nor ugly. She was young and beautiful and could easily support herself and her son on her earnings.

"I'll . . . be fine now," Sarah said weakly.

Chad saw a vein pulse at her temple and wondered just how fine she really was. Her eyes were closed and her lips had turned white. A sudden impulse made him push a wayward lock of hair from her forehead. His hand fell away when her eyes flew open.

"What are you doing?" She looked scared and he frowned. He'd done nothing to frighten her.

"Relax, I don't attack helpless women. The doctor will be here in a few minutes." When Sarah continued to look unconvinced, he said, "Look, I don't want to be here any more than you want me here. I'll be out of your hair just as soon as the doctor arrives and I know you'll be all right. All this is partly my fault, you know."

Sarah started to reply but a ruckus at the door forestalled her.

"I'm back," Abner called as he slammed the door behind him. "I did it! I brought the doctor for Mama."

Moments later a short, portly man with thinning gray hair bustled into the bedroom. "What seems to be the trouble? This little scamp pulled me away in the middle of a consultation." He saw Sarah stretched out on the bed and frowned. "Reckon the boy knew what he was talking about. What happened, Sarah?"

"An accident," Chad said, speaking for Sarah. "Miss Temple fell into a tub of scalding water. You'd better have a look at her."

Doctor Clayter eyed Chad curiously. "Who are you?"

"The name's Chad Delaney. I happened to see a group of boys beating up on Abner as I rode through town and rescued him. Can't we talk about this later? Your patient needs tending."

"Indeed she does. Take Abner into the other room, Mr. Delaney, I'll do my best for Sarah."

"Come on, boy," Chad said, turning Abner toward the door. "Let's wait outside. I'm sure the doctor will take good care of your mother."

"Do I have to go?" Abner whined. "Are you sure Mama's gonna be all right?"

"Go on, Abner, I'll take good care of your mama," Doctor Clayter said as he opened his bag and began removing various bottles and jars.

Chad hustled the child from the room, having no idea how to entertain the worried little boy. Finally he asked, "Are you hungry, Abner?"

"I haven't eaten lunch yet. Can you cook?" he asked hopefully.

Abner's guileless question brought a smile to Chad's face, softening his stern countenance. "I'm not very good at it but maybe your mama has something already prepared."

Chad walked into the tiny kitchen, frowned at the dilapidated cookstove that looked like it had seen better days, and eyed the cupboards with misgiving. When he'd looked for the lard earlier he hadn't noticed much in the way of food. A little flour, a bit of sugar and salt, some beans, coffee, a half loaf of bread, cornmeal, three shriveled potatoes, and an onion. Then he spied a pot sitting on the back of the stove and gave a sigh of relief.

Lifting the lid, Chad was disappointed to find it filled with starch. "Shit!"

"I'm not supposed to say that word."

"Sorry," Chad muttered. "There's not much here, Abner."

Abner shrugged. "Mama was going to the store after she got paid for doing Mrs. Kilmer's laundry. I'm not very hungry, anyway."

"How about if we finish off this bread," Chad asked as he brought the bread to the table and hunted for a knife. He found one in a drawer and neatly cut the bread into thick slices. "What about butter? Do you have any?"

Abner shook his head. "Lard with a little sugar

sprinkled on top is good." Suddenly he brightened. "There's a jar of jam on the shelf."

"Then jam it is," Chad said.

They had just polished off their bread and jam when Doctor Clayter entered the kitchen. "Sarah is sleeping. I gave her a sedative. She's in quite a bit of pain."

"Can I see her?" Abner asked, sliding off his chair.

"If you're very quiet," the doctor said. "You can sit beside her, she'll know you're there."

Abner scampered off and Doctor Clayter regarded Chad with speculation. "You must be new in town. What brings you to Carbon, Mr. Delaney?"

"I'm a bounty hunter. Maybe you can help me. Ever hear of a man named Freddie Jackson?"

"Sure. Who hasn't? Use to live in these parts. That's before I settled here."

"I heard he has family in Carbon."

"He *had* family in Carbon. Unfortunately his pa died over three years ago and his ma followed six months later. His two sisters moved east with their husbands shortly after Freddie left town. Don't know the particulars about why or how he became an outlaw, though."

"Have you seen Jackson around town lately?"

"Wouldn't know him if I saw him. Forget Jackson. Let's talk about Sarah. What do you intend to do about her?"

"What in the hell are you talking about? Sarah Temple isn't my responsibility."

Clayter glared at Chad from beneath bushy brows. Chad squirmed uncomfortably beneath his piercing regard, wondering if the doctor had the ability to see into his soul. If so, Chad wondered if he saw the emptiness there, or recognized the black hole where his soul once dwelled.

"Someone's got to take responsibility," Clayter finally said. "Sarah's in bad shape. Both her arms and hands were badly scalded in the accident and she's swathed in bandages up to her shoulders. She'll be a long time healing. She and Abner will starve to death if someone doesn't assume responsibility. It will be many weeks before Sarah can work again."

Chad felt a rush of anger. He wasn't going to get roped into something that was none of his concern. He had an outlaw to catch. "Does Sarah have no one in town to help her? What about relatives? Is none of her family living?"

Clayter gave a snort of disgust. "She has parents and siblings, but you'll get no help from that quarter. They have no use for her. Well, I've got to get back to my patients. I'll be back tomorrow to check on Sarah. She may develop a fever. If that happens, give her a spoonful of the medicine I left on the nightstand. I also left laudanum for pain."

"How much do I owe you, Doctor?"

"Can you pay? I know Sarah can't."

Chad's mouth thinned. "I can pay."

"Very well. Two dollars should cover my services."

Chad dug in his vest pocket, found two silver dollars, and handed them to the doctor.

"Thank you. I'll see you tomorrow, Mr. Delaney."

"Not if I can help it," Chad muttered. "How long will Sarah sleep?"

"Until morning, I should think. If she awakens

during the night, give her another dose of laudanum."

Chad gave a slow shake of his head. "It won't be me feeding your patient laudanum, I'll be long gone by then. Give me the name of her parents."

"Reverend and Mrs. Temple, for all the good it will do you."

Chapter 2

Chad stood at the foot of the bed, watching Sarah sleep. She looked uncomfortable lying there fully dressed and he wondered if he should do something about it. Fearing his clumsy fumbling would do more harm than good, he decided not to attempt to remove her dress and underthings. Her relatives could do that when they arrived.

His gaze settled on Sarah's face, noting her pallor and the dark smudges beneath her eyes. She looked exhausted and he remembered the piles of dirty clothes outside, waiting to be laundered. Did she do that every day?

Intrigued, Chad couldn't turn his gaze away from the pulse beating at the base of her throat. A very white throat, he noted. Her skin was smooth and flawless, like fragile porcelain. His gaze followed the long line of her throat to where her full breasts rose and fell beneath the bodice of her patched dress. Sarah Temple was a feast for the eyes, but Chad had neither the time nor the inclination to enjoy the banquet. Women were dangerous. A woman had come close to ruining his brother's life; but even before that Chad's disillusionment with women had begun with his own mother.

"Mama is sleeping a long time, mister."

Abner came up behind Chad, his big blue eyes wide with concern. "When is she gonna wake up?"

"Doc Clayter gave her something to make her sleep. Let's hope she doesn't wake up until morning, 'cause when she does, she's going to be in a lot of pain. She's not going to be able to use her hands or arms for a long time."

Big tears rolled down Abner's cheeks and he dashed them away. "What are me and Mama gonna do?"

"Don't worry. I'll find someone to help you," Chad promised. "Doc Clayter said your grandparents live in town. I'm going to bring them here to take care of you and your mother."

Abner gave him an incredulous look. "I didn't know I had any grandparents. I don't have a papa, either."

Chad didn't have time to argue the point, or to wonder why Sarah chose not to tell her son about his grandparents. The sooner he found someone to care for Sarah and Abner, the sooner he could get back to the business of finding Freddie Jackson.

"I have a few errands to run, Abner. Will you be all right here with your mother while I'm gone?"

"You're coming back, aren't you, mister?" Abner's fear was palpable and the wall around Chad's heart developed another crack.

"I'll be back." Not to stay, but he didn't tell the child that. "Why don't you call me Chad? All my friends do."

Abner beamed. "Sure, Chad, I can take care of

Mama while you're gone. Can we eat supper when you come back? I'm hungry."

Chad cursed beneath his breath. Abner was a growing boy and needed nourishing food. Maybe Sarah's parents could remedy that, too.

"I'll see what I can do about supper, son. I hope to have all your problems solved by the time I return."

Chad left the house, his face taut with determination. A niggling suspicion prickled the back of his neck at the thought that Sarah had never mentioned her parents to Abner. He was so engrossed with his thoughts he nearly collided with a woman coming up the path to the house. She gazed at Chad a moment, then sneered in derision.

"I knew Sarah Temple would revert back to her old ways," she said contemptuously. "Once a whore, always a whore. The least she could do is keep her activities confined to the nighttime. She sets a poor example for that bastard son of hers."

Chad had no idea who this obnoxious woman was but he didn't like her. "Who are you?"

"I'm Mrs. Kilmer. I've come for my laundry. I told Sarah I wanted it by this afternoon."

Chad thought of the dirty clothes littering the backyard and couldn't help smiling. "Sarah won't be doing your laundry any time soon, Mrs. Kilmer. I suggest you take it home and do it yourself. You'll find it in the backyard."

Mrs. Kilmer's mouth fell open. "Well, I never! I don't know who you are, young man, but one word from me and Sarah Temple will never get work in this town again." Her eyes narrowed. "Ah, I understand now. Sarah has another source of income, one more lucrative. As I said before, once a whore, always a whore."

Chad's hands curled into fists at his sides. He didn't have time for this. Getting involved in someone's life was the last thing he wanted. He'd left home because he wanted no responsibilities to tie him down. He was still running hard to escape memories that had scarred his soul.

"I suggest you gather your soiled laundry and take your vile tongue elsewhere, lady. I'm not in a good mood right now and listening to your insults is making it worse."

Mrs. Kilmer took one look at Chad and backed away. Edging around him, she literally flew around the corner of the house to the backyard. Chad didn't wait around to see if the woman gathered her laundry as he mounted Flint and reined him toward the church steeple across the tracks.

Chad found the clapboard parsonage nestled beside the church. The sign stuck in the front lawn of the church said it was the United Methodist Church of Carbon, and that Hezekiah Temple was the preacher. Chad tied Flint to the hitching post and marched up to the parsonage. He didn't know why he should be the one to inform the Temples of their daughter's accident and beg for help, but the sooner he did it the sooner he could be on his way.

Raising his fist, he pounded on the door, composing words in his head while he waited for someone to answer. A few minutes later the door opened, revealing a gaunt, stern-faced man dressed in unrelenting black. Permanent frown lines marred his brow and his thin, flattened lips had probably never known a smile. He was younger than Chad had imagined; his dark hair was gray at the temples and swept back from his high forehead.

"Do you have business with me?" the preacher asked.

"Are you Hezekiah Temple?"

"I am."

"I've come about your daughter."

Hezekiah raised his eyebrows in askance. "What about Ruth? I saw her just last week and she and the children were fine."

"I'm talking about your other daughter."

Hezekiah's lips flattened even more, if that was possible. "I have only one daughter. Her name is Ruth. She's married to a good man. They have two children. Since we have nothing more to discuss, I bid you good day." He started to close the door.

"Wait!" Chad's superior strength won out as he held the door open. "You have another daughter. Her name is Sarah."

"Who is it, dear?" A short, full-bodied woman peeked out at Chad from behind her tall husband.

"Someone asking about Sarah. I told him we had no daughter named Sarah. Perhaps he'd like to hear it from you, Hazel."

The woman's gaze shifted to the floor. "My husband is correct. We have only one daughter and one son." She glanced up at her husband for approval and received it.

What was wrong with these people? Chad wondered. "I know you have a daughter named Sarah. She lives nearby and takes in laundry for a living. She has a son named Abner. I'm here on her behalf. She's had an accident and needs your help."

Hezekiah seemed not at all moved by the news

of his daughter's plight. "Who are you?"

"The name's Chad Delaney. You don't know me but I know Sarah and Abner."

"Are you one of Sarah's . . . customers?" Hazel asked timidly.

Chad grit his teeth in frustration. Did these people have no hearts? "You're a man of God, Reverend. Have you no compassion? Sarah fell into a tub of boiling water and suffered serious burns to her arms and hands. She won't be able to take care of herself and Abner for some time. You're her parents, I'm appealing to you for help."

"Sarah sinned against God's laws," Hezekiah intoned in his best fire and brimstone voice. "She committed fornication then had the gall to lie about it. I'm a man of God, Mr. Delaney, I do not condone fornication. Sarah is an embarrassment to her family and to the town of Carbon. We disowned her years ago."

"What about your grandson, did you disown him, too?" Chad noted that Hazel said nothing, meekly deferring to her husband. Did the woman have no mind of her own?

"The result of Sarah's sins is her responsibility," Hezekiah intoned. "We want nothing to do with her or the bastard she gave birth to."

Chad felt like smashing the hypocrite in the mouth. "Whatever happened to forgiveness? Doesn't your church believe in giving someone a second chance?"

"We will speak no more of it, Mr. Delaney. Sarah made her bed, now she must lie in it. I might have relented and forgiven her for sinning, but when she lied about what she had done I knew she was beyond redemption. Some souls cannot be saved and must be surrendered to the devil. Sarah is one of those lost souls."

"You're a hypocrite and a fanatic, Reverend," Chad snarled. "I pity you. Your soul is as barren as your heart."

Chad's words gave him pause for thought. They were startling because he could have been describing himself instead of the Temples.

"Hezekiah is a good man," Hazel claimed. "None of the town's prominent citizens criticize us for disowning Sarah. Hezekiah says she should have left town."

Chad had wasted enough time with these unnatural parents. They were clearly never going to change. Personally he thought Sarah was brave, albeit foolish, for staying in Carbon and trying to restore her reputation. Unfortunately the townspeople seemed disinclined to give her a second chance. The situation was growing desperate. Dusk was approaching and he still hadn't found anyone to assume responsibility for an injured woman and her child. This was going to take longer than he thought and he wasn't happy about it.

"I can see I'm wasting my time here," Chad said. "I'm really sorry for you. Good day, Reverend and Mrs. Temple. You don't deserve a grandson like Abner."

As he walked away, Chad heard Hazel Temple say to her husband, "Perhaps I should . . ."

"It's none of our business," Hezekiah answered as he slammed the door.

Chad had a difficult time reconciling the Sarah he knew with the Sarah described by her parents. Of course he hadn't known Sarah very long. But whores didn't take in laundry. Whores usually had food in their cupboards and wore decent clothing. Had the town never forgiven her for having a child out of wedlock, he wondered, and labeled her a whore despite the fact that she was trying to live a respectable life? Chad had no idea why he cared. He intended to light out of town as soon as he found someone to tend Sarah and her son.

It was dusk when Chad entered the ramshackle shanty where Sarah and Abner lived. He was loaded down with groceries he had purchased after leaving the parsonage. He wasn't much of a cook but he knew Abner would be hungry. Hell, he was hungry, too.

"You came back!" Abner came running to the door to meet him, his eyes shining with happiness.

"I told you I would. How's your mother?"

"She woke up once but went back to sleep. She wanted some water and I held the glass to her lips."

"You did good, boy. How would you like some bacon and beans? I bought some tinned stuff too; peaches and things."

Abner's eyes grew round. "Peaches? Really? I've never tasted them. I'll bet they're good."

"You'll find out as soon as I fire up the stove, fry some bacon, and open a few cans. Got fresh bread, too. The last loaf in the bakery."

Chad struck a light to the oil lamp sitting on the kitchen table and looked for the woodbox. He found it next to the stove. The supply was low but Chad found enough wood to start a decent fire. In no time at all he had cooked a meal of sorts and was sharing it with Abner. When he opened the tin of peaches, he watched in amazement as the lad devoured the entire contents.

"I'll do the dishes," Abner offered as Chad began to clear the table. "Mama does them on the back porch. There's a tub out there. You can pour the water in the tub for me and I'll do the rest."

"It's a deal," Chad said. "I'll look in on your mama while you're doing the dishes."

The bedroom was dark when Chad entered. He saw a lamp on the nightstand and lit it, turning it down low. Sarah was still sleeping but she looked uncomfortable with her skirts twisted around her legs. Chad knew most women wore corsets and hers had to be digging into her ribs by now. Cursing her parents for being such callous bastards, Chad realized it was up to him to make her comfortable.

Determination tautened his jaw as he strode to the dresser and rummaged in the drawers for a nightgown. He found a white shapeless garment and pulled it out, giving it a shake to free it of wrinkles. Plain, high-necked, and worn thin from countless washings, it didn't look like a nightgown a whore would wear. He carried it to the bed, wondering how he was going to get Sarah into it without hurting her.

Fortunately her dress buttoned down the front. He made short work of the buttons then slid his arm beneath her to lift her so he could work her bodice down her shoulders. Sarah moaned but didn't awaken.

Damn, he felt like a blasted nursemaid! He had to find someone . . . anyone! to take over this burdensome task. Tomorrow he was out of here for sure. Chad still hadn't spoken with Sarah's brother or sister. Surely one of them would be willing to help their injured sister. Regrettably it would have to wait until morning.

Carefully Chad worked Sarah's dress down her shoulders and over her injured arms. Then he removed his arm from beneath her and concentrated on pulling the dress down her hips and legs. That wasn't too difficult, he thought as he removed her shoes and reached beneath her petticoat to where her stockings were fastened with ribbons above her knees. His fingers skimmed along smooth white flesh and abruptly he withdrew his hand as if burned. He gave a shaky laugh, chiding himself for being so skittish. Sarah was only a woman and he'd seen and felt more than his share of women's legs . . . and everything else.

He quickly stripped off her stockings and released the tape on her petticoat, tossing it atop the dress on the floor. Trying to keep his gaze from settling on her full breasts, he wondered how he was going to undo her corset strings since they laced down her back. He was still pondering the situation when Sarah opened her eyes and stared at him.

"What are you doing? Why are you still here?"

"I'm still here because your parents refused to help or acknowledge you," Chad said in a low growl. He didn't mean to sound surly but his patience, what little he possessed, was hanging by a slim thread. "What I'm doing is trying to get you out of your clothes and into a nightgown."

She glanced down at her nearly nude body and gave a cry of dismay. "You can't . . . you shouldn't . . ."

"There's no one else," Chad said grimly. "Turn

on your side so I can unlace your corset. You're much too thin to wear one of these contraptions, anyway. My sister-in-law Zoey wears denim trousers and plaid shirts. Makes sense to me. In my opinion nothing is worse than lacing yourself so tight you can't breathe. Don't argue, just turn and let me do the rest."

Sarah didn't have the energy to argue. She hurt like the very dickens and was still groggy from the laudanum the doctor gave her. When Chad nudged her on her side, she did not resist. She even sighed in relief when he used his knife to cut the strings then slid her corset away from her body.

"Now the chemise," Chad said as he raised the hem on the brief garment that saved her from total nudity.

"No, please."

Chad ignored her as he eased the chemise up over her head. He reached for her nightgown, pausing a brief, unintentional moment to stare at her nude body. Her pale flesh gleamed silver and gold in the lamplight and his breath caught in his throat. She was exquisitely made; small, delicate, and all female. Generous by any standards, her full breasts were tipped with delicate pink nipples. Her waist could easily be spanned by both his hands and her gently curved hips merged into a pair of shapely legs. His eyes lingered a moment too long on the dark triangle at the juncture of her thighs. He had to forcibly restrain himself from running his fingers through the lush thatch of thick dark hair covering her womanhood.

Realizing where his thoughts were taking him, Chad pulled the nightgown over Sarah's head and carefully eased her arms into the sleeves. It wasn't until the nightgown was pulled down to her feet that he was able to breath freely again.

"Are you hungry?" he asked as he settled Sarah beneath the blanket. "There's some bacon and beans and . . ."

Sarah nearly gagged at the thought of beans and bacon. "Nothing, thank you. What about Abner? Has he eaten?" Suddenly she recalled the bareness of her cupboards. "I don't have any bacon. I'm not even sure there's beans."

"You have both bacon and beans now. Don't worry about Abner. His tummy is full for a change. I bought a piece of beef, someone can make soup with it tomorrow." The words "after I'm gone" were implied but not spoken aloud. "Are you in pain?"

The white lines around Sarah's mouth spoke more eloquently than words.

"Doc Clayter left a bottle of laudanum. I'll give you a another dose. Open your mouth."

He poured a spoonful of medicine and brought it to her lips. She opened dutifully, swallowed, and grimaced. "Water."

Chad obliged, then perched on the edge of the bed. "Where does Abner sleep?"

"There's a trundle. It slides beneath the bed in the daytime and pulls out at night. Why are you still here?"

"Because no one else volunteered," Chad said harshly. "Playing nursemaid isn't exactly my line of work. I've got an outlaw to catch so I reckon I'll move on tomorrow."

No response was forthcoming. Sarah had already dropped off to sleep. He reached over to douse the light and noticed that her face was flushed. He placed a hand on her forehead and felt heat against his palm. She was feverish and it made him feel angry and helpless. He'd never asked to be placed in this predicament, never bargained for a chore for which he had no training. It was just like a woman to trap him into a situation beyond his control. He was glad his brothers couldn't see him now. They'd tease him unmercifully.

Well, it wasn't a damn bit funny.

"Is Mama sleeping again?" Abner asked as he walked into the room. He stifled a yawn with the back of his hand.

"Yes, it's the best thing for her. Are you tired?"

"A little. Where are you going to sleep?"

"Let's get you settled first." He pulled the trundle from beneath the bed and smoothed the covers in place. He was about to tell Abner to climb in when he heard Sarah moan. "Tell you what. You can sleep on the sofa and I'll take the trundle. Your mama might wake up during the night and need something."

Abner thought about that a moment and decided it would be great fun. He'd never slept on the sofa before.

The house was quiet as Chad tugged off his tight buckskin trousers and jacket, removed his white linen shirt, then turned the lamp down low and climbed beneath the covers of the trundle. Weary to the bone, he closed his eyes and waited for sleep to claim him. He hadn't been in bed ten minutes when he heard Sarah thrashing about. When he went to check on her he found her burning with fever and shivering at the same time. She was shaking so hard the entire bed was shaking with her.

Cursing the unlucky star that brought him to Carbon, Chad found the medicine the doctor left for fever and painstakingly spooned a measure down Sarah's throat. When her shivering continued unabated, Chad sighed helplessly, shucked off his longjohns, pulled back the blanket, and slid into bed beside her. Sharing his body heat was the only way he knew to warm her. When he took her into his arms, a tiny breath slipped past her lips and she burrowed into him. His loins tightened and he could feel his body responding to the soft woman's flesh molded against him.

Chad groaned as he tried to turn his lustful thoughts to something less dangerous. It didn't work. The woman in his arms was still there, still snuggled against him, making him hard as stone, and there wasn't a damn thing he could do about it. Except leave. And he'd do that as soon as he found someone to care for Sarah and her boy. Chad wanted no responsibilities, no commitments, no entanglements. He had left Dry Gulch and a prosperous ranch to escape obligations he couldn't handle.

During the night Sarah's fever broke and Chad left her bed. He knew she wouldn't appreciate waking up and finding him beside her, no matter what his excuse. He still hadn't decided whether Sarah Temple was a laundress or a whore and he told himself he didn't care. All he wanted was out of here.

Chad was up and dressed when Sarah awoke. She appeared startled to find him in her bedroom. "I thought you'd be gone by now."

"I'm fixing to leave soon. How do you feel?"

"Better. I just need to get these bandages off."

"That won't be for a while. Are you hungry? I'll fix something for you and the boy to eat before I leave."

Sarah refused to look at him, recalling how he had stripped her bare last night before slipping her nightgown over her head. "There's very little food in the house. I was going to the store as soon as Mrs. Kilmer paid me for doing her laundry. The laundry! I have to get up and finish it."

She tried unsuccessfully to get out of bed, crying out in pain when she put pressure on her arms. She was utterly helpless and she didn't like the feeling. She had depended on herself too many years to let this injury stop her from taking care of herself and Abner.

"You won't be doing anyone's laundry for a long time," Chad said. "Mrs. Kilmer took her dirty clothes back home yesterday and all I can say is good riddance. What a vicious woman."

Sarah groaned in dismay. "That woman is my bread and butter. I hope you didn't offend her."

Chad shrugged, recalling the heated exchange between him and Mrs. Kilmer. "Forget the woman. You probably don't remember that I bought groceries yesterday after I called on your parents. I know how to cook oats, would you like some?"

All vestiges of color drained from Sarah's face. "You went to see my parents? Whatever for? How did you know about them?"

"Doc Clayter told me who your parents were and where to find them."

"How dare you interfere in my life!"

"Look, lady, I could have just ridden out of town and left you and Abner to fend for yourselves but I thought your parents should know about your accident. Someone has to take care of you and the boy."

"It won't be my parents, as I'm sure you found out. They disowned me years ago."

Chad searched her face, wondering how she could speak about it so calmly. "So they told me. I never met a more self-righteous pair of fanatics in my life. What happened?"

"It's a long story. One I'm sure won't interest you since you'll be leaving soon. Goodbye, Mr. Delaney."

Ungrateful wretch, Chad thought but did not say. What would she have done had he left? "I'll be more than happy to turn this job over to someone else. I'm not any good in the sick room. I'll fix something for you and Abner to eat, then I'll be leaving for awhile." He turned toward the door.

"Wait!" Sarah said. She hated to ask Chad Delaney for anything but this matter was most pressing. "Could you please help me get out of bed before you leave? There is something I . . . need to do."

Chad started to refuse but the pained look on her face changed his mind. It suddenly occurred to him what she might need. He nodded then returned to the bed. With Sarah's help he managed to raise her without hurting her too badly.

"Anything else you need?" Chad asked with wry amusement. Color had returned to her cheeks and he suspected it was due to embarrassment.

"There's a chamberpot inside the commode," she said, refusing to look him in the eye. "Just remove it and set it on the floor beside the bed, please."

Chad did as she asked. "Do you need any help?"

Sarah shook her head. It was bad enough that a

virtual stranger had undressed her. Her bodily functions were private and she was determined they remain that way. It would be difficult but somehow she'd manage this on her own.

Abner was waiting in the kitchen for Chad to prepare breakfast. "I already washed," Abner said, showing Chad his hands. "Can we eat now?"

"As soon as I fire up the stove and cook the oatmeal. I'll bet your mama is hungry, too. Why don't you go on in and see her while I put on the coffee and cook us up a pot of oats. That ought to fill your empty tummy."

Abner skipped out of the room and Chad set to work. A half-hour later he found a tray and carried coffee, a bowl of gruel, and a slice of browned bread into the bedroom. He found Abner sitting on the bed chatting with his mother. The chamberpot was nowhere in sight so he assumed Sarah had managed on her own.

"Your breakfast is on the kitchen table, Abner. Go on in and eat while I feed your mother."

Sarah watched warily as Chad set the tray down on the bed and brought a spoonful of oats to her mouth. "You don't have to do this."

"Dammit, just shut up and eat. I'm not here because I want to be and I'd appreciate it if you didn't make this any harder for me than it already is."

Sarah opened her mouth for a scathing reply and found it filled with oatmeal. He kept her so busy chewing and swallowing she found little opportunity to say anything. Before she knew it the bowl was empty and the coffee cup drained down to the last dregs. Replete, she settled back against the pillows and sighed.

"Thank you, I guess I was hungrier than I

thought. It's been a long time since I could afford coffee."

"You should eat more. You could use some meat on your bones, you're skinny as a rail."

Red patches blossomed on Sarah's cheeks. Chad Delaney was no gentleman. No doubt he had looked his fill when he'd helped her off with her clothes last night. How in the world had something like this happened? She was as helpless as a kitten and dependent upon a strange man. A man who exuded danger, but one who possessed a tiny spark of compassion despite his rough exterior. Chad Delaney was a hard man on the outside, but Sarah suspected that deep down there was goodness in him. Dimly she wondered what had made him that way, and what it would take for him to rediscover his inherent kindness.

Chad walked into the doctor's office just as Clayter was bidding goodbye to a patient. He spotted Chad and motioned him into his examining room. "How's my patient? I planned to look in on her later."

"Sarah seems better this morning, but that's not why I'm here. I spoke with her parents yesterday and the 'good' reverend and his wife refused to acknowledge their daughter. They ignored her plight and flatly refused to help her. There has to be someone who will take care of Sarah and Abner for a couple of weeks. I understand Sarah has a brother and sister."

The doctor gave a snort of derision. "You'll find no help there."

"Nevertheless, I have to try. Tell me where to find them."

"Don't say I didn't warn you, Delaney. I'll write their addresses down for you. Ruth lives outside of town but Jacob resides in Carbon with his wife and children."

"Wish me luck, Doc. I can't stick around town much longer. I'm not cut out to be a nursemaid. Besides, I've seen the havoc women cause and don't need that kind of trouble."

"There's a world of anger inside you, Delaney," Doc said. "Just see that you don't direct it at Sarah and her boy."

Chapter 3

Chad was angry. Angrier than he'd ever been in his life and that was saying a lot. Talking to Sarah's brother had been an utter waste of time. Jacob Temple had refused to discuss his sister Sarah, or even admit he had a sister by that name. Chad got the impression that Jacob was as unbending and unforgiving as his father. He spouted scripture and claimed to be a deacon of the church. He'd said he had no sympathy for whores and wouldn't lift a hand to help one.

Chad had left before the urge to smash the sanctimonious fool in the face became too strong to repress. Now he was on his way to the home of Ruth Temple Stout, Sarah's sister. Chad had no idea what he'd do should Sarah's sister refuse to lend a hand. He cursed beneath his breath. If he didn't have bad luck he wouldn't have any luck at all. His life was going from bad to worse.

Chad arrived at the neat clapboard ranch house situated at the end of a dusty road. Everything about the ranch exuded modest prosperity. A woman came out on the porch to meet him before he could dismount. Two small children clung to her skirts. She looked like an older version of Sarah but in Chad's opinion she had none of Sarah's appeal.

"My husband isn't here. Do you have business with him?"

"I came to see you, ma'am," Chad said, doffing his hat. "You are Ruth Temple, aren't you?"

"Ruth Temple Stout," she corrected. A wary look came over her face as she slowly backed toward the door. "I don't know you. What business do you have with me?"

Chad dismounted and Ruth's alarm increased. Chad sought to ease her fear. "I mean you no harm, ma'am. I came about your sister."

"Sister? I have no sister. Perhaps you'd better leave."

Chad grit his teeth in frustration. "What about Sarah? Have you disowned her, too?"

Ruth had the grace to flush. "Sarah chose the kind of life she leads. She's an embarrassment to our family, to the entire town, if you want the truth of it. Father disowned her years ago and I'd be disloyal to the family if I acknowledged her. Why are you here? Who are you?"

"I'm Chad Delaney. I know your sister."

Ruth rolled her eyes. "I'll bet you do. Please state your business, Mr. Delaney, then kindly leave."

For all the good it would do him, Chad decided to appeal to Ruth's compassion, if she possessed any. "Your sister was injured in an accident yesterday and she needs your help. Both her arms and hands are swathed in bandages and she's unable to care for herself and Abner."

Ruth gave him an incredulous look. "And you expect me to help? I'm sorry, but you've come all this way for nothing. My reputation in this town is exemplary and I won't have it besmirched by associating with Sarah. I've risen above her sinful reputation and maintain my standing in town despite it. Good day, Mr. Delaney."

Has the whole world gone mad? Chad wondered. He'd thought his own problems were formidable but Sarah Temple's were overwhelming. Now what in the hell was he going to do? Come what may, he was going to ride out of Carbon and forget he'd ever met a woman named Sarah Temple, he told himself as he mounted and rode away.

When Chad returned, Doctor Clayter was at the house. He'd just changed Sarah's bandages and was packing up to leave. He welcomed Chad with some relief. "Ah, there you are, Delaney. Sarah said you'd left town."

Chad's expression was grim. "I'm still here but not for long. If you're ready to leave, Doctor, I'll walk you to the door."

Sarah watched Chad and the doctor leave, her thoughts in a turmoil. How had this stranger come to be so important to her in such a short time? she wondered. What would she and Abner have done without him? She felt so helpless, so utterly alone. For the first time since Abner was born she began to doubt her ability to provide for herself and her son. This accident had been the last straw in a long chain of disastrous events that had changed her young life forever.

Chad Delaney was going to leave and Sarah was relieved. The man was dangerous; he had too many secrets. There was a dark side to him. She felt real fear at the chaotic tumble of emotions he roused within her. The unleashed energy he exuded and the hidden secrets she glimpsed in the depths of those hazel eyes gave hint to his torment. He was running from something . . . or someone. Was it a woman? Sarah didn't want a bitter man like Chad around Abner. Her son was young and impressionable and was becoming too fond of the bounty hunter.

Sarah blushed every time she recalled Chad's hands on her, undressing her. She tingled all over when she remembered his gentle touch upon her body. Complicating matters was Sarah's vague memory of a hard male body holding her during the night, pressing her against solid male contours. She knew it was a dream but just the thought of Chad lying beside her made her hot and restless and she buried it deep inside her. Chad Delaney was a temptation and the good Lord knew she couldn't afford to succumb to the renegade when she'd been trying so hard to maintain an unblemished reputation in a town where everyone thought her a whore.

Chad walked Doctor Clayter to his carriage, determined to speak with him about Sarah's situation. "I spoke with Sarah's brother and sister," he said without preamble.

"I warned you, didn't I? I knew you wouldn't find any help there. I didn't open my practice in Carbon until after Sarah . . . er . . . got in the family way. I delivered her child, and she's been doing my laundry for free ever since to pay for it. Truth to tell, she paid her bill long ago but she still refuses to take money from me. I've treated Abner for various childhood diseases and once for a broken arm. Sarah can't pay with hard cash and so she continues to do my laundry."

"What do you know about Sarah besides what you've already told me?"

"Not much. Oh, there's gossip and rumors aplenty, but I don't put much store in them. From what I gather, Sarah's parents never forgave her for sinning with a man. Some say she was raped, but since the rumor was never confirmed, no one really knows and the townspeople refuse to buy it."

Chad's mouth flattened. Rage seethed through him. "Do you know the name of the man who was supposed to have raped her?"

"No, and I don't know if anyone else does, either, but I'm willing to bet that's the way it happened. Sarah is no whore, I'd stake my life on it. You find me one man who's paid for her services and I'll give you a hundred dollars, that's how sure I am."

"I'm not interested in your money," Chad said, frowning. "I can't stick around long enough to get involved in Sarah Temple's life. I make my living by bringing outlaws to justice and it's time I got on with it. Sarah and Abner are complications I don't need. I can't afford entanglements at this time in my life."

"You're going to leave Sarah and Abner?" Clayter asked, his voice ripe with accusation. "I understand you were responsible for Sarah's injury."

Chad's jaw hardened. "Did Sarah tell you that?"

"Not in so many words. But Sarah has been taking in wash for a number of years now and never had an accident until you showed up. I don't know who you are, Delaney, or what happened between you and Sarah, but if you have any compassion you'll stick around until she can manage on her own."

"Compassion!" Chad snorted. "What about Sarah's parents? What about her brother and sister? There's not an ounce of compassion between them. Why should I take responsibility for Sarah when her own family won't? I'm a stranger, for God's sakes!"

Clayter stared at Chad, his sharp gaze seeing things Chad had tried hard to bury. "Let your conscience be your guide, son. I'm a pretty good judge of character and I don't think you'll disappoint me."

"You're wrong," Chad charged. "You don't know me at all."

Clayter stared at him. "I know something soured you on life. You're bitter and disillusioned, but I can see through that tough exterior to your better qualities. You can fool a lot of people, but not me."

"You're wrong, Doc, dead wrong. This is likely to be the last time I'll see you so I'll bid you goodbye. Do I owe you anything for Sarah's care?"

"You've already paid me," Clayter said gruffly. "Tell Sarah I'll return in a couple of days to check on her."

He climbed into the carriage and slapped the reins against his horse's rump. Annoyed, Chad watched the carriage disappear down the rutted road. The doctor's lecture had irritated Chad. Clayter couldn't possibly know about the vile things he'd seen and done, or been aware of the tragic events that had occurred when he'd involved himself in other people's lives. Nothing was going to force him to become involved again.

Nothing!

Chad returned to the house in a foul mood. He went straight to the bedroom. He found Sarah sitting on the edge of the bed, attempting to rise.

"I'm leaving," Chad said, hardening his heart against Sarah's helplessness. "I've already stayed longer than I intended."

Chad tried to avoid looking at Sarah but seemed unable to turn his eyes away. Even wrapped in her voluminous nightgown she looked seductive in an innocent sort of way that contradicted everything he'd been told about Sarah Temple. He recalled with clarity her nude body, her womanly curves, and her long, supple legs. She'd felt so damn good in his arms; he could still recall the incredible heat of her lithe body pressed against him. Sweat popped out on his forehead and he felt himself thicken with desire.

"I'm surprised you remained this long. I'm not ungrateful, you know. You've been a great help to me and Abner and I thank you."

Despite his resolve to get the hell out of here while he still could, he seemed rooted to the spot. "How will you survive without help?" he heard himself ask. Would he never learn to stay out of other people's business?

Sarah's chin rose fractionally. "I'll be fine. Abner is a big help to me."

Chad nodded curtly, thinking there was only so much a five-year-old could do and biting his tongue to keep from saying it. "Well, it's certainly been interesting knowing you, Sarah Temple. Take care of yourself."

Chad strode out of the room and shut the door quietly behind him. He leaned against the panel for a moment, indecision warring within him, then his expression hardened and he shoved himself away from the door.

"Chad!" A small body hurtled toward him, clinging to his leg. "I wondered where you were. I tried to start a fire in the stove but there wasn't any wood in the firebox."

Chad closed his eyes and fought to control his temper. He didn't know with whom he was angrier, himself or Sarah Temple. Fate was conspiring against him. There could be no other explanation for it.

"I was just leaving, Abner, but I reckon I can gather enough wood to last you and your mother a spell."

Abner's face fell. "You're leaving? For good?"

"That's right." God, he couldn't stand to see Abner's disappointment but there was no help for it. "I have to make a living and I can't do it sitting around here playing nursemaid. It's up to you to take care of your mother."

"I can do it," Abner said with false bravado.

"I know you can. I'll go cut that wood."

The hillside was covered with trees and fallen branches. Chad didn't have far to go to find wood for the stove. Dimly he wondered who would be cutting wood for Sarah when winter came. Soon Chad had gathered a huge armload of wood and returned to the house. Abner was waiting for him in the kitchen. He wasn't alone. Sarah had joined him. Still clad in her nightgown, she was balancing a jar of jam between her bandaged hands.

Chad realized what was going to happen, but before he could react the jar slipped from Sarah's hands, hit the floor, and shattered into a hundred pieces, spewing jam and broken glass all over the place.

"Oh, no!" Sarah cried, staring at the mess. Standing barefoot amidst a field of broken glass, Sarah seemed bewildered by her predicament. Before Chad could stop her, she took a step forward. Her face contorted with pain and she cried out when a piece of glass found her tender instep.

Cursing roundly, Chad's footsteps crunched across the floor as he scooped Sarah up and carried her back to her room. "Don't touch anything until I clean up the mess," he called over his shoulder to Abner.

"You're a walking disaster," Chad said as he sat Sarah on the edge of the bed. "What in the hell do you think you were doing just now?"

"Trying to feed my son," Sarah contended. "Do you have a better idea?"

His hot gaze raked her from head to toe. "Yeah, a lot of them but nothing that will do me any good right now," he growled. He grasped her ankle and placed it on his knee. "Let me have a look at your foot."

Sarah gave a shriek as Chad plucked a sliver of glass from her instep. A gush of blood poured forth and he grabbed a towel from the washstand to stanch it. "Does it hurt?"

"Not much. It seems I'm in your debt again."

Chad merely grunted. "I'll need a bandage."

"In the top drawer of the dresser. Left side."

Chad found a strip of cloth and bound it around her foot. Then he stood back to inspect his handiwork. "I'd best get back to the kitchen and clean up that mess." Suddenly a thought occurred to Chad. "Do you have a neighbor you're friendly with? Someone who would be willing to help out until you're on your feet again?"

"There's only Carrie Barlow and we're barely acquainted. The poor woman is burdened with five children and another on the way. Her husband was injured in a mine accident and can't work. She has her hands full taking care of her family. The residents of Shantytown are too busy making a living to neighbor."

Chad could understand that. The rows of shanties beyond the tracks sheltered people who barely scraped out a living.

Chad strode from the bedroom without revealing his intentions to Sarah. After cleaning up the kitchen with Abner's help, he fired up the stove, cut up the chunk of beef he'd purchased the day before, and placed all the ingredients for a stew in a pot to cook. He asked Abner to point out the Barlows' shack then sent the boy to the bedroom to keep his mother company. With a purposeful glint in his eyes, Chad marched up to the Barlows' and rapped sharply on the door.

A heavily pregnant woman answered the door. She held a baby in one arm while a toddler with a runny nose clung to her skirts. In the background he could hear the clamor of youthful voices.

Lank hair the color of mud and drawn features gave Chad the impression of a woman past her middle years. It wasn't until she raised tired eyes to Chad that he realized she was still a young woman.

"Are you Carrie Barlow?" he asked.

"I am. If you've come about the rent money, we don't have it. Charlie is still unable to work. He's . . ."

"It's nothing like that Mrs. Barlow. I'm a friend of Sarah Temple."

A glimmer of interest brightened Carrie Barlow's tired eyes. "Has something happened to Sarah? I saw the doctor's carriage parked in front of her house."

"She's had an accident. Unfortunately she'll be laid up for a spell."

"What kind of accident?"

"She suffered severe burns to her hands and arms."

"A pity," Carrie said, shaking her head in commiseration. "She told me once she didn't have anyone. It ain't easy to survive nowadays. My man is laid up and hasn't earned a penny in weeks. An' me with another baby on the way."

"How would you like to earn some money, Mrs. Barlow?" Chad asked, heartened by Carrie's reply.

Carrie's eyes lit up, then just as quickly dimmed. "A sick husband and five children to care for don't give me much time to earn extra money."

"I realize you're limited in what you can do, but perhaps we can reach an agreement. Sarah is going to need help. She can't dress or bathe herself, or properly care for Abner. I'll pay a decent wage if you can find time to help her."

Carrie shook her head. "There just ain't no way, mister. Lord knows I need the money, but I can barely take care of my own brood."

Frustration gnawed at Chad. He could sympathize with Carrie Barlow even though her response disappointed him. He was between a rock and a hard place and saw no solution.

Carrie must have sensed Chad's dilemma for suddenly she brightened. "Tell you what, mister. I can come over before the children get up in the morning and help Sarah bathe and dress. Then maybe I can sneak over again at bedtime and settle her for the night. Abner can stay here during the day and play with my kids. One more ain't gonna make much difference. Except . . . well, there ain't hardly enough food to set on the table as it is and it would be a chore to feed another mouth."

Relief such as he'd never felt before washed over Chad. "I can pay five dollars a week. Doc Clayter said Sarah will be laid up two, three weeks at the most. I'll pay you three weeks in advance. How does that sound?"

Carrie's eyes widened in disbelief. "Five whole dollars a week? I declare. There really is a God."

"I feel the same way." Chad reached into his pocket and found three five-dollar gold pieces, placing them in Carrie's outstretched palm. Carrie closed her fingers around them as if she feared Chad would snatch them back.

Jubilant, Chad returned to Sarah's house to tell her the good news. He was free! Free to cast off the bonds of responsibility and resume his life again. The first order of business was Freddie Jackson. The outlaw was still on the loose and a five-hundred-dollar reward sounded damn good right now.

The savory aroma of stew filled the small shack and Chad's mouth watered. Maybe he'd stay long enough to share supper with Sarah and Abner. Then a troubling thought occurred to Chad. Sarah couldn't feed herself. Nor could she cook or buy food. He had no idea how long it would be before she was able to take in laundry again but the vision of Sarah bending over a tub did not appeal to him.

He stirred the stew and went in to see Sarah.

Despite her mixed feelings about Chad, Sarah was glad to see him. And surprised. "I thought you'd be gone."

"Not yet. I spoke with Carrie Barlow. She's agreed to come over in the mornings to help you wash and dress, and return again in the evenings to put you to bed. She's also agreed to keep Abner during the day."

"What! In case you didn't notice, Carrie Barlow is expecting again. She has her hands full taking care of her own family."

"The woman needs the money, Sarah. She's earning hard cash for helping you. I'm really doing her a favor."

Sarah's violet eyes blazed with defiance. "You're taking advantage of Carrie's desperate situation."

"I'm doing this for you."

"You're doing this for yourself. You want to leave and are willing to do anything to escape with your conscience intact. I don't need you, Chad Delaney. I got along just fine before you showed up."

Chad laughed mirthlessly. "You don't say. You look pretty helpless to me. You can't use your hands or arms and you've injured your foot. What else can go wrong?"

"Plenty if you stick around!" Sarah shot back.

"Why are you arguing with my mother?" Abner asked, clearly frightened.

Chad turned his attention to Abner. The last thing he wanted was to frighten the boy. It was a damn shame his mother was too proud and obstinate for her own good.

"We're not really arguing, Abner. Your mother doesn't agree with what I've done, that's all. Don't worry about it. Are you hungry? I'll bet that stew is done. What do you say we go in the kitchen and dish us up some?"

"I *am* hungry," Abner admitted. "Can Mama eat with us?"

"Of course."

Without waiting for Sarah's permission, he scooped her from the bed and carried her into the kitchen, placing her in one of the rickety chairs. Then he dished out the stew. He and Abner made a game of feeding Sarah and soon all three had eaten their fill.

"You make a tolerable stew, Mr. Delaney," Sarah said. "A few herbs and a smidgeon more of salt would make it even more palatable."

It was a backhanded compliment but Chad let it pass. "You may as well call me Chad." He gave her one of his rare smiles. "We've come to know one another quite well for strangers."

Sarah flushed and gazed down at her bathrobe tellingly. "You're no gentleman to remind me of . . . of . . ." She looked at Abner and fell silent.

"I never said I was a gentleman. I seriously doubt you've ever met a real gentleman." The moment the words left his mouth he wished he could call them back. He had hurt her. The anguish on her face told him exactly how much.

Sarah arose abruptly and limped back to the bedroom. "I'll bid you goodbye now, Mr. Delaney, to save you from saying it later. Come along, Abner, it's time for bed. You can crawl in with me tonight."

"What about Chad?"

"He can stay at the boardinghouse."

"Goodbye, Chad. I'm gonna miss you," Abner

called as he disappeared into the bedroom with his mother.

"I'm going to miss you too, kid," Chad muttered to himself.

Chad bellied up to the bar and ordered whiskey. He chugged the generous shot down quickly and poured himself another. His room at the boardinghouse seemed empty and cold and he had wandered down to the One-Eyed Jack Saloon to pass the time until bedtime. Since he was still in town he decided it couldn't hurt to ask some questions about Freddie Jackson. A few weeks ago Chad had met a man who knew Jackson and didn't mind talking about him. That's how Chad had learned that Jackson hailed from Carbon.

Fortified by a second swig of whiskey, Chad engaged the man next to him in conversation. They chatted a few minutes about the town and then the man, who said his name was Cal Bork, asked, "You new in town, mister?"

"Just rode in yesterday," Chad said. He stuck out his hand. "The name's Delaney. Chad Delaney."

"Pleased to meet you, Delaney. My folks own the general store. Lived here all of my life. Did you come to Carbon for any particular reason?"

"I'm looking for man named Freddie Jackson. You know him?"

"Sure do, but he ain't been around in a long time. At least five or six years. Rumor has it he's wanted for bank robbery."

"Does he have family in town?" Chad asked.

"Not anymore. His parents are dead and his sisters married and moved away." He scratched the dark stubble growing on his chin. "Funny thing about Freddie. Always wondered why he up and left town so sudden like. It wasn't long after that we heard he'd turned outlaw."

"Freddie Jackson is wanted for bank robbery in both Montana and Wyoming."

"You a bounty hunter?"

"Yeah, I'm looking for Jackson. But I'll be moving on tomorrow. Looks like all my leads have grown cold." Chad grew thoughtful. "Did Jackson have any friends in town?"

"Freddie was a ladies' man. I heard he was involved with a woman before he left. Freddie was a secretive sort, he didn't say much about his private life. A friend of mine said he saw Freddie with the same woman on more than one occasion, but he never did see her face."

"No one ever saw her?"

"Naw. Like I said. Freddie was close-mouthed about his lady friends. The woman might have been a whore, or maybe a respectable woman who didn't want it known that Freddie was screwing her."

Chad grew pensive. Was he missing some pertinent piece of information? he wondered. Was there something about Freddie Jackson and the mysterious woman that he should know about? It was something to chew over, he decided. Chad and Cal Bork parted company a short time later. Returning to the boardinghouse, Chad spent a fitful night, tossing and turning in the lumpy bed, wondering how Sarah and Abner were faring without him.

* * *

Carrie Barlow entered Sarah's house early the next morning. Sarah was already awake, having spent a sleepless night worrying about her shaky future.

"I don't have much time," Carrie said as she wielded her bulky form into the bedroom. "The kids will be up soon and looking for their breakfast. I'll fire up the stove and heat some water for a sponge bath. How does that sound?"

"Wonderful, Carrie, but I feel guilty for imposing on you like this. Mr. Delaney shouldn't have approached you. You have enough to do without taking on another responsibility."

"Don't worry about it, honey. Mr. Delaney is a godsend. I didn't know where our next meal was coming from before he turned up on my doorstep. Charlie still can't work. Doc Clayter says it will be another couple of weeks before he's up and around. Our money was all gone and when Mr. Delaney offered to pay me for helping you, I was happy to accept."

Sarah brooded in silence as Carrie busied herself in the kitchen. She'd never met a man like Chad Delaney. She sensed the secret darkness festering inside him. Whatever bothered him hadn't completely corrupted him, for his innate goodness shone through his tough exterior. He exuded an earthy quality, like a sturdy oak upon which one could lean. He tried to hide his decency but he didn't fool Sarah.

Sarah knew Chad hated playing nursemaid, that he couldn't wait to be rid of her and Abner, and she couldn't blame him. She was nothing to him. For all he knew she was the whore the townspeople and her parents called her. Just when she was convinced he was the worst kind of renegade though, he did something completely out of character. He bought food for her and Abner and paid someone to come in twice a day to help. He didn't have to do it, which said a lot about his character.

Despite his compassionate nature, Chad Delaney had an arrogant streak a mile wide. He was a man, and Sarah had learned the hard way not to trust men. Everything men did was suspect. Their brains hung between their legs and they did and said whatever it took to satisfy their lust. She knew firsthand how a man's raging lust could ruin an innocent woman.

Carrie returned a short time later with a basin of warm water and a threadbare towel. With quick efficiency she helped bathe and dress Sarah and brushed her hair into a semblance of order.

"You look much better," Carrie said approvingly. "I'll just empty this chamberpot for you and see about breakfast."

Sarah followed Carrie into the kitchen, wishing she could do something to help. A few minutes later Abner wandered in from outside.

"Is breakfast ready yet?"

"Just like my kids," Carrie said, smiling. "They're always hungry." She stretched and rubbed her back. "I'll whip up something before I leave."

"Are you all right?" Sarah asked, noting Carrie's obvious discomfort.

"I'm fine. I woke up with a nagging pain in my back. Too much lifting, I reckon."

Carrie found oatmeal in the cupboard and set a pot of water on the stove to boil. Ten minutes later it was done and she spooned the thick gruel into two bowls and set them before Sarah and Abner. Abner dug in immediately but Sarah sat looking at hers with longing. Her bandages didn't allow her hands to bend around a spoon. She watched Abner eat, intending to ask him to help her when he finished.

Suddenly the door flew open and Carrie's oldest daughter rushed up to her mother. "The baby is awake, Mama, and cryin' somethin' fierce. Papa says you gotta come home now."

"Oh, dear," Carrie said, realizing she had lingered too long. "My family needs me, Sarah. If Abner is finished he can come along and play with my brood."

"Can I go, Mama?" Abner asked hopefully. It wasn't often he got to play with children who didn't call him names he didn't understand.

Sarah wished life could be better for her son but circumstances wouldn't allow it. If playing with the Barlow children made him happy, then she certainly wasn't going to deny him. "Go on, honey. I'll be just fine."

Abner scampered off behind Carrie and her daughter, leaving Sarah staring wistfully at her bowl of oatmeal. Unless she wanted to lap up her cereal like a dog, she'd get no breakfast today.

Chad awoke early, ate with the other boarders, and paid for his night's lodging before setting out for the livery, where he'd boarded Flint. The walk to the livery was just long enough for Chad to ponder his next move. The logical thing was to try to pick up Freddie Jackson's trail. But as he mounted Flint and headed out of town, his thoughts took him in another direction.

He wondered how Sarah and Abner would survive once all the food he'd bought was consumed. The staples he'd purchased wouldn't last forever. He hated being saddled with responsibility. The feeling that he was abandoning Sarah and Abner made him angry. He didn't owe them a damn thing.

Chad looked around to get his bearings and groaned in dismay when he saw what he had done. Without realizing it, he had ridden straight to Sarah's house.

Chapter 4

Chad had desperately wanted to turn Flint around and ride hell for leather out of town, but something stopped him. That something had a name. It was Sarah Temple. He hadn't wanted to come here. He hadn't expected to see Sarah again, but some perverse demon demanded that he dismount and go inside. It was almost as if he could hear Sarah's plea for help and it annoyed the hell out of him.

Chad despised the idea of being needed. He didn't want to feel any strong emotion for a woman. Yet something had drawn him to Sarah's house like a bee to honey. Resignation set his feet into motion as he approached the front door. He didn't knock. He merely opened the door and stepped inside. The house was small. He could see straight through the parlor into the kitchen, where Sarah sat staring with consternation into a bowl of oatmeal.

Sarah sensed his presence and swiveled around to face him. "If you've come to tell Abner goodbye, he's not here."

Chad strode into the kitchen, noting with satisfaction that, for the first time since her accident, Sarah was fully dressed in a gray gown that looked as if it had seen better days. "Mrs. Barlow must have been here this morning. I'm glad it's working out."

Sarah glared at him. "Why are you here?"

"Damned if I know." He glanced at the bowl of oatmeal sitting in front of Sarah. "That's going to get cold. Don't you like oatmeal?"

"I . . ." She glanced down at her hands and shrugged. "Carrie had to leave and my hands won't hold the spoon."

Chad spit out a curse. This wasn't going to work, he could see that now. Carrie Barlow's family came first and Sarah was likely to starve before she was capable of feeding herself. With resignation he sat down and picked up the spoon.

"Open your mouth." His voice was harsher than he intended but he was so damn frustrated he couldn't think beyond the fact that Sarah was this way because of him.

Sarah's chin jutted out. "You don't have to . . ."

"Yes, I do. Just do as I say."

Sarah's mouth fell open and Chad shoved a spoonful of oatmeal into it. She chewed and swallowed and opened her mouth again when the spoon returned to her lips. In a surprisingly short time the bowl was empty.

"Have you had enough?"

"Yes, thank you."

"You could pretend to be grateful."

"Why? I wouldn't be helpless now if you hadn't turned up on my doorstep."

"I rescued your son from a beating."

Sarah grit her teeth. "I already thanked you, what more do you want from me?"

Chad stared at her, his expression troubled. "I wish I knew."

Sarah felt the searing heat of his gaze and stared into the carved, compelling contours of his face. Her insides clenched as she nervously dampened her lips. She sensed a recklessness in him; a kind of raw energy that was now focused on her and it unnerved her.

Chad tried to control the stirring in his blood, cursing the way it thickened and settled in his lower regions. His gaze settled on Sarah's full breasts, uncomfortably aware of the way they rose and fell with her breathing, pressing against the worn material of her dress. He recalled how firm and white they were and he ached to test their weight in his hands. He didn't want to remember the softness of her shapely body but that single glimpse he'd had when he'd undressed her made him desperate to have her.

Whatever she was, whatever she had been in the past, the fact remained that Sarah Temple was a beautiful young woman, shapely, sensuous, and alluring. Unwelcome as the notion was, Chad admitted that he wouldn't mind sharing a night or two of passion with Sarah.

Suddenly Chad noticed a tiny drop of oatmeal clinging to the corner of Sarah's mouth and he leaned close. His glittering gaze held her immobile as he flicked out his tongue and lapped the oatmeal from her lips. A groan slipped past his throat. She tasted delicious and that one taste wasn't enough. Leaning closer, his lips covered hers. He felt Sarah stiffen when his tongue delved deep, devouring her with shameless satisfaction.

Chad wanted to pull her against him, to mold the length of her warm body to his, but feared he'd hurt her. He had to satisfy himself with cupping her breasts in his large hands and rolling her nipples between his fingers.

He heard her whimper of protest and wondered if any man had touched her since Abner's conception. He could tell she enjoyed his touch, and he felt something powerful and erotic jolt through him at the thought. He began to gently massage her breasts, savoring their softness.

He felt Sarah stiffen and pull away from him. "No! Stop! I can't do this."

Chad's jaw hardened. "You should have told that to Abner's father."

Sarah looked as if she'd been struck and Chad felt a brief stab of remorse. She rose awkwardly to her feet and shrugged him away when he offered to help. Unable to use her arms, she lost her balance. Chad saw what was happening and swept her into his arms scant moments before she toppled over. He held her against him, barely able to contain his amusement.

"Where do you wish to go?" Chad asked.

"The parlor will do," Sarah said, "but I can walk. There's nothing wrong with my legs."

The corners of Chad's mouth tilted upward into a wolfish grin. "Damn right there isn't. Your legs are damn near perfect."

"You're incorrigible, Chad Delaney," Sarah said, glaring at him.

"Guilty," Chad agreed. He lowered his head as if to kiss her again.

Sarah stiffened in his arms. "Don't do that!"

Chad remembered the blood-pounding desire he had felt when he'd kissed her, the way she had returned the kiss for those brief few moments, and he wanted to feel her mouth soften beneath his again. His lips hovered inches from hers as he stared into her compelling violet eyes, stunned by the turbulent emotions he saw stirring deep within them.

Suddenly the front door was flung open. It hit the wall with an explosive bang.

"Harlot! Thank the merciful Lord we're here in time to prevent you from sinning again. You have been seduced by the devil. He forces you to fornicate with any man with coin to pay for your services. You are doomed, I say!" the reverend intoned loudly. "Doomed to everlasting hell."

"Father! Mother!" Sarah shuddered.

"So, the rumors are true," Hezekiah charged, eyeing Chad with righteous indignation. "You are living in sin with this man. Repent now or suffer the fires of hell."

Chad set Sarah carefully on her feet, his temper dangling by a slim thread. "You have a poor opinion of your daughter, Reverend."

"I have but one daughter, her name is Ruth," Hezekiah intoned. "Ruth is a fine, God-fearing woman."

Chad's unrelenting gaze bored in on Sarah's mother. "Have you come to help Sarah, Mrs. Temple?"

"I wish to bring a sinner back to God," Hazel said, glancing submissively at her husband. "I pray for Sarah's soul every day."

"Wouldn't you like to see your grandson?" Chad asked.

"Chad, please," Sarah begged.

"No, Sarah, I'd like to know what your sanctimonious parents think about their grandson. Abner is a fine boy; they should be proud of him."

"The boy is a whore's get," Hezekiah claimed in a holier-than-thou voice. "He is nothing to us. Isn't that right, Hazel?"

A fleeting look of remorse crossed Hazel's face, but it was so brief Chad thought he must have imagined it. "Yes, Hezekiah, you're absolutely right. The boy is nothing to us."

A strangled sob escaped from Sarah's throat. "Say whatever you want about me, Father, but please leave Abner alone. He's an innocent child and doesn't deserve your scorn. If you opened your heart to him you'd . . ."

"I did not come here to talk about your bastard," Hezekiah said, his thin chest puffed out with self-righteous fury. "I've come to redeem a sinner. To turn her away from the devil. But I see now that Sarah does not seek redemption.

"Sarah is an embarrassment to my family and must be punished. Fornicating openly, without shame or remorse, is evil."

"Father! I'm not what you think. You must believe me."

Hezekiah snorted in derision. "Do you even know who fathered your child? How many men had you lain with before conceiving the devil's spawn? And don't think for a minute that I believe your story about being forced. Even as a child you were disobedient, unruly, and a liar, nothing like your sweet sister."

"I'm sorry you feel that way, Father. I've been truthful with you but you refuse to believe me." Her chin raised fractionally. "I no longer care what you think. Nor will I allow you to hurt my son. You cannot make me leave Carbon. I have no other place to go."

Chad's hands clenched at his sides. He wanted to toss the preacher out on his ear so badly he had to exert tremendous restraint to keep from doing so. He moved closer to Sarah, unconsciously lending support.

"You leave me with no choice," Hezekiah thundered as he pointed a bony finger at Sarah. "On your knees, sinner! It is my duty to beat the evilness out of you."

He turned to Chad as he removed a leather strap from somewhere beneath his rusty black coat. "I suggest you leave, sir. I strongly advise that in the future you curb your lust. Consorting with whores will lead you to perdition."

Chad eyed the length of leather in the reverend's hands and snarled in outrage. "And I strongly advise that you leave this house and not return. If you raise that strap to your daughter, you're placing your life in serious jeopardy."

Sarah refused to cringe beneath her father's hurtful words. In her heart she knew she'd done nothing of which to be ashamed. What really distressed her was the fact that Chad had to hear all this. This was the first time her father had turned up on her doorstep since he'd disowned her, and she prayed it would be the last.

She stared with awe at Chad. No one had ever defended her before. She had managed on her own before Chad Delaney walked into her life and she could do so again.

"I can defend myself, Chad. Father beat me once but I won't allow it to happen again."

Her words had no effect on Chad, and in fact, Sarah had no idea whether Chad had even heard her, so intent was he on the reverend.

"Your daughter has suffered enough for her mistake, Reverend, and paid a hefty price. Leave her alone, she's not bothering you."

The leather strap wavered in Hezekiah's hands. "Sarah's presence in town upsets my family. She knew what she was doing when she first sinned with a man. You do not know her evil nature, sir. Be off with you and leave the sinner to me."

He took a menacing step toward Sarah, but Chad deliberately blocked his path. "Are you going to leave or must I throw you out?"

Hazel pulled on her husband's arm. "He means what he says, Hezekiah. Perhaps we should leave and return at another time. He will tire of Sarah soon and leave town. His kind never sticks around long. They flit indiscriminately from whore to whore."

Sarah made a strangled sound in the back of her throat. To be called a whore by her own mother deeply saddened her. She knew her mother was completely dominated by her overzealous father but she'd harbored a slim hope that her mother would relent one day. That hope was now shattered, just as quickly as her life had been ruined by a man. Fortunately Chad intervened before Sarah broke down completely and made a fool of herself.

"Listen to your wife, Reverend," Chad advised.

"Leave now while you still have two good legs to carry you."

"Are you threatening me, sir?"

"You're damn right I am! Get out, get out now."

Hezekiah sent a threatening glance at Sarah, then grasped his wife's elbow and headed for the door. "Very well. I cannot abide the stench of corruption," he said, directing his words to both Sarah and Chad.

"And I cannot abide a sanctimonious sermonizer who sees only black and white. Good day, Reverend."

Hezekiah dragged Hazel out the door as if the devil was nipping at his heels. He did not look back as he marched away, his body rigid with outrage.

Sarah watched her parents leave, her eyes awash with tears. She thought they had broken her heart years ago, but that was nothing compared to what she now suffered. How could they be so unfeeling toward their own daughter, so unforgiving? A preacher's duty was to save sinners. Not that she had sinned, for she had been sinned against, and was paying dearly for it. As a result, her trustful nature had been seriously impaired and her innocence lost forever. Fresh tears flowed down her cheeks in silent mourning as she turned her face away from Chad.

Chad cursed beneath his breath. He'd known heartless people before but the Temples topped the list. He glanced at Sarah, saw her tears, and felt something inside him give. He marveled at the fact that he cared so much. He thought he'd lost that ability long ago. Women were devious creatures; he didn't want to feel anything for them. Sarah had a son but no husband. The townspeople called her a whore. Her own parents had disowned her. Who and what was the real Sarah? he wondered.

Despite his grave misgivings, Chad reached for her, moved by the perplexing urge to offer comfort. Carefully he brought her into his arms and lifted her face to his.

"Don't cry. They're not worth it."

"It's not just them," Sarah admitted. "It's everything. This town, the people, the difficulty of putting food on the table. I'd take Abner far away if I could, but I can barely feed us let alone find the money to settle in another town. I'm not a whore, no matter what you've heard. Granted I'm an unwed mother, but that doesn't make me a bad person."

Raw emotion surged through Chad, primitive and undeniable; an emotion he'd never expected to genuinely experience.

"I don't know what happened, Sarah, and I don't really care. I do know that your parents have no business treating you like an outcast. Everyone makes mistakes; no one is perfect. I'd say you've paid dearly for your mistake."

Sarah blinked away her tears. Despite the small spark of compassion Chad displayed upon occasion, there was an aloofness about him, a dangerous, unreadable temperament that made him hard to understand. He confused her, and she found that unsettling. Then all thought vanished as Chad's mouth claimed hers.

Chad tasted the sweetness of Sarah's mouth and groaned. Reason bid him stop. Inexplicable need urged him on. He wanted Sarah Temple. Not just sexually; he wanted to protect her and Abner from the people of this town. From her own parents. What had started as an unaccountable need to comfort Sarah had grown all out of proportion. He'd never felt this way before, never thought he was capable of giving solace. Not only that; he wanted to give her more pleasure than any man before him had.

Sarah whimpered as he pressed her closer.

"Don't," she said, dragging her mouth away from his.

Painfully aroused, Chad was barely able to think beyond the pressing need between his legs. "I want you, Sarah," he muttered against her throat as his lips teased the wildly beating pulse there. "Let me comfort you. I won't get you pregnant, if that's what you're worried about. I know how to prevent it."

His words were like a dash of cold water. "Let me go." Her voice was deadly serious.

Chad's arms dropped away and he stared at her in consternation. There was nothing wrong with two lonely people wanting each other, was there? He searched her face. What he saw shocked him. There was a wounded look to her eyes and mouth. He had somehow hurt her and for the life of him he couldn't think what he had done.

"What's wrong? What have I done?"

Chad's words shamed Sarah. She'd tried so hard to live a respectable life despite the town's groundless condemnation. Then Chad Delaney had marched into her life and made her feel things that frightened her. She disliked men intensely. Yet something about Chad made her think sweet, romantic thoughts instead of dark sin and pain. His kisses evoked irresistible pleasure. Nothing had prepared her for the shattering effects of desire. It puzzled, humiliated, and terrified her. For a brief moment, though, she had reveled in the unique taste and scent of him.

The pressure of his body against hers had felt good and right despite knowing it was wrong. But it was Chad's careless words that had brought her to her senses. He considered her a whore, like everyone else in this town. Would Chad believe her if she told him she'd been raped? Would he pass judgment and call her a liar and a sinner?

"I repeat, Mr. Delaney, I am not for sale. The One-Eyed Jack Saloon has a variety of women who I'm sure would suit your needs."

Chad's eyes narrowed with contempt. "Are you holding out for a better price? I should have known. Women are all alike. All they do is take. I finished giving a long time ago, Miss Temple."

"I never asked you for a thing, Mr. Delaney. Your opinion of women is appalling. Experience has taught me that men can't be trusted. What soured you on women, Mr. Delaney?"

"What soured you on men?" Chad shot back.

Sarah gave a harsh laugh. "Need you ask? Look at me. Look at my circumstances. My own parents despise me, and do you know why?" Chad opened his mouth to speak but Sarah forestalled him. "I'll tell you why. Because I believed a man's sweet talk. I was a trusting, naive child who fancied herself in love. And then . . ." Her words fell off and she looked away.

"So you fell for some man and he got you pregnant. I'm surprised your parents didn't make him marry you."

"That's not exactly how it happened," she said

bitterly, "but close enough. My parents refused to believe the truth and disowned me when I told them I was pregnant."

"What is the truth?"

Sarah stared at him. "The truth, Mr. Delaney, is that you're like every other man I've ever known."

They were still glaring at one another when Abner rushed into the house, nearly bursting with excitement.

"Mama, Mrs. Barlow is having her baby. Doctor Clayter is there now."

Chad looked at Abner in disbelief. How could this be happening to him? He thought he'd solved the problem of Sarah's care and now he faced a new dilemma. With a new baby added to her other responsibilities, Carrie Barlow would not be able to help Sarah or care for Abner. Now what? Chad wondered. How in the hell did he get himself into these messes?

"Isn't it exciting, Mama?" Abner enthused. "Doctor Clayter sent me home and said he'd be over as soon as he's through at the Barlow house. Can I go out and play, Mama? I like Danny Barlow, he doesn't call me names."

"Go out and play," Chad said, answering for Sarah. "And stay out of trouble."

Chad could not imagine a worse scenario. He had no clue where to find Freddie Jackson. He had arrived in Carbon looking for an outlaw and had unwittingly inherited responsibilities he couldn't seem to escape from. His entire life was going to hell in a handbasket. At one time life had been damn near perfect. He had his brothers, his ranch, money, and all the women he wanted. Now he was a moderately successful bounty hunter saddled with a woman and child he couldn't wait to get rid of. His pockets were nearly empty and the man he was hunting was still at large. What else could go wrong?

"I'm going over to the Barlows to see if I can help," Sarah said, heading out the door.

Chad's gaze settled on her bandaged arms, and he raised one eyebrow in surprise. "How do you propose to do that?"

"Carrie and I have never been close but she's always been kind to me. The least I can do is lend moral support."

She swept out the door and Chad felt obliged to follow. The Barlow shack wasn't far. Chad rapped on the door when Sarah stared at her useless hands and stuck her foot forward to tap the door. A large man on crutches answered.

"I'm Sarah Temple," Sarah said. "I've come to lend whatever support I can for Carrie. Is the doctor in with her?"

"Come in. I'm Charlie, Carrie's husband. I don't believe we've met." His gaze swung to Chad.

When Sarah offered no introduction, Chad jumped into the void. "I'm Chad Delaney, a friend of Sarah's."

"Friend, indeed," Sarah mumbled beneath her breath as she walked into the tiny parlor. Just then Doctor Clayter came out of the bedroom, wiping his hands.

"You have a fine son, Charlie. The baby arrived a bit early and is rather small, but he'll be fine. You can go on in and see Carrie and your son now if you'd like. But first, a word of advice. Let Carrie rest a year or two before putting another babe in her belly. She's had too many children in too short a time. This one is healthy but I can't guarantee the next one will be if you don't give her time to recover fully."

Charlie had the grace to flush. "I'll be careful, Doc. We don't need any more mouths to feed. By the way, when can I get this cast off my leg? I need to get back to work to support my family."

"I'll come out early next week to remove it. Meanwhile, see that Carrie stays in bed for a few days. You can manage that long without her, can't you?"

"Sure, Doc," Charlie conceded. "I'll see that you get paid, too. Just as soon as I get back on my feet again."

Chad said nothing as Charlie disappeared into the bedroom, but he couldn't help thinking how privileged he'd been compared to the kind of poverty the Barlows and Sarah experienced on a daily basis. The Delaney ranch was a prosperous business that supported all three brothers rather well. Some years were leaner than others but there had always been money for the little extras that made life enjoyable.

"I planned to stop by just as soon as I finished here, Sarah," Doctor Clayter said.

"I came to see if I could help."

"There's nothing for you to do. I gave Carrie something to make her sleep and she'll be dropping off soon. Charlie can handle the children until Carrie's on her feet again. Go on home, I'll be there directly."

Sarah headed for the door, then paused when Charlie hobbled from the bedroom and motioned to Chad.

"Carrie asked to see you, Mr. Delaney. Make it quick, she's exhausted."

"Are you sure she asked to see me?" Chad wanted to know.

"Yeah, very sure. Go on in."

Chad glanced at Sarah, shrugged, then entered the bedroom. Carrie looked very small and fragile lying in the big bed. A tiny bundle rested in her arms, nuzzling at her breast.

"You wanted to see me?"

Carrie looked up, a worried look on her face. "It's about the money you gave me to help Sarah. The baby came early and I won't be able to live up to our agreement." She flushed and looked away. "I already spent the money on food. I'm sorry. As soon as Charlie is on his feet again we'll pay you back."

"Keep the money, Mrs. Barlow," Chad said gruffly. "You need it more than I do."

"Who will assist Sarah? She's so . . . helpless . . . and she has no one." Her eyes were glazing over and it was obvious the laudanum was taking effect.

"Don't worry about Sarah. I'll take care of her." No sooner had the words left his mouth than the portent of what he said dawned on him. He had just committed himself, something he'd vowed never to do again.

Sarah couldn't imagine why Chad Delaney was still here. It worried her. Men like Chad didn't do anything without wanting something in return. He'd already admitted he wanted her sexually. His thrilling kisses had made her forget the fragile state of her reputation. She didn't need a man in her life, especially one who was bound to be here today and gone tomorrow. Chad Delaney wanted one thing from her. What she didn't understand was why he just didn't take it while she was helpless and then leave for parts unknown. That's what Freddie Jackson had done.

Sarah retired to the bedroom directly after supper. Abner and Chad were still in the kitchen doing up the dishes. Very carefully she pulled out the dresser drawer with her bandaged hands and removed her nightgown, feeling very satisfied with herself for being able to do at least that much on her own. The last thing she wanted was for Chad to undress her.

Sarah gazed in dismay at the several buttons marching down the front of her dress. Her burns no longer pained her like they did shortly after the accident, but manipulating the buttons was beyond her meager capabilities. She wanted to scream in frustration.

Chad knocked once and entered the room. Sarah blinked away her tears. Being dependent on a man for things she had done herself all her life angered her. She didn't want to be indebted to anyone.

"Can I help?" Chad asked as he lit the lamp Sarah hadn't been able to manage on her own.

"Where's Abner?"

"He fell asleep on the sofa while I was finishing up in the kitchen. I'll put him on the trundle as soon as you're settled in bed."

"I think I'll sleep in my clothing tonight."

His big hands moved to the buttons on her bodice. "You'll rest more comfortably without your dress."

Sarah fairly dripped from her words. "What did I ever do to deserve such kindness?"

Chad grinned. "Nothing that I'm aware of. I'm here because I'm responsible for your accident and I can't find anyone to help you. Now be quiet and let me concentrate on these buttons."

Sarah's lips clamped together as Chad's hands moved over her breasts. His touch was light, experienced, and she wondered how many women he'd undressed in his lifetime. Plenty, she'd wager. She tried to remain stoic but the tingling sensation in those places he'd touched gave her butterflies in the pit of her stomach.

"Can't you hurry?"

"There," Chad said, releasing the last button. "I'll just work your dress down your arms and hips now."

Sarah stood absolutely still as Chad carefully removed her dress and petticoats. When he tried to lift her shift, Sarah planted her arms at her sides and gave her head a vigorous shake.

"Leave the shift," she said tightly. "It can serve as a nightgown."

Chad gave her a wicked grin. Did she have no idea how appealing she looked? Her back was to the light, rendering her shift nearly transparent. The shimmering outline of her body sent blood pounding through his veins. He wanted . . .

Sarah.

Chapter 5

"Get in bed, Sarah," Chad said gruffly.

Sarah felt as if she'd just stepped into a raging inferno as Chad's heated gaze slid over her. His hazel eyes were shot with pure fire and his face darkened with what Sarah could only describe as raw desire. She shuddered, recalling the last time a man had looked at her like that and the painful results. When Chad ordered her into bed an unspeakable fear shot through her. Was he finally going to show his dark, dangerous side? Would he take her without her permission? Would he hurt her?

Sarah raised her chin fractionally. She'd let no man do that to her again. "I'll get into bed as soon as you leave."

A muscle twitched in Chad's jaw. Did she think he was going to attack her like a wild animal? His anger slowly faded when he realized that's exactly what she thought. Her previous experiences with men must have been bad to instill such fear in her, he reflected.

"Very well. Get into bed while I fetch Abner. I'll take the couch tonight."

"You don't have to stay," Sarah said unconvincingly. "Abner and I can manage tonight."

"I've already given up my room at the boardinghouse. Money is tight right now. If I don't find Freddie Jackson soon I'm going to have to find another outlaw to bring in."

Sarah's face turned a sickly shade of green. "Freddie Jackson? You're hunting Freddie Jackson?" Her knees grew weak and she leaned against the bed for support.

Her violent reaction to the mere mention of Jackson gave Chad pause for thought. "You know Jackson?"

She blinked up at him, her eyes wary. "Vaguely."

"When did you see him last?"

"Please, I'm tired. Can't we speak of this in the morning?"

Chad searched her face. She did indeed look tired. But there was something else. Some deep hidden fear. How well did Sarah know Jackson? Was there a connection there someplace?

"Jackson left town over five years ago. You must have been very young at the time," Chad persisted.

"I . . . I want to go to bed." She sat on the edge of the bed and tried to slide her legs under the covers without using her hands.

Chad moved instantly to help her, lifting her legs onto the bed and pulling the blanket over her. Instead of leaving immediately he perched on the edge of the bed, his gaze intent upon her face. "How well did you know Jackson?"

"Leave me alone! You have no right to question me. I don't know anything about Freddie Jackson."

Chad wasn't so sure. For someone who professed to know nothing about Jackson, Sarah had become inordinately distraught at his line of questioning. He could see that to continue questioning Sarah tonight would get him nowhere so he decided to give it up for the time being.

"Very well, Sarah. Go to sleep. We'll talk tomorrow."

Sarah collapsed in relief when Chad bid her goodnight and left the room. He was dredging up hurtful memories she preferred to forget. Her parents had punished her for crying rape so she saw no purpose in revealing the man's name to anyone. Freddie Jackson had already left town by the time she learned she was pregnant and her pride wouldn't let her confront his elderly parents with his evil deed. They had thought the world of their son. Telling them would have destroyed them.

Sarah had been so young and naive when Freddie had attacked her. She'd been too ashamed to tell anyone about it, until she'd turned up pregnant and was forced to reveal her shameful secret to her parents. Their negative response had taught her a valuable lesson. She'd learned it was far better to suffer in silence than to tell the truth and be reviled for it. She'd also learned to loathe and distrust men.

She didn't want anyone to know that Freddie Jackson was Abner's father. The man was an outlaw and a rapist. Her son meant everything to her and she prayed he'd never discover the identity of his evil father. Abner had been conceived in pain and shame but he was the only person in the whole world who loved her unconditionally. She'd do everything in her power to protect him. She'd fight tooth and nail to keep the world from learning that he was Freddie Jackson's son.

* * *

Abner was sound asleep on the couch when Chad returned to the parlor. He lifted the boy into his arms, thinking how comfortable Abner's slight weight felt against him. Abner murmured in his sleep as his arms went around Chad's neck. Chad's arms tightened around the boy. Never had he felt so fiercely protective toward another human being.

Suddenly Abner's eyes opened and he smiled up at Chad with such wide-eyed innocence that Chad's heart lurched in his chest.

"Are you gonna stay with us forever, Chad?" the boy asked.

"I can't, Abner. I've got a job to do. As soon as your mama is able to care for herself I'll be moving on."

Abner's smile faltered. "I wish you could stay forever. Since you've been here Mama hasn't cried once."

"Your mother's been crying?"

Abner nodded solemnly. "All the time. She doesn't want me to know but I hear her at night when I'm supposed to be sleeping. She works too hard and sometimes goes without food so I can eat."

"You're a brave boy, Abner. And smart, too."

"I have to be brave. I'm the only man in the house. I don't have a papa." He looked at Chad speculatively. "Would you like to be my papa?"

Chad stifled a groan. Abner's question left him speechless, and more than a little discomfited. "That's a mighty fine offer, son, but I'm not cut out to be anyone's papa. One day your mama will find the right man to be your papa."

Abner's face fell. "I don't think so, but that's all right. I'll take care of Mama."

Chad felt a stab of pity but quickly shoved it aside. He thought he'd buried all those maudlin emotions, not that he'd had all that many, the day he left Dry Gulch. He wasn't about to let a small boy or his entrancing mother lasso him into a situation he didn't want and wouldn't tolerate.

"Off to bed with you, boy. Be quiet now, your mama's already asleep."

Chad carried Abner into the bedroom and eased him onto the trundle. Reluctantly Abner removed his arms from around Chad's neck. Then he did something that utterly unnerved Chad. Abner raised his head and planted a kiss on Chad's cheek. Chad quickly withdrew and left the room as if the devil was on his heels.

The following days were as difficult for Sarah as they were for Chad. Having Chad around on a daily basis, allowing him to perform intimate chores, such as dressing and undressing her, made her aware of him as she'd never been aware of another man. Lord knows she didn't want to think of Chad as someone special but she couldn't help it. He was so patient with Abner it sometimes brought tears to her eyes.

Yet with her he was often short-tempered and grumpy. And the way he looked at her utterly unnerved her. As if he wanted to devour her. He hadn't tried to kiss her again but sometimes she wished . . . Her head whirled in confusion. There wasn't a thing she wanted from Chad Delaney, or any other man.

In another few days her bandages would be removed and it couldn't be too soon for her. Abner was becoming too fond of Chad. He was going to be dreadfully hurt when Chad walked out of their lives but that's the way it had to be. She wasn't ungrateful. Had Chad not stayed with her Sarah didn't know what she would have done. Doubtless she and Abner would have starved to death before her family came to her aid, but now it was time for Chad to move on.

Sarah owed Chad more than she could ever repay. It was clear to her that the man hated every moment he had to spend with her, even though he seemed to be fond of Abner. Only his deep-seated sense of honor kept him here. Sarah wasn't fool enough to think Chad was anything other than a hardened drifter who had been hurt by life. She also knew that a woman was responsible for at least some of his pain. To Chad's credit, he had retained a spark of decency that softened his hard edges. Whether he intended it or not, Chad wasn't as hard-bitten as he pretended.

Chad chafed impatiently at his lack of freedom. He should be out looking for Freddie Jackson, not playing nursemaid. Somehow he managed to put food on the table and with great difficulty to keep his hands off Sarah, although truthfully the latter was becoming more difficult with each passing day.

Chad felt as if he knew every glorious inch of Sarah's body without having actually tasted her charms. She might be thin but she was nicely proportioned. Her breasts just fit his hands. He was carrying around a permanent erection and it was damn uncomfortable. Thank God he knew better than to seduce Sarah. Nothing would spell his doom or seal his fate faster than bedding Sarah Temple. He didn't want attachments. Being a bounty hunter and living precariously, without setting down roots, suited him just fine.

"Shall we continue our conversation about Freddie Jackson?" Chad asked several days later when he found himself alone with Sarah.

Sarah forced a calm she didn't feel. "I thought we'd already explored that subject."

"Why are you so reluctant to talk about Jackson? How well did you know him?"

Sarah hesitated only a moment before saying, "I knew him casually. My parents were strict; I knew few men socially."

Chad's eyebrows rose a good half inch. "That's hard to believe. There was at least one man you knew intimately."

Sarah flushed and looked away. "I don't need you to remind me, Chad Delaney. Nor do I wish to discuss this further. I think I'll go see how Carrie and the new baby are doing. Charlie went back to work this morning."

She left the house without a backward glance.

Chad stared at her departing back. Questions formed in his mind. Questions about Sarah and Jackson, and he didn't like what he was thinking.

Sarah flexed her fingers and stared at the reddened, raw skin on her hands and arms. There was some soreness but at least she was no longer hampered by those cumbersome bandages and was once again able to take care of herself. Reveling in her freedom of movement and restored independence, she looked first at Chad at then at Doctor Clayter.

"You've still got to be mighty careful for awhile," Clayter warned. "You can perform simple tasks but you're not to plunge your arms into hot water until you're completely healed."

Sarah's head shot up. "That's impossible, Doctor." Sarah exclaimed. "I earn my living by taking in laundry. I planned to contact my old customers as soon as possible and let them know I'm in business again."

"You heard me, Sarah," Clayter said sternly. "No laundry. Not until I say it's all right."

Sarah gnawed her bottom lip, her brow furrowed in consternation. Would fate never stop dealing harshly with her? Without her livelihood she had no way to support her son.

Clayter must have sensed her distress for he said, "Try not to fret, Sarah. Perhaps I can find some other kind of work for you. Something less arduous. Well, I must be off. Can't keep my patients waiting. Don't forget what I said, Sarah. No laundry until I say so."

"It was kind of Doctor Clayter to offer to find you other work," Chad said.

"Doc Clayter has a good heart. He's always been kind to me, but he knows darn well there won't be a job for me. Not in this town. My father made certain of that. People only bring me their laundry because I do a better job than anyone else."

"How will you support yourself?" Chad asked, wishing he could take back the words. He didn't care, didn't even want to know. He just wanted to walk out of here and forget he'd ever met Sarah Temple and her son Abner.

"Don't worry, I'll find a way."

"There's always a way for a woman to earn money," Chad said evenly. "Especially a beautiful woman. Have you explored any of those options?" The suggestion was outrageous and he knew it.

"You may find this hard to believe, Mr. Delaney, but I'd go begging before I'd whore for a living. Does that answer your question?"

"Perfectly. Since I've done all I can for you, I reckon I'll be on my way. I'm no longer needed here, thank God. There's still plenty of light. Guess I'll head out immediately." He turned to leave, paused, then spun around to face Sarah. "You've got gumption, Sarah, I'll give you that. I'm sure you and Abner will do just fine."

Sarah wondered why she wasn't relieved that Chad was finally leaving. She had to confess she'd grown accustomed to him. No man had ever done the things Chad had done for her. No one, including her family, had ever cared about what happened to her and Abner. Though he did it grudgingly, Chad had displayed more concern for her and her son than anyone ever had. She had no idea what had turned Chad away from his home and family, but he couldn't hide the fact that inside he was basically good and honorable. She hoped that one day he would meet a woman who would gave him back his self-respect. A woman who could earn his trust and love.

A lone horseman rode into town. His skin was darkened from the sun and a thick black beard covered the lower half of his face. With the brim of his hat pulled down over his eyes, he hoped no one, except perhaps for those who had known him well, would recognize Freddie Jackson.

Jackson tied his horse to the hitching post, glanced furtively around, then walked through the swinging doors of the One-Eyed Jack Saloon. His narrowed gaze swept the room before deeming it safe to approach the bar. He ordered a whiskey and gulped it down, savoring the rush of heat to his innards. A few minutes later a man bellied up beside him. He ordered a whiskey and glanced at Jackson in a friendly manner.

His eyes widened as he stared curiously at Jackson. Then he slapped Jackson on the back and said heartily, "Say, ain't you Freddie Jackson? I'm Cal Bork, remember me? We had some good times together before you left town."

Freddie gave him a nervous smile. How unlucky could he get? He'd never expected to meet someone who knew him his first night in town. "I remember. How have you been, Cal?"

"Couldn't be better. What are you doing in town? Isn't it dangerous? A bounty hunter's been nosing around, asking questions about you."

Freddie spit out a curse. "I ain't gonna stay long. Just came to see my parents. They're getting up in years. I had business nearby and decided to pay them a visit. Thought I'd lost that damn bounty hunter weeks ago."

"Sorry to be the one to give you bad news, but your folks died three or four years back and your sisters married and moved out of town."

"Shit! It was a dumb idea anyway. Reckon I'll hightail it out of town before that bounty hunter finds me."

Jackson tossed back the last of his whiskey and

made as if to leave. Suddenly he turned back to Cal. "Whatever happened to that preacher's daughter. What was her name . . . Oh, yeah, I remember now. It was Sarah. Sarah Temple."

Cal laughed. "You'd never guess. The pious little tart lifted her skirts for some man and got herself knocked up. Her parents disowned her and kicked her out. She and her bastard son are living in a shack across the tracks. She takes in laundry for a living. Some say she takes in tricks."

Jackson's attention sharpened. "She has a son? How old is the kid?"

"Let me think . . . Must be five or six by now. Cute little fella. Too bad."

"Thanks, Cal, you've been a big help. Take care of yourself."

Abner was subdued when Sarah served him supper that night. She knew he felt Chad's loss keenly but there was nothing she could do to make him feel better.

"Are you sure Chad left town, Mama?"

"That's what he said, honey."

"Why did he have to leave? Why can't he stay with us and be my papa?"

"Mr. Delaney doesn't want attachments. And besides, I don't want a husband. His leaving is best for everyone. You wouldn't want him to be unhappy, would you?" Abner shook his head. "He'd be very unhappy if he had to stay here with us. Men like Chad come and go with the wind."

A furtive knock on the door brought the conversation to a halt.

"Chad!" Abner cried, running to open the door. "He's come back!"

Against her will Sarah found herself moving expectantly toward the door, just steps behind Abner. It had to be Chad, she reasoned, for no one else ever visited. Certainly not her parents, and she had no friends.

Abner reached the door and flung it open. His face fell when he saw a strange man standing on the doorstep. Jackson didn't wait to be invited in. He merely shoved inside and closed the door firmly behind him.

Sarah grabbed Abner and pushed him behind her. "Oh my God! It's you. What do you want?"

"I thought you'd recognize me. Ain't you glad to see me?"

Sarah stared at Freddie Jackson, her fear escalating. She'd recognized him immediately. How could she forget him? Her knees nearly buckled beneath her and she clutched Abner's hand so hard he cried out.

"Mama, you're hurting me!"

Sarah barely heard him, so great was her shock. What was *he* doing here? Freddie Jackson was her worst nightmare come true. For the first year or two after Abner's birth she'd lived in terror, fearing Jackson would return and learn that he had a son. As time passed her fear began to wane, especially after Jackson's parents died and his sisters moved away. She reckoned he'd have no reason to return to town now. She'd been wrong! Dear Lord, she'd been wrong.

"What do you want?" Sarah hissed, swallowing past the lump in her throat. "I prayed I'd never see you again."

"So you do recognize me," Jackson said. His probing gaze settled on Abner, who was peeking around his mother's skirts. The boy's eyes were bright with curiosity, not in the least fearful. Jackson liked that in a kid.

"Is that the boy?" Jackson asked. "Handsome little fellow. How old is he?"

"I'm five," Abner sang out to his mother's horror. "Why are you scaring my mama?"

"Brave, too. I like that. He's got my eyes, Sarah. What did you name him?"

"My name is Abner." Abner glared up at Jackson, assessing and judging him with a child's astute perception of good and evil. "I don't like you."

Sarah gasped in horror. "Abner! Go to your room. Let Mama handle Mr. Jackson."

"I have to protect you, Mama," Abner protested.

Jackson stepped forward, gripping Abner's arm and pulling him forward. Grasping Abner's chin, Jackson raised his little face to the light as he searched the boy's features.

"Don't touch him! Leave him alone!" Sarah cried, flying to her son's defense.

"Well, well," Jackson muttered, grinning at Sarah, "what do you know. Looks just like me. He's my kid, ain't he, Sarah?"

"No!" The word burst forth in an angry rush of denial. "Go away! Abner is my son . . . *my* son, do you hear? You have no right to him."

"The boy needs a man to raise him. You'll make a sissy of him."

Sarah sneered in derision. "Look at you. You're an outlaw, a man on the run. You can't possibly think that you . . ." The thought was so horrendous she couldn't find proper words to express it.

"That's exactly what I am thinking," Jackson said, staring at Abner. "I gotta lay low for awhile.

I got a snug little hideout on Elk Mountain and a squaw to look after the kid. All I gotta do is knock over one more bank and I'll be set for a long time."

Sarah's mind worked furiously. This couldn't be happening. No one was going to take Abner from her. She and Abner had gone through too much together. He was hers and hers alone.

"Sooner or later the law will catch up with you. What will happen to Abner when they do? A bounty hunter was in town looking for you. Leave now, Freddie, before he comes gunning for you."

Jackson sent Sarah a fulminating look. "You're no longer that innocent little girl who worshipped me."

"Thank God. I know you for what you are now, Freddie Jackson. You're a despicable bastard. If not for you I'd still be innocent."

"Watch what you say in front of the kid," Freddie warned. "Besides, you wanted it."

Sarah wanted to tear out Jackson's eyes, but not in front of Abner. "Go to bed, Abner. I'll be in as soon as Mr. Jackson leaves."

Jackson didn't stop Abner as he reluctantly obeyed his mother.

"You have no rights where Abner is concerned, Freddie," Sarah spit out once Abner was gone. "You raped me and left me lying on the ground, hurt and broken. I was a child when you ripped away my innocence."

Freddie frowned. "That ain't the way I remembered it. I hear your pa disowned you. You been turning tricks for a living?"

Sarah raised her hand to slap him but he caught her wrist in his big hand, bringing her up against him. "Don't raise your hand to me, woman. You're nothing but a whore. You ain't fit to raise my son. Pack up his clothes, I'm taking him with me."

"I'm more fit than you!" she screamed at him.

"At least with me he won't be no sissy."

"Why? Why are you doing this?"

"Maybe I took a shine to the kid. Maybe because he's mine. And don't try to tell me otherwise, he's the picture of me when I was his age. Maybe being a father appeals to me. Go on, pack his clothes."

"No. You can't have Abner."

He pulled a Colt .45 from his holster and pointed it at Sarah. "I got a friend here who says I can have anything I want. Are you gonna get the kid or shall I?"

Sarah lunged at him. Jackson retaliated by knocking her aside with the barrel of his gun. Stunned, Sarah fell to the floor, unable to move, unable to speak as Jackson stepped over her and stalked into the bedroom.

Minutes later he returned with a wildly protesting Abner. Jackson held him tucked under one arm as he nudged Sarah with the toe of his boot. "Get the kid's clothes. I ain't got all day."

Coming out of her stupor, Sarah scrambled to her feet. Raising her hand to her temple, she pulled it away stained with blood. She ignored the pain. "Where are you taking him?"

"I told you. I got a hideout on Elk Mountain."

"I understand the area is crawling with hostile Indians who have left their reservations. You're deliberately placing my son in danger."

"Naw, the Indians won't hurt me. Spotted Deer is a Shoshone."

"Take me with you," Sarah pleaded frantically.

"I can take care of Abner better than Spotted Deer. I'm his mother."

"Mama! Don't let the bad man take me away!"

"I'm your pa, kid. Get used to it."

"Please, Freddie, take me with you," Sarah repeated.

Jackson frowned. "I got no use for you, Sarah. There's too much hate in you." His gaze raked her with contempt. "You're too skinny. Spotted Deer suits me better. You're as cold as an icicle in winter, if I recall. I was the first with you and I liked that, but you ain't my type.

"Are you gonna get the kid's clothes or shall I take him like he is? It gets cold in the mountains at night. He'll freeze without a jacket to keep him warm."

When Sarah didn't move fast enough, Jackson gave her a vicious shove. Sarah stumbled, righted herself, then dragged herself into the bedroom. Numb with grief, she gathered Abner's clothing and stuffed it into a pillowcase. Why, after all these years, did Freddie Jackson have to turn up? And why did he want his son? Nothing made sense. Of one thing Sarah was certain. Freddie Jackson wasn't going to take her son from her without a fight. She'd follow him to hell and back if necessary.

"Hurry," Jackson growled.

Sarah grabbed the pillowcase and Abner's heavy jacket and hurried back to the parlor. "This is everything," she said, handing the pillowcase to Jackson.

"Tell your mama goodbye, kid," Jackson said as he dragged Abner out the door.

"Mama! Mama! Don't let him take me!"

Sarah couldn't stand it. Disregarding her own safety, she lunged at Jackson, gripping him around the middle in a futile attempt to stop him. Jackson spit out a curse and flung his arm back, tossing Sarah aside like a rag doll. By the time she regained her wits, Jackson had already mounted his horse and had Abner perched in front of him.

Abner was nearly frantic now, trying to dislodge himself from Jackson's grasp. Sarah shook her head to clear it and picked herself off the floor. "Don't worry, honey. I'll find you. Be brave."

No answer was forthcoming. Darkness was all around her, suffocating her as pounding hoofbeats echoed in the distance. Sarah didn't waste precious time crying and carrying on. She knew what she had to do and there wasn't a moment to spare. If only Chad were here, she thought dimly. Chad would help her, she knew he would. But Chad had already left and she was on her own. Grabbing her jacket from the nail by the door, she rushed out into the night.

All was dark and silent inside the Barlows' shack. Sarah knew they kept a swaybacked nag stabled in a small lean-to next to the house and she silently prayed for forgiveness as she saddled the animal and led him away. She hoped the Barlows would understand. Stealing was nothing compared to the lengths she was prepared to go to in order to save her son.

Mounting the horse, Sarah set a course toward Elk Mountain. She couldn't be too far behind Jackson. With a little luck she would catch up to him by morning. Brilliant moonlight flooded the night as Sarah scanned the horizon. Then suddenly she saw him. He was riding east along a ridge, clearly outlined against the moonlit sky. Sarah offered a silent prayer of thanksgiving and took off after him.

Chapter 6

Chad made camp in a canyon beneath a sheltered overhang a few miles east of Carbon. He saw no reason to continue on to Medicine Bow that night. He'd all but given up on finding Freddie Jackson. After he made a campfire and ate a meager meal, he retrieved a stack of wanted posters from his saddlebags and sat down on a rock to study them by firelight. Three other outlaws were known to be in the area and he decided to question the leader of the local vigilante group in Medicine Bow in the morning. Perhaps Sean MacKay could give him a good lead on the other men.

Chad built up the fire to ward off wild animals, hoping that hostile Indians, known to be roaming the area, wouldn't see it. Rolling up in his bedroll, Chad searched for sleep and failed to find it. He was restless and disturbed by things that shouldn't bother him. Sarah and Abner were nothing to him. He'd given more of himself to Sarah than he'd given any other woman. The day his mother had left three small boys for a lover was the day he'd developed a deep distrust of all women.

Of the three brothers, Pierce had found a woman

he could trust, a woman who loved him unconditionally, but Chad didn't expect miracles where he was concerned. Cora Lee Doolittle, may she rest in peace, had come close to destroying the lives of all three Delaney brothers. Chad vividly recalled the day Cora Lee had died, and the changes that fateful moment had wrought in his life.

For two years he'd drifted aimlessly, hoping to escape his demons. Then he'd met Sarah and Abner. Somewhere within his barren soul he'd discovered a tiny spark of compassion he thought he'd lost forever. He realized now that compassion was the emotion that had kept him in Carbon. He'd fought against accepting responsibility but couldn't find it in his heart to leave Sarah and Abner to fend for themselves. Even now he felt a pang of guilt for having taken off like he did.

A part of his conscience argued that he should have stayed longer. He should have been more concerned about how Sarah and Abner would survive after he left. Yet a darker, deeper place inside him whispered that he'd done more than was required of him, more than most men would have done under the circumstances. Though the thought was new and frightening, Chad prided himself for not bedding Sarah when he wanted her so badly. Had he bedded her, he wouldn't have been able to leave her. He realized that making love to Sarah would mean he would lose himself to her. Thank God he hadn't let his loins rule his head. If he hadn't left when he did he knew he would have succumbed to the desire pounding inside him and taken Sarah.

Chad imagined Sarah's slim body stretched out beneath him and felt himself harden. He gave a snort of disgust. Obviously he needed a woman. His first order of business upon reaching Medicine Bow was finding a willing whore to ease his discomfort. Unfortunately he feared that no woman but Sarah could alleviate the persistent ache inside him. Flopping over on his stomach, he welcomed sleep when it finally arrived.

Freddie Jackson kept up his furious pace until he reached Medicine Bow, unaware that Sarah trailed behind him. He reined in before the High Rollers Saloon and dismounted. It was very late. Abner was sound asleep and he eased the boy from the saddle and carried him inside the saloon.

One of the girls ambled over to him, eyed Abner, and asked, "What have you got there, Freddie?"

"A kid," Freddie said. "My kid. Will you do me a favor, Sadie?"

Sadie's eyes narrowed. "What kind of favor? I don't know a thing about kids."

"I got an errand to do. Will you watch the boy for me? I won't be gone long."

"How much?"

Freddie snorted with disgust. "Ten dollars. That's more than an hour of your time is worth."

"Take him in the office, the boss is gone tonight," Sadie said, indicating a doorway. "He won't wake up, will he?"

"Naw, the kid's dead tired."

"He better not or it will cost you more."

"I said I won't be gone long." He placed Abner on a leather sofa and made a hasty departure.

Freddie stripped the saddlebags from his horse and crept along the shadows of the nearly deserted street until he reached the bank. He'd passed through Medicine Bow on his way to Carbon and had already cased the town and the bank. Medicine Bow was a small town hardly worthy of the name. It consisted of a depot and baggage room, a store, two eating houses, a saloon, a bank, and several shanties. About thirty buildings in all.

The bank was newly constructed and not very secure. Few people knew that the railroad used the bank to deposit its payroll. But Freddie knew and had been planning this job for a long time. He walked around to the back and pried open a window. No alarm gave him away as he crept through the dark bank to the small safe in the back office.

He lit a match, got his bearings, located the floor safe, and knelt before it. The safe was no different than a dozen others he'd cracked. He'd have it opened and the money out in record time. He fiddled with the dials, listening to the clicks as he slowly spun it first to the right and then to the left. When he began to detect a pattern he memorized the numbers and continued on. Forty-five minutes passed before the last tumbler fell into place and the heavy door opened.

Freddie smiled grimly. He could have used dynamite, it was quicker, but he'd have to leave fast and wouldn't have had time to go back for Abner. Besides, he was an expert at manipulating combination locks. This way was quiet; the robbery wouldn't be discovered until morning, allowing him plenty of time to escape. He began packing money in his saddlebags. When they were full he stuffed bills into his vest, jacket, and trouser pockets. When he could carry no more, he left the same way he had arrived, returning the saddlebags to the horse's back before returning to the saloon.

Freddie found Sadie sitting in the back room watching over Abner. "You done good, Sadie. Thanks. I'll take Abner off your hands now."

"Where did you go?" Sadie asked suspiciously.

"Don't ask questions, you'll live longer."

Opening his coat, he reached into his pocket and pulled out a hundred-dollar bill. "Here's a little bonus. See you around, Sadie."

Sadie had seen more than Freddie intended. When he opened his coat she'd spied sheaths of money sticking out of the inside pockets. She also noted his bulging trouser pockets. She couldn't recall them bulging like that when he'd first come into the saloon. Sadie put two and two together and came up with the right answer. She might be a whore but she was an honest one.

Sadie gave Freddie enough time to mount up and ride off before hightailing it to Sean MacKay's house.

Sarah rode into Medicine Bow in time to see Freddie ride away from the saloon with a sleeping Abner resting across his knees. Lines of exhaustion marred her brow and her still tender hands hurt dreadfully from hanging onto the reins. She wished she had thought to bring gloves but she'd been in too much of a hurry to think beyond the fact that Freddie had taken Abner away from her.

Sarah dug her heels into her horse's flanks and took off after Jackson. In another hour or so dawn would lighten the skies, decreasing the difficulty of following him. Unfortunately it would also make it easier for Freddie to see her, but she didn't care. She wanted Freddie to know she was following him. As she rode out of town she could have sworn she heard someone shouting, "Bank robbery!"

* * *

Jackson was five miles out of Medicine Bow before he realized he was being followed. Not by a posse, it was too soon for that. Unless it was the bounty hunter, he had no idea who it could be. When he passed a large boulder, he rode his horse out of sight behind it. The moon was a bright beacon in the sky, providing sufficient light to see by as he pulled his gun free of his holster and waited.

Freddie had dropped from sight and Sarah grew frantic. She had no idea how he had eluded her. Had he turned off someplace? Had he . . . ?

Her questions were answered when Jackson shot out from behind a boulder, directly into her path. Her horse shied, nearly throwing her, but she hung on, staring at the gun in Jackson's hand.

"Aw, shit! What in the hell are *you* doing here?"

Abner awoke with a start, saw his mother, and screamed for her.

"I want my son!" Sarah shouted, gaining control of her frightened horse with difficulty. "Give him back to me."

"You might as well turn back 'cause you can't have him. You babied him for the first five years of his life, now it's time to turn him into a man. Ain't that right, kid?"

Abner's chin lifted belligerently. "I *am* a man. I want my mama."

Jackson cocked his gun. "I oughta get rid of you right now, Sarah. You're making me mad."

"Don't you dare hurt my mama!" Abner cried. "I'll hate you forever if you do."

Abner's words gave Jackson pause, and he uncocked his gun and rammed it back into his gunbelt. He didn't want his kid to hate him for killing his mother. "Get out of here before I change my mind."

"I'm not going anywhere," Sarah charged. "I'll follow you to the ends of the earth, if need be."

Jackson looked fit to be tied. The sky was changing from black to gray and streaks of dawn colored the western horizon. Once the robbery was discovered the vigilantes would be hot on his trail. He didn't know how much Sadie had seen or guessed at, or if she would keep her mouth shut, but he couldn't count on her silence. He wouldn't be safe until he reached his hideout on Elk Mountain.

Having Sarah tag along behind him was dangerous. She knew where he was going and would spill her guts if he forced her to turn back. He really didn't want to kill her. She was Abner's mother, and besides, he didn't like killing women.

"You win, Sarah. You can come with me as long as you can keep up. I don't aim to be caught by the vigilantes."

"Vigilantes!" Suddenly Sarah recalled the words she'd heard in Medicine Bow. "You robbed the bank!"

"Yeah," he admitted, "but they'll never find me."

Freddie said nothing more as he gouged his spurs into his horse's flanks. The animal leaped forward and Sarah followed.

Chad arose at dawn, packed up his gear, and mounted up without taking time to fix himself anything to eat. He'd awakened this morning feeling perturbed and out of sorts. Though he tried to deny it, he was worried about Sarah and Abner. Indecision plagued him. Or was it his conscience? Chad could fight it no longer. He had to return to Sarah and Abner. He had argued with himself all the way to Medicine Bow before admitting he'd been defeated by that lone spark of compassion in him. Sarah and Abner needed him, he felt it in his bones.

He couldn't live with himself for deserting them while their future was so shaky. The least he could have done was wait another week or two, until Doc Clayter said she could start taking in laundry again. He frowned and shook his head. The thought of Sarah with her arms submerged in hot water was not a pleasant one. Sarah needed rest and plenty of good food. She was far too thin. He'd tried to tell himself it was none of his business but it didn't work. Fate had decreed otherwise. He had to go back to Carbon.

Suddenly he noticed a group of riders headed in his direction. His curiosity piqued, he reined in and waited for them to approach. As they drew near, he recognized Sean MacKay, the local vigilante leader. He'd crossed MacKay's path many times in the last two years. Alarm bells went off inside his head.

"Morning, Delaney," MacKay said when he reached Chad and drew rein. "Who are you after this time?"

"Morning, MacKay," Chad replied. "You seen anything of Freddie Jackson around these parts lately?"

"Strange that you should mention him," MacKay said. "He robbed our bank last night. I had hoped you'd seen him."

"I wish I had. In which direction was he headed?"

"Don't know. Sadie reported the robbery right

away, but it took time to gather a posse. By then Jackson's trail was cold. You want to join us?"

The alarm bells in Chad's head grew louder. He didn't know why but the need to return to Carbon was urgent. Chad's intuition seemed to be working overtime. He had no reason to think anything was amiss with Sarah, or to link her in any way to Jackson, but his gut told him otherwise.

"I just remembered something I forgot in Carbon. Think I'll head back that way."

"If you find Jackson, I reckon you'll be taking him in for the reward."

"I reckon so," Chad contended.

"Good luck, Delaney. We're gonna hang him on the spot if we find him first."

They left Chad in a cloud of dust. Turning his horse around, Chad rode back to Carbon. Late afternoon shadows had lengthened by the time he reached the dreary little town. The dingy, sunbaked buildings presented an appearance of peace and respectability, but Chad knew better. The town's "respectable" citizens were small-minded and judgmental, and their preacher was the worst offender of all.

Chad rode directly to shantytown and dismounted before Sarah's small shack. A strange premonition twisted his gut when he saw no sign of Abner, or any other movement about the shanty. Chad's worst fears were realized when a gust of wind caught the door and it swayed open on rusty hinges.

His fears escalated when Chad walked through the house and found it empty and cold. The yard was as deserted as the house. Where could Sarah be this time of day? He glanced across the way at the Barlow shack, feeling a welcome rush of relief. If Sarah wasn't at home perhaps she was with Carrie Barlow. His long legs carried him across the distance to the Barlows'. He rapped sharply on the door, chafing in impatience until one of Carrie's brood appeared to open it.

Chad stepped into the house. Carrie saw him immediately and came to greet him, her newborn babe nestled at her shoulder.

"Why, Mr. Delaney, what brings you here? I thought you'd left town. Is something wrong?"

"I was hoping you could answer that question, Mrs. Barlow," Chad said grimly. "Sarah isn't home. You haven't seen her, have you?"

Carrie shook her head. "Why, no, I haven't. Perhaps she stepped out for a spell."

"Perhaps she did," Chad said uncertainly.

Carrie grew thoughtful. "Come to think of it, I haven't seen Abner since yesterday. The little scamp usually turns up to play with one of my kids."

Chad began to have a bad feeling about this. "Thanks, Mrs. Barlow. Is there anything else you can think of? Did anything unusual happen yesterday or today?"

"Now that you mention it, our horse disappeared from the lean-to next to the house. Charlie is fit to be tied. He'd sure like to get his hands on the horse thief who stole it. That horse was Charlie's pride and joy."

Chad didn't have time to chat about a missing horse when he was so worried about Sarah and Abner. "Sorry about the horse, Mrs. Barlow. If you'll excuse me, I'm going to see if I can find Sarah and Abner."

Chad hurried away. He had another stop to make before jumping to conclusions. He mounted Flint and rode to the parsonage. Hezekiah himself answered Chad's knock. He scowled when he saw Chad standing on his doorstep.

"Have you come to seek redemption, Mr. Delaney? I seriously doubt you're worth saving. Get thee gone, Satan."

"Is Sarah here?" Chad asked brusquely. He wasn't here to beat around the bush with a man who saw evil in everything.

"If you're referring to Sarah the harlot, no, she is not here. She is not welcome in my home."

"Do you know where she is?"

Hezekiah's stern features hardened. "In some man's bed, I suspect."

"I hope you rot in hell," Chad said, whirling on his heel. He was wasting time here and knew it.

Chad rode into town, tied Flint to the hitching post in front of the One-Eyed Jack Saloon, and walked down one side of the street and up the other, looking for Sarah in each of the businesses he passed. It appeared as if Sarah and Abner had disappeared into thin air.

"Hey, Delaney, you still in town?"

Chad whirled on his heel toward the sound of the voice. He saw Cal Bork coming out of the general store and waited for him to approach.

"Yeah, I'm still here. What of it?"

"Don't get your dander up, I was just curious. I was in the storeroom taking inventory when I heard you asking Pa about Sarah Temple."

"That's right, Bork. Have you seen Sarah? She's not at home and I haven't been able to find her anywhere."

"Can't say as I have." He gave Chad a speculative look. "Are you still looking for Freddie Jackson?"

"Yeah, why do you want to know?" Now it was Chad's turn to become suspicious. "Has Jackson been in town recently?"

"Er . . . no. Not that I know of." His eyes shifted away from Chad. "Reckon I'd better get on back to the store."

Chad was astute enough to recognize a lie when he heard one. He grasped the lapels of Bork's shirt and pulled him close, until they were nose to nose. Chad stared him down. "If you value your life, I suggest you tell me what you know. Jackson is an outlaw with a price on his head. You look like a reasonable man, so I'm appealing to your sense of honesty. Was Jackson in town yesterday?"

"Yeah, Jackson was in town yesterday, asking about his parents. I told him they were dead and that was the end of it. I haven't seen him since so I figured he hightailed it out of here."

Chad tightened his grip on Bork's lapels. "Is that all, Bork? Think hard. What else did he say?"

Beads of perspiration popped out on Bork's forehead. "Now that I think on it, Jackson did inquire about someone else." He swallowed convulsively. "He asked about Sarah Temple."

Everything Chad feared had come to fruition. Ever since Sarah's strange reaction at the mention of Jackson's name, Chad suspected a connection between the two. He'd tried to convince himself that he'd been imagining things, that his fancy was working overtime, yet the gut feeling had remained. Abruptly he released Bork's lapels. "I suppose you told Jackson where to find Sarah."

Bork gave a jerky nod. "I might have mentioned it. He seemed interested in that kid of hers. Wanted to know how old he was. I thought it odd but Jackson always was a strange one."

Taking advantage of Chad's distraction, Bork slowly backed away. "That's all I know, Delaney, I swear it."

"Did Jackson say where he was heading? Did you know he meant to rob the bank in Medicine Bow last night?"

"No! That's all he said. I don't know anything about a bank robbery, or where Jackson was heading. Can I go now?"

"Go on, get out of here."

Chad needed to think. All kinds of possibilities were running through his mind and he needed time to sort through them. His growling stomach reminded him that he hadn't eaten all day so he headed for the nearest eating house. After ordering a thick steak, fried potatoes, apple pie, and coffee, he sat back and stared out the window while his mind sorted through the facts.

Fact one: Sarah and Abner were missing.

Fact two: Jackson was in town asking about Sarah.

Fact three: No matter how much the thought riled him, Sarah and Jackson had to be more than casual acquaintances.

Now came the questions. Was Abner Jackson's son? Did Sarah go off willingly with Jackson? Her house showed no signs of a struggle. Did Sarah love Jackson? That thought caused him no small amount of consternation. After listening to Sarah's disparaging remarks about men, Chad got the impression that she neither trusted nor liked them.

Was Jackson the cause of her distrust? What had he done to her? And why would she go with him?

His meal came then and Chad ate slowly, mulling over the options open to him. If Sarah had willingly accompanied Jackson, then it was none of his business. The reward for capturing Jackson was still a consideration, however. There was also something else to consider. If Jackson forced Sarah to go along with him, Chad would brave hell and high water to find her. Abner was a good kid. A man like Jackson would be a bad influence on him. Surely Sarah knew that.

By the time he'd eaten the last bite of pie and drained his coffee cup, Chad had made up his mind. He couldn't abandon Sarah and Abner to a violent man like Jackson. He would find Jackson and rescue her, even if she didn't want to be rescued.

Women! They didn't have the sense they were born with. The fact that Jackson was Abner's father, if indeed that was true, didn't give Jackson the right to take Sarah and Abner. God, he was confused. Had Sarah gone with the outlaw willingly or did Jackson take her and Abner by force?

Suddenly another thought occurred to Chad. Did the Barlows' missing horse have anything to do with Sarah's disappearance? His gut told him it did. Chad's face was grim with determination as he left the eating house. Fortunately, Chad knew this area like the back of his hand. Jackson was no dummy. He knew he couldn't show his face around here without risking capture. Common sense told him Jackson would lay low for awhile. Medicine Bow sat at the foot of Elk Mountain.

Wouldn't it make sense for Jackson to have a hide-out somewhere on Elk Mountain? Chad thought it did and that's exactly where he headed after replenishing his supplies at the general store.

Jackson led Sarah along a winding trail to an abandoned miner's shack. It was protected on one side by a ridge, making it difficult for passersby to see. Nearby, a clear creek meandering down from the mountain top bubbled over a stony bed. It was a peaceful setting, and Sarah thought the air much cleaner than the soot-drenched air she breathed in Carbon.

Though remarkably beautiful, and despite being within a day's ride of Medicine Bow, the area was remote and uninhabited. She was more alone than she had ever been in her life. If only Chad . . . No, she wouldn't allow herself to think about Chad. He was far away by now and probably glad to be shed of her and Abner.

"We're here," Jackson said, setting Abner on the ground and dismounting behind him. "Lots of wide-open spaces. No one will find us here."

"What about Indians?" Abner asked fearfully.

"Indians ain't gonna hurt us, kid. Spotted Deer won't let them."

Just then an Indian woman appeared in the doorway of the crude cabin. Her face seemed carved from stone as she stared at Sarah and Abner. The woman was handsome rather than pretty, with dark skin, penetrating black eyes, and a statuesque figure. Her malevolent glare caused a shiver to skitter down Sarah's spine. Sarah recognized something cruel about the woman, something dangerous in her eyes that made Sarah want to take Abner and run.

"Who is the woman?" Spotted Deer asked in guttural English. "Why is she here?"

Jackson pushed Abner forward. "This here's my kid. His name is Abner. And that's his ma. Her name is Sarah. I wanted the kid with me. His ma followed. She don't mean a thing to me, Spotted Deer."

Spotted Deer approached Sarah, her eyes dark with contempt. "Her skin is pale and her eyes are strange. Send the woman away, Fred-die."

"Aw, forget her, honey. I got no feelings for Sarah. She can clean and cook for us so you won't have to work so hard."

Jackson's eyes glittered with lust as his gaze settled on Spotted Deer's breasts. "What say you and me go inside so you can give me a proper greeting?" he said, pulling her toward the cabin. He paused in the doorway and turned back to Sarah. "You and the kid stay here until we're finished. Don't even think about running because it won't work. If the wild animals don't get you, the Indians will."

Sarah waited until Jackson and Spotted Deer were inside the cabin before leading Abner to a fallen log and sitting down beside him. She had no idea where she was or how to get back to civilization. She could steal a horse now, while Jackson was occupied, but she wasn't sure she could find her way back to civilization. She was exhausted and so was Abner. Her hands were so raw she doubted she could hold the reins properly. When the time came for her and Abner to escape she wouldn't hesitate, but at the moment she was too tired to try.

"Why did that bad man take me away, Mama?" Abner asked, laying his weary head in Sarah's lap. "Is he really my papa?"

The answer to that question wasn't easy for Sarah to give. Biologically Jackson was Abner's father, but in all the ways that counted, Abner had no father. How could she explain that to a five-year-old?

"Freddie Jackson really is your father, honey, but I never wanted you to know. I'm sorry to say he's not a good man. I wanted to spare you this. You might never have known if Freddie hadn't shown up in Carbon and found out about you."

"He didn't know about me?" Abner asked, his interest piqued.

"No. Someday, when you're older, I'll explain it to you."

"I don't have to like him just because he's my papa, do I?"

"No, honey, you don't. But if I were you I wouldn't say anything to make him mad. I'm going to try to find a way for us to escape. That will be our little secret."

Abner seemed to accept that. "I'm hungry, Mama."

"So am I. When Freddie comes out of the cabin I'll ask about getting us something to eat."

Fifteen minutes later Freddie exited the cabin. His shirt was unbuttoned, and he was in the midst of fastening his trousers. "Get inside and fix us something to eat," he barked. "You insisted on coming along, now make yourself useful."

"Come on, Abner," Sarah said, rising quickly so as not to rouse Jackson's anger.

"The kid stays," Jackson growled. "He's too much of a mama's boy for my liking. You've turned the kid into a sissy. From now on Spotted Deer will see to his needs. She can teach him some of her people's ways. Shoshone discipline will do the boy good."

"If that squaw hurts Abner I'll make her sorry she left her people," Sarah warned. "Abner is a good boy; he doesn't need to be taught discipline."

Jackson's face hardened. "Do as I say and don't argue. I'm still mad at you for following me. You don't want to see me when I get really angry." His tone held a threat Sarah wasn't prepared to challenge at the moment. Turning abruptly, she walked into the squalid cabin.

The place was filthy. Spotted Deer was sprawled across the rumpled bed, her clothing awry. Suddenly she leaped off the bed to confront Sarah, her face twisted with fear and hatred.

"Why are you here, white woman? I am Freddie's woman. He doesn't need you."

"You're welcome to Freddie Jackson. I wouldn't have him on a silver platter. I loathe the man. The only reason I'm here is because of Abner."

Spotted Deer looked unconvinced. "Why do you hate Fred-die? You have his son."

"Freddie Jackson raped me. I didn't want what he did to me. Abner is the result of his attack. But I don't love Abner any less because of what his father did to me. Abner is all I have in the world and no one is going to take him away from me."

Spotted Deer smirked. "You talk brave, white woman. Ab-ner is *my* son now, and you are our slave." She grabbed a broom sitting by the door and started beating Sarah with the handle.

Sarah howled in pain and outrage but could not escape the irate woman's vicious attack. It wasn't until Jackson came into the cabin to see what the ruckus was about and took the broom away from Spotted Deer that the beating stopped.

"Cut it out, Spotted Deer," Jackson said crossly. "Let Sarah do her job, I'm hungry."

Abner started to run to Sarah's defense but Jackson snatched him up before he reached his mother and handed him to Spotted Deer. "The boy is yours, Spotted Deer. You always wanted a kid. Take him outside while Sarah fixes us some grub."

Spotted Deer's dark eyes glittered with malice. "If you take the white woman to your bed, I will cut out your heart."

"Aw, Spotted Deer, why would I want a bag of bones like Sarah? You got nothing to worry about."

Still smarting from Spotted Deer's blows, Sarah sincerely hoped it was true. Had she known how intently Jackson was watching her as she built up a fire in the hearth and set a frying pan over the flames, she would have been terrified.

Chapter 7

Sarah shifted uncomfortably on the hard floor. The thin blanket provided meager protection against the chill mountain air that seeped through every crack and crevice of the drafty cabin. She wished Abner had been allowed to sleep beside her but Freddie had insisted on sending her son up to the loft. At least the loft had a plump layer of straw to keep Abner warm, Sarah reflected as she pulled the blanket closer around her.

Freddie had crawled in bed beside Spotted Deer and before long, sounds of their rutting reverberated through the cabin. Sarah put her hands over her ears but it didn't help. Freddie and Spotted Deer were vocal lovers. His harsh grunting and her squeals, combined with the creaking ropes beneath the mattress, nearly drove Sarah mad. The vulgar noises made her recall the night Freddie had raped her and the pain and degradation returned as if it had happened yesterday. God, how she hated him. If he laid a hand on her again she'd kill him.

It seemed like forever before the sex sounds turned into sated snoring and Sarah was able to relax. Sleep finally came but it was hard won.

A gray misty dawn had floated down from the top of Elk Mountain when Sarah was rudely kicked awake. She opened her eyes to find Spotted Deer leaning over her.

"We need wood for the fire, white woman. My man and my child will require food soon. If you do not hurry I will beat you again."

Sarah dragged herself from the floor, wrapped the blanket around her shoulders, and left the cabin. When she returned with an armload of wood, Jackson was standing in the middle of the room, stark naked. He scratched himself with obvious enjoyment, ignoring Sarah's startled gasp. Sarah looked around for Spotted Deer but couldn't find her.

"What's the matter?" Jackson asked, sending her a wicked grin. "I know you've seen naked men before. Maybe you forgot how well endowed I am. Are you hankering for a little of what I got, Sarah?"

Sarah averted her eyes, walked to the hearth, and dropped her load of wood on the grate. "You've got nothing I want, Freddie Jackson."

Jackson came up behind her, pressing obscenely against her. "I've been thinking. You turned into a fine-looking woman. There's no reason you and Spotted Deer can't share me. I got enough for both of you."

Spotted Deer walked into the cabin, saw Jackson molded intimately against Sarah and flew into a rage. "What are you doing with my man, white woman? Keep away from him. He's mine."

"My name is Sarah! Tell your lover to keep away from me! All I want from him is my son."

Jackson sent the Indian woman a fulminating look. "You don't own me, Spotted Deer, just remember that. Your jealousy is beginning to bore me. Be good or I'll send you back to the reservation with your father. If I want to have a little fun with Sarah, it's none of your concern."

"Over my dead body," Sarah hissed.

Abruptly Jackson turned away, aware of Spotted Deer's malevolent glare. It would serve her right, he thought, if he sent her away and took another woman. Sarah's soft white flesh was beginning to look damn good to him.

During the following days Sarah lived in fear. Jackson was getting bolder where she was concerned and Spotted Deer was still jealous of his interest in her. It took little provocation for the Indian woman to pick up the broom and beat Sarah for no apparent reason. One day Sarah grabbed the broom from the vicious woman and gave her a taste of her own medicine. That only enraged Spotted Deer, who found various ways to punish Sarah for her defiance, none of them pleasant. Soon Sarah was covered with numerous bruises, her tender flesh black and blue from being beaten, pinched, and slapped.

Abner fared a great deal better. Spotted Deer seemed to have a soft spot for the boy and treated him sternly but with none of the harshness she displayed with Sarah. Even Jackson seemed taken with Abner. Unfortunately Jackson had no idea what a young boy needed in terms of love. He displayed a gruff fondness toward Abner, but mostly he just ignored the boy.

Spotted Deer did her best to keep Sarah and Abner apart. She allowed virtually no conversation between mother and son and Jackson didn't care enough to intercede when Sarah pleaded for his help. Sarah could take the beatings, accept the harsh treatment, but she couldn't bear being separated from her son.

Sarah let five days pass before she seriously began looking for a means of escape. The problem with any plan she formulated was that she and Abner were seldom alone and thus unable to communicate. Then something happened that made Sarah's situation truly desperate.

Sarah returned to the cabin with the bucket of water she'd been sent after that morning, shocked to find Jackson and Spotted Deer engaged in a violent argument. From what Sarah could gather, Spotted Deer wanted Jackson to send Sarah away and Jackson had refused. When she walked through the door, Abner, who had been cowering in the corner, ran to her, hiding behind her skirts.

"I do not like the way you look at Sarah," Spotted Deer charged. "There is no room in this cabin for two women."

"No one tells Freddie Jackson what to do," Jackson retorted. "You're too damn bossy, Spotted Deer. I'm getting tired of you haranguing me about Sarah. In fact," he said cruelly, "I'm just plain tired of you. Get your things together and get the hell out of here."

Spotted Deer's dark eyes narrowed. "You want me to leave?"

"Yeah. You're no longer welcome here." He turned away from her, which was a big mistake. Spotted Deer grabbed a knife from the kitchen table and lunged at him.

Sarah's cry of alarm alerted Jackson and he whirled in time to deflect the wicked blade. Wrest-ing it from Spotted Deer's hand, he struck her across the face, sending her flying across the room.

"Don't ever try that again," Jackson growled as he kicked Spotted Deer in the ribs for good measure. "Now get up and get out of here. Go back to your people where you belong."

"You are a bad man, Fred-die," Spotted Deer hissed as she painfully picked herself up from the floor. "The Shoshone are a proud people. One day you will pay for this with your life."

"Don't threaten me," Jackson warned. When Spotted Deer continued to glare at him he took a menacing step toward her, his fist raised to strike her again.

Sarah flew to her defense. "Let her alone, Freddie. She's hurt. Besides, you're frightening Abner."

Jackson spared a glance at Abner then lowered his fist. Spotted Deer took advantage of the lull and fled out the door.

"Good riddance," Jackson muttered darkly. "No woman tells me what to do. Remember that, Sarah."

Sarah wasn't sure Spotted Deer's leaving was a good thing for her. Being alone with Jackson was going to be difficult. The way he looked at her made her skin crawl. What did he expect of her now that Spotted Deer was gone?

Sarah learned the answer to that question sooner than she wished.

"Go on outside and play, kid, I want to talk to your mother," Jackson told Abner.

"No, stay!" Sarah cried, clutching Abner against her.

"That's not a good idea, Sarah," Jackson said evenly. "Let Abner go."

His tone brooked no argument. "Do as Mr. Jackson says," Sarah said, pushing Abner away from her. "Go outside and play. It's okay."

Reluctantly Abner left, wandering off into the woods where he'd seen a rabbit scampering by.

"What do you wish to talk about?" Sarah asked, backing away from Jackson.

"I'll be needing a woman now that Spotted Deer is gone."

"What has that got to do with me? Go find yourself another squaw."

"Use your brain, Sarah. I've been watching you. You're a damn fine looking woman and I want you. You must have learned a few tricks in the five years since Abner's birth. I still remember how tight you were the first time I took you." He rubbed his groin obscenely. "You'll be sharing my bed from now on."

"Like hell!" Sarah objected. "I didn't want you then and I don't want you now."

"You got no choice, woman. I just sent my whore packing and it just so happens there's another one here to take her place."

He advanced toward her. Sarah retreated until she was backed up against the door. She felt behind her for the knob but it was too late. Jackson was upon her, grinding his loins against her.

"Your skin is so white," he said as he stroked her neck with rough, seeking fingers. "I always did fancy white skin. Spotted Deer served her purpose until something better came along."

His hand slipped down to her breast, squeezing until she cried out for him to stop. "You're hurting me!"

"Spotted Deer never complained." His hands slid down to her waist, then lower, raising the hem of her skirt on his upward journey.

Casting about desperately, Sarah said, "What if Abner walks in? You wouldn't want him to think you're hurting his mother, would you?"

"I don't give a damn what the kid thinks," Jackson said, moments before his mouth slammed down on hers.

Panic shuddered through Sarah. It was his rape of her all over again. All the pain and degradation she'd suffered that day resurfaced with the same terror she'd experienced all those years ago. She searched for and found the strength to shove him away.

Jackson cursed and reached for her again. Then suddenly a scream rent the air, putting a halt to Freddie's attack. "What's that?" he asked as a second scream was abruptly cut off.

"Abner!" Sarah cried, recognizing her son's voice. "Something's happened to Abner."

Sarah pulled open the door and rushed outside, Jackson hard on her heels. There was no sign of Abner. Sarah called his name. He didn't answer. The silence was terrible, broken only by birdcalls and the rush of water over rocks. Sarah dashed into the woods but had no idea which way to turn. There was no sign to indicate the direction the small boy had taken.

"Do something!" Sarah shouted to Jackson. "Find my son."

"I'll get my horse and comb the woods," Jackson said, sprinting toward the lean-to at the back of the cabin where the horses were tethered. He came to a screeching halt at the sight of the empty shed. "They're gone! The horses are gone!"

Sarah skidded up beside Jackson, stared into the empty lean-to, and felt the world rock beneath her feet. "What's happening? What does it mean?"

"Spotted Deer!" Jackson spat. "The vindictive bitch wasn't satisfied with Abner, she took the horses."

The color drained from Sarah's face. "Where did she take him?"

"To her people, that's where. Spotted Deer took a shine to the kid."

"No! You've got to go after them!"

"Not me! I value my life. Spotted Deer's got it in for me now. I ain't gonna be taken by savages."

"We're talking about a child, Freddie. Your child. Or have you conveniently forgotten that?"

"The Injuns will be good to the kid. I told you, Spotted Deer likes him."

"Damn you, Freddie Jackson! I'll go after him myself."

Jackson grasped her arm. "You ain't going no place. How far can you get on foot? Get inside and fix me something to eat while I think on what's to be done. We need to get us a horse before we can do anything."

Ignoring him, Sarah started to walk off. "I'm going after Abner. You can stay here if you want."

Jackson's grip on her arm tightened as he dragged her toward the cabin and shoved her inside. Then he pulled the door shut and barred it from the outside. Since the windows were too narrow he didn't worry about Sarah crawling through the opening. Then he set off into the woods. There was a slim possibility that Spotted Deer had released his horse once she was a safe distance from the cabin.

He returned a short time later in a rotten mood.

"Did you find any sign of them?" Sarah asked hopefully.

"Shut up and get me something to eat. When I find that bitch I'm gonna skin her alive."

When Sarah opened her mouth to speak, Jackson warned, "Don't say a word, Sarah, not a damn word." His glittering gaze rested on her breasts. "We can make another kid easy enough." His meaning was clear, but Sarah refused to accept it.

Chad had been on Elk Mountain ten days. He'd cut Jackson's trail several times but still hadn't found his hideout. Small tracks he'd found at various watering holes indicated that one of the riders with Jackson was a woman. Since there was no sign of a struggle, Chad surmised that Sarah was Jackson's willing companion. That thought made the blood congeal in his veins.

It was late afternoon when Chad heard a strange sound. He peered into the dense woods surrounding him and saw nothing. Then he heard the sound again and slightly altered his direction. He was surprised when he came upon an old Indian trail. He spotted movement up ahead and moved into the trees where he couldn't be seen. Then he spotted an Indian woman on horseback ahead of him on the trail. She was leading a second, riderless horse. He watched in dismay as the woman dismounted and pulled a small boy from the saddle. Chad's expression turned grim when the woman gave the boy a rough shake and spoke earnestly to him.

Abner! Chad could see his small, tearful face

clearly. His features were contorted with fear as he struggled with the Indian woman. Fortunately the woman was so intent upon subduing Abner that she didn't hear Chad approach. Abner saw him, however, and his little face lit up with joy.

"Chad! You came! I knew you would."

Spotted Deer spun around just as Chad dismounted. Abner ran into his arms and he quickly set the boy behind him, out of harm's way. Spotted Deer stared at Chad with fear in her eyes, and turned to flee.

"No you don't," Chad said as he lunged at her. "You're not leaving until you tell me what you're doing with Abner."

Spotted Deer's lips turned downward, refusing to answer. Chad noticed her bruised face and split lip and wondered who had beaten her.

"Spotted Deer took me away," Abner explained.

"Where's your mother?" Chad wanted to know.

"Back at the cabin with Mr. Jackson. Did you know he's my papa? I don't like him. Mama said it's all right not to like him."

"Fred-die is a bastard," Spotted Deer offered, sending Chad a sullen look. "He sent Spotted Deer away so he could bed his new woman. Spotted Deer took Abner."

"Where is Jackson?" Chad asked, increasing his grip on the woman's arm. "What do you know of him?"

"I am his woman," Spotted Deer said with a sneer. "Or I was until he returned with that skinny white woman. You will find him at the cabin. I took his horses so he goes nowhere."

"Where is the cabin? I've been combing the mountain for days looking for it."

Spotted Deer pointed toward a ridge visible in the distance. "There, below the ridge." She tried to escape from his biting grasp but Chad's grip was firm. "You let Spotted Deer go now."

Chad's grip relaxed. "Go, but Abner remains with me. Leave one horse, I'll need it."

Spotted Deer hesitated but a moment before leaping atop Jackson's horse and disappearing into the forest.

"Are you all right, son?" Chad asked, dropping to his knees before Abner. "I heard you screaming. Did Spotted Deer hurt you?"

Abner shook her head. "I was screaming at her to take me back to Mama. When I wouldn't stop she got off her horse and tried to make me behave. Are we going after Mama now? Mr. Jackson is mean to her."

"In a minute. Why did you and your mother go with Jackson?"

"We had to. Can we go now?"

Chad wasn't satisfied with the answer but it had to suffice. Abner appeared to be worried about Sarah and the boy wasn't one to exaggerate. Truth to tell, he was worried about Sarah himself. Chad had no idea what had transpired between Sarah and Jackson these past ten days but obviously it was enough to make Spotted Deer jealous.

"Yes, we can go now," Chad said, lifting Abner aboard Flint's broad back and mounting behind him. "But we have to be careful, son. Jackson is a dangerous man. We don't want him to hurt your mother."

"You can help Mama, Chad, I know you can." Abner's vote of confidence warmed Chad's heart.

The horse he'd taken from Spotted Deer trotted beside him as Chad grasped the trailing reins and started off toward the ridge Spotted Deer had pointed out. A short time later Chad caught a glimpse of the old miner's cabin. It butted up against the foot of the ridge, camouflaged by the rocks, trees, and earth that blended cleverly with the weatherbeaten logs. No wonder he hadn't been able to find it.

Chad reined in a safe distance from the cabin and dismounted. He tethered both horses, then lifted Abner from Flint's back. He squatted down on his haunches, placing himself at eye level with the boy.

"I'm going to get your mother, Abner, but you're going to have to obey me."

Abner nodded solemnly. "What do I have to do?"

"Stay out of trouble, for one thing. See that boulder over there?"

Abner glanced at the large rock. "I see it."

"You're to hide behind that rock and not come out until I return. Is that clear? No matter what you hear or see, you're not to come out. Can you do that? It's growing dark. You won't be frightened, will you?"

"I'm not afraid of the dark. Are you sure I should stay here?"

"Yes, very sure. I'll have my hands full and don't want to worry about you. Do I have your promise?"

"I promise."

Chad smiled, took Abner by the hand, and led him to the boulder. Then he gave the lad a quick hug and left, praying that he understood the danger and would obey. Surprise was the only element

Chad had going for him. Once Jackson realized what was going on he could turn on Sarah, or use her to gain his escape. Crouching low, Chad carefully made his way through the gathering gloom toward the cabin.

After Jackson finished eating he sat back and stared at Sarah through slitted eyes. Sarah watched warily as he arose abruptly and struck a match to the lamp.

"I want to see what I'm getting," he said, eyeing her greedily. "I ain't had my dessert yet and you're going to provide it. Take off your clothes."

Sarah shot out of her chair and raced to the door. Jackson reached it before she did, catching her in his arms. Then he dragged her to the bed. Roughly he pushed her down on the rumpled surface while shedding his gunbelt. Then he fell on top of her, pinning her beneath him.

"You ain't going nowhere, woman. We're gonna make us another kid. I kinda like the idea of being a daddy."

Sarah's throat went dry, and she gagged. The idea of being intimate with Freddie Jackson made her physically ill. She fought and scratched like a madwoman, unwilling to become his victim again. She wasn't the innocent she'd been six years ago.

"Damn you!" Jackson cursed. "Hold still."

With great difficulty he managed to open his trousers. When Sarah continued to struggle, he dealt her a stunning blow to the cheek. Sarah screamed and went limp, all the fight beaten out of her.

"That's more like it," Jackson grunted as he released his sex. He was attempting to raise Sarah's skirt when the door burst open and Chad charged into the room.

Jackson leaped to his feet, reaching for his gun and cursing when he realized it wasn't where it was supposed to be. He saw it lying on the floor and dove for it. Nimbly Chad kicked it under the bed.

"Who are you?" Jackson wanted to know. He didn't like looking down the barrel of a six-shooter.

"Your worst nightmare. I'm taking you in, Jackson. There's a five-hundred-dollar reward on your head."

"So you're that damn bounty hunter who's been tracking me. I can make it worth your while to let me go."

"The name's Chad Delaney and I don't want your tainted money. Step away from the bed."

Jackson obliged, moving gingerly toward the door, giving Chad his first good look at Sarah. "You bastard! What have you done to Sarah?"

"You know her?" Jackson asked curiously. "Are you one of her customers? Listen, you can have her. Just let me go."

Chad moved toward the bed, alarmed by Sarah's pallor. She was so still he wasn't certain she still breathed. Concern for Sarah made Chad careless. He turned his eyes away from Jackson for the space of a heartbeat. Taking advantage of the brief lapse, Jackson made a mad dash through the open door. Chad fired a shot at him, heard a yelp, and ran to see if he'd hit Jackson. But Jackson had already disappeared into the dark forest. Briefly he considered giving chase, but claiming the reward for Jackson's capture no longer seemed important. Sarah and Abner needed him.

Dimly Sarah was aware of the ruckus taking place around her. Jackson's blow had stunned her and things happened so fast after that she wasn't certain what was going on. When her head finally cleared, she saw Chad bending over her.

"Are you all right? What did Jackson do to you?"

"Chad . . . How? Why? I can't believe you're here."

"Yeah, well, neither can I. It's a long story." His voice was thick and unsteady and edged with concern. "Did he hurt you?"

Sarah sat up slowly. "I'm fine except for a few bruises that aren't important." Her voice held a desperate note. "Forget about me. You have to find Abner. Freddie's Indian squaw took him. He's just a little boy. He must be frightened to death."

"Abner is safe, Sarah. I came across Spotted Deer not far from here. She didn't object too vigorously when I took Abner from her and sent her packing."

Sarah leaped to her feet. The abrupt movement left her head spinning and she reached for Chad to steady herself. Chad's arms slipped around her. He groaned, his body remembering every subtle nuance of hers as his hands slid down to her waist to hold her more firmly against him. She was warm and soft and clinging sweetly to him.

Chad had no idea how it happened, but a moment later he was kissing her, fervently, madly, as if he'd been starving for the taste of her. And by some crazy quirk of fate she was kissing him back, their bodies melded together, their mouths fused. His hands slid down over her hips to grasp her bottom, pressing her against the hard ridge of his arousal. He thought he heard Sarah moan but couldn't be sure.

Sarah's mind went blank. Chad's scorching, searing kiss blotted out all thought. Her arms curled around his neck as his tongue parted her lips, seeking entrance. She granted it eagerly, savoring the clean taste of him as the memory of Freddie's repulsive kiss faded from memory.

Chad broke off the kiss. His eyes were dark and inscrutable as he searched her face. "God, Sarah, you can't imagine how worried I was about you and Abner. I have to know. Did you go with Jackson willingly? Is he Abner's father?"

Sarah stiffened, pulling away from him. "You think I went willingly with Freddie Jackson?"

"I don't know, that's why I'm asking you."

She turned away from him, her shoulders slumping with disappointment. Why is everyone so eager to believe the worst of her? "Think what you want, Chad Delaney, you will anyway. I want my son, where is he?"

Abner! Chad had been so caught up in the moment he had almost forgotten the boy. "I'll go get him."

Sarah sagged in relief as Chad left the cabin. She didn't know what had gotten into her. She'd been so glad to see Chad she'd responded wantonly to his kisses. He wanted her. She could feel the proof of his need pressing against her through the barrier of her clothing. His eager kisses had almost convinced her that he cared for her, then his words made a mockery of her thoughts. Yet the fact remained that Chad was concerned enough to follow her. Or was it Abner he cared about?

Chad returned to the cabin with a sleeping Abner in his arms. Sarah gave a cry of alarm and flew to his side.

"He's all right, Sarah. The poor boy's exhausted. I found him asleep right where I left him. Where shall I put him?"

"In the loft," Sarah said, indicating a rope that pulled down a retracting stairway. "I fixed a bed for him up there."

She pulled on the rope and the stairs came down. Chad ascended the rickety staircase and laid Abner down on the pallet of straw and blankets. Sarah followed him up, tucked him in and placed a kiss on his forehead. When she would have lingered, Chad placed an arm around her shoulders and led her back down the stairs.

"Let him sleep. He'll be fine tomorrow." His gaze slid over her bruised face. "Are you sure you're all right?"

"I will be as soon as I leave this place."

"Why don't you get some rest? You look exhausted."

"You'd be tired too if you had to chop wood, carry water, and cook for four people."

"I'm sorry. I've been searching for you since the day after you'd disappeared. If I hadn't come across Spotted Deer I might still be looking. This cabin isn't easy to find."

Sarah saw Chad's expression change abruptly from concern to intense, unrelenting anger. "I should have wrung Jackson's neck while I had the chance. When I saw you both on the bed, all I could think of was how badly I wanted to kill him."

"You got here in time. Spotted Deer served him in bed, not I. He turned to me after he sent her away."

"Come here," Chad said, grasping her hand and leading her over to the bed. "Sit down and tell me what happened."

Sarah perched on the edge of the bed. "Will you believe me?"

"There are certain things in my past that make it difficult for me to trust a woman, but I'll try."

"We're more alike than you know," Sarah muttered.

"Why don't you start at the beginning," Chad urged. "How well do you know Freddie Jackson?"

"Not well at all. I guess I never really knew him. I met him at a church social about six years ago. I don't know why he took a shine to me. I was a painfully shy, awkward sixteen at the time and he was a smooth-talking man of twenty-five. I admired him. I even thought I . . . was in love with him."

"What did your parents think about that?"

"Nothing. They didn't know I was taken with him. I never even shared a private word with him until he found me alone one day in the church and asked me to meet him that night in the barn behind the parsonage. I was young and impressionable and thought he was a gentleman. He swore he only wanted a moment or two of conversation with me, that no one would ever know I'd sneaked out to meet him."

"I take it Jackson wasn't an outlaw at that time."

"No, he was just a restless young man without much direction. His parents doted on him, giving him everything he wanted within their means. Obviously it wasn't enough." Painful memories made her voice crack.

"I thought it romantic that Freddie wanted to

meet with me alone. I had girlish dreams like any other innocent girl of sixteen."

"What happened?" Chad asked, fearing he already knew the answer.

"Talk was the last thing Freddie wanted. The moment I entered the barn he threw me on the ground and brutally raped me. I was afraid to tell my parents and that's what he counted on. When I was finally able to pick myself up off the ground I felt as if my life had been destroyed by that one cruel act. The only way I could survive was to pretend it never happened. Then my world shattered when I learned I was pregnant. By then Freddie had already left town to begin his life of crime."

"You never told anyone who hurt you?" Chad asked with disbelief.

"What good would it have done? Freddie was gone. Accusing him of rape would have hurt two old people who loved their son. Telling my parents I was pregnant was the most difficult thing I had ever done. They refused to believe I'd been raped. They called me a sinner and cast me from their house in disgrace."

"Jackson never knew he had a son?"

"Not until he returned to Carbon recently. Somehow he learned about Abner and turned up at my door. He saw Abner and decided he wanted his son."

"So you both went along with Jackson," Chad said evenly.

Sarah leaped to her feet. "No! It wasn't like that at all. He took Abner without my consent. Do you think I'd let my son go without a fight? I stole the Barlows' horse and followed. Freddie had no choice but to take me along when he saw me following him up Elk Mountain."

Chad pulled Sarah down on his lap, stunned by the tender feelings she aroused in him. For a man who shunned responsibilities, he had suddenly become the unwilling protector of one small woman and her son.

What was happening to him?

Chapter 8

"What you did was very foolish and very brave," Chad said. Despite her fragile appearance, Sarah possessed more gumption than any woman he had ever known. "You should have gone to the sheriff. I understand Carbon has had a sheriff for some time now."

"There wasn't time," Sarah revealed. "Besides, I didn't want anyone to know Freddie Jackson was Abner's father. Abner has suffered enough cruelty in his young life, he didn't need another cross to bear."

Chad's arms tightened around her. He didn't understand this strange, savage need to protect Sarah from everyone and everything. From the beginning he'd been determined not to care for Sarah Temple. Yet here he was, holding Sarah in his lap and loathe to let her go.

"Chad, I . . . I think you should let me up," Sarah said breathlessly.

"I don't think I could let you go right now even if I wanted to," Chad whispered against her cheek. "I'm going to kiss you, Sarah. I'd like to do a lot more if you'd let me. I wanted you from that first moment I saw you. I can't fight it any longer."

"Is that why you followed me here?" Sarah asked.

"I suppose that's one of the reasons," he said moments before his lips touched hers. Her mouth was sweetly inviting and he deepened the kiss, drawing a tiny, shuddering sound from her.

"Sweet, so sweet," Chad groaned against her mouth. He wanted to be inside Sarah so badly it was tearing him apart. He was trembling from the force of it as he eased her back on the bed and came up over her.

He kissed her hungrily, ravenously, allowing her scant time to think about the right or wrong of what they were doing. His hands covered her breasts, finding her nipples and rolling them between his fingers. He smiled as Sarah writhed beneath him, pleased to find her so responsive. Anxious to render her naked, his fingers tugged at her buttons. Sarah uttered a protest and moved her hands to stop him.

"Don't make me stop, sweetheart, I don't think I can."

"Chad . . . I . . ."

He silenced her with a kiss. A scorching, voracious kiss that effectively put an end to her objections. When he felt a tiny bubble of fear in her, it suddenly dawned on him what was troubling her.

"How long has it been since you've been with a man, Sarah?"

Sarah glanced up at him, then her glance skittered away. "Freddie was the only man, and that was rape."

Chad went still. "You've never been made love to?"

"No," she said in a small voice.

"Then it's about time. First we have to get your clothes off."

"All of them?"

Chad searched her face, cursing himself for going too fast. Her degrading experience with Freddie Jackson had left Sarah scarred; she knew nothing about lovemaking, or the pleasure to be gained from a relationship with a man who cared about her.

"We'll go slow, Sarah, I swear it. I won't hurt you. You've been hurt enough in your life. I want to give you pleasure."

"Why?"

"Because you deserve it," Chad said uneasily. If there was another reason, he chose to ignore it. "Will you trust me?"

"Trusting is difficult, and it hurts," Sarah observed.

"Do you want me, Sarah?"

He felt her shift beneath him and the fragility of her slender frame had an unsettling effect deep inside his gut. He sensed her tension, her fear, her agonizing loneliness and commiserated with her. Those were the same emotions he had experienced nearly every day since leaving Dry Gulch. He wanted to make Sarah smile, to hear his name on her lips when she cried out her pleasure. He wanted . . .

Sarah.

The ensuing silence nearly killed him. When she finally spoke he had to strain to hear. "I do want you, Chad. God help me, I do, and it frightens me. All these years I've done my best to preserve my reputation, though God knows I had little of it left to save. Give me pleasure, Chad. I want to experience it at least one time in my life and I want you to give it to me."

Her words touched something deep and inviolate inside him. "You won't be sorry," he vowed. "I've never abused a woman and don't intend to start now."

She threw her arms around him, pulling him down for her kiss, surprising Chad. Their lips met and melded. His senses whirled as his hands tangled in her hair and he deepened the kiss.

Chad was shocked at the way Sarah's kisses affected him. He'd worked so hard to feel nothing for Sarah but lust. He knew he'd hungered for Sarah sexually, but hadn't realized till now that he wanted something deeper than physical pleasure. It scared the daylights out of him.

Chad managed to release the buttons on her bodice and untie the ribbon on her chemise, baring her breasts to his kisses, her soft sighs delighting him. Then he drew a velvet nub of nipple into his mouth. It hardened instantly, deliciously sweet and enticing. He suckled her, absorbing her warmth, her femaleness, her very essence. He cradled her breasts and pressed them together, burying his face in their sweet crevice. He felt the pounding of her heart and knew that his matched it.

"Help me," Chad whispered, tugging at her clothing. Sarah obliged, lifting her shoulders then her hips as her dress and underclothes were stripped away. Then he stood up and tore off his own clothing, tossing them to the floor.

Sarah watched him from beneath lowered lids, admiring the latent power and masculine beauty of his naked form. His legs were long and perfectly sculpted. His hips were slim and his torso broad and impressive. His stomach was ridged with corded muscles. Even in the dim light she could see a fine dusting of brown hair on his arms and legs. She'd never initiated sex in her life, but now it seemed the right thing to do. She held out her arms to him but Chad didn't move into them immediately.

"I want to look at you first. You're beautiful."

His gaze traveled the length of her lithe curves, coming to rest on the dark mound at the junction of her thighs. He had dreamed of her like this, her yielding body flushed with passion, soft, voluptuous, welcoming him in every way.

With a groan of surrender he came down on her. His mouth found hers. Within seconds she was responding to the urgent demands of his lips, her tongue sparring with his, her mouth clinging with quiet desperation.

Beneath his touch her breasts swelled, and her nipples hardened. He heard her whimper and understood her need as he lowered his mouth and suckled the stiffened crests. His hands and lips were everywhere at once. Her back, her buttocks, her trembling thighs. He pressed kisses along her shoulders, her breasts, her stomach. He nudged her legs apart, his warm breath whispering over her most intimate place. Then his mouth touched her there and she arched up against him.

"Please, Chad."

"I want to be sure you're ready, sweetheart," Chad said in a voice made husky with desire. His sex was heavy, primed to burst, but still he held back. He wanted to make this memorable for

Sarah, to banish all those bad memories of her first time.

His caressing hand moved over the curve of her abdomen, trailing through the dark curls, touching her moist flesh below. His thumb rubbed across the tiny nub at the entrance to her sex, and when his fingers found her secret place, Sarah tried unsuccessfully to hold back a scream.

She's tight, Chad thought, testing her with his fingers. If he'd had doubts about her celibacy these past few years, they were quickly dispelled. She couldn't be having sex regularly and be this tight. His fingers teased, sliding inside her with slow, deep strokes.

Sarah gave a long, drawn-out sigh.

"I'm going to come inside you now, Sarah. You're tight, so it might hurt. That's why I spent so much time preparing you."

Sarah was past caring. She wanted him. All of him. And she wanted him now. She felt the moisture gathering between her legs and knew she was as ready as she'd ever be. She arched up against him in blatant invitation and he accepted, pressing inside her slowly but surely. She felt herself stretching to accommodate him. There was a moment of discomfort but it wasn't painful. The delicious sliding friction quickly created an inferno within her.

When Chad realized he wasn't hurting Sarah, his relief was enormous. Flexing his hips, he pressed deep, filling her with himself. She was hot, tight, and wet, challenging his control.

"Don't move," he warned as she shifted her hips beneath him. His breathing was shallow, his muscles taut as he fought to master the instinctive need to spill himself.

"What is it?" Sarah asked, frowning.

"I don't want this to end too soon. I promised you pleasure and you're going to get it. Hang on, sweetheart, we're going for one helluva ride."

Clutching his shoulders, Sarah clung to him. He felt his muscles tremble beneath her hands, stunned by his response to her touch. Her hips arched upward, driving him more deeply. He gazed down at her and saw a look of pure joy on her face.

Sarah never dreamt such ecstasy was possible as waves of pleasure broke over her. This was nothing like the terrible act that had remained in her memory all these years. This was bliss, pure and simple, yet she knew there was more and she strained to find it. She heard herself pleading with him as her body raced out of control, heard Chad's voice in her ear, whispering encouragement as he thrust and withdrew in long, piercing strokes. And then she felt the slow tide of pleasure washing over her, sweeping her into a whirlpool of churning sensations. She cried out his name, dimly aware of his culmination—that one deep thrust that brought him to climax, sending his seed spilling into her. Moments later he collapsed against her and cradled her in his arms.

Chad pulled a blanket over them and curved himself around her body. Moments later blessed sleep claimed them. Shortly before daybreak Sarah drifted into wakefulness. She cuddled closer to Chad, warm and no longer lonely. She felt loved. Oh, yes, definitely loved, even if it was lust driven. Sarah was no fool. She knew where she stood with Chad. He was a man and men wanted sex with no attachments. He had wanted her, and now that he had taken her he would disappear from her life.

Sarah didn't regret what had happened between them. She was grateful in a way. Chad had single-handedly proved that pleasure could be obtained from an act she'd once thought ugly and dirty. But she certainly wasn't going to do this with any other man. Making love with any man but Chad sounded revolting. Her one night of rapture would have to last a lifetime.

Sarah saw nothing but a life of hardship and drudgery in her future. She supposed she'd be the town laundress until the day she died, rejected by her parents even though she led an exemplary, celibate life. She released a long, loud sigh.

"What are you thinking?"

Sarah started violently. She had no idea Chad was awake. "Nothing important."

"Are you regretting what we did?"

"No," she said, giving him a quick smile. "I was just thinking about my future."

He pulled her into his arms, wanting somehow to comfort her. Taking her back to Carbon was the last thing on his mind now. He wanted her again. Once was not enough. The way he felt now it would never be enough. Sarah was still such an innocent. Awakening her to passion had been a profound experience. There was something sweetly vulnerable and terribly appealing about Sarah Temple, and that made her dangerous. He didn't want to feel anything for Sarah except lust, and right now he was feeling plenty of that.

Sarah snuggled against him, content just to lie there and remember all those wonderful feelings Chad had aroused in her. Then she felt the hard ridge of his sex stirring against her stomach and she stared at him in surprise. His cheeky grin sent heat spiraling through her veins, a seething warmth that brought back provoking memories. Memories she wouldn't mind revisiting.

Chad apparently sensed her thoughts for he pressed her more tightly against his hardening body. His hand stole beneath the blanket to caress her. She sighed, her hips moving in languid rhythm to his caresses. This time there was no long foreplay, no slow arousal. They came together in heat and passion and wild need. Mouths fused, bodies melded, they rode the crest together. Chad locked his arms around her and thrusted uncontrollably. The shattering force of his passion seared her as he spilled himself inside her. She writhed against him, shuddering, finding her own fulfillment at the same instant Chad reached his.

Chad rolled away and collapsed beside Sarah, staring at the ceiling. The thin gray light of early morning bathed the shack's meager furnishings in dirty shadows, making Chad wish he could have found a better place to introduce Sarah to passion. The hard ground beneath the moon and stars would have been better than this, but he seriously doubted he could have waited. That's how desperately he'd wanted Sarah.

"Why are you frowning?" Sarah asked.

"This is a damn poor place to make love for the first time. This shack can't have good memories for you."

"You made new memories." She slid her feet over the side of the bed. "Abner will be up soon. It wouldn't do for him to find us in bed together. I'll fix breakfast if you build a fire in the hearth."

Chad pulled on his underwear and bent to tend

to the fire. Sarah hastily donned her shift and poured water from a pail into a bowl so she could wash. By the time Chad had a fire going, she had bathed and dressed.

"I'll wash, shave, and dress outside," Chad said, gathering up the rest of his clothing. "Then I'll tend to the horses."

Sarah watched him, heat flushing her cheeks as he moved about the cabin. He seemed at ease and totally comfortable with his near nakedness as he gathered his discarded clothes. He must have sensed her eyes on him for he turned to smile at her. Sarah quickly looked away, but not before she saw his sex stir and harden beneath his drawers.

"Reckon I'd better get out of here," Chad said, glancing down with a grin. "Next time you'll think twice about looking at me like that."

Sarah's mouth fell open, but before she could form a retort Chad had already walked out the door. What was wrong with her? she wondered. She had granted Chad what she'd denied every other man and had thoroughly enjoyed it. Her thoughts skittered to a halt when Abner came bounding down the stairs from the attic.

After breakfast, Chad collected the weapons in the cabin so Jackson wouldn't claim them should he decide to return. During his search he found the money from the Medicine Bow bank robbery.

"We'll drop this off in Medicine Bow," he said as he packed the money and weapons in his saddlebags. By the time he finished, Sarah and Abner were ready to go.

Chad lifted Abner in front of him on the saddle and Sarah rode the horse she had borrowed from the Barlows. She hoped they would forgive her for taking him without asking first and was relieved that she'd be able to return him in good shape.

For a disquieting moment, Sarah recalled the intimacies she'd shared with Chad last night. In the light of day her wanton behavior embarrassed her, yet she didn't regret it. How could she when Chad had given her such pleasure?

"You seem lost in thought," Chad said when he held back to ride beside her.

Sarah flushed and looked away. There was no way she was going to tell Chad she had been recalling their lovemaking and the profound affect it had on her. It was unlikely she'd ever be with Chad again. Once he took her home he'd leave her and never look back. It was a mystery why he'd followed her, but she suspected it was because he wanted the reward for Freddie Jackson. Jackson had been his motivation from the beginning.

"Are you by any chance reliving last night?" Chad asked when a long silence ensued.

"No," Sarah was quick to deny. "I was wondering what the Barlows would say when I returned their horse." It wasn't exactly the truth but it would have to suffice. She'd never admit her thoughts were so filled with Chad that she could think of little else.

"We'll find out soon enough. Medicine Bow is up ahead. By nightfall we'll be in Carbon."

Sarah and Abner waited outside the bank while Chad returned the money. It hadn't taken them long to come down Elk Mountain. It surprised Sarah that Freddie's hideout had been so close to town.

"I'm hungry," Abner complained when Chad

came out of the bank. "Is it lunchtime yet?"

Chad laughed and ruffled Abner's blond curls. "I reckon we can find an eating house in this town. I can use a decent meal myself."

An hour later, their stomachs full, they continued on to Carbon. Chad had learned in town that the vigilantes were still hunting for Jackson and he sincerely hoped they found him. It bothered him to think that Jackson might return to Carbon looking for Sarah and Abner and tried not to let it matter. He had better things to do than hang around the mining town, waiting for Jackson to show up. He had done his duty where Sarah was concerned, now it was time he got on with his life. Sticking around Carbon was dangerous to him in more ways than one.

Chad worried that he was becoming terribly fond of Sarah and Abner. He had too many dark memories complicating his life. Until he came to grips with the traumatic events that had sent him fleeing from his home, he had nothing to offer a woman. He was empty, a mere shell of the man he once was. Deep in his heart Chad knew he wasn't responsible for what happened, but those brooding demons inside him wouldn't give him peace.

Sarah felt a sense of desperation as she rode into Carbon. The town held so many bad memories for her. The thought of returning to her old backbreaking job of taking in laundry sent her spirits plummeting. But what else was there for her? She was an outcast, and she was resolved to that, but it was Abner she felt sorry for. The boy deserved so much better than she could give him.

Carbon looked even more somber and unremarkable than usual as they rode down the main street. Coal dust clung to the rooftops like a thick cloud, clogging their throats and burning their eyes. Sarah didn't remember the town looking so shabby, but she'd never been in the mountains before, breathing clean, unpolluted air.

"We're here," Chad said, reining in before her shack.

"I'm going to return the Barlows' horse," Sarah said. "I feel so guilty about taking him. Would you take Abner inside? I'll be back soon. If you can stay awhile, I'll fix supper for us when I return."

Sarah didn't wait for his answer. Whatever Chad decided, she'd accept. She owed him more than she could ever repay and was determined to ask nothing more from him.

Carrie Barlow answered the door, her eyes widening when she saw Sarah standing on the doorstep. "Sarah, come in! Where in the devil have you been? I was worried about you when Mr. Delaney said you were missing. Would you like some coffee?"

Sarah stepped into the noisy room crowded with children engaged in various activities. "I can't stay, Carrie. I've got a confession to make and I hope you'll forgive me."

Carrie frowned. "Forgive you? Whatever for?"

"I took your horse. But don't worry, I brought him back. He's just fine. I left him in the shed out back."

"You took our horse?" Carrie asked, dumbfounded. "Why would you do a thing like that? Charlie will be so relieved to have him back."

"I desperately needed a horse, Carrie, and yours was handy. Abner was kidnaped by his father and

I had to follow. I feared I'd never see my son again if I waited too long to go after him. That's why I didn't rouse you from bed to ask permission. I couldn't waste time on explanations. Please forgive me."

"Of course. Do you want to tell me about it?"

"I'm not proud of my association with Abner's father. It's a story best left untold. I have Abner back, that's all that matters."

"Did that nice Mr. Delaney help you? I think he's sweet on you. He seemed so concerned when you were hurt."

"He held himself responsible for my accident," Sarah explained. "He merely did what his conscience demanded."

And he wanted the reward for capturing Freddie Jackson, Sarah thought but did not say.

"About Abner's father," Carrie began, curious about the man Sarah had never mentioned before.

"I don't wish to talk about him," Sarah said curtly. "I'm sorry, Carrie, but Abner's waiting for me. I have to leave. We'll talk more later. I'm really sorry about taking your horse."

Sarah left before Carrie's curiosity brought questions Sarah didn't want to answer. Chad was still there when she returned to her shack. He and Abner were searching the cupboards for something to eat.

"You stayed," Sarah said, feeling foolish for making such an obvious statement.

"Yeah," he said succinctly. He'd been doing a lot of thinking on the ride back to Carbon. He didn't like the conclusion he'd arrived at but no other solution was available.

"You and Abner can wait in the parlor while I

fix us something to eat. It won't be fancy but it will fill our stomachs." She took stock of her empty cupboards and shook her head. "I hope my former customers will return with their laundry. I'm going to need the money."

Her words served only to reinforce Chad's decision. He would present it to Sarah after they'd eaten and Abner was put to bed. Sarah might put up an argument but he was determined to have his way. He was too fond of Abner, and yes, dammit, too fond of Sarah to leave her to the likes of Freddie Jackson.

After a supper of beans, bacon, and biscuits, Abner's head began to droop. Sarah hustled him off to bed and returned to the kitchen to do the dishes. Chad sat at the table, sipping his coffee.

"We need to talk, Sarah."

"About what? If it's about what happened last night, forget it. I don't regret it, nor do I expect anything from you. You saved me and Abner, and for that I'll always be grateful to you."

A muscle twitched in Chad's jaw. "Is that why you let me make love to you? Out of gratitude?"

Why should her words disappoint him? Chad wondered. Gratitude was all he wanted from a woman, the most he would accept.

Sarah sensed Chad's troubled thoughts and sought to diffuse them. "No, Chad, there's more to it than that and you know it. But I don't think either of us wants to explore feelings we're not comfortable with. Is there something else you wanted to discuss?"

Chad's fingers pushed through his thick brown hair as he rose and came to stand behind her. "I've thought a lot about this, Sarah. I've decided you can't remain in Carbon. There's no guarantee Jackson won't return for Abner. I can't stay here forever to protect you."

"I've never asked for your protection. It's something you decided on your own. I've taken care of myself and Abner since I was sixteen. It hasn't always been easy but we've survived."

"How long do you think you'd survive if no one brought their laundry to you? Mrs. Kilmer was so angry the day I turned her away that she vowed no one in town would bring their laundry to you in the future. I suspect she meant it."

Sarah was stunned. "What did you say to her?"

"Quite a lot, actually. She called you a few choice names, hinting that you were earning money in other ways and didn't need her business. I fear I lost my temper."

Sarah's knees started to buckle and Chad steadied her. "Are you all right?"

"Yes. You just dealt me a shock I wasn't prepared for. Your burst of temper quite possibly cost me my livelihood. What are Abner and I going to do now?"

"That's what I want to talk to you about." Lifting her in his arms, he carried her to the sofa in the parlor and sat down beside her. "I'm going to take you to my brother and sister-in-law in Rolling Prairie, Montana. The Circle F Ranch is large and prosperous, and Zoey will be delighted to have another woman in the house. It gets lonely for her out there."

Sarah looked at Chad as if he'd just grown two heads. "You want to take me to the home of complete strangers and dump me? I can't possibly impose on people I don't know. No, it's impossible."

"I don't see where you have any choice, Sarah. You have no guarantee Jackson won't return to Carbon for Abner. Or that the law will catch up with him any time soon. And another thing, how are you going to support yourself and Abner? You've got to think of your son."

"How do you know your brother and his wife will take me in?"

"Because I know. Zoey and Pierce have a child about two years old. There are countless chores to perform on a ranch, you won't find yourself idle."

Sarah chewed over Chad's words, arriving at and discarding several options to his suggestion. Without a means of support she and Abner wouldn't survive long on the charity of her poor neighbors. She'd always managed on her own and her pride wouldn't allow her to beg her parents for food for her child. There was only one other way to earn a living and that didn't appeal to her. She was no whore.

"Maybe I can do your sister-in-law's laundry," Sarah offered. "Or take care of her child to free her for other duties. I can cook and clean and . . ."

"Whoa. I wasn't hinting that you should become their slave. Leaving you with Pierce and Zoey is one way of coping with my conscience when I take off. I'm surprised I actually have a conscience. I thought I'd left it behind in Dry Gulch but I reckon I'd merely misplaced it. You helped me to find it again but I'm not sure it's something I want to keep."

His gaze was so intent upon hers that Sarah found it difficult to breathe. She wanted to lay her hand along his stubbly chin, to run her fingers through his thick brown hair, and place her head on his shoulder. She longed to tell him she'd go anywhere with him if he promised to stay with her. No matter how much he belittled himself Sarah knew him to be a kind, caring man who'd been adversely affected by some tragic event in his life. She didn't want to, never expected to, but she feared she was falling in love with him. But the last thing she wanted was to become a burden to Chad.

Her thoughts must have conveyed themselves to Chad, or maybe it was the way she looked at him, for he reached for her and pulled her onto his lap. With a sigh of surrender, she offered him her lips.

Chapter 9

Chad kissed her roughly. The effort to summon his usual self-control and quell the gnawing hunger sweeping through him was beyond his capabilities. To touch Sarah was to want her. He didn't know what was happening to him. With whores he'd bedded there had been pleasure—easy, forgettable pleasure. Nothing beyond the uncomplicated satisfaction of easing his lust and gaining release. But with Sarah, the grinding need to possess her never let up. It was constantly with him.

Chad moaned when Sarah reached out trembling fingers and touched his face. Her hand trailed downward over his torso, past his hips, to shyly rest upon his shaft straining against his clothing. He gasped and pressed himself into her hand.

Sarah flushed and jerked her hand back.

"Go ahead, sweetheart," Chad encouraged as he reached for her hand and drew it down to his manhood. "Touch me. It feels good. Damn good."

Her hands returned to his body. His own hands were not idle as he swiftly and efficiently removed her dress. Her chemise was about to go in the same manner as her dress when Chad paused, glancing toward the closed bedroom door. "What about Abner?"

"Abner could sleep through an earthquake. He won't awaken."

The sofa was narrow and uncomfortable but didn't hinder them as the rest of their clothes melted away as if by magic. When they were both naked, Chad sprawled across the sofa and lifted Sarah atop him. His breath came in short gasps as he guided her hand to his erection, teaching her the rhythm. Amazed at her boldness, Sarah wanted to explore and caress every inch of him, from his engorged shaft to his corded, muscular torso.

"Take me inside you," Chad urged in a tormented whisper.

Raising up, she took him inside her. He slid full and deep into her, so deep he felt her stretching to accommodate all of him.

His hands went to her breasts. They were full and generous despite her thinness. Her nipples were dark, taut and rigid beneath his fingers. Chad lost himself in the pure pleasure of touching her, of hearing her moan, of seeing desire darken her violet eyes.

His thrusts accelerated, and he knew his movement sent raw pleasure pounding through her. They moved together in a wild frenzy and he thrust and withdrew as the need within him built, becoming unbearable. Unspeakable rapture shone in her eyes as she threw her head back and rode him shamelessly, surrounding him with her tight, wet heat. She cried out his name and he felt her spasms just as he bucked, sending his seed splashing against the walls of her womb, branding her forever. And then the ability to think ceased.

"That was incredible," Chad said on a gasp. "I wish . . ."

"What do you wish, Chad?"

"I wish things could be different. I have nothing left to give a woman. I care for you and I don't want you to think that we . . . that you and I . . ."

"How can you say you have nothing to give after what we just experienced together? I'm not an expert, but feelings like that are . . ."

"Lust, sweetheart, pure and simple. We're explosive together. Your sweet innocence is like an aphrodisiac. I can't get enough of you. But I'm incapable of feeling deep emotions. What we just did makes us both happy, but don't read too much into an act that was driven by lust."

"I was going to say rare."

Sarah felt like such a fool. Chad didn't love her; he never would. She didn't believe in miracles. She knew that wanting and loving were two entirely different emotions, yet she'd harbored a slim hope that Chad felt something deeper than lust for her. She wondered at the event that had crippled him emotionally.

She reached for her clothing, suddenly embarrassed by her nakedness. Perhaps the townspeople were right. Maybe she was a whore at heart. She couldn't bring herself to feel guilty. Making love with Chad had seemed natural and right. It had meant a great deal to her. She'd always be grateful to Chad for proving that all men weren't rapacious bastards.

"I'm sorry, Sarah. I never meant to hurt you. I just wanted you to know that my life is an emotional wasteland. Until I resolve my problems I have nothing to offer a woman except sex. But don't get me wrong, I care about what happens to you and Abner. For what it's worth, you're the first woman to attract me in a helluva long time."

"Is that all, Chad? Is physical attraction all you feel for me? What happened to make you so cynical?"

"It's a long story."

"I've got time. What happened in Dry Gulch? I know there was a woman involved. Did you love her?"

"Love? Hah! I don't believe in it. Love is empowering to a woman and I'd never trust a woman with that kind of power."

"She must have hurt you badly."

"No, it wasn't like that at all. But you're right about a woman being involved. If you must know, it began when a neighbor, Cora Lee Doolittle, accused my brother Pierce of getting her with child."

"Did he?"

"Absolutely not! Pierce didn't even like Cora Lee. The lying bitch told the vigilantes that Pierce beat her up when she told him she was pregnant and begged him to marry her. Pierce barely escaped with his neck intact. The vigilantes were going to hang Pierce if he didn't marry Cora Lee. He fled and was seriously wounded. Zoey Fuller found him and nursed him back to health."

"He married Zoey," Sarah remembered.

"Eventually. That's another long story. Suffice it to say, they're happily married today. The vigilantes found Pierce and brought him back to Dry Gulch. They demanded that he either marry Cora Lee or face the hangman."

"Why did Cora Lee lie?"

"That, too, is another story. Anyway, Pierce couldn't marry Cora Lee because he was already married to Zoey by then. So Cora Lee and her brother Hal hatched a plot to gain Cora Lee a husband and share in the Delaney wealth. They insisted that I marry Cora Lee and give her bastard a name. I had to do it to save Pierce."

"You said you weren't married."

"I'm not. Oh, I married the witch, all right. I'd have done anything to save Pierce's life. But it wasn't a real marriage."

He fell silent, brooding over the tragic events that followed. A woman's lies had started a chain of events that had produced fatal results.

"Something happened."

Chad's thoughts turned inward, recalling that fateful day. "I went to see Cora Lee at her ranch a few days after our marriage." His voice was hard, tinged with bitterness. "I found Cora Lee and her brother in bed together. To make a long story short, Hal was the father of her child. Hal drew on me. He missed, I didn't."

"You killed him?"

"Yes."

"His death wasn't your fault, Chad. The man drew on you." She gave a delicate shudder. "You must have been shocked to find Cora Lee in bed with her own brother."

"I was thoroughly sickened. The disastrous events that followed Hal's death will remain with me forever."

She looked into his shadowed eyes and saw his pain. She longed to reach inside him and release his demons, but didn't know how.

"Tell me about them."

"Cora Lee and Hal's father was a sick man. He heard the shots and got up from his sickbed to investigate. When he saw his only son lying dead on the floor it was more than the poor man could take. He dropped dead of a heart attack."

"How dreadful. But that still . . ."

"There's more, Sarah. Cora Lee went into premature labor. The baby didn't survive. Neither did Cora Lee."

Sarah paled. Dear God. She understood now. Chad had reacted to all those senseless deaths by shouldering the blame. Until he could shed his guilt he would remain emotionally empty. She wondered if his distrust of women started with Cora Lee or went back farther than that.

"Cora Lee was probably a weak person," Sarah surmised. "Hal was as much or more to blame than she was. Perhaps he forced his sister to do those terrible things, then made her lie about them when she became pregnant. We'll never know. Needless to say, Cora Lee paid the ultimate price for her sins. You should put your demons to rest."

"I reckon I realize now that Cora Lee was Hal's victim. I pity her. She didn't deserve to die. Neither did an innocent babe. You can't begin to imagine how those deaths affected me. I can't help thinking that if I hadn't killed Hal things might have ended differently. When I drew my gun, I aimed to kill. The sight of Hal rutting on his own sister set something off inside me I couldn't control."

"So you left your home and everything you held dear because you killed a man in self-defense," Sarah repeated, trying to understand Chad.

"Those deaths, particularly those of Mr. Doolittle and the babe, weighed heavily on me. I had to get away. I needed space and time to come to grips with those events. In trying to save my brother's life, I inadvertently caused four deaths. I had to get away from Dry Gulch and all those disturbing memories."

"Is Cora Lee the reason for your low opinion of women?"

Chad gave her a slow grin. "Don't get me wrong. I like women. They have their place in a man's life. I just don't trust them. My brothers feel the same way. Pierce was dead-set against marriage until he met Zoey. We've all had bad experiences with women, beginning with our mother. She left my pa for another man. We were just young boys at the time and couldn't understand why our mother didn't like us enough to stay with us. That distrust has carried through into our adult lives."

"All women aren't alike. You said Pierce found a good woman. There must be others out there."

"Perhaps there are but I'm not sure I could handle one. I'm emotionally incapable of loving."

"Someday a woman will steal your heart when you're least expecting it, Chad Delaney." I wish it could be me, Sarah thought but did not say. When and if Chad married he'd want an innocent girl, not a less than respectable woman with an illegitimate child.

"This talk of marriage is a waste of time. Unless . . ." He searched her face, then shook his head. "I suppose every woman wants a husband. Once you get to Rolling Prairie, Zoey will introduce you to suitable young men. I hope you choose wisely. Abner needs a man in his life."

"Damn you, Chad Delaney! We've just made love and already you're trying to get rid of me. For your information, I don't intend to marry . . . ever. No man would love Abner like I do. It would take a special man to forget Abner is illegitimate."

Chad reared up and began pulling on his pants. "Any man who loved you would love Abner without reservations."

"Where will I find a man like that?" Sarah contended.

Chad frowned. *He* loved Abner but he didn't count. He wasn't husband material. And unless he wanted to be roped into marriage he reckoned he'd best keep his lust under control and his fly buttoned. The last thing he wanted was to make Sarah believe he was interested in marriage.

"I'm sure there are any number of men who will appreciate you." This conversation was beginning to make him uncomfortable. The thought of Sarah with another man was not a pleasant one. "Perhaps you should go to bed. There's much to be done tomorrow. I need to purchase a wagon so you and Abner can travel to Montana in comfort. You probably have some household goods you'll want to transport."

"I don't have all that much. Some bedding and dishes, a few articles of clothing. None of the furnishings are mine. But you're right, Chad, I am tired. You can sleep on the sofa, if you like. Good night."

Sarah didn't get very far. Chad reached for her, pressing her against him. The thrust of her firm breasts against his chest sent his resolve flying out the window. His shaft stirred restlessly as he lowered his head and kissed her. When Sarah leaned into his kiss, he reluctantly recalled his vow to contain his lust and abruptly broke off the kiss.

"Good night, Sarah. Sleep well."

Chad couldn't sleep. Dredging up those tragic events from his past made him reluctant to return to Dry Gulch. Perhaps he wouldn't have to go all the way to Dry Gulch, he reasoned. He could leave Sarah and Abner in Rolling Prairie with Pierce and Zoey and take off for parts unknown. There were still plenty of outlaws to catch out there, including Freddie Jackson.

Sarah's thoughts were as troubled as Chad's. His story had answered a lot of questions about Chad Delaney, but it didn't make her love him any less. Chad's problems originated from within his own conscience. He held himself responsible for four deaths that were none of his doing. It occurred to Sarah that Chad was possessed of an innate goodness that he'd be the first to deny. The sad truth was that those events had drained him emotionally and his conscience denied him peace. He'd fled all he loved and held dear in order to escape his demons, but time and distance had failed to erase his memories.

An uneasy sleep finally claimed Sarah. She was shaken awake the next morning by Abner.

"Mama! Chad is gone. Is he coming back?"

"Would you be sorry if he didn't?"

"I like Chad, Mama. Why can't he stay with us?"

"Chad wants to take us to Montana to live with his brother and sister-in-law," Sarah said. "They live on a big ranch."

Abner's eyes shone with excitement. "Do they have horses?"

"I suppose. Chad doesn't think we should stay in Carbon. He's afraid Freddie Jackson will return and take you away again."

Abner frowned. "I don't like that man. He was mean to you. I don't believe he's my papa. I'm going to pretend Chad's my papa."

Oh, God, she was going about this all wrong. "That's not wise, honey. Chad cares about what happens to us but that's as far as it goes."

Abner's frown deepened. "What do you mean?"

"You're not old enough to understand, honey. Wait in the kitchen for me. I'll join you after I've dressed. There's much to be done today, and it won't get accomplished if we lie in bed all day."

Chad bought breakfast at an eating house and was the first in line when the bank opened. He had a letter of credit on the Delaney account but this was the first time he'd needed to use it. He felt guilty taking money he hadn't earned, even though he was an equal partner with his brothers. Before he left Dry Gulch he'd done his share of the work and spent his share of the profits. But for the past two years he'd contributed nothing to the ranch and felt uncomfortable taking from it.

Until now. He was damn near broke and he needed a wagon and supplies to get Sarah and Abner to Montana. The bank manager offered no argument when Chad withdrew a substantial sum of money.

Chad's next stop was the livery, where he was able to purchase a small covered wagon and four sturdy horses to pull it. Then he bought supplies for the trip and stored them in the wagon. Chad's last stop was the general store. He felt a little awkward purchasing women's clothing, but Sarah was going to need something besides the rags she called a wardrobe. He bought three day dresses made of sturdy material and another of velvet that he couldn't resist because it was the exact shade of her violet eyes. He added a warm coat and boots. He had to guess at the sizes but the clerk proved helpful in that respect when Chad mentioned they were for Sarah Temple.

Chad found it easier to buy clothing for Abner. Before he left the store he'd bought the youngster several flannel shirts, denim pants, underwear, boots, jacket, and headgear. He even purchased new boots and trousers for himself, adding a leather vest and sheepskin jacket that had taken his eye. They were headed for high country and he knew that the weather could turn at a moment's notice.

While Chad was conducting his business Sarah packed their meager belongings. When she finished, there was one last thing she had to do. No matter what her parents thought of her, she couldn't leave town without telling them goodbye. They had never actually met Abner and suddenly she felt it very important that Abner meet his grandparents. She tried to explain the situation to the child in words he would understand.

"Why didn't my grandma and grandpa ever come to see me?" Abner wanted to know after listening to Sarah's explanation. "Don't they like me?"

"They never gave themselves a chance, honey. They were angry at something I did so they deliberately cut me out of their lives. But I think they should meet you before we leave town." Her expression turned wistful. "I want them to know what they're missing."

They left the house after a lunch of leftovers from

breakfast. Sarah composed words she wanted to say in her head while Abner skipped along beside her. They didn't see Chad, who was on his way back to the house after having completed his errands.

Chad was puzzled when he spied Sarah and Abner walking down the street. He wondered where Sarah was going and what she was up to. Then she rounded a corner and it occurred to him that she was going to call on her parents. He spit out a curse. Hadn't she taken enough abuse from them? He followed close behind as she walked up to the parsonage and knocked on the door.

Hazel Temple opened the door. Her startled gaze swept over Sarah and settled on the boy standing beside her.

"Hello, Mother. I know I'm the last person you want to see but I wanted you to meet Abner before we left town. This is likely to be the last time you'll see either of us."

"You're leaving town?"

"It's what you and Father have always wanted, isn't it?"

Hezekiah appeared in the open doorway beside his wife. "It's exactly what we want. Why are you here, Sarah?"

Sarah's chin rose fractionally. "I wanted you to meet your grandson."

Hezekiah's stern gaze settled briefly on Abner. "We've never acknowledged your bastard. Why bring him here now?"

"I wanted him to know that he has grandparents before we leave. And I wanted to tell you both goodbye." She nudged Abner.

"Goodbye, Grandmother, goodbye, Grandfather. Can we go now, Mama?"

"Where are you going?" Hazel asked, ignoring her husband's disapproving frown.

"We're going to Montana," Abner piped up. "We're going to live with Chad's family."

"Delaney is a fool if he marries you," Hezekiah said with derision. "Are you sure he knows what you are? His family won't approve of you if he's stupid enough to take you to his home."

Hezekiah's hurtful words were a bitter reminder of his rigid nature. "Chad knows exactly what I am, Father. Neither of us wants marriage. We're good friends and will remain friends, no matter what you think of me."

"You're his whore, Sarah, you'll never be anything else to him."

"Father!"

The truth hurt. Sarah would never stop wanting Chad. She could deny it until her face turned blue, but all Chad had to do was touch her and she shattered. If that made her a whore, then so be it.

"You've said enough, Reverend," Chad said, stepping up beside Sarah. No one had seen him leave his horse at the hitching post and quietly follow behind Sarah and Abner. "Sarah came here to tell you goodbye. She still has feelings for you, though God knows why."

He took her arm and Abner's hand and determinedly turned them away from the door. Sarah didn't look back as she followed Chad, but her eyes were suspiciously moist. She had tried so hard to understand her parents, and in a way she did. She had humiliated them before their flock. Her very presence was an embarrassment to them.

"Wait!" Suddenly Sarah's mother broke free of her father's iron grip and darted past him to where Sarah and Abner stood.

Sarah's heart leaped with joy as her mother placed a restraining hand on her arm."You have a fine son, Sarah. I know I've treated you badly in the past, but what you did was a sin." She paused to smile down at Abner. "I couldn't let you leave without telling you . . ."

"Telling me what, Mama?"

"I'm sorry. That's all. I'm sorry."

Abruptly she turned and hastened to her husband's side. Hezekiah was scowling fiercely as he pulled her inside and slammed the door.

"You shouldn't have come here, Sarah," Chad chided.

"I wanted them to see their grandson before I took him away."

"All you did was open yourself to more heartache."

"Did you hear what my mother said, Chad? She said she was sorry. That alone was worth the trip. It's the most I've ever had from either of them."

A lump formed in Chad's throat. It took so little to make Sarah happy. He'd never known a woman like her. Had he any inclination toward marriage he'd . . . Shit! He was thinking with his loins again. Sarah appeared to be different from his mother and Cora Lee, but these days he couldn't trust his own judgment.

"Forget your parents, Sarah. My family will make you welcome. You'll have everything you need at the Circle F."

Everything but you, Sarah reflected sadly. "I hope I'm doing the right thing. What if Jackson has given up on Abner? I could go on taking in laundry and raising Abner just like I've always done."

"You'd die before your time if you continued on like you were. This is the best way, Sarah, believe me."

Sarah wasn't so sure but she gave Chad the benefit of the doubt.

All was in readiness early the following morning. The wagon was packed and Chad was waiting beside it for Sarah and Abner to return from the Barlows, where they had gone to bid Carrie and the children farewell. An unwelcome visitor arrived before Sarah and Abner. Chad was unpleasantly surprised to see a buggy pull up to the house and Mrs. Kilmer climb out of it. Behind her, a maid struggled with a basket of laundry.

"I decided to give Sarah another chance with my laundry," Mrs. Kilmer said, looking down her nose at Chad. "She's the only one who can get the starch right in my husband's shirts." She spied the wagon and looked askance at Chad. "Are you going somewhere?"

"I'm leaving town," Chad said succinctly.

"Good riddance," Mrs. Kilmer sniffed. "Where is Sarah?"

"Saying goodbye to Mrs. Barlow. I'm taking Sarah and Abner with me to Montana."

The haughty woman's mouth dropped open. "You're marrying Sarah?"

"I didn't say that."

"Well," she huffed, "I should think not. Men don't marry Sarah's kind."

Chad's fists balled at his sides. If he'd had the slightest doubt about taking Sarah with him he no longer did. "I suggest you take your laundry and leave, lady. The town will have to find some other helpless victim to pick on."

"Well, I declare! I wish you joy of your whore." Lifting her nose in the air, she spun around and stalked back to her buggy.

Chad would have done something he'd regret if he hadn't spied Sarah and Abner walking down the road toward him.

"Wasn't that Mrs. Kilmer? What did she want?" Sarah asked as the buggy shot past her.

"She brought you her laundry. I sent her packing. Forget her." He lifted Abner into the wagon. "Are you ready to go, son?"

Abner nodded excitedly. "Will I like it in Montana?"

"I guarantee it." He turned to Sarah, lifted her onto the seat and vaulted up beside her.

"I don't think I'm going to miss this at all," Sarah said, glancing back at the rundown shanty that had been her home for the past six years.

Sarah felt no regret over leaving, despite her apprehension about her new life in Montana. After Chad dumped her with his relatives, she might never see him again. As they left the town of Carbon behind, Sarah vowed to use this time alone with Chad to make him love her.

Most nights Sarah and Abner slept in the wagon and Chad under it. The weather was brisk but not too cold. Chad had made no effort to renew their intimacy, though sometimes Sarah caught him gazing at her in a manner that could only be described as predatory. She was astute enough to know he wanted her and that he was deliberately holding himself in check. Did he fear he might become too fond of her? Was he afraid that involvement meant he'd have to place his trust in a woman?

One night, while Sarah cooked supper over the campfire Chad had built, unexpected company dropped in. Chad reached for his shotgun.

"Howdy, mister, didn't mean to startle ya. Smelled yer coffee. We ran out of coffee two days ago. Could ya spare a cup fer me and my partner?"

Both men were scruffy-looking characters. Both wore stained buckskins and sported shaggy beards.

Chad took note of their pack mules. "Are you prospectors?"

"Reckon ya could say that," the bigger of the two men said. "I'm Justice Crumb and this here's Tolly Rinker. About that coffee . . ."

Chad uncocked his gun and rested it against a log. He didn't like the looks of these men, but they didn't seem threatening. "Sit down. Sarah will pour you each a cup of coffee. I'm Chad Delaney."

"That your wife and kid?" Rinker asked, staring intently at Sarah.

"Yeah," Chad acknowledged tersely.

Sarah looked startled but did not contradict him.

"But Mama . . ."

"Time for bed, son," Sarah said, cutting Abner off in mid-sentence. "Go inside. Mama will tuck you in later."

"But Mama . . ."

"Do as your mother says," Chad said quietly. Abner took one look at Chad's taut features and scampered into the wagon.

"This is mighty fine coffee, missus," Rinker said. He hadn't taken his gaze from Sarah since entering their camp.

Sarah shifted uncomfortably beneath Rinker's hungry gaze. As soon as she'd served the coffee, she excused herself and climbed into the wagon with Abner.

"That's a fine-looking woman," Crumb said. "Bet she's a nice warm armful on a cold night." He guffawed lewdly and poked Rinker in the ribs. "Me and Rinker ain't had a woman fer almost a year. How much will ya take fer a few minutes with her? Won't take long."

Chad calmly reached for the shotgun. His voice was as cold as a winter storm. "I suggest you two move on. Sarah's not for sale. I don't share what's mine."

The moment the words left Chad's mouth, he realized how possessive he'd become of Sarah. He'd kill any man who touched her.

"Don't get yer dander up, mister. Just thought you'd welcome some extra money. But I can see now we made a mistake."

"Damn right you did! You'd best move on before I take exception to what you said and load your backsides with buckshot."

Crumb heaved his bulk from the log he'd been sitting on. "Come on, Rinker, time to move on."

"But Crumb, I'm hard as a brick," Rinker whined. "There's two of us and only one of him."

"Not this time," Crumb said, sizing Chad up. "The woman ain't worth my life. There's a cathouse in the next town, we were headed there anyway."

"Much obliged fer the coffee, mister," Crumb called over his shoulder. "Take care of that woman and kid of yers."

Chad watched them ride away, the shotgun poised in the crook of his arm.

"Do you think they'll come back?" Sarah asked as she climbed down from the wagon to join him.

"You heard?"

Sarah shivered, suddenly chilled. "I heard. I feared they'd try to jump you. I had a gun inside. If they had tried anything, I would have shot them."

Chad's arm came around her. "I wouldn't let them have you, Sarah. You were never in danger."

He turned her in his arms, disregarding the warning bells that went off inside his head as he claimed her lips.

Chapter 10

Chad's lips moved on hers with almost desperate yearning. Sarah thought she could actually hear turbulent winds of need howling across his soul. Something dark and despairing swirled in his eyes. Sarah recognized the hopelessness in them and sympathized with the depths of emotions he was experiencing, for she was feeling those very same emotions.

She'd give her own soul to be able to help him banish his painful memories and overwhelming sense of guilt. Until he regained emotional stability she didn't stand a chance with him. His heart was as closed to her as if he'd built a wall around it. The only thing she had going for her was the fact that Chad wanted her. Chad's lust was intact even if his heart wasn't.

The kiss seemed to go on forever. Sarah clung to him, her mouth soft and trembly beneath his. When it ended she stepped away, breathless and shaken.

"What if those men come back?" she asked, glancing furtively around the campsite.

"They won't."

His confidence was reassuring, but Sarah was still doubtful. "How do you know?"

"They know they'd never succeed with whatever they tried. They are prospectors, not murderers. Being a bounty hunter has taught me a lot of things. One is to judge men's characters. They didn't want a woman badly enough to risk their lives. I'll keep watch for awhile, but I'd bet money that they're on their way to the nearest town."

Sarah shuddered. "I hope you're right."

"Sit with me for awhile," Chad invited.

"Let me check on Abner first."

Sarah climbed into the wagon, saw that Abner was sound asleep, and her heart nearly burst with love. Abner was her life. Without him she'd have nothing. Unless Chad . . . She sighed, warning herself not to let her fancy run away with her. Chad wanted a woman for only one thing. Changing him wasn't going to be easy, she decided as she grabbed her shawl and climbed down from the wagon to join Chad.

Sarah was surprised to see that Chad had spread his bedroll out beneath the stars. He reached for her hand, helped her to sit down and sprawled beside her. A tense silence ensued as both Sarah and Chad stared into the star-studded night.

"Did you like the clothes I bought for you and Abner? You haven't mentioned them."

"You shouldn't have spent money you couldn't afford on us. I know you were counting on the reward for capturing Jackson. How did you manage to buy a wagon? You said you were running short of cash."

"I *was* running short of cash. I visited the bank before we left. The Delaney family is fairly well off.

I used a letter of credit to obtain funds."

"I'll pay you back," Sarah vowed. "I don't want to be a burden to anyone. Dumping me and Abner on your brother and sister-in-law might sound like a good idea to you, but not to me. As soon as I find a job in town I'll be moving on. What are your plans?"

Chad went still. It was almost as if he'd withdrawn from her. "I'm going back to doing what I've been doing. I'm not ready yet to return to Dry Gulch." He gazed off into the distance. "Someday, maybe. But don't worry, you'll like Pierce and Zoey."

"When you return—if you return—I'll probably have moved on myself. I only agreed to come with you because I'm afraid Freddie would return to Carbon for Abner."

"Is that the only reason, Sarah?" He spoke in an odd yet gentle tone.

Sarah stared at him. What did he want from her? An admission of her feelings for him would be disastrous right now. Their relationship was one-sided. The only love involved was the love she had for Chad. Telling him how she felt would do more harm than good. He wasn't ready yet to open his heart to love.

"I don't know what you want me to say, Chad. I doubt you'd want to hear the truth."

Chad didn't know what he wanted to hear from Sarah, but he knew what he wanted her to *do*. He wanted her to stay at the Circle F ranch where she'd be safe, but he knew that was asking too much from her. He had no authority where Sarah was concerned. He'd asked for no commitment and wanted none. It was better that way. He'd just make Sarah's life miserable with his painful memories and relentless guilt. He'd hoped to leave all his guilt behind when he fled Dry Gulch, but it hadn't worked that way. His problems followed him. His best moments in the past two years had been those times he'd spent making love to Sarah.

"Sarah, I wish . . ."

"We've already been down that road, Chad. I don't expect anything from you. I've always known exactly where I stand with you. You're a compassionate man, I appreciate everything you've done for me and Abner."

"I shouldn't have made love to you. I've hurt you and I never meant to."

"Don't blame yourself, I could have stopped you had I wanted to. Until you made love to me, I thought the act was vile and disgusting. I'm grateful to you for showing me how wonderful it could be."

"It won't happen again if you don't want it to."

Chad might as well have asked her to stop breathing. If she was to have so little of him she wanted to make every minute count.

Her eyes were brilliant reflections of the stars as she gazed at him. "I want it to happen again."

Chad went utterly still. "Are you sure?"

"Very sure. Maybe I truly am the kind of woman my parents accused me of being."

"You're no whore, Sarah."

"I am with you, Chad."

His hands clamped around her shoulders, giving her a gentle shake. "Dammit! Don't talk like that. Your parents were wrong, the town was wrong. You were taken advantage of by a vicious rapist."

"You healed me when you made love to me. I

wish I could do the same for you. Then maybe you'd . . ." She flushed and looked away. "I'm sorry, I don't want to place any pressure on you. You've already done more for me than any other person."

"Sarah . . ." Her name was a groan on his lips. "You *have* helped me. You and Abner have restored something inside me I thought I'd lost. For a long time I'd been unable to feel anything. I was an empty shell, then I met you and realized I'd merely misplaced my compassion, not lost it. I've still got a long way to go, but it's a start."

"Why not stay in Dry Gulch and face your demons?"

He pulled his eyes away from her. "I'm not ready for that."

"I didn't think so."

The beginning of a smile tipped the corners of his mouth. "Is this conversation leading someplace?"

She felt a warming glow flow through her. "I hope so. I want you to kiss me, Chad."

He regarded her warily. "I won't be able to stop with just a kiss. You know where I stand, Sarah. I have nothing left to give but passion."

"I'll settle for that right now."

"I don't deserve you, sweetheart," Chad said as he gently lowered her to his bedroll. "I feel like a bastard for taking advantage of you, but I want you too desperately to listen to my conscience. If you had any sense you'd realize I'm no good for you."

"I guess I'm just plain stupid. Besides," she teased, "Abner likes you so you can't be all bad. Are you going to kiss me or not?"

"I'm going to kiss you."

His large hand took her face and held it gently. She put her arms around his neck and pulled him against her. His breath was warm and moist against her face. Her heart raced with excitement. Chad was the only man she wanted. The only man she'd ever need. All she had to do was convince him that his heart wasn't as barren as he thought.

His tongue traced the soft fullness of her lips before he joined their mouths. His kiss sang through her veins. She returned his kiss with reckless abandon, disappointed when he abruptly ended it.

"Let's move inside the wagon," he whispered against her lips. "I can move Abner to my bedroll under the wagon. It's a fine night, he'll enjoy it."

He spread his bedroll beneath the wagon bed, then climbed inside the wagon. He reappeared a few moments later with the sleeping child in his arms. "Go inside, I'll join you as soon as I settle Abner." When Sarah moved to obey, he placed a hand on her arm and said, "Take off your clothes, sweetheart. I want you naked."

The wagon was small, barely large enough for two pallets placed side by side. Tonight she and Chad would lie upon them and make love. Sarah shivered with anticipation as she undressed. By the time Chad climbed into the wagon she was lying naked beneath the blanket.

The warmth from the glowing lantern turned Chad's flesh to molten gold as he knelt beside Sarah and hastily stripped. The sight of Chad's nude body made Sarah gulp in an unsteady breath. His shaft was hard, heavy, and fully erect. His eyes were dark and unreadable as he pulled aside the blanket and gazed down at her.

She sighed as he lay down beside her. His lips found her mouth and he kissed her thoroughly, hungrily. Then his mouth began to roam. He found the pulse at the base of her throat, a pouting nipple cresting a firm breast, the inside of a quivering thigh, triggering ripples of reaction in the acutely sensitive places his lips had just visited. She trembled in response to his lips as they moved along her upper thigh, higher, until his heated mouth claimed her most secret place.

She gasped as his tongue stroked into the delicate flesh. The pleasure was inexpressible, more potent beyond any sensation she'd ever known. Dizzily she wondered how anything so sinful could feel so wonderful. Surely her father was right. She'd burn in the deepest hell for gaining pleasure from this.

Then Sarah felt his fingers sliding inside her, inflaming, teasing, even as his mouth worked its magic on a sensitive bit of flesh she'd been unaware of until now. Wildfire blazed through her in glorious, undulating waves; she cried out his name. For several thudding heartbeats she was awash in a sea of ecstasy, sucked into a whirlpool of swirling delight.

When the turbulence subsided, she felt Chad caressing between her legs with the blunt tip of his sex. A moment later he pressed inward with a luscious, sliding friction that reignited the flame that had burned so hotly scant moments ago. Her hips lifted to him as he buried himself inside her. Her face blazed with incredible joy as she wrapped her arms around him, bringing him closer.

Her hips moved again, inviting him deeper. Chad gave a harsh groan, his strokes, now swift and hard, thrust uncontrollably into her. It was madness. Heat was building, threatening to consume her. Then the firestorm within her burst forth, shattering the world around her. She twisted against him, shuddering as he spilled himself inside her. The meaning of true fulfillment was suddenly clear to Sarah. No matter how desperately Chad railed against it, Sarah felt that they were destined to be together. She was his, he was hers.

They both dozed. Sometime during the night, Chad was awakened by the strange feeling that he and Sarah were no longer alone. He started to reach for his gun and realized there was no need for it.

"Abner? Is that you?" He moved over to make room for the boy, who was squirming to fit himself between him and Sarah.

"I got lonesome by myself. I want to sleep with you and Mama. Did you get lonesome, too, is that why you're sleeping with Mama?"

Chad groaned in dismay. It was unfortunate that Abner had found him in bed with Sarah. He'd been careless. So much for his resolve to keep his hands off Sarah. Somehow he had to satisfy the boy's curiosity without making too much of it. He glanced at Sarah and saw she was still sleeping. No help there, it was up to him. He decided to make light of it.

"I do get lonesome sometimes. But I'm glad you're here now. Go back to sleep."

Abner smiled sleepily. "I like you a lot, Chad. I wish you were my papa."

"I like you a lot, too, Abner, but I don't think I'd make a very good papa."

The sound of voices awakened Sarah. When she

realized Abner had climbed into the wagon and was snuggled between her and Chad, she felt a sense of rightness. When she heard Abner announce that he wished Chad was his papa, tears sprouted from the corners of her eyes. Why did Chad have to be so stubborn? Why couldn't he see that they belonged together? What did she have to do to make him understand that he needed them in his life? Whatever it took, she vowed to find a way.

Chad had been right. The men who had burst into their campsite hadn't returned. As they crossed the Wyoming border into Montana, Sarah relaxed and began to enjoy the scenery. The dusty trail they followed passed through towering green spruces and craggy granite peaks that seemed almost to touch the glowing blue sky. The days were still mild but the nights were turning colder now.

To Sarah's consternation, Chad had become somewhat remote since their night of incredible passion. Only Abner seemed able to coax a smile from Chad. Sarah wondered if Chad was upset because Abner had found them in bed. Did he think she'd demand things of him he wasn't willing to give? She might love Chad to distraction, but she'd never force him into marriage. That was a decision he'd have to make himself.

Summer was waning and the days were growing shorter. As they neared Rolling Prairie there was a definite chill in the air. Sarah was grateful for the warm coats Chad had purchased for her and Abner for they were definitely needed after the sun went down. Not for the first time Sarah wondered why Chad had been so generous with his time and money when he owed her nothing. He had to care for her just a little, didn't he? People didn't just help someone they didn't care about.

Sarah was driving the wagon with Abner seated beside her when Chad rode up on Flint. He had ridden ahead this morning and when he returned he was smiling from ear to ear. He'd been so dour of late that his smile was a welcome sight.

From Chad's expression, Sarah deduced that they must be close to their destination. Soon she and Abner would have a safe place to stay. She supposed the responsibility Chad had shouldered on their behalf was becoming a burden. He probably didn't like it that Abner was becoming too fond of him and probably suspected that what she felt for him was more than simple passion. By now Chad must be beginning to feel pressured and would probably be glad to be rid of them.

"We're on Circle F land," Chad confirmed as he rode up beside the lumbering wagon. "We should reach the ranch house soon."

"Do all those cattle grazing on the hillsides belong to the Circle F?"

"It's a good ranch. Zoey almost lost it when her father was killed but Pierce saved it for her and made it a prosperous enterprise. I'm going to ride ahead and tell them to expect company. Just follow the trail, it leads directly to the ranch house." He rode off in a cloud of dust.

A short time later Chad galloped into the yard, scattering chickens and geese. He dismounted, wondering where everyone was. He saw an old man limping toward him from the barn and walked over to meet him.

"Where is everyone?" Chad asked.

"Who wants to know?"

Chad smiled. "You must be Cully. You're just as crusty as Zoey said." He stuck out his hand. "I'm Chad Delaney."

Cully squinted up at him. "Delaney. You must be the brother who run off. You oughta be ashamed of yourself, young fella. Pierce and Zoey have been mighty worried about you."

"Where is my brother?"

"All three of 'em, Pierce, Zoey, and the boy, went to Dry Gulch."

"They have a son? I never did know what they had."

"They named him Robbie, after Zoey's pa."

"When will they return?"

"I don't expect 'em back for at least a month. They go a couple times a year to check on things at the Delaney ranch. I'm in charge when they're away. What can I do for you?"

Chad seethed with frustration. What else could go wrong? It wouldn't be right to just drop off Sarah and Abner without permission. And he didn't want to stick around for a month or longer. There was no help for it. He had to take Sarah and Abner to Dry Gulch, the place he had avoided for nearly two years.

"I'm not alone," Chad told Cully. "A friend and her young son are following in a wagon. I reckon we'll have to go on to Dry Gulch. Is it all right if we spend the night?"

Cully scratched his grizzled white head. "Reckon so. Just make yourself at home. Pierce and Zoey would want it that way. You can bed down in the two empty bedrooms." He sent Chad a piercing look. "You and your lady friend can divide them up any way you want. There's plenty of food in the larder, I hope your friend can cook."

"We'll manage," Chad said. "Where are the hands?"

"Off on a cattle drive. Ain't nobody here but me."

Chad glanced up and saw the wagon coming down the road. "There's Sarah now."

Cully shaded his eyes against the sun as he watched the wagon lumber into the yard. Abner jumped down the moment it pulled to a stop.

"Chad! Where are the horses? I wanna see the horses."

Chad helped Sarah down and brought her over to meet Cully. Cully stared at her with avid curiosity, obviously wondering about their relationship but too polite to ask.

"Cully, meet Sarah Temple and her son Abner. Cully is Pierce and Zoey's right-hand man," Chad explained to Sarah.

Sarah offered her hand and found it enveloped in a warm, surprisingly strong, calloused grip. "Pleased to meet you, Mr. Cully."

"Just Cully, ma'am. That's a mighty fine looking young'un you got, there. Howdy Abner," he said, offering his hand to the boy.

"Howdy, Cully. I'm glad we're finally here. Can I see the horses?"

Cully gave him an indulgent smile. "Help yourself, boy, they're behind the barn. Just don't open the gate. Wouldn't want you to get hurt."

Abner raced off toward the barn, his face alight with excitement.

"Where is your brother?" Sarah asked.

"There's a small problem," Chad explained. "He took his family to Dry Gulch. We'll stay the night and leave in the morning. Cully said the larder is full and we should make ourselves at home."

"You're taking me to Dry Gulch?" Sarah asked, stunned. "You said . . ."

"I know what I said, but things have changed. Lord knows I'm not thrilled about returning to Dry Gulch, but I can't just dump you here without talking to Pierce and Zoey first."

Sarah decided not to pursue the subject as she turned her attention to Cully. "I appreciate your hospitality. Perhaps you'll join us for supper."

"Much obliged," Cully said with a grin. "Ain't had a decent meal since Miz Zoey left."

"Will you show me around?"

"Sure thing, Miz Sarah." Cully led the way into the house.

"I'll see to the team," Chad muttered crossly.

He wasn't in the best of moods. He wasn't ready yet to return to Dry Gulch. He wasn't sure he'd ever be ready. Just being this close to his home brought back memories he'd been running from for two years. His mood lightened considerably when Abner came running toward him. The little scamp's smile was infectious.

"I'm gonna like it here," Abner said as he skidded up beside Chad. "But I'd like it better if you stayed." His expression grew serious. "Mama said you don't wanna be with us."

Chad dropped to his knees beside the boy he'd grown to love as much as a man with dead emotions could love. "You and your mother have nothing to do with my reason for leaving. Some bad things happened a long time ago, things you're too young to understand. Those events messed me up inside. There's a lot of bitterness inside me. You and your mother deserve better than what I can offer." He searched Abner's face. "Do you understand any of what I've just said?"

Abner shrugged. "I think so, but does that mean you don't love me? It's all right, Chad. I can still love you, can't I?"

Chad felt something give inside him. He pulled Abner into his arms, holding him close. "No matter what happens, always remember that it has nothing to do with you. I care for you, Abner. I always will."

"What about Mama?"

Chad chose his words carefully. "Your mother is a fine woman. She'll make some man a wonderful wife. The problem is mine. I'm not the kind of man your mother needs."

Abner gave Chad a slow smile. "You're wrong, Chad. You're 'zactly the kind of man Mama needs. I'm going back to see the horses," he said, running off.

Chad shook his head in dismay. The kid had a way of getting under a man's skin. He could understand why Jackson wanted his son. If he was Jackson he'd do everything in his power to claim the boy.

Everyone, Cully included, enjoyed the supper Sarah put on the table that evening. Cully had killed a chicken for the occasion and Sarah found the ingredients for noodles. With mashed potatoes, biscuits, and fresh green beans, the meal was memorable.

"Thanks fer the grub, Miz Sarah," Cully said, patting his stomach. "Reckon I'll take myself off to the bunkhouse. I'll be up in the morning before you leave."

"Good night, Cully," Sarah said, stifling a yawn. "You're not the only one who's tired."

"I'll take Abner up to bed," Chad offered. "He looks about done in."

"Will you tell me a story?" Abner begged. "It's been a long time since anyone's told me a story."

Chad didn't have the heart to refuse. "Sure, son, if you can stand one of my wild tales."

Abner was asleep before Chad finished his story. He pulled the covers up to the boy's neck and tiptoed from the room. He met Sarah on the stairs.

"Which room did you put Abner in?" Sarah asked. "I hope the bed is big enough for both Abner and me."

Chad gave her a teasing smile as he searched her lovely features. Her violet eyes were smudged with dark circles, attesting to her exhaustion. Her lush red lips were parted invitingly. He recalled with alacrity how sweetly those lips clung to his when he kissed her.

"Actually, the bed is a single one. I saved the room with the double bed for us."

"For . . . us?"

"This is likely to be the last time we'll be together, Sarah. I don't intend to stay long in Dry Gulch." His eyes glittered. "I want to make love to you tonight. I haven't been able to think of much else since that night in the wagon. My problems seem to dissolve when I'm making love to you."

His words shocked her. How could he say those things and still believe he didn't love her? What would it take to bring him to his senses?

"Had I known a woman's body could be so soothing a tonic for my troubles, I would have spent more time in bed and less time chasing outlaws. There's a lot to be said for lust."

Sarah's head buzzed with anger. She knew he'd been using her, but her love for Chad had blinded her to everything but her need to be with him. She knew now what a foolish dreamer she'd been. Lust was all Chad was ever going to feel for her. She'd let him make love to her, wanting him, needing him, pretending that one day he would realize that he loved her. She knew now it just wasn't going to happen. She could keep giving and giving. He would keep taking and taking. What hurt the most was the knowledge that almost any woman would serve his needs.

In the beginning Chad's honor and compassion had kept him in Carbon. He'd felt pity for her. He cared only for Abner. How could she expect Chad to want her when she was utterly unlovable? She had a child and no husband. As long as she allowed him in her bed, he'd keep taking, giving nothing of himself in return. She had asked for no emotional ties and received none. She could love him till doomsday, but he would never love her.

"Find yourself another woman," Sarah said, stepping around him. "You used me for the last time."

"What's wrong? Are you suddenly too good for me?" His anger was palpable. "I thought you were one of the few honest women left in this world, but I was mistaken. Now that I've taken you away from the hard life you led you no longer want me, is that it?" He snorted derisively. "And here I was worried about hurting you because you were becoming too emotionally involved with me. You knew where I stood from the beginning."

"Don't, Chad, please. Of course I knew where you stood. But a girl can hope, can't she? You're just like the men in Carbon who thought I was fair game. You were the only man I thought worth my time. Being with you meant something to me even if it meant nothing to you. Are you going to tell me which room is Abner's?"

A nerve twitched in his chin. "Third door on the right. Sleep well."

Trembling from the force of her anger, Sarah entered Abner's room, leaning against the closed door for support. Tears rolled down her cheeks. She should have known better than to trust a man. She was a fool to believe she could make Chad love her. She realized now that he'd always been a hard, bitter man. One who had little use for women beyond the pleasure they gave him. His one redeeming quality was the spark of compassion that had somehow survived. Someday, some woman would unlock the secrets of his heart. She wished that woman well.

Chad's glittering gaze followed Sarah as she made a hasty departure. Why must he be such an unfeeling bastard? The answer was simple: Because he feared he was becoming too fond of Sarah and Abner. Acquiring a wife and child meant a man had to settle down, and he wasn't ready for that. He still had his demons to battle.

Saying hateful things to Sarah hurt him as much as they hurt her but he felt they needed to be said in order to keep an emotional distance between himself and Sarah. Leaving was going to be damn difficult for him and he could imagine what it would do to her.

Chapter 11

"We're home," Chad said. Today he was driving the wagon. Abner was sitting between him and Sarah.

Sarah gazed absently at the lush acres of pasture surrounded by foothills and towering peaks. The grazing cattle looked fat and content; the fences appeared to be in good repair.

"Where's the house and barn and all the buildings?" Abner asked excitedly.

Chad smiled at his exuberance. "You'll be able to see them when we round the next bend in the road."

Sarah stared mutely ahead. She and Chad hadn't spoken more than a few words to one another since the angry words they had exchanged at the Circle F. It hurt to think that she had no future with Chad. All her hopes and dreams had been pure fantasy.

Chad cast a surreptitious glance at Sarah. His feelings about their relationship were mixed. Sarah had known where he stood from the beginning. She'd been foolish to expect things he couldn't give her, and he was confident that he hadn't led her to believe otherwise. He'd been honest about his aversion to marriage, so Sarah had no right to expect anything but passion from him. On the other hand, he shouldn't have initiated lovemaking when he knew she'd probably misinterpret his intentions. Lust was a powerful driving force. His lust for Sarah was intensely motivating and pleasurable.

"Aren't you excited, Mama?" Abner asked, jumping into the void. "This is where Chad used to live."

"We won't be staying long, honey," Sarah said, refusing to look at Chad. "Coming here with Chad was a mistake. If it wasn't for Freddie Jackson we'd still be in Carbon, doing what we've always done. Maybe we'll return after Chad catches him. Would you like that?"

Abner made a face. "I don't wanna go back there, Mama. The boys there are mean to me."

"Abner is right," Chad said succinctly. "You can't return to Carbon. There's nothing there for you."

Sarah gave him the full benefit of her displeasure. "What is there for me here? I'll do what I darn well please, Chad Delaney."

Damn stubborn woman, Chad thought irritably. Then his thoughts skidded to a halt when the Delaney ranch came into view. Chad let his gaze devour the house in which he'd grown to manhood. It looked the same after two years. Ryan had repaired the roof, he noted. The same roof he and his brothers had slid down to sneak away and raise hell in town when they were boys. And what hell they'd raised!

As they matured, they no longer had to sneak out to play cards at the saloon, or get into fights, or visit whores. Chad recalled a yellow-haired whore named Nellie, who demanded nothing from him but his lust and a night's pay, and wondered if she was still available. If anyone could cure him of his hunger for Sarah, it was Nellie. He hoped he'd find time to visit her before he left Dry Gulch.

Chad experienced a mixture of anticipation and foreboding as he drove the wagon into the yard. He recognized several of the hands and waved to them as he drove by. Within minutes the wagon was surrounded by excited men.

"Well I'll be damned. It's Chad Delaney," a young hand said, grinning from ear to ear. "About time you came home."

"Howdy, Rusty," Chad greeted. "Are my brothers around?"

An older man Chad didn't recognize pushed through the crowd. He held his hand out to Chad. "I'm Chuck Harper, foreman here. Pleased to meet you. Welcome home."

Chad jumped down from the wagon and grasped Chuck's hand. "Howdy, Chuck. Didn't know Ryan hired a foreman. Never needed one before."

"Probably didn't while you were here. Pierce spends most of his time at the Circle F with his family, and Ryan had a hard time keeping up here. He hired me right after you left."

Chad noted a hint of censure in Chuck's voice but wasn't angered by it. He'd left Ryan in a bind the day he rode away and couldn't fault Chuck for sympathizing with his brother.

"Where are my brothers?" Chad repeated. "I stopped first at the Circle F and learned that Pierce and his family were visiting Ryan."

"They all left three days ago for the cattle auction in Butte. Ryan is looking to buy one of those fancy English bulls he'd heard so much about. Pierce decided to go along and look them over. Mrs. Delaney didn't want to stay here alone so she and little Robbie tagged along."

Chad stifled a groan. Fate was conspiring against him. Ryan and Pierce would be gone at least a week. Maybe longer since they were traveling with a woman and child. That meant he'd be stuck in Dry Gulch until they returned.

"Hey, Chad, introduce us to your wife," one of the hands called out.

"I don't have a wife," Chad countered. "The lady's name is Sarah Temple. She's a friend." He reached into the wagon for Abner while three men leaped forward to help Sarah down. "And this is Abner, her son. They're going to be guests here for awhile."

"All right, back to work," Chuck said after everyone had greeted Sarah and Abner. "Rusty, take the wagon to the barn. You and Slim can unload it and carry the things into the house."

"Much obliged, Chuck," Chad said.

"Anything else we can do to make your guests comfortable?" Chuck offered.

From the corner of his eye Chad saw Abner chase one of the dogs into the barn. "Have the hands keep an eye out for Abner. He's a curious little boy. I reckon he'll be underfoot a lot. I'd hate for him to get hurt. When the newness wears off he'll learn what's dangerous and what isn't."

"Sure thing, Chad. We'll keep an eye out for the boy."

"Are you sure Abner will be all right?" Sarah

asked anxiously. "This is all so unusual to him. He's like a kid with a new toy." She gazed wistfully at the wide open spaces. "It's a wonderful place to raise children. Best of all, there isn't a layer of coal dust hanging in the air and clogging our throats."

"He'll be fine," Chad insisted. "Come on into the house, I'll show you around. Maybe Cookie has some milk and cookies to tide Abner over until supper."

"You have a cook?"

"Cookie has been with us a long time. If he had a name, I can't recall it. You didn't expect three bachelors to do their own cooking, did you?"

"I've never known anyone who had a cook."

"We have a housekeeper, too. Or we did. Mrs. Lester was getting on in years. She may have already retired."

Chad held the front door open and Sarah stepped into the foyer. She could see the parlor from where she stood and was duly impressed. The house was even roomier than it looked from the outside.

"I'll show you around," Chad said with a hint of pride. He had fled to escape tragic memories, but his home was still dear to his heart. The absence of a mother had affected the Delaneys in many ways, but it did not diminish their sense of family and the happy times he'd shared with his brothers.

Sarah followed Chad through the parlor, dining room, office, kitchen, storeroom, and pantry, then he ushered her upstairs to the bedrooms.

"There are five bedrooms," Chad said. "One was Pa's. Pierce, Ryan, and I had our own rooms.

There's one guest room. You can have Pa's room and Abner can take the guest room. I reckon Pierce, Zoey, and their son are sharing Pierce's old room."

Chad opened the door and ushered Sarah inside a small but comfortable room. The bed was covered with a colorful quilt and gingham curtains hung at each of the two windows. The view beyond the windows delighted Sarah as she gazed out at the lush green pasture topped by lofty, snow-capped mountains.

"My room is between yours and Abner's," Chad said. "Make yourself at home. I'll bring your belongings up as soon as I find Cookie and tell him we have guests."

They were behaving like strangers, Sarah realized. Polite strangers who had never shared intimacies. It was as if making love was nothing special to Chad. He'd changed during their trip to Dry Gulch, Sarah thought. He'd become remote and unreachable. Since arriving in Montana, Chad seemed obsessed with leaving as soon as possible. She willed herself not to care.

Sarah heard the door close and knew Chad had left. She gazed out the window and saw him emerge from the house a few minutes later and walk toward the barn. Abner was running alongside him, keeping up a steady conversation.

An older man whose tall, lanky frame was wrapped in an enormous white apron must have seen Chad and Abner for he came out of the barn to greet them.

Cookie? He must be, Sarah decided, before she was distracted by the sight of her son trailing behind them. Sarah decided to go downstairs to make sure Abner wasn't making a nuisance of himself.

She found him in the kitchen, munching on an apple.

"Mama, look what Cookie gave me!" Abner exclaimed, holding his half-eaten apple up high.

Chad saw Sarah and called out a greeting. "Sarah, come and meet Cookie. He's the one who's kept us from starving all these years. Cookie, this is Sarah Temple, Abner's mother."

"Howdy, Miss Sarah. Any friend of Chad's is a friend of mine. I wish you can convince him to stick around. Ryan and Pierce were powerful worried about him."

"I'm pleased to meet you, Cookie. Unfortunately, I haven't the influence to make Chad do anything," Sarah said.

Chad cleared his throat. "Cookie said Mrs. Lester's health failed and she left to stay with her daughter a short time ago. Ryan hasn't gotten around yet to hiring a new housekeeper."

Sarah sensed that Chad was making small talk and wondered why he felt it necessary to do so. "Finish your apple, Abner. Perhaps there will be time for a nap before supper."

"No nap," Abner protested. "I'm too old for that baby stuff. I want to go back outside and play with the dog."

"Let him go, Sarah," Chad urged. "The trip has been a long one. The boy needs to stretch his legs. The hands will keep an eye on him. Besides," he added, "we need to talk. I'll carry your bags up to your room and we can talk there."

His last sentence had an ominous ring to it. Sarah suspected he was going to tell her he was leaving and she steeled herself, refusing to let him see how deeply his leaving would hurt her.

Sarah was gazing out the window when Chad entered her bedroom and placed a small trunk at the foot of the bed. "What do you think of the ranch?"

"I can see why you love it."

Chad walked up behind her. "Are you satisfied with the room?"

She felt the heat emanating from him and deliberately moved away. "The room is very nice. Nicer than anything I've ever known. But I don't intend to impose upon your family any longer than necessary. What is it you wanted to say to me, Chad? If it's about your leaving, I already know you don't intend to stick around."

Chad followed her across the room. When he reached her, he placed his hands on her shoulders and turned her to face him. "Sarah, stand still, will you? No matter how badly I want to leave, I can't. Not yet. Not until my brothers return. I'm not going to dump you and Abner on strangers and walk away. I'm not a total bastard."

Sarah eyes softened. "No, you're not."

Some of the hardness left Chad's features. "Dammit, Sarah, why are we pretending to be strangers? We're lovers, for godsake!"

"Are we?"

Chad's eyes glittered. Her question had an unsettling effect on him. "You want me, Sarah, just as much as I want you."

His hands tightened on her shoulders. She felt them scorching her through the barrier of her clothing. He was standing so close she could see the golden flecks floating in his hazel eyes. She couldn't move, couldn't breathe, as Chad's mouth covered hers. She could have turned her head away, but she didn't. She let him kiss her, let him pull her against him, let his tongue part her lips and push inside. She felt his shaft stir against her and gave a strangled cry of protest.

Somehow she found the strength to escape the compelling potency of his kiss. "Don't."

Chad's hands fell away. "You wouldn't have kissed me like that if you didn't want me."

"What I want and what I need are two different things," Sarah claimed. "Why are you tormenting me like this?"

"Do you think I'm not tormented?" I've been in Dry Gulch less than one day and already my demons are stirring. I'm eager to move on. There has to be somewhere I can go to escape."

Chad's words rattled Sarah badly. What could she say to him that hadn't already been said? She was saved from replying when Abner called to her from the bottom of the staircase. "Abner needs me. I have to go."

Sarah's thoughts were in a turmoil. Being with Chad tied her in knots. She seriously doubted he'd ever solve his problems.

Sarah thoroughly enjoyed the supper Cookie placed on the table that night. It was nice not to have to cook or clean up afterward. She knew she wouldn't have that luxury for long, but while she did she intended to savor it fully. After supper she excused herself and took Abner up to bed. He offered only a mild protest as she bathed him, put him into his nightclothes, and tucked him in.

Earlier she had asked Cookie about a bath and was informed that the ranch had a bathing room with piped-in hot water. That kind of extravagance was unheard of in Sarah's world and she couldn't wait to soak in a hot tub. She'd seen Chad go out to the bunkhouse after supper to talk with the hands and decided to take advantage of the privacy.

Chad trudged up the stairs. He'd lingered in the bunkhouse until the men began drifting off to their beds, the thought of returning to an empty room unappealing to him. He ducked into Abner's room to check on him. The boy was sleeping soundly so he tiptoed out, closing the door behind him. He paused briefly before Sarah's door, then continued on to the bathing room.

He should have noted the light shining under the door, but his mind had been preoccupied. He opened the door and came to an abrupt standstill. The breath slammed from his lungs and he lost the ability to think when he saw Sarah standing beside the tub, gloriously nude, her body rosy from her bath, her dark hair falling in damp ringlets over her shoulders. His gaze lingered on her breasts, then traveled down to the thatch of black curls between her legs. He felt his body swell and harden.

Stunned, Sarah stood rooted to the spot. He was staring at her intently; the heated centers of his eyes sent hot and cold shivers down her spine.

"I'm finished," Sarah said, reaching for the towel with shaking hands. "You may have the bathing room." Chad still hadn't said a word as she slipped past him and hastened to her room.

There was a reason why Chad hadn't spoken. He couldn't. Seeing Sarah gloriously nude had stolen his speech and left him needy as hell. If he had any sense he'd go into town and look up Nellie. Regrettably, he didn't want Nellie. Willing himself to move, he closed the door and went about his bath.

Sarah lay awake, aware of the wind whistling through the trees and the slap of branches against her window. She heard Chad return to his room after his bath and still sleep eluded her. The clock in the foyer struck two. She had just dozed off when an eerie cry jolted her awake. She leaped from bed and rushed into Abner's room, fearing something had happened to him. The lad was sound asleep, his head resting on his hands, an angelic look on his face.

Then she heard the cry again, and garbled words, coming from behind Chad's closed door. "Damn you, Cora Lee! I killed them. They're all dead."

Sarah rushed into Chad's room without considering the right or wrong of it. In all the times Chad had slept within her hearing, she'd never heard him cry out or thrash so. Had returning to Dry Gulch done that to him?

The room was dark except for a slash of moonlight that fell across the bed. She gasped in dismay when she noted the mess surrounding Chad. The bedding was twisted about him, and he continued to mumble and thrash in his sleep. Gingerly Sarah approached the bed. She could make out his words clearly now."No! I can't stay, Pierce. Don't try to talk me out of leaving. It's my fault, all my fault!"

His anguished words tore at Sarah's heart. She was too compassionate to allow his nightmare to continue. She grasped his shoulders and shook him. "Chad, wake up. You're dreaming."

Still deeply immersed in his nightmare, Chad

shook himself free. Undaunted, Sarah grasped his shoulders and shook him harder. Suddenly Chad growled deep in his throat, grabbed her in a bear hug, and pulled her down onto the bed, rolling on top of her.

"Chad! What are you doing?"

Chad had emerged from sleep slowly, saw something bending over him in a threatening manner, and reacted mechanically. He'd trained himself to respond instantly to danger and ask questions later. Before Sarah realized what was happening, Chad had pulled her beneath him on the bed, reached under his pillow for his gun, and pressed it against her temple. Sarah went still beneath him, wondering if she'd live to see the light of day.

"Chad, it's Sarah. Please don't hurt me."

"Sarah?" The gun came away from her head and he heard Sarah heave an enormous sigh. "What in blazes are you doing in my bed? Not that I'm complaining."

"You were having a nightmare. I tried to wake you."

"Sorry," Chad muttered. He shifted his weight but didn't let her up. "This is the first nightmare I've had in a long time. I reckon coming back to Dry Gulch set it off."

She heard the note of pain in his voice—and something else. The sharp edge of rising desire.

"Let me up, Chad."

"Why? You came to me, I didn't come to you."

"Tell me about your nightmare. Maybe I can help," Sarah said, trying to diffuse the volatile situation. Chad was much too close for her peace of mind.

"There's only one way you can help me. Is that what you're offering, Sarah?"

Sarah refused to be baited. "I'd rather hear about your dream. It must have been disturbing."

"Forget the nightmare. It's always the same. People dying while I'm standing over them with a smoking gun."

"What else?"

"I'd rather not talk about it." He kissed the corners of her lips. "You can help me by letting me love you. Only you can banish my demons."

Sarah gnawed at the tender inside of her lip as she considered his words. "You want to love me for all the wrong reasons. I can understand your mistrust of women, but you should know by now that I'm different."

"I do know you're different, Sarah. I reckon I've always known it. And I do care for you and Abner."

Her voice trembled. "What are you trying to tell me?"

"I reckon I'm saying that if I could shed this guilt and lose my demons, you're the woman with whom I'd want to share my life. Unfortunately miracles don't happen overnight. The blame and the burden are mine alone to bear. It isn't fair to share them with anyone."

A bold slash of moonlight fell across his face, revealing his anguish. "Isn't wanting you and caring for you enough right now? I'd like to offer more, but I can't."

She gasped as he lowered his head and caressed her lips with his tongue, outlining the contours before covering them completely. The caress changed from teasing to intense as he deepened the kiss, thrusting boldly with his tongue. The blood hammered through her veins as he stroked her breasts, her stomach, her thighs, igniting a desperate wanting inside her.

"Raise up," Chad whispered against her lips. "I want to remove your shift."

"I didn't come to your room for this."

"Why did you come?"

"I heard you cry out and wanted to help."

"You can help me by letting me love you. Give me respite from these clawing demons that plague me."

"You don't need my help to banish your demons," Sarah told him. "Guilt is a terrible burden. You have no reason to blame yourself for what happened. Your intentions were good. You married Cora Lee to help your brother. What happened after that couldn't be helped. You were innocent of those deaths."

"I never considered myself an innocent, but I lost any claim to innocence I might have retained the day I found Cora Lee rutting in bed with her brother. The deaths that followed could have been prevented if I hadn't killed Hal Doolittle. Don't try to make excuses for what I did, Sarah. Those deaths altered my perception of life and human nature. Cynicism, pleasure, lust, those are emotions I can understand."

"Don't forget compassion, Chad. Like it or not, you do have more than your share of compassion. You proved it when you married Cora Lee to save your brother, and when you wouldn't abandon me and Abner when we needed you."

"No one but you would consider me compassionate, Sarah. Not even my brothers, and they know me best. Somehow you and Abner bring out a side of me no one else sees, so don't give me more credit than I deserve, sweetheart. I know exactly what I am. I'm emotionally unable to provide the things a woman wants from a man. But that doesn't mean I'm not capable of giving pleasure."

Sarah refused to believe Chad was as uncaring as he claimed. Those comments about himself came from a disillusioned man, not an emotional cripple. He might think he lacked sympathy and the ability to love, but a man who displayed Chad's abundant compassion lacked none of those qualities. It was up to her to prove that he was worthy of being loved. Taming a renegade was going to be a formidable task; she prayed she was up to it.

"Chad, just tell me one thing. Do you truly think I'd be here with you now if I didn't care for you?"

Chad was silent a long time. Finally he said, "I believe you *think* you care for me. You haven't had much experience with men. You'll get over it."

"What if you're mistaken? What if I really *do* care for you, and you really *do* have the ability to love?"

"What if pigs could fly? Sarah, don't agonize over me like this. I'm not worth it. Maybe it would be best if you went back to your room. If you stay, I'll take advantage of you."

"Kiss me, Chad."

"Didn't you hear what I just said?"

"I heard, but I don't believe you."

Chad's face hardened. "You're a fool, Sarah. A sweet, trusting fool. I'm leaving as soon as my brothers arrive home. Do you still want me to kiss you?"

Sarah closed her eyes and offered up a quick prayer. She was staking her future on making Chad love her, on proving to him that he was capable of feeling strong emotions, emotions that had nothing to do with lust or pleasure. And finally she prayed for courage to persevere, for without Chad she had no future.

"I want to chase away your demons, Chad. Kiss me. Let's both forget the past and concentrate on pleasure. You do give me pleasure, Chad, the kind I never knew existed. If not for you, I'd have gone on forever believing lovemaking was vile and disgusting."

"I don't deserve you, sweetheart. I can promise you little beyond pleasure, but as God is my witness, you'll have that in abundance until the day I leave."

With a minimum of effort, Chad rid Sarah of her shift. Then he pulled her into his embrace. He groaned his approval as she swept tiny nipping kisses over his chest, his shoulders, his chin, and teasingly lower. Fire spread across his stomach as her lips continued their downward path. She made him forget to breathe. And her mouth . . . dear God, her mouth! She kept edging down lower, lower still, until her lips closed over his swollen sex. When he whispered encouragement, she kissed along the length of him. She was awkward at first, but her innocent enthusiasm more than made up for it. Chad closed his eyes and allowed her to consume him.

It was agony. He was going to die.

It was heaven. He was going to die.

Either way, it was a death he welcomed. Only when he knew he was about to spill his seed did he stop her.

"Enough!" He was panting as if he'd run a great

distance as he gently pulled away from her.

"You taste . . ." She flushed and lowered her voice. "It's not at all what I expected."

"You didn't have to do that, sweetheart."

"I wanted to taste you. With any other man, that same act would have been repugnant. Didn't you like it?"

"I'd have to be dead not to like it. Now it's my turn to give you pleasure."

He knelt over her, cupped her buttocks in his hands, and roughly lifted her against his open mouth. The heady scent of woman and sweet musk filled his senses as he stroked her with his tongue, in, then out, again and again, until she was whimpering for blessed release. His expression turned almost feral as he raised up, spread her thighs, and thrust into her with one forceful surge.

Her body was ready for him. She was hot, wet, and her sweet moans told him she was as wild with need as he was. He filled her completely, withdrew, and filled her again . . . and again.

"Now, sweetheart," Chad gasped hoarsely. "Come to me now!"

"Chad! I feel . . . Oh, God, I feel as if I'm losing my soul!"

Chad felt her tense, felt her muscles spasm, and lost what little control he still retained. With a hoarse shout, he spilled himself inside her. Even after his breathing had slowed and his heart had quit pounding, he didn't move. He didn't want to leave her, didn't want to quit holding her.

He was content for the first time in years. Yet even as the thought occurred to him, he rebelled against it. He was in lust with Sarah, he'd known that from the very beginning. His heart wasn't prepared to accept another explanation. How could he feel anything when he still carried around a heart full of guilt?

Sighing heavily, Chad lifted himself off Sarah and settled down beside her. She was already half-asleep when he pulled her into his arms and curved his body around hers. Sleep came swiftly after that.

Chad awakened hours later. He smiled to himself when he felt Sarah's warm body pressed against him. Then his smile faded into a puzzled frown. The body was far too small to be Sarah's. He opened his eyes, more than a little startled to see Abner nestled between him and Sarah.

"I was lonesome again," Abner said sleepily. "I wish I could sleep between you and Mama every night."

Chapter 12

Sarah awakened slowly, stunned to find Abner in bed with her and Chad. Thank God the child was too young and innocent to suspect what they'd been doing. But if it happened too often, Abner would certainly question it; he was an astute lad, wise beyond his years. She was more than a little unsettled when Abner asked, "Mama, why do I have to wear nightclothes when you and Chad don't wear any?"

Even Chad appeared dismayed by that question. She couldn't remember the answer she'd given but it must have satisfied Abner, for a moment later he bounded out of bed and announced that he was going downstairs to ask Cookie to please make hotcakes for breakfast.

"This can't go on," Sarah said, once Abner was gone.

"I'm sorry, Sarah. I didn't mean for this to happen."

"It's not fair to Abner. I can't imagine what he's thinking, and I'm afraid to ask. I should have woken earlier and gone to my own room."

"It's my fault," Chad contended. "I like waking up with you in my arms."

Sarah reached for her shift and pulled it over her head and down her hips. By the time she climbed out of bed, she had reached a decision. "I can't be your whore, Chad. I don't want your family to think badly of me. This 'lust' we have for one another is getting out of hand." Lust didn't really describe what she felt for Chad, but Chad didn't want to hear the truth.

Chad got out of bed and pulled on his pants. "I reckon I'll be sleeping out in the bunkhouse from now on," he said. "I can't trust myself to sleep in the same house with you and not touch you."

Sarah nodded jerkily, then turned to leave.

"Wait!" She paused, her hand on the doorknob. "There's one more thing I want to say." She waited expectantly. He appeared to be having difficulty choosing his words. "Marrying you would be one solution, but it wouldn't be right to burden you with my problems. I'm doing you a favor by walking out of your life."

Sarah closed her eyes against the burgeoning pain his words inspired, then opened them quickly. It wouldn't do for Chad to see how very much she wanted them to be together forever. "Don't do me any favors. I've never asked you for a commitment, Chad. Everyone has to do what their heart tells them."

Chad's eyes gleamed with purpose as he gripped her shoulders with his large hands. "What about your heart, Sarah? What does it tell you?"

Sarah was silent so long it appeared as if she meant to ignore his question. At length, she said, "What my heart wants doesn't matter. It's never mattered before, why should it now? Giving Abner a good life is what's important to me."

"There isn't a selfish bone in your body or a mean thought in your head," Chad said. "I've never known a woman like you. Sometimes I can't bear the thought of leaving. Then, at other times, when my demons possess me, I feel the best thing I can do for you and Abner is to walk away and not look back."

His hands tightened on her shoulders and he bent his head until their foreheads touched. "Someday you'll thank me for not messing up your life like I've done mine." His arms fell away. "You'd best get dressed and see to Abner."

Sarah backed away toward the door. Then she turned and fled. Chad had returned to Dry Gulch against his wishes, and now he was forced to wait for his brothers to return before he could leave, and guilt rode her. Chad didn't need her and Abner to complicate his life.

Sarah saw little of Chad during the following days. He had fallen into a familiar routine, helping the hands with their chores and making decisions on behalf of his absent brothers. It was as if he had never left and Sarah knew this was where he truly belonged. Chad was in his element here, working the land he loved. Sarah never tired of watching him doing odd jobs around the barn or corral. Whether he was breaking horses or plying a hammer, Chad excelled at everything he did.

With Abner as his shadow, Chad displayed exemplary patience with the boy, which never ceased to amaze Sarah. She had no idea what they talked about, but Abner chatted endlessly, and she knew that would have driven most men crazy. Abner was going to miss him, Sarah reflected, and so would she.

One day a visitor arrived at the ranch. It was Otto Zigler, a neighbor who had leased the Doolittle ranch for his sons. He asked to see Pierce. Sarah explained that Pierce wasn't here, invited him into the house, then sent Abner for Chad, who was in the barn and hadn't seen Zigler ride up. A few minutes later Chad greeted Zigler with a hearty handshake.

"What brings you to the Delaney ranch, Otto?" Chad asked.

"I didn't know you were home, Chad, or I would have asked for you instead of Pierce. The Rocking D is your property, after all," Otto explained.

Chad's face turned to stone. He didn't want to talk about anything that reminded him of the Doolittles or what happened on the ranch two years ago. "What about it? I gave Pierce authority to sell the Doolittle property before I left."

"Pierce leased the property to me and my sons. My two boys worked the ranch and made it a profitable enterprise. Then Herman got married and moved to Douglas so he could help his wife's papa with his spread. Now Karl wants to go to California and I can't work two spreads by myself. You won't have any trouble finding someone else to lease the property. Maybe you'd prefer to sell it outright. It's a good piece of land. The boys hired six hands. They're still on the place. If you want to keep them, you'd best get out there and talk to them."

Chad stared mutely at Zigler. Where in the hell were his brothers when he needed them? Returning to the Doolittle ranch now would surely stir up a hornet's nest of problems. Problems he'd been trying to forget. He doubted his emotions could survive intact if he returned to the place where four senseless deaths had occurred.

"Well, I'd best be going," Zigler said, rising from his chair. "Here are the keys to the house." He handed Chad a set of keys he retrieved from his jacket pocket, then clapped his hat on his head. "If I were you, I'd get out to the Rocking D as soon as possible. The hands won't be sticking around long. My boys sold off their cows, but the Delaney herd is large enough to run half of them on Rocking D land."

Chad accepted the keys, staring at them as if he expected them to bite him. Sarah showed Zigler out the door then returned to Chad's side. He was still staring at the keys.

"What are you going to do?"

"I never wanted to set eyes on that place again." His voice sounded like a hollow parody of itself; his eyes were bleak with despair. "If I hadn't returned to Dry Gulch, either Ryan or Pierce would have taken care of this for me."

Sarah's heart went out to him. "Perhaps returning to the Rocking D is the best thing that could happen to you."

"How can you say that?" he asked with disbelief.

"The only way you can lay your ghosts to rest is to revisit the past," Sarah continued, undaunted. "Go to the Rocking D in a spirit of reconciliation. It's the only way to let go of the guilt riding you."

"What makes you an expert?" Chad asked harshly.

"I've been there," she reminded him. "I suffered

the same kind of guilt you're feeling. For a long time I thought I was responsible for what Freddie Jackson did to me. I felt that he must have seen something in me I wasn't aware of myself, and that I deserved my fate. In time I came to realize it *wasn't* my fault. I guess having Abner made me realize I had to lose my guilt and live for my child. Having to work to support Abner left me little time for self-pity."

"I appreciate what you're trying to do, Sarah, but you've never killed anyone. You don't know what it's like to see innocent people die because of something you've done."

"I'll go with you to the Rocking D," Sarah offered, deciding not to belabor the point with Chad. It was going to take more persuasion than she was capable of to convince him to set aside his guilt.

"I'll go tomorrow," Chad said. "Maybe Pierce will return before then and handle it for me." He paused in the doorway. "Thank you, Sarah. I don't deserve you." Then he was gone.

Sarah hugged Chad's words to her as if they were a precious mantle. She wanted to be the kind of woman Chad needed, even if she had to convince him that he *did* need her.

To Chad's chagrin, his brothers didn't return to the ranch, not that day or the next. Whether he liked it or not, he had to go to the Rocking D himself. He was in the yard hitching a horse to the buckboard for the trip when Sarah walked up to him.

"Have you seen Abner?"

Abner ducked from beneath the buckboard. "What do you want, Mama?"

"Time for your nap, honey."

"Aw, Mama, I'm too big to nap. Besides, Chad's gonna take me for a ride in the buckboard."

"I was going to ask if you wanted to come along," Chad said. "It's a decent day. Maybe the last one for awhile. Abner could use an outing."

"You're going to the Rocking D." When Chad did not refute her words, Sarah said, "Of course, I'll come with you. Give me time to get warm wraps for me and Abner. Is it far?"

"No, not far at all. Get your wraps while I finish up here."

"I wish I had my own pony," Abner said wistfully.

"Perhaps that can be arranged," Chad said absently.

"Did you hear that, Mama?" Abner said, jumping up and down with excitement. "My very own pony!"

Sarah heard and didn't like Chad's raising the boy's hopes. It was unlikely they'd be around long enough for Abner to own a pony. "We'll see," she hedged.

A short time later they were seated side by side on the wagon's unsprung seat, jostling over a rutted dirt road skirting Delaney land. The days were growing colder; there was a promise of snow in the air. Abner was too excited to notice the chill.

They had been on the road less than an hour when Sarah noted a long line of freshly painted fences and a ranch house beyond. Suddenly Chad drew rein. Sarah watched him closely, wondering what he was thinking. She didn't have long to wonder.

"That's the Doolittle ranch up ahead."

It occurred to Sarah that not all of Chad's demons were inside him; many of them existed in that house. His reluctance to continue down the rutted road gave Sarah a hint of what was going on inside him and her heart went out to him.

"It's too late to turn back now," Sarah said quietly. Chad must have agreed for he took up the reins and set the horse into motion.

A man came out of the barn to meet them as they pulled into the yard. "Are you Chad Delaney?" he asked. Chad nodded. "Mr. Zigler said you'd be coming around. A good thing, too. Winter is coming on, there isn't enough work around the place to keep the hands busy and they're starting to drift off." He stuck out his hand. "I'm Griff Henry, the foreman."

Chad dismounted, lifted Abner from the buckboard, and shook hands with Henry. "I won't lie to you, Henry. I don't intend to keep the place. I'd prefer to sell it, but if I can't find a buyer, I'll lease it."

"I reckon you'll want to have a look around," Henry said. "The Zigler boys kept the place in fine shape."

"I'm cold, Mama, can we go inside the house?" Abner asked.

The wind was coming out of the north, giving a definite bite to the air.

Chad handed Sarah the keys. "Go on inside and warm up. Build a fire if you can find wood in the house."

"There's wood stacked next to the back door," Henry said. "There's plenty of food in the bunkhouse, too. I'll send one of the hands over with something to hold your family over until you return home."

Sarah wondered why Chad didn't correct Griff Henry when he referred to them as a family. She let it slide as she took Abner's hand and led him to the house. Truth to tell, she was more than a little curious about the place that held such unspeakable memories for Chad.

Sarah shivered as she entered the house. It was cold inside, but not cold enough to cause the chill that ran down her spine. Despite being occupied by another family after the Doolittles, the atmosphere literally reeked of misery, of sin. Now she knew how Chad must feel, for she could almost touch the corruptness that permeated every nook and cranny of the dwelling.

Shaking off her disquiet, Sarah found her way to the kitchen. The wood was piled outside the back door, just where Griff Henry said it would be. Abner helped her carry in enough wood to start a fire. In no time at all she had a blaze going, dispelling the bone-numbing chill in the room. A few minutes later, one of the hands appeared at the kitchen door with a plate of roast beef sandwiches, a bowl of potato salad, and a pot of coffee. There was even a mug of cider for Abner.

"Thank you," Sarah said as he set the food on the kitchen table. "Has Mr. Delaney finished his inspection?"

"Don't know, ma'am. He's still in the corral with Griff."

"Would you ask Mr. Delaney to come up to the house for a bite to eat?" Sarah requested.

"Sure thing, ma'am." He doffed his hat and departed.

Suddenly Sarah realized that Abner had disappeared. She wondered what mischief the little scamp had gotten into. "Abner, where are you?"

"Upstairs, Mama," Abner answered. It sounded like his voice was coming from a long way off.

"Come down this minute!"

"I can't. I'm stuck."

"Stuck where?" Sarah asked on a note of panic.

"Up here. Come get me."

Sarah raced up the stairs two at a time. "Where are you, Abner?"

"Here, Mama."

Sarah had no idea where "here" was. She could only go by the sound of his voice. "Keep talking, honey, I'll find you."

She found him in one of the bedrooms, wedged between the wardrobe and the wall. "What are you doing back there?" Sarah wanted to know.

"I found a ball and wanted to play with it. It rolled behind the wardrobe and I tried to get it. I'm stuck, Mama. Can you help me?"

Clucking in exasperation, Sarah attempted to move the wardrobe but found it beyond her strength. Then she tried pulling Abner out from behind the heavy piece of furniture and ended up hurting him, he was wedged in so tightly.

"I'm going to need help, honey. I'll go find Chad. He'll have you out in no time."

"Hurry, Mama."

Sarah could tell he was trying to be brave, but the catch in his voice told her he was close to tears. She turned in a rush and flew down the stairs. She opened the front door and ran headlong into the solid wall of Chad's hard chest. He caught her up in his arms.

"What's the hurry? Has something frightened you?"

"It's Abner," Sarah said breathlessly. "He's gotten himself into a tight place and I need your help to free him."

"Where is he?"

"Upstairs." She grabbed his arm. "Hurry, he's frightened."

Chad balked, reluctant to step into the house. "I hadn't intended to come in. It's time to leave; I've seen all I want to see of this place."

A mewling sound drifted down from the upper floor. "Dammit, Sarah, I never intended to enter this house again. I swear fate is conspiring against me."

"Hurry," Sarah urged, grasping his hand and dragging him toward the stairs.

"Is Abner hurt?"

"No, just scared. He's gotten himself stuck behind a wardrobe and can't get out." The cries were becoming louder now. She pounded up the stairs; Chad was right behind her. "He's in there," Sarah pointed, leading the way down the hallway.

Suddenly she sensed that Chad was no longer following her. She glanced over her shoulder, skidding to a halt when she saw Chad staring into a vacant room as if it were occupied by ghosts. She groaned with dismay, fearing that his demons had just caught up with him.

The sobbing grew louder. "I'm coming, Abner. Don't cry," Sarah called to her frightened son as she returned to Chad's side.

The lack of color in Chad's face worried Sarah. He appeared to be in shock as he pointed to the bed. "That's where it all started." His voice sounded as if it had been scraped raw.

"It's over with, Chad. That happened a long time ago."

"Hal died first," Chad continued as if he hadn't heard her. "My shot hit a vital spot; he died almost instantly. Ed Doolittle died right where I'm standing. The sight of his dead son brought on a fatal heart attack."

His eyes were glazed over, so Sarah gave him a vigorous shake. "Dammit, Chad! If you won't help me free Abner, I'll have to get one of the hands to do it."

Chad blinked and shuddered. He reached deep inside himself for the strength to overcome this crippling journey into his past and found it. The glaze left his eyes, but not the darkness. It felt as if he were coming out of a bad dream.

He mentally shook himself, searched for sanity, and found it. "Where is Abner?"

"He's down the hallway. The little scamp got himself wedged behind a wardrobe and it's too heavy for me to move. I don't think he's hurt, but he's mighty scared."

Chad followed close on Sarah's heels. He took control the moment he entered the room.

"Are you hurt, son?" he asked in a voice that was still thick with emotion.

"Chad! Get me out of here. I'm not hurt, but it's awfully tight in here."

"Hang on, Abner."

Chad put his shoulder to the massive wardrobe and heaved against it. It moved an inch or two, but not enough to free Abner. Chad tried again, this time making considerably more headway. The wardrobe slid several inches away from the wall and Abner literally popped out. Sarah caught him in her arms.

Chad straightened slowly, working the kinks out of his back. "Are you all right, son?" Abner's smile answered the question.

"Let's get out of here. It's spitting snow and I want to get home before it turns into a blizzard."

"I'm hungry," Abner complained.

"Griff Henry sent over some sandwiches and coffee," Sarah pointed out. "It wouldn't be polite to leave them. Why don't we eat a bite before we leave?"

Sarah wasn't too surprised by Chad's lack of enthusiasm, but when he offered no objection, she took Abner's hand and descended the stairs. She found coffee mugs and plates in the kitchen cupboard, then removed the cloth from the food. Abner dug in with gusto, but Chad's appetite appeared to have deserted him. Sarah's attempt to engage Chad in conversation was met with marginal success.

"Did you decide to keep on the ranch hands?" Sarah asked.

"Winter is a slow time. I let them all go except for the foreman and one cowboy. I don't want this place, Sarah. It came to me through a tragedy. I'd like to get rid of it as soon as possible. Once I'm gone, Pierce can deal with it. I washed my hands long ago of everything having to do with the Doolittles. I'd just as soon give the place away."

There was nothing Sarah could add to this, so she concentrated on her food. When they'd eaten their fill, Sarah wrapped up the leftovers and sent them back to the bunkhouse with Abner. They left the Rocking D in the wake of a brewing storm. It had grown bitter cold, but Sarah didn't complain. She was happy to leave a place that caused Chad so much pain.

Chad's brothers had returned from their trip during their absence. When he saw them striding from the house to greet them, Chad's mood lightened considerably. Bear hugs were exchanged all around. Sarah and Abner were introduced, then they all hustled into the warm house, where Sarah met Zoey and Robbie.

"Chuck told us Chad brought friends with him," Pierce said, smiling at Sarah. "Sorry we weren't here to give you a proper welcome, Sarah."

Pierce is a handsome man, Sarah thought, *but not as handsome as Chad.* He was every bit as tall and broad as Chad, but his hair was darker and his eyes were a vivid, compelling green. Sarah wondered if Zoey loved Pierce half as much as she loved Chad.

"How long have you known Chad?" Zoey asked.

Leave it to a woman to get right to the heart of the matter, Sarah reflected as she studied Zoey's lovely features. She thought Zoey breathtakingly beautiful, but wondered why she insisted on dressing like a man. Her snug denims hugged a pair of curvaceous hips, and her flannel shirt could not hide the fact that her breasts were unfettered by a corset. Sarah wished she had the courage to flaunt convention and dress like Zoey.

"Sarah and I met a few weeks ago," Chad answered for Sarah.

"I'm sure there's a story here somewhere," Ryan commented.

Sarah's gaze shifted to the youngest Delaney

brother. Ryan was slightly taller than Chad and Pierce. His piercing green eyes were keenly intelligent, but alight with skepticism. Sarah had a feeling that of the three, Ryan was the most stubborn. The bold slash of his eyebrows above the hard planes of his handsome face must draw women like flies, she reflected. Though not quite as black as Pierce's hair, Ryan's dark brown locks enhanced his tanned features and lent him a dangerous appeal. Instinct told her that he was a rogue and a womanizer.

"Why don't we all go into the kitchen?" Zoey suggested. "Hot coffee would taste good right now. I can't wait to hear what Chad has to tell us. He's been gone a long time."

Everyone must have thought it a good idea for they all trailed into the kitchen. Cookie was working over the sink. When he saw the Delaneys troop in, he sensed their need to be alone. "I'll keep the young'uns occupied while the grownups talk. Help yourself to coffee and cookies." He took each boy by the hand and led them off.

Once the adults were seated around the table, Zoey poured mugs of coffee for everyone and passed around a plate of cookies. Then she took a seat beside Pierce.

"We're all anxious to hear why you stayed away so long, Chad," Pierce prompted once Zoey had settled into place. "We haven't heard a word from you in over two years."

Sarah thought he sounded like a father scolding one of his children.

"Where in the hell have you been?" Ryan asked.

"Around," Chad said, refusing to elaborate.

"Why haven't you withdrawn funds from the

bank account?" Pierce wanted to know.

"I didn't need it," Chad replied. "I earned enough money as a bounty hunter to meet my needs."

"Bounty hunter!" Pierce and Ryan exclaimed in unison.

Chad's expression turned stony. "It's an honest living."

"So is ranching," Pierce contended. "I can't believe you preferred chasing outlaws to working the land you've always loved."

"Dammit, Pierce, you know why!"

"Leave Chad alone, Pierce," Zoey said, coming to Chad's defense. "Have you forgotten that Chad rescued me from Samson Willoughby? Let him explain in his own way. I'm sure we'll understand once we know the facts. He *has* returned, let it go at that."

Chad sent Zoey a grateful smile. "Much obliged, Zoey. At least someone in this family has good sense. You all should know, though, that I won't be staying long."

"What!" The word exploded from Ryan in an angry expulsion of breath. "Why in the hell did you return if you don't intend to stay? What about Sarah? We thought . . . Hell, we *hoped* you'd found someone and returned home to settle down."

Sarah flushed. Nothing could be further from the truth. All Chad wanted to do was dump her and leave.

"I know I've got some explaining to do," Chad began, "and I'll try to answer all your questions. As for settling down in Dry Gulch, you all know my feelings about that. Nothing has changed in that respect."

"Then why *did* you return?" Ryan repeated.

"I came to ask if one of you would take Sarah and Abner in. You both have large houses, and they desperately need a place to stay."

Pierce's eyes narrowed, sensing things Chad wasn't telling them. "You'd better explain."

Sarah felt the color drain from her face. She prayed Chad wouldn't tell his brothers more than they needed to know, but she could think of no way he could explain without mentioning that Abner was illegitimate. She'd experienced people's scorn and disapproval before, but it was important to her that Chad's relatives think highly of her.

"Sarah and Abner are in danger. An outlaw named Freddie Jackson may be stalking them," Chad began. "He's a bank robber and a rapist. Jackson is Abner's father, but he's not Sarah's husband. He's already taken the boy from his mother once."

Sarah paled beneath the keen perusal of Chad's family. Chad's rather terse explanation had all but named Freddie her rapist. She wanted to disappear into the woodwork.

"Oh, you poor thing," Zoey said, understanding perfectly what Chad had only hinted at. "We're glad Chad brought you and Abner to us, aren't we Pierce?"

Pierce nodded absently as he searched Chad's face for a hint of his brother's feelings for Sarah.

"I don't want to impose on your generosity," Sarah insisted. "I didn't want to come here, but Chad was determined. You know how persuasive Chad can be when his mind is set on something."

They did indeed. The Delaneys had tenacity in common.

"Chad wants us to believe that his relationship with Sarah is a platonic one," Ryan said knowingly. "He brought Sarah to us because he is concerned for her safety." He sent Chad a wicked grin. "I don't buy it."

Chapter 13

"What kind of damn fool statement is that?" Chad bit out. "Sarah and I are friends, no other explanation is necessary. You're embarrassing Sarah."

Chad knew precisely what his family was thinking. They knew it wasn't like him to bring strangers into their home unless they were people he cared about. Nor was it his style to dump someone on them and take off. But he'd changed during the two years he'd been away. Chad was surprised his brothers didn't recognize the differences in him. He'd always been stubborn and hardheaded; now he was bitter and disillusioned.

"All I ask is that you protect Sarah and Abner from Freddie Jackson," Chad continued. "I'm going after him as soon as I leave here, but it might take a while to catch him."

"You can count on us, Chad," Pierce said. "It's time we returned to the Circle F. Sarah and Abner can accompany us."

"Accepting charity is new to me," Sarah said with quiet dignity. "I've provided for myself and Abner since the day he was born. My son's well-being is all that matters to me and I'd do anything to keep him safe. I've worked hard all my life, I don't want to become a burden to anyone. I intend to work for our keep. I can cook and sew and clean and do laundry. Taking in laundry is how I made my living in Carbon."

"We wouldn't dream of making you work for your board," Zoey said, aghast. "You'll be our guest. The pleasure of your company is all we'll ask of you. It gets pretty lonesome on the Circle F. Our nearest neighbors live miles away."

"Your generosity overwhelms me," Sarah said with feeling. "Unfortunately I can't accept on those terms. I wouldn't be comfortable with accepting charity and giving nothing in return."

"I have another solution," Ryan injected before Zoey could reply.

Zoey frowned at her brother-in-law. "What other solution can there be? Sarah and Abner will be our guests for as long as they wish to stay."

"Suppose we let Sarah decide," Ryan suggested. "I need a housekeeper. Mrs. Lester left some weeks ago, and I haven't gotten around to replacing her. The hands and I can protect Sarah and Abner just as well as Pierce. If Sarah wants to work for her keep, then I say we should let her."

Sarah was grateful for Ryan's understanding. He must have known she was uncomfortable with Zoey's offer and countered with one more acceptable to her.

Chad glowered at his brother. "Sarah isn't a servant, Ryan. She'd be better off accepting Pierce's hospitality. Hard labor nearly ruined Sarah's health. She was recently scalded and only newly recovered. I don't want her to work that hard again."

A bubble of anger rose up inside Sarah. Chad should know by now that she wouldn't be content to live on charity. She had no money of her own, and accepting Pierce's hospitality wouldn't add a cent to her financial security. Accepting gainful employment would salve her pride and provide much needed funds to set aside for the future.

"It's my decision, Chad," she reminded him. "Pierce and Zoey don't really need me, but Ryan does. I want to be useful." She turned a brilliant smile on Ryan. "If the job is still open, I'd be happy to accept the position of housekeeper."

Ryan's answering grin was potent enough to set most women's hearts to pounding. Sarah pitied the poor smitten women who had lost their hearts to a rascal like Ryan. "The job is yours, Sarah. And don't worry about Jackson. If he's stupid enough to show up on Delaney land, he won't get past the hands. We'll set guards, if we have to."

Sarah prayed that was so. But Freddie was a sly one, she'd put nothing past him. "It's settled then. I'll accept the same arrangements you had with Mrs. Lester. You won't be sorry, Ryan."

Sarah didn't like the way Chad looked at Ryan. It was as if he thought his brother had designs on her. If that was Ryan's intention, she'd set him straight on her own.

"Sarah is old enough to make her own decisions, even if I don't agree with them," Chad said with ill humor.

"I can't say I'm not disappointed," Zoey sighed regretfully. "Robbie would have enjoyed a playmate."

"If that's settled, we'll leave for the Circle F in a day or two," Pierce decided.

"I wish you'd stay," Chad persisted. "Otto Zigler was here the other day. He's giving up the lease to the Rocking D. I was hoping you'd take care of it for me."

"I'm not covering for you this time, Chad," Pierce told him. "I filled in for you once, but you're here now to take care of the matter yourself. The Rocking D is your responsibility."

"Dammit, Pierce, I told you I wasn't going to stick around long. If you won't handle this for me, I'll get Ryan to do it."

"Not me," Ryan drawled. "I've got enough to do around here. Pierce is right. It's time you faced up to your responsibilities. You're not to blame for what happened on the Rocking D. Ghosts don't exist, Chad. It's time to put your guilt behind you and get on with your life."

Ryan's words had little impact on Chad as he rose abruptly. The chair behind him crashed to the floor. "Fine brothers you are! I know why you're doing this and it's not going to work." Whirling on his heel, he strode angrily from the room.

"What do you think he'll do?" Ryan asked worriedly.

"Chad always was stubborn," Pierce said. "Once he cools down, he'll probably go to town and have our lawyer handle everything for him."

"He's going to leave," Sarah said with conviction. "It never was his intention to stay. He never wanted to come to Dry Gulch. His plan was to dump me and Abner on Pierce and Zoey and take off again. Pierce wasn't home so he was obliged to continue on to Dry Gulch."

"We had so hoped that Chad had finally found a woman to love," Zoey said wistfully.

"Chad doesn't believe in love," Ryan guffawed. "Pierce is the only one who believes in love, and even he didn't succumb until he met Zoey. Marriage works for him, but it's out of the question for me and Chad."

"What a terrible thing to say!" Zoey scolded. "Chad isn't as hard-hearted as you seem to think. He wouldn't have brought Sarah and Abner here if he was."

Zoey's rebuke brought a flush to Ryan's face. "Sorry, Sarah, I didn't mean to imply . . ."

"It's all right, Ryan. I know exactly where I stand with Chad. I've never asked for a commitment, nor have I expected one. Chad has been very good to me. I owe him a great deal. He's too good a man to carry around the daunting burden of guilt. He's told me everything, you know."

"You must be very close if he told you everything," Zoey said thoughtfully.

Sarah's cheeks reddened. "We're just friends." Lovers would have been an apt description, but she didn't want to share that information with Chad's family. "Chad took care of me and Abner when an injury rendered me nearly helpless."

"I worry about Chad," Pierce said. "He has to help himself, none of us can do it for him."

Pierce's sobering remark brought a halt to the conversation. Sarah took advantage of the lull to excuse herself. If she was to function as housekeeper, she needed to consult with Cookie about supper, and make a thorough inspection of the house.

Sarah found Cookie with the boys in the bedroom. She shooed the children out so she could ask Cookie about her duties.

"Where are you going?" Zoey asked when the boys skipped into the kitchen, where they all sat around the table.

"Out to the barn," Robbie lisped.

"Not without a wrap," Zoey replied. "It's cold outside. Both of you come upstairs with me, I'll see what I can find for you to wear."

"My jacket is hanging on a hook by the door," Abner said. "I'll wait here for Robbie."

"Sit down, son," Pierce invited, indicating an empty seat beside him. Abner slid into the chair.

"Are you and Ryan as nice as Chad?" Abner asked shyly.

"You think Chad is nice?" Ryan asked with surprise.

Abner nodded emphatically. "Mama thinks so too. I asked Chad to be my papa, but he said it wasn't a good idea. Do you think you could ask him? He might listen to you."

Ryan and Pierce exchanged startled glances. "We don't have much influence over our brother," Pierce said kindly.

"Mama and I didn't have enough to eat before Chad came to our house. We were lonesome, too. Now when I get lonesome, I crawl in bed between Chad and Mama. I wanted to sleep naked like they do, but Mama said I couldn't do that." He sighed hugely, innocently unaware of the information he'd just revealed. "I'm sure gonna miss Chad when he leaves."

Abner's revelation was met with gaping silence and shocked expressions. Abner seemed not to notice. Robbie returned to the kitchen a few minutes later, and the boys skipped out the back door.

"I'll be damned," Ryan muttered, sharing a knowing glance with his brother.

"I suspected as much," Pierce contended.

"What are we going to do about it? What if Chad leaves Sarah in the family way? In my opinion, Sarah isn't the kind of woman who shares her favors with just anyone. According to Chad, Sarah was the victim of rape."

"I suggest that we have a talk with our brother," Pierce said. They both rose and strode off to find Chad.

Chad was in the corral when he saw his brothers shoot from the kitchen and head in his direction. He groaned aloud when he noted the determined looks on their faces. He wanted to walk away, but when they got their dander up they were like dogs panting after a bone. They had something to say and Chad knew from experience they wouldn't let him rest until they said it.

"You lied to us, brother," Pierce charged. "You told us that you and Sarah were merely friends."

"So?" Chad contended. "What of it?"

"You can start by telling the truth," Pierce demanded.

"I don't answer to you, Pierce. I'm twenty-eight years old and capable of handling my own affairs."

"Like hell! Not an hour ago you asked me to handle your affairs for you."

"Dammit, Pierce, what's the point of all this?"

"You're sleeping with Sarah!" Ryan charged. "You brought her here, asked us to protect her, then lied about your relationship. Do you still intend to leave?"

"That's always been my intention. Sarah knows

it and hasn't questioned my decision."

"I don't suppose you know why she's so accepting," Pierce challenged.

Chad didn't appreciate this interrogation. Then he recalled that he had challenged Pierce two years earlier about his relationship with Zoey, using nearly the same words. "Since you're so smart, you tell me."

Pierce cursed beneath his breath. "I'm smarter than you are. I married Zoey. It's obvious to everyone but you that Sarah loves you."

Chad gave a shout of laughter. "You don't know Sarah if you think that. She doesn't want marriage any more than I do. She doesn't love me. She's grateful to me, but that's as far as it goes."

"Does she make a habit of sleeping with men out of gratitude?" Ryan retorted. "How many men have there been before you?"

Rage exploded in Chad's head. "No one talks about Sarah like that and gets away with it." His words were punctuated with a smashing blow to Ryan's chin. Ryan reeled backward, but came back swinging. Soon both brothers were rolling on the ground, exchanging punches.

With difficulty, Pierce separated the two of them and held them apart. "Enough of this. You're damn protective of someone for whom you profess simple friendship, Chad. We're not condemning you for your relationship with Sarah. Lord knows I was as stubborn as you are, until Zoey finally convinced me we belonged together. The difference between our situations is that Zoey and I were married before we slept together. But if you're going to leave Sarah with Ryan while you run off to escape your demons, he deserves to be told the truth about you and Sarah."

"Exactly," Ryan concurred. "And if you're not interested in Sarah romantically, does that make her fair game? Sarah is a beautiful woman, I wouldn't mind . . ."

His sentence ended abruptly when Chad darted around Pierce and flung himself at Ryan. Another scuffle ensued. It ended in a draw when Abner and Robbie came out of the barn and saw the fight. In a surprised move, Abner flung himself on Ryan's back and started screaming at him to stop hitting Chad.

"I'm all right, Abner," Chad said, picking himself off the ground. "You and Robbie go on up to the house. It's time to wash up for supper."

Abner's little face screwed up into a frown. "Why were you and Ryan fighting?"

"You wouldn't understand. Do as I say, son. Go on now. I promise there won't be any more fighting."

"I promise, too," Ryan added when Abner glared at him.

"Abner's a smart little kid," Ryan said as Abner and Robbie trudged off toward the house. "You think a lot of him, don't you, Chad?"

"Yeah," Chad growled, dusting his hat off on his pants and clamping it back on his head.

"He's going to miss you. I suggest you search your heart carefully before you leave. You might not find it as barren as you think. Thank God compassion is foreign to me," he added. "No woman is going to tie me in knots. Love has no place in my life. Love 'em and leave 'em, that's my motto."

"You're talking nonsense," Chad argued. "You

know damn well I have nothing to offer a woman. I'm emotionally bankrupt. I'm not a womanizer like you, Ryan. You need a woman in your bed to make you happy."

"I know what and who I am," Ryan said. "Are you ready to talk about Sarah now?"

"What about her? You promised to protect her and Abner."

"I intend to," Ryan declared. "Both Pierce and I are of the opinion that you should do the honorable thing where Sarah's concerned. She's already been hurt by a man. Rape is a horrible thing for a woman to suffer."

"I think, and Pierce agrees, that you care more for Sarah than you're letting on."

"You two just don't give up, do you?" Chad muttered. "Neither of you understand. I *do* care for Sarah. I'm actually doing her a favor by walking out of her life. I don't want to make a mess of her life like I did mine. She's better off without me."

"Why don't you let Sarah decide," Pierce challenged.

"She'd agree with me."

"Which brings us back to the question Ryan asked earlier," Pierce said. "With you out of the picture, is Sarah fair game for other men?"

"If Sarah finds a man to love, I won't be around to object," Chad said. "She deserves better than what I can offer."

"Damn fool," Pierce bit out. "You two had better see to your bruises before supper. The women don't need to know about your little fray."

"Stubborn wretch," Ryan muttered as he walked away.

"I'm charging you with keeping Ryan in line

while I'm gone," Chad told Pierce. "I don't trust him around Sarah. All women are fair game to him. You and I both know he won't marry Sarah."

"For what it's worth, I'd advise you to stick around and protect your property," Pierce threw over his shoulder as he walked off.

Chad watched his brothers leave, the two people he cared the most about. Well, maybe not the only two. There were Sarah and Abner. If he even suspected Ryan would seduce Sarah in his absence, he'd beat his brother bloody.

Abner and Robbie had already given their version of the fight between Chad and Ryan to the women before the men reached the house. It really wasn't necessary, though. The bruises on their faces gave them away.

"Do you want to tell us about it?" Zoey asked when they sat down to the evening meal.

"No," Chad and Ryan said in unison.

"They have always settled their differences with their fists," Pierce said by way of an explanation. When Ryan and Chad remained mute, it became apparent that the women were going to get nothing more.

Sarah wasn't sure she wanted to know what Chad and Ryan had fought about. It would be disheartening to learn she was the cause of the fight. She'd leave before she'd let herself come between Chad and his brothers.

Two days later, Pierce and his family returned to the Circle F, deciding to travel while the weather still held. Sarah began her housekeeping duties with enthusiasm. In truth, the work wasn't hard. With winter fast approaching, Chad, Ryan, and the hands were busy preparing for harsh weather. Hay was hauled in for feed, the cattle driven to lower ground, and the outbuildings were reinforced to withstand blizzards.

Somehow Ryan had convinced Chad to return to the house to sleep and he now occupied his old room, but Sarah saw little of him in the ensuing days. She knew he was eager to leave and couldn't imagine why he was sticking around. She supposed it was due partly to the problem he was having getting rid of the Rocking D, and partly because Ryan kept finding work that desperately needed Chad's attention.

One day Frank Frasier, who was new to the area, strolled up to the house. Looking to buy a ranch, he had been told in town that the Rocking D was for sale and to inquire at the Delaney ranch. When Chad asked Ryan to take Frasier to the Rocking D, Ryan politely declined, declaring himself too busy to spare the time. In the end, Chad was obliged to show Frasier around the spread. They left immediately, and Sarah spent the next several hours worrying over Chad's reaction to another visit to the Rocking D.

Chad returned shortly before supper. He was quieter than usual; his face was colorless, his expression bleak. Sarah wanted to comfort him, but didn't know how.

"I sold the Rocking D to Frank Frasier," he said when they had all gathered for supper. "He'll bring the money around in a day or two. I intend to deposit the funds in Sarah's name, then I'll be moving on."

Sarah didn't realize she'd been holding her breath until it exploded from her throat. "I don't want your money! The wage Ryan pays me is sufficient for my needs."

Chad's expression hardened. In this matter he was inflexible. "Nevertheless, the money is yours."

"Have you thought this over carefully?" Ryan asked. "This is your home, Chad, there's no need for you to leave."

"I'm going after Jackson. Sarah and Abner won't be safe until he's behind bars. I don't want them to go through life wondering and worrying about him."

"I'm sure Freddie has forgotten all about Abner," Sarah claimed. "I doubt he'll follow us all the way to Montana."

Chad turned a deaf ear to Sarah's logic. Sarah wondered if he'd heard anything she'd said. There was a darkness in him that hadn't been there since his last visit to the Rocking D. She watched in dismay as he rose abruptly and exited the room without a word to anyone.

Ryan shook his head. "I thought I was hardheaded, but my brother's stubbornness surpasses even my own. Two years have passed since the tragedy at the Rocking D. Chad should have conquered his demons by now and moved on with his life. It isn't good for him to live in the past. I don't want him to leave, Sarah. Can't you think of a way to keep him here? He might listen to you."

"Chad has to fight this battle on his own," Sarah said on a sigh. "I can't force him to do anything he doesn't want to do. Though Chad will be the first to deny it, he's a kind, compassionate man. In time those good qualities will emerge from the darkness inside him. We have to let him find his own way, Ryan."

Ryan gave her a crooked smile. "I'm thinking of giving him a little nudge. Have you ever been courted, Sarah?"

Sarah's violet eyes widened. "Courted? Why no, I don't believe so."

"Well, prepare to be courted by me. I'm considered quite a catch, you know. I'm known as Rogue Ryan in town. How do you suppose Chad would react if he thought I wanted you?"

"I'm not sure he would react at all."

"I think you're wrong, Sarah. Chad knows me. He's aware of what I want from a woman. If I pretend to seduce you, he's going to be madder than hell. Will you play along?"

Sarah frowned. "For what purpose?"

"To get my brother's attention. To make him admit he has strong feelings for you. Marriage isn't for me, but it's working for Pierce and it might be exactly what Chad needs to bring him to his senses. I'd rather see him married to you than drifting aimlessly, weighed down by his conscience."

Sarah's mouth worked wordlessly. Ryan's startling proposal had stolen her ability to string words together. After several minutes of stunned silence, she found her voice. "What makes you think I'd marry Chad?"

Ryan gave her a radiant smile, obviously pleased with his ability to arrive at the heart of the matter. "You love him. Women are funny that way. It's so easy to read them. Zoey was the same way. Both Chad and I knew she was head over heels for Pierce long before Pierce knew it. Just because I'll never marry doesn't mean I don't want to see my brothers happy. I think you'll make Chad happy,

Sarah. I think he's already in love with you, and he's crazy about Abner."

"So you want to pretend to court me in order to make Chad jealous," Sarah said slowly.

"It's the only way to keep Chad from leaving."

"I think you're wrong."

"About you loving Chad?"

Sarah's cheeks pinkened. "I . . . I suppose you're right about that. It's been difficult to admit it because of my distrust of men. No man has ever been as good to me as Chad. I think you're wrong about Chad loving me, though. He feels responsible for me, and he does care for me in so far as he's able to care for any woman. But love is a strong emotion. And we both know Chad's emotions are on shaky ground. He's utterly consumed by what happened at the Rocking D. There's no room in his heart for me and Abner."

"Shall we disprove your theory?" he challenged. He gave her a dimpled, heart-stopping smile that would have made most women swoon.

"Do you truly think the subterfuge will keep Chad from leaving?"

"I'm willing to give it a try. How about you?"

Sarah nodded slowly. She didn't know Ryan very well, but he seemed to have his brother's best interests at heart. She prayed it was so, and that she could trust him.

Chad suspected something was going on between Ryan and Sarah, but he had no idea what it could be. In the following days, he noticed that Ryan and Sarah were often together, their heads bent in intimate conversation. He couldn't imagine what they had to talk about. It made him madder than a wet hen to see Ryan coaxing a smile out of Sarah, and treating Abner with easy affection.

He tried to tell himself he didn't care, that once the sale of the Rocking D was completed and the money banked, it didn't matter what Sarah did with her life. He'd asked for no commitment, nor did he extend any hope that he'd return to Dry Gulch any time soon. He just hated to see Sarah get mixed up with Ryan. He loved his brother dearly, but Rogue Ryan wasn't the type of man Sarah needed. Once he got what he wanted from Sarah, he'd go on to his next conquest. It made Chad spitting mad to think that Ryan had seduction on his mind when he hired Sarah as housekeeper.

One day Sarah announced that she was going to the hen house to gather eggs. When Ryan followed a few minutes later, Chad decided to tag along behind his brother. He found them both in the barn, apparently meeting there for a prearranged tryst. Chad saw red as he slipped noiselessly into the barn. It took a moment for his eyes to adjust to the dim interior. Then he saw Sarah in Ryan's arms and the breath slammed from his chest. His anger was such that he feared he'd kill someone if he didn't leave immediately. He spun on his heel and stormed out of the barn.

"I think he saw us," Sarah whispered when she saw Chad make a hasty departure. "He looked mad."

"I knew he'd follow me when I left the house minutes after you did."

A worried expression marred Sarah's delicate features. "What if we're wrong? What if Chad doesn't give a hoot what I do?"

"You saw how he reacted. He's cross-eyed jealous. But even if he isn't, I kind of enjoyed our little flirtation." His eyes sparkled with mischief. "Holding a beautiful lady in my arms isn't hard to take."

Sarah blushed and stepped away. She didn't know how to take Ryan. Did he really have his brother's best interests at heart? Sometimes she wondered.

Chad spent the rest of the day fuming in impotent rage. Every time he visualized Sarah in Ryan's arms, he wanted to do someone bodily harm. Sarah was headed for trouble if she succumbed to Ryan's seduction. He knew what his brother wanted from a woman. Hell, he'd been just like Ryan two years ago. It was amazing how time and events changed a man.

Chad shoved his food around on his plate that night at supper, annoyed at the way Ryan was teasing and flirting with Sarah. If Sarah's blushes and shy smiles were any indication, she appeared to be enjoying every minute of Ryan's flirtation. He decided abruptly that it was time to have a talk with Sarah. Given any encouragement, Ryan would have Sarah in his bed before she could blink her eye. It was up to him to warn her about his brother's reputation as a womanizer.

Sarah tucked Abner in bed that night, then went to her room. Ryan had gone out to the bunkhouse after supper and she had no idea where Chad was. He appeared angry and withdrawn at supper and Sarah was surprised that Ryan's charade was working so well. Chad had said nothing more about leaving, and the longer he stayed the less likely he'd be to get out before spring. Weather had been exceptionally mild of late, but the winter was well on its way.

Sarah shivered as she undressed, washed, and slipped into a flannel nightgown. The nightgown had just settled around her ankles when the door burst open and Chad stepped into the room. He closed the door and leaned against it, glancing around as if surprised to find Sarah alone.

"Where's Ryan?" he asked harshly.

Sarah froze, shock and anger warring within her. "How should I know?"

Chad shrugged, walking deeper into the room. "You and Ryan are awfully close these days."

Sarah felt a surge of joy. Had Ryan been right? Was Chad jealous? "What of it?"

Anger sizzled through Chad. "You don't know Ryan. He's a womanizer. He'll break your heart. You're an innocent, Sarah. Falling for Ryan isn't in your best interest. Have you bedded him yet?"

Sarah stepped back as if struck. How could Chad say such a mean thing to her? Lashing out at him seemed her only defense. "What if I have? You don't want me."

Chad nearly leapt across the room to reach her. Seconds later she was a captive in his arms, molded against him, chest to chest, thigh to thigh. He stared down at her, his teeth bared in a feral smile.

"Not want you? Where in the hell did you get that idea? Not a minute goes by that I don't want you."

Chapter 14

The breath caught in Sarah's throat. The wanting was mutual. She needed Chad as desperately as he needed her. She could pretend that he loved her as much as she loved him, but her heart knew better. In this relationship, love was one-sided. Falling in love with Chad had truly surprised her. Her experience with Freddie Jackson had led her to believe that all men were brutal animals who took what they wanted when it wasn't freely given. Nothing in Sarah's life had prepared her for Chad Delaney.

Life had treated Chad nearly as shabbily as it had her, Sarah reflected. He wore the burden of guilt willingly, believing himself responsible for four deaths, when in truth he was blameless. Chad was a remarkable man. Sarah found no flaws in his character. He was basically kind and exceedingly compassionate. He made love to her as if she were special. He gave her back her self-worth.

Chad regarded Sarah with trepidation as he waited for her to either deny or confirm her involvement with his brother. When she continued her silent introspection, he gave her a little shake.

"Dammit, Sarah, tell me. Have you let Ryan make love to you?" His voice sounded as if it had been scraped raw.

"What would you do if I said yes?"

Chad's expression hardened, his arms tightened around her like a vise. "I'd beat him to a bloody pulp. He's only playing with you, Sarah. You don't know Ryan like I do."

"Ryan has been awfully good to me and Abner."

"Ryan isn't a monster. He isn't cruel or heartless. He's merely a womanizer. He can't help it. It's in his blood."

"I don't expect a commitment from Ryan," Sarah informed him.

"If you're bedding him, you damn well better ask for a commitment," Chad growled.

Sarah lowered her voice to a whisper. "I never asked *you* for one, Chad."

"We're not talking about me, we're talking about Ryan."

"You're the only man I've made love with, Chad. I don't count Freddie Jackson. What he did to me was an obscenity."

A great shudder passed through Chad. He stared at her for the space of a heartbeat, then lowered his head and claimed her lips. At first his kiss was hard, demanding, possessive, then his mouth softened, becoming teasing and seductive. He nibbled at her lip, then drew her full lower lip between his teeth. His hands cupped her face, holding it in place while his mouth ravished hers. Blood pounded in his veins, seared his skin, and pooled between his legs. He wanted to make love to her; he needed to be inside her, to taste her sweet passion once again.

Her lips were warm, pliant against his, and when she began to make frantic little cries deep in her throat, he knew there was no turning back.

"I want to make love to you," he whispered hoarsely.

"I want that too," Sarah moaned, clinging to him as if he were her anchor in a storm that threatened to sweep her away.

"Can you accept me the way I am, sweetheart? I don't know if I'll ever defeat my demons, but if I do . . ." His sentence ended abruptly. He didn't want to give Sarah false hope. He couldn't predict the future.

"I didn't always trust you, but I've always accepted you, Chad. You've been a wonderful friend to me and Abner."

Her words shamed him. It made him feel as if he were using her. "You make me feel like a heel. You deserve better than me. Perhaps I should leave."

Sarah's arms tightened around his neck. "Don't go." Her voice held a note of desperation. "I need you. Make love to me, Chad."

"Are you sure?"

"Very sure."

He gave her a dazzling smile and gently disengaged her arms from around his neck. Gazing deeply into her eyes, he began to unbutton her flannel gown. Seconds later, he whisked it over her head and tossed it aside. She stood utterly still as his admiring gaze swept the length of her, pausing briefly on her breasts before continuing down past her flat stomach, to the curly black patch between her legs.

Abruptly he dropped to his knees, grasped her

bottom, and pressed his lips to her stomach. He was aware of nothing but her enticing scent, her delicious taste, the feel of his hands on her, and his blood thickened with sweet languor. Yet there was a power to it. He'd never felt stronger in his life.

His hands slid between her thighs, parting them so his mouth could find her. His tongue darted into the fragrant, dewy folds, holding her hips as his mouth devoured her. He felt her go rigid, heard her cry out, felt her fingers dig into his hair. He made a gurgling sound deep in his throat. His shaft was hard and heavy and ready to burst.

The buzzing in Sarah's ears grew louder. She felt her knees grow weak as Chad's mouth worked unspeakable magic on her pliant flesh. When his thumb began to massage the hard little nub at the apex of her thighs, she went wild. She exploded in a rush of pleasure so intense she thought she'd die of it. Then she did. When she came to her senses a few minutes later, she was lying on the bed beside Chad. He had removed his clothing and was bending over her, smiling down at her.

"What happened?" she asked as she lifted her hand to the hard planes of his face.

"Did you like it?"

"It was . . . wonderful." She glanced down at his sex and saw that he was still massive and fully aroused. "Can I do that to you?"

The mere thought of Sarah's mouth on him made his shaft jerk and spit. "You don't have to."

She leaned up on her elbow and stared into his eyes, her own darkened by desire. "I want to."

His heart hammered in his ears as he clasped her head between his hands and slowly brought it down to his groin. She nuzzled blindly against his belly, stroked him with her tongue, then drew his erect flesh into her mouth.

She tasted him fully, moving her mouth up and down the pulsing staff as her hands roamed his naked flesh, memorizing every glorious inch of his powerful form. The scent of his arousal titillated and provoked as she savored the saltiness of him on her tongue. She felt him stiffen, knew he was close to the edge, and reveled in her own sense of power. Then suddenly he lifted her and brought her on top of him.

"Take me inside you," he said on a breathless gasp. "God, woman, you can't begin to imagine what you do to me." He raised her slightly, flexed his hips, and thrust forward, impaling her in one long slide.

Sarah could find no reply to match the indescribably erotic feeling of Chad's turgid flesh pushing into her as she thrust down against him, bringing him deeper. Then all conscious thought fled as she lost herself in the pleasure of his loving. When her climax came she embraced it fully, gloriously, vaguely aware when Chad shouted her name and spilled inside her.

Sarah came to her senses slowly. She gave Chad a languid smile when she felt his lips grazing across her shoulder blades, stopping briefly to press against the rapidly beating pulse at the hollow of her throat. She gave a gurgle of contentment when his mouth continued down to her breasts, plying the tip of his tongue to her nipples.

"What are you doing?" she managed to whisper.

He raised his head and gave her a wicked smile. "I was so eager for you, I didn't love you properly the first time."

Sarah sent him a provocative grin. "I thought you did just fine."

Chad thought so too, but that didn't stop him from loving her again.

While Sarah slept blissfully in Chad's arms, a thousand thoughts marched through his head. He was jealous, there was no doubt about it. Jealous of his own brother. Of any man, should the truth be known. The emotion was so foreign to him, it left him stunned. What in the hell was he going to do about it? Before he could include Sarah and Abner in his future, he had to mend the emotional shambles he'd made of his life.

After struggling a time with the problems he had to resolve, Chad arrived at a decision he couldn't have made had he not met Sarah. He wasn't going to leave the ranch. Not yet, anyway. Leaving would give Ryan free rein with Sarah, and he didn't want his roguish brother to break her heart. With his life finally falling into place, Chad eased out of bed so as not to disturb Sarah, dressed quickly, and departed. He stepped out of Sarah's room and ran into Ryan.

"Are you coming or going, brother?" Ryan asked with a hint of amusement.

Chad sent Ryan a fulminating look. "Come into my room. We need to talk."

Ryan nodded, following Chad into his room. "What do you want to talk about?" he asked, closing the door behind him.

"Sarah. Don't think you can add her to your list of conquests. Admit it. You're just amusing yourself with her."

Ryan gloated in secret mirth. He'd been right

about his brother. Chad *was* jealous. Ryan shrugged, pretending indifference. "Why should you care? You're leaving soon. You said so yourself. If you cared about Sarah, you wouldn't leave her."

"I brought Sarah here for protection. You're my brother. I expected you to protect her, not seduce her."

Ryan grinned. He understood his brother better than Chad understood himself. "You realize, of course, that leaving now is not in Sarah's best interest. She could be carrying your child."

"Are you suggesting that I marry Sarah? You, a man dead set against marriage?" Chad laughed harshly. "Since when have you become an advocate of marriage?"

"Since you came home and I saw how good Sarah is for you, and how much you care about her and Abner. But," he added by way of warning, "if you leave now, beloved brother or not, Sarah becomes fair game."

"Well, *beloved brother*, I'm staying."

Ryan wanted to whoop with joy.

"But don't get your hopes up. And don't give me one of your sanctimonious sermons. Sarah's father has given me enough of those to last a lifetime. I admit Sarah and I are . . . more than friends, but I won't marry her until I'm sure I can be the kind of husband she needs. There are ghosts rattling around in my past. Unless I can banish them, Sarah is better off without me."

"I don't know who is more stubborn, you or Pierce," Ryan said, shaking his head. "Seriously, though, I'm glad you're staying. The only way you can confront your problems is to face them head on. Running from them won't work."

"What about your problems, Ryan? You're just as fearful of marriage and distrustful of women as I am."

Ryan's eyes sparkled mischievously. "I *like* women, Chad. They have a definite place in my life."

"In your bed," Chad muttered. "That's one place Sarah will never occupy."

"That's up to you," Ryan challenged. "At least I have the good sense not to fall in love. I'm perfectly happy bedding whores, obliging widows, and ladies willing to sacrifice their virtue for pleasure."

Chad stiffened. "In which of those three categories have you placed Sarah?"

"Perhaps I'll create a special one for Sarah," Ryan said easily.

Chad gave his brother a rueful smile. "You'll get nowhere with Sarah. I've already warned her to steer clear of Rogue Ryan." He clapped his brother on the shoulder, unable to remain angry. "I don't want to fight with you, Ryan. I know you wouldn't hurt Sarah. We're arguing over nothing."

Ryan returned his grin. "Welcome home, brother. I'm glad you decided to stay. As for Sarah, don't keep her waiting too long. She's not the kind of woman who beds a man without making a commitment to him. Whether you know it or not, she wouldn't give me a second glance with you around. Good night, Chad."

"Good night, Ryan."

Chad removed his clothes and climbed into bed. He still had a lot to think about and many things to resolve within himself. Tomorrow he'd take the first step toward healing his emotions. He'd do whatever was necessary to banish his demons forever.

Sarah awoke from a wonderful dream. Or had it been a dream? Did Chad really say he wasn't leaving? She glanced out the window, saw that it was still early, and decided to bathe before the household stirred. She could feel the sticky residue of Chad's seed between her legs, and as much as she loved his scent upon her, it needed to be washed away. She donned a robe and went down the hall to the bathing room. She met Ryan in the hallway. He gave her a conspiratorial smile as he set the buckets down on the floor.

"It's working, isn't it?" he asked gleefully. "Chad is so jealous he can't see straight." He thought it best not to mention that he saw Chad leaving her room last night.

"Chad is difficult to read," Sarah murmured. "He *did* seem perturbed, though, didn't he?"

"Perturbed is too mild a word." He gave her a quick hug. "I've done my part, Sarah, the rest is up to you."

Chad watched the tender scene from his open door. "What's going on?"

Both Ryan and Sarah whirled at the sound of Chad's voice. Nonplussed, Ryan said, "Not a thing. Sarah is on her way to take a bath. We met in the hallway by accident."

He stared hard at Ryan before accepting his explanation with a curt nod. "I suggest we leave Sarah to her bath." He motioned for Ryan to precede him out the door.

Sarah bathed quickly, then hurried down to the

kitchen. Cookie was doing dishes. "Where are Chad and Ryan?"

"Already gone," Cookie said.

"Did they mention where they'd be today?"

"Ryan said he was going out with the hands to distribute hay to the stock in the south pasture. Chad didn't say where he was off to. Sit down, Miz Sarah, I'll have a hearty breakfast before you in no time. You could stand a little meat on your bones."

Sarah ate mechanically, barely tasting her food. She was almost finished when Abner trailed into the kitchen and announced that he was starving. While Abner ate, Sarah stared absently out the window. She saw Chad riding Flint out of the yard, saw him head north, and wondered where he was going.

"Cookie, what's north of here?" Sarah asked casually.

"Not much, Miz Sarah. The stock has already been moved down from the north pasture. 'Course there's the Rocking D, with nothing in between but empty acres, hundreds of 'em."

"That's all?"

Cookie scratched his head, rearranging the thatch of sparse gray hair growing there. "There's a cemetery between here and the Rocking D. Some of the families in the area use it to bury their loved ones."

Sarah glanced out the window again. The leaden skies held a promise of snow, but so far the weather had been exceptionally mild. Sarah didn't know where Chad was going, but she felt strongly that she should be with him.

"Would you keep an eye on Abner for me?" Sarah asked Cookie.

"Sure thing, Miz Sarah. Bundle up, it's cold out there."

She donned coat, muffler, and gloves, then hurried out to the barn. She saddled a horse and a few minutes later, took off after Chad.

Two men who were hiding in the woods behind the house watched her ride off.

"Is that the woman, Freddie?"

Freddie Jackson gave his swarthy companion a cocky grin. "Yeah, Sanchez, that's her."

"Should I go after her, señor?"

"Naw, it's the kid I want. My kid," he added proudly. "As soon as I get him, we're gonna head to Mexico. The money from the bank we robbed in Dry Gulch yesterday is gonna help us get there. I'm taking my kid with me. I'll find some sweet little señorita to take care of both of us."

"There's no one at the ranch house now, señor. We've been watching since dawn, they all rode off except your kid and the old man."

"Yeah, let's do it now, Sanchez. We ain't never gonna have another chance like this."

Sarah caught up with Chad at the cemetery. It was located in a peaceful valley surrounded by forest and lofty mountains. But Sarah could see no serenity in the slump of Chad's shoulders as he stood with his head bowed before a cluster of graves.

Sarah dismounted and quietly watched from the cover of tall pines, unwilling to intrude upon his solitude. She was more than a little startled when she saw Chad fall to his knees and bury his head in his hands. He looked so forlorn, so utterly dejected, that Sarah could almost feel his pain. She started forward, determined to offer what little comfort she could. At the sound of her soft footsteps, he raised his head and turned in her direction.

"What are you doing here?" he asked with a slight edge of wariness.

"I followed you."

He let out a furious oath and turned away. "How did you know about the cemetery?"

"Cookie told me."

"You've come out here for nothing," Chad said harshly. "Go back to the ranch."

Sarah shook her head emphatically. "I'm staying. I'm not going to leave you alone, Chad."

The stark planes of his face stood out in vivid contrast to the burning intensity of his eyes. "Dammit, Sarah, don't coddle me. Healing has to come from within myself. No one can help me."

He returned his gaze to the graves he'd been contemplating just moments before. Sarah's stomach clenched painfully when she read the names on the markers. Doolittle. Cora Lee, Hal, Edward, and Baby Doolittle. She gazed at Chad in silent commiseration. His face was a study of intense pain and deep concentration. She could almost feel his anguish, see him struggling with some dark force within himself.

She remained absolutely still, watching, waiting for some sign to indicate he'd won his battle. The wind whistled through the trees, breaking the eerie silence of this desolate place, and she shivered as an icy blast penetrated her coat. Nothing short of imminent death could make her leave Chad now.

Suddenly Chad leaped to his feet, grasped his horse's reins, and threw himself upon his back. He would have ridden off without so much as a thought for Sarah if she hadn't called out to him. He appeared to have forgotten she was there.

"Chad! Where are you going?"

Chad reined in sharply. "To the Rocking D."

"Wait! I'm coming with you."

He offered no objection as he waited for her to mount. Her feet had barely settled in the stirrups when he kneed Flint into a brisk gallop. She reached the Rocking D several minutes behind Chad. She found him standing on the porch talking to Frank Frasier, the man who was buying the ranch. She dismounted and walked over to join them.

"Howdy, ma'am," Frasier said, doffing his hat. "I was just telling your husband that I got the loan from the bank and was on my way to town to pick up the money. Was there something special you wanted?" he asked Chad.

"Just wanted to take a last look around," Chad said. His face gave away nothing of the turmoil roiling inside him.

"Sure thing, take your time. I'm fixing to leave, but you know your way around. I'm keeping on the foreman and hiring back the hands that were let go, so I'm kinda anxious to get going and sign them on before someone else does."

"Don't let me stop you," Chad said. "This isn't going to take long."

Frasier nodded and headed to the barn to get his horse. Chad waited until Frasier rode off before he let himself into the house.

"Why are you doing this?" Sarah asked as she followed Chad through the door.

"Because I have to. Ryan was right. I can't go on

running forever. Problems have a way of following wherever you go; you can't outrun them. All my problems are directly related to this house."

Chad paused at the foot of the stairs, resting his hand on the newel post. He was surprised to find his fingers shaking and he jerked his hand away, struggling to gain control. After a moment he was able to pull himself together, and he reached for Sarah's hand. She grasped it, and they ascended the staircase together.

Sarah felt Chad tense and tighten his hand around hers when they reached Cora Lee's bedroom. She could almost taste the fierce battle waging within him as he stepped inside the room and stared at the bed. She wondered what he was thinking as one emotion after another flashed across his face, each more profound and seething than the previous, each expanding and spilling over, stunning Sarah with the sheer intensity of his pain.

"Say something," Sarah whispered, squeezing his hand. "What do you feel?"

"Drained. Tired of living in the past and sick of fighting guilt."

His feet dragged as he approached the bed and glanced down at the floor where Hal Doolittle had died in a pool of blood. He shuddered and pulled Sarah into his arms, holding her so tightly she could hardly breathe. "I want it to be over," he said on a groan. "Help me, Sarah."

He lifted her face with his thumb and forefinger and kissed her. She had no idea what was going on inside Chad now, but whatever it was, she was willing to help.

"Make love with me now, Sarah. Here, in this

house, on this bed." His voice held a note of desperation. "I need you."

Sarah gaped at him, then at the bed. The bed where Cora Lee and her child had breathed their last. "Are you sure this is what you want, Chad?"

"I've never been more sure of anything in my life. Make new memories for me, sweetheart. I want to banish the past. You're the only one who can help me."

Sarah didn't know how to interpret his words. "Are you saying you love me?"

"Loving you wouldn't be difficult," Chad admitted. "Even though I'm not sure I know what the word means. Perhaps I just need time to come to grips with the idea. Will you let me make love to you? Here? Now?"

Sarah shook her head. "It's not a good idea. It would be for all the wrong reasons."

"You're wrong, Sarah. It would be for all the right reasons. Making love to you in this room will help to restore my peace of mind. You can give me new memories to replace the painful ones associated with this house. Give me pleasure to remember instead of death."

Sarah tried to dispute Chad's logic, but couldn't. He had given her more hope for a future with him in these last few minutes than he had in all the previous weeks and months they had been together. If new memories were what he wanted, then she'd give them to him. No matter what happened between them after today, he'd still have his new memories. She stepped out of his arms and began to undress.

Their loving was slow, tender, and achingly poignant. If Sarah felt uncomfortable in this house, her discomfort vanished the moment Chad touched her, the second his lips claimed hers, the instant his tongue invaded the sweet warmth of her mouth. He brought her to climax without spending, then aroused her again, bringing them both to shattering completion.

"I feel as if I've just emerged from a long tunnel into the light," Chad murmured into her ear.

"No more demons?"

"I hope not. I feel as if I'd just been released from two years of hell."

Chapter 15

Jackson and Sanchez emerged from the cover of lofty pines wearing a dusting of snow, which was now falling in abundance from the leaden skies. They spied a party of riders approaching the Delaney house and ducked back out of sight.

"Dammit!" Jackson cursed. "Vigilantes. Let's get the hell out of here."

"What about the kid? Are we going to Mexico without him?"

"Not on your life, Sanchez. When I go to Mexico, my kid is coming with me. The vigilantes won't expect us to stick around in Dry Gulch after robbing the bank. Remember that old line shack we passed a ways back? Nobody will be using it at this time of year. We can stay there until the coast is clear. When the time is right, we'll nab Abner and head south to Mexico. If we wait long enough, we're bound to find the kid alone. Plenty of cover here. We'll just sit tight and wait for the right time."

"What are we gonna do about food? We can't just mosey into town and stock up at the local grocery store. Somebody is bound to recognize us."

"Don't need to. We'll steal what we need from the local ranchers. Come on, Sanchez, let's get the hell out of here."

Chad and Sarah met the vigilantes on their way home from the Rocking D. Riley Reed and his men intercepted them about a mile from the Delaney ranch. It was snowing steadily now, and Chad chaffed at the delay.

"Well, well, if it ain't Chad Delaney," Reed said, reining in beside Chad. "When did you get home?"

"A while ago," Chad said shortly. There was no love lost between Reed and the Delaneys. Reed and his vigilantes had come so close to lynching Pierce that his brother still wore the rope burns on his throat. "What brings the vigilantes out on a cold day like this?"

"We're looking for bank robbers." His gaze shifted to Sarah. "That your wife?"

Chad ignored his question and posed one of his own. "Who are you chasing this time, Reed? Not another innocent man, I hope."

"The men who robbed the bank in town are guilty as sin," Reed returned. "They got clean away, but we'll find them. They couldn't have gotten far. We figure they're heading south. Have you seen a couple of suspicious characters around here?"

A shiver of dread crept along Chad's spine. Bank robbers. He didn't like the sound of that. His first thought was that Jackson had traced Sarah and Abner to Dry Gulch. Was that lowlife still determined to have his son?

"What did they look like?" Chad asked.

"One was a short, dark Mexican. The other was

tall with blue eyes. Both wore hats pulled low over their foreheads and bandannas covering the lower part of their faces."

"We haven't seen anyone matching those descriptions," Chad said. "Any idea who they are?"

"Some say it was Freddie Jackson and a Mex named Sanchez. They pulled off a robbery over in Roundup a couple weeks back and the federal marshal there recognized them. Can't say for sure, though, not till we find them." He peered up at the sky. "This snow will help us track them down."

"Good luck," Chad said distractedly as he watched them ride away. He didn't hold out much hope of the vigilantes catching Jackson. Jackson was a wily bastard. Chad had good reason to know. He hadn't caught the man after tracking him for over two weeks.

"Chad, are you thinking what I'm thinking?" Sarah asked. Her face appeared as white as the falling snow and Chad could taste her fear.

"We're not sure it was Jackson who robbed the Dry Gulch bank," Chad reminded her. "It could be anyone."

"But what if it was Jackson? What if he followed us to Montana? Several people knew I'd left with you. I recall telling Carrie where to find me."

"Even if you hadn't told Carrie it wouldn't be difficult for a resourceful man like Jackson to learn our destination. Don't worry, Sarah, Ryan and I will protect you and Abner."

"I'm not worried for myself. Freddie wants Abner, not me. Why would a man like that want to be a father all of a sudden?"

"Abner is Jackson's link with immortality, I suppose. Let's get back to the ranch."

"Oh God, yes. I want to make sure Abner is all right."

"Jackson is no fool. He's probably miles away by now."

Chad prayed he was right. His gut told him Jackson was closer than he'd like to think. And over the years, Chad had learned to listen to his gut.

Sarah rushed into the house, vastly relieved when Abner ran up to greet her.

"The vigilantes were here, Mama!" he cried excitedly. "They were looking for a bad man."

Sarah snatched him up into her arms and gave him a fierce hug. "I know, honey. We saw them."

He squirmed out of her arms. "It's snowing outside. Can I go out and play?"

There was no way Sarah was going to let Abner out of her sight if there was any possibility that Freddie Jackson was in the vicinity. "Not now, Abner. I . . ."

"I'll take you out," Chad offered. He'd walked into the room in time to hear Sarah refuse Abner permission to go outside to play. He couldn't blame her for wanting to keep the boy close, but the look of disappointment on Abner's face had gone straight to his heart. "There's chores that need doing in the barn, I'll keep an eye on him."

Abner gave a whoop of joy and ran to the kitchen to put on his outdoor gear.

"You're still worried, aren't you?" Chad asked.

"Can you blame me?"

"No, that's why I'm going after Jackson."

Sarah stared at him. "You're what?"

"I'm going to find Jackson. His capture is long

overdue. I don't want you and Abner to have to worry about him ever again."

"You can't go! The weather isn't good. It's snowing."

"That's why I have to go now. He'll be easier to track in the snow. Ryan will look after you in my absence. There are ten armed men on the ranch."

"What's this about a bank robbery?" Ryan asked as he entered the room. "Cookie told me about it the minute I walked in the back door. He said the vigilantes paid us a visit."

"We think Freddie Jackson is in the area," Chad explained. "He's probably miles away by now, but I'm going after him to make certain he doesn't bother Sarah again."

"That's a job for the vigilantes," Ryan said.

"I'm a bounty hunter, remember? I understand outlaws and how their minds work. I've tracked them in all kinds of weather and gotten into some tight places, but I've always gotten my man. I'm not going to fail with Jackson. Will you take care of Sarah and Abner in my absence?"

"You know I will. Nothing will happen to them while you're gone."

"You can't let him go, Ryan!" Sarah exclaimed, alarmed.

"I can't stop him, Sarah."

Chad regarded Ryan solemnly. "I'm trusting you not to seduce my woman while I'm away."

"*Your woman*!" Ryan repeated. "Did something happen today that I should know about?"

Chad sent Sarah a tender glance before answering Ryan's question. "You could say that. We'll talk about it when I return."

Abner picked that moment to run into the room,

bundled to the eyebrows. "I'm ready, Chad. Can we go outside now?"

"Sure thing, son. Don't worry about Abner," he said to Sarah. "I'll keep an eye on him."

"I don't have a good feeling about this," Sarah said after Chad left with Abner. "I don't want Chad to leave. Not now. Not when he and I . . ." She flushed and dropped her gaze.

"What happened today, Sarah? Did you and my brother come to an understanding?"

"I followed Chad to the cemetery," Sarah revealed. "Something happened to Chad out there, something that defies explanation. It was as if a great upheaval was taking place inside him. His anguish was almost palpable. I was shocked when he decided abruptly to go to the Rocking D. I couldn't let him go alone, so I followed. When we reached the house, we climbed the stairs together and went into Cora Lee's room. He struggled with his demons a long time before he reached some kind of a decision."

Ryan was intrigued. "What happened next?"

Sarah hesitated, then decided she had nothing to lose by telling Ryan the truth. "We made love on Cora Lee's bed."

Ryan was visibly shaken. "You what?"

"Chad asked me to make love with him. At first I didn't think it was a good idea, but the longer I considered it the more reasonable it sounded. He needed new memories to associate with the Doolittle house; I provided them for him."

"Alleluia!" Ryan crowed delightedly. "Maybe I'll get my brother back now. Chad has changed. He isn't the same man I'd grown up with. He's lost the joy of living. If not for you, he might never have returned home. Did he ask you to marry him?"

"I'm not sure Chad wants marriage any more than you do. I'd like to think he's ready for a commitment, but I'm not going to wish for things that might never be. I do believe, though, that he's finally defeated his demons, but," she added sadly, "I'm not sure he wants me and Abner in his life."

"He called you his woman," Ryan reminded her.

"In some ways, I am, but that's for Chad to decide," she said, blushing.

With nothing more to add to that, Ryan returned to his chores and Sarah went to her room. Today's events had been both draining and exhilarating, leaving Sarah with much to think over. Unfortunately, she still didn't know where she stood with Chad.

Chad planned to leave at first light. He had gathered his gear, packed his saddlebags, and conferred with Cookie about trail food. He figured he'd head south, and if he found nothing to indicate that Jackson was traveling in that direction, he'd head on back to the ranch and search the surrounding area. Common sense told him Jackson was too smart to stick around, but his gut told him Jackson could still be in the immediate vicinity. He decided to follow common sense first and, failing a result that way, he'd go with his gut.

Even if Jackson was still around, Chad seriously doubted the man would attempt a bold abduction with ten armed men protecting Abner. Jackson would have to be either damn stupid or cocksure of himself.

Supper was a subdued affair that night. When

Chad announced that he intended to leave at dawn, Sarah was visibly shaken. She excused herself a few minutes later and ran from the room, glad that Abner had already been fed and put to bed so he couldn't see how upset she was.

She didn't know Chad had followed her up to her room until she tried to close the door and found it blocked. She was surprised and a bit dismayed when Chad stepped into the room and closed the door behind him.

"What was that all about?" he wanted to know.

"If you don't know, I'm not going to tell you."

"You know I have to do this, Sarah. I won't be satisfied until Jackson is in jail."

"What about me? What about us? Is there an us?"

"I know we haven't discussed the future, and I intend to remedy that when I return. Until today, sharing my bleak future with a woman was unthinkable. For the first time in two years I'm thinking clearly again. I have you to thank for that."

Sarah's denial was emphatic. "You owe me nothing. Your healing came from within, from your strengths, and from your indomitable character. It was inevitable. I knew that one day you'd return from the hell you dug yourself into."

"I want to stay with you tonight, Sarah. I want to awake in the morning with you in my arms. I know you're tired. We don't have to make love. Just holding you will be enough for me. I don't know how long I'll be gone, but I won't return until I've turned Jackson over to the law. I'll track him to the ends of the earth, if I have to."

Words she'd feared to voice rang within the silence of her mind. Suddenly the burden of withholding them became too great, and she blurted out all those gut-wrenching emotions she'd kept hidden for so long. "I love you, Chad. I can say that now without any reservations. I want your arms around me, forever, if possible."

Chad agonized so long over his answer that Sarah knew he wasn't ready yet to declare himself. Marriage meant he'd have to place his trust in a woman, and accept responsibility as a husband and father.

"Did you know I fancied myself in love once?" Chad said, dropping his arms away from her. "I was even engaged to be married."

Sarah couldn't imagine such a thing. "No, tell me about it. What happened?"

"She was considered the town beauty. I felt honored that she chose me to marry. She wanted me to leave the ranch and move to the big city. She hated the thought of living on a ranch and tried to convince me to settle in Denver, or San Francisco. I didn't take her seriously. Both Pierce and Ryan were more aware of her capricious nature than I, but I refused to heed their warning. Pierce had already been burnt in a bad marriage and was quick to note that she wasn't right for me."

"Did you finally see the light and break the engagement?"

Chad gave a rueful laugh. "I was left standing at the altar, so to speak. The day before the wedding, she ran off with an eastern dandy who was in town visiting relatives. Last I heard, they were living in New York City."

"She must have been crazy to leave you for another man," Sarah said wistfully.

Chad smiled and brought her back into his arms.

"What I'm getting at, love, is that saying the words you want to hear is difficult for me. My own mother deserted me when I was a small lad, and my father instilled in us a fear of marriage. I never thought I'd learn to care for a woman like I do you. And you know I'm crazy about Abner."

"Deny it all you want, but I know you love me, Chad. You've proven it in so many ways. Sometimes action speaks louder than words. One day you'll feel comfortable saying what I want to hear. I can wait. But I won't wait forever," she warned. "I don't want a man who can't love me with his whole heart and soul."

"You left out body, Sarah. I can love you with every fiber of my body, if you'll let me."

"And I will love you with every fiber of mine," Sarah replied, gazing deeply into his eyes.

God, she loved him. She loved him enough for both of them, enough to last until he found the courage to speak what was in his heart. No other woman could love him as much or give him more, she thought fiercely as she lifted her face for his kiss.

Chad's mouth seized hers with almost desperate yearning. Surely he must love her, he told himself. Nothing else could be so confusing yet feel so wonderful. With a sigh, he reached for the courage to bare his soul and failed to find it. He had no difficulty finding passion, though. Passion he had in abundance, and all of it for Sarah.

He carried her to the bed and undressed her, his tongue writing lovenotes on her skin as he bared it to the heat of his mouth. One hand slid down her naked back to her waist, then continued down to trace her spine to the cleft of her bottom. He heard her sigh and murmur with pleasure as he drew a nipple into his mouth.

"Take off your clothes," she gasped on a note of raw desire.

Buttons flew as Chad all but ripped off his clothing. His body was hot, he was swollen and heavy, so hard and full he ached.

Suddenly the leashed passion in him erupted. With a deft motion he spread her thighs, lifted her bottom, and pushed into her, his hands gripping her hips and thrusting until she felt him touch her womb. He was not gentle; Sarah was surprised he hadn't hurt her considering the fury of his passion and his powerful entry.

It didn't take long; just a few piercing strokes of his sex deep inside her brought her to a shattering climax. He peaked and yelled his own release seconds later.

His breath was harsh and raw. He felt the drain in his body, the easing of his lust. But the need for Sarah was still vibrant, still a raw ache inside him. If this was love, then he had almost died of it. The emotions roiling inside him were the fiercest he'd ever experienced. His heart pounding, he buried his face in her neck and whispered, "I love you, Sarah."

No answer was forthcoming. The even cadence of her breathing told him she had fallen asleep. He kissed her forehead, drew her into the curve of his body, and joined her in slumber. There was plenty of time to bare his heart to her.

Chad had been gone a week, and Sarah missed him desperately. The weather had turned surprisingly mild for late October, almost like Indian summer. Ryan remained close to the house during Chad's absence and Sarah felt guilty for keeping him from his work. Abner moped around the house, keenly aware of Chad's absence and clearly missing him.

One day, when a cowboy rode in from the south pasture to confer with Ryan, Sarah and Cookie went outside to see what was wrong. Ryan explained the problem to them. Three calves had gotten themselves stuck in mud in a deep gully and the hands were having trouble freeing them. Runoff from the early snowfall had filled streams and gullies with gluey, sucking mud. Sarah could tell that Ryan was torn. He felt the need to give his men a hand to free the calves but was reluctant to leave Sarah and Abner because of his promise to Chad.

"You needn't stay because of me," Sarah told him. "Cookie is here, and I know how to use a gun. Jackson is probably long gone by now. He wouldn't be dumb enough to stick around and risk capture."

"I'm inclined to agree, but I promised Chad I wouldn't leave for any reason."

"I'm right handy with a gun," Cookie said. "Don't worry, Ryan, go take care of your cows. I'll keep my eyes peeled for trouble."

Though reluctant to do so, Ryan rode off with his men to help free the stranded cows. Since the day was so fine, Sarah decided to tackle the wash. She had just stripped the bed linen from Chad's bed when Abner skipped into the room. He was dressed for the outdoors.

"I'm going to the henhouse with Cookie," Abner informed his mother. "We're gonna gather eggs for a cake. Cookie said he'd make a chocolate one for me because that's my favorite."

Sarah gave him an indulgent smile. "Try not to break any eggs, the hens aren't laying well. And stay close to Cookie," she warned. "Don't go running off."

"You worry too much," Abner threw over his shoulder as he danced away.

Sarah shook her head. Such an active little scamp like Abner couldn't be kept in the house for long. She suspected Cookie was going to the henhouse simply because Abner was bored with playing inside. She knew Cookie carried a shotgun with him whenever he ventured from the house, so she wasn't worried about Abner's safety.

Humming to herself, she gathered up the sheets and carried them downstairs to the laundry room. Immersed in her task, time ran away with her and she didn't think about Cookie and Abner again until she wrung out the sheets and carried them outside to hang on the clothesline. She had just hung the last sheet when she became disturbed by the ominous silence. There was no sign of Cookie or Abner, no voices to indicate they were nearby. She thought it highly unlikely that they were still in the henhouse, but she hadn't seen them leave.

Fear, stark and vivid, raced through her. She tried to keep her fragile control as she ran to the henhouse. Ducking inside the long, low building, her worst fears were realized when she spied Cookie lying on the ground, his head resting in a congealing pool of blood.

She rushed to his side and dropped to her knees, praying he wasn't dead. The shallow rise and fall of his chest sent a shudder of relief coursing through her. Examining him more closely, she discovered a wound on his head. He'd been struck with enough force to break the skin. The bleeding had slowed but the swelling around the wound was impressive. Sarah ripped off the hem of her petticoat and pressed the folded scrap to his head.

Cookie groaned and his eyes fluttered, as though trying to summon the strength to awaken.

"Cookie, wake up," Sarah pleaded, nearly beside herself with worry. "Who did this? Where is Abner?"

The panic he heard in Sarah's voice overcame Cookie's inclination to close his eyes and shut out the pain. With great difficulty, he opened his eyes. "That you, Miz Sarah?" His voice sounded as if it had been scraped over sandpaper. He tried to rise, but Sarah wouldn't let him.

"What happened, Cookie? Where is Abner?"

"They took him, Miz Sarah."

"Who took him?"

"That Jackson fella. Heard his partner call him by name before I passed out. Me and Abner were gathering eggs when they snuck up behind us. Jackson bopped me on the head with the butt of his gun before I could swing my shotgun around. Don't recall much after that."

The thought of Abner with a man like Jackson shattered Sarah. She didn't believe Jackson would hurt his son, but in all likelihood he'd take Abner away where she would never see him again. The thought of life without Abner nearly tore her apart.

"I'm going to help you into the house first, then I'm going to find Ryan. Jackson can't have gotten too far. Did he say where he was taking Abner?"

Cookie's leathery brow furrowed as he tried to

recall what Jackson had said before blackness closed in on him. His head hurt like the very devil, the thought kept slipping away before it fully formed in his mind.

"Think, Cookie. What did Jackson say?" Sarah prodded. She hated to keep plaguing the poor man, but she and Ryan had to know in which direction Jackson was headed.

Cookie concentrated and finally found what had eluded him. "I recollect now, Miz Sarah. I heard Jackson say they were going to Mexico and live like kings."

Sarah blanched. Jackson may as well be taking Abner to the ends of the earth. "Let me help you up, Cookie. Can you walk?"

"I think so. Might need a little steadying, though."

Sarah lent him her shoulder and managed to get him upright. Together they made slow progress to the house. Once inside, Sarah wet a cloth and gave it to Cookie to hold to his head.

"I'll send someone to town for the doctor as soon as I find Ryan. Will you be all right?"

"Don't worry none about me, Miz Sarah. It's all my fault. I should have been more careful. I want that boy back as much as you do."

"It's not your fault, Cookie. I reckon we all became too complacent. We should have been more vigilant, but it seemed ridiculous to assume that Jackson was still in the area. I'll be back as soon as I can."

Sarah saddled a horse and rode like the wind. About a mile from the house she spied a group of riders and rode out to meet them. She prayed it was Ryan and the hands returning to the house. But as she drew closer, she noted that the horses were moving at a snail's pace, and that one horse was pulling a travois, consisting of two long poles with a blanket fastened between them. Sarah's heart sank when she saw a man lying on the makeshift stretcher. Even before she saw his face, she knew it was Ryan.

The grimace of pain upon Ryan's face did not bode well for his condition. "What happened?" she asked anxiously.

The foreman answered her question. "Ryan went down in the gully to try to boost one of the calves from the mud. The animal slipped and landed on top of him. I think his leg is busted. I've sent Clem to town for the doctor."

Through a blur of pain, Ryan had the presence of mind to wonder what Sarah was doing out riding. It didn't take him long to draw the right conclusion. He spit out a string of colorful oaths. "Something happened, didn't it?"

"Abner's gone," Sarah said on a sob. "Jackson surprised Cookie and Abner in the henhouse. He struck Cookie down and abducted Abner. Cookie lost a lot of blood. He may have a concussion."

Trying to remain lucid through a mist of pain was proving difficult for Ryan. "So you came looking for me. Dammit! This wasn't supposed to happen. I'm pretty sure my leg is busted. How much of a head start does Jackson have?"

"A couple of hours. He's taking Abner to Mexico. I've got to go after him, Ryan."

"Not alone, you're not. Take some of the hands with you."

"No. You'll need them while you're laid up. Besides, this isn't their fight, it's mine."

"Don't be stubborn, Sarah. You can't go alone. What do you expect to gain?"

"My son. I'll accompany you back to the house and pack a few supplies before I leave."

"I'll send for Pierce."

"I can't wait that long."

"If I can't talk you out of this, then your best bet is to ride to Fort Ellis and ask the army for help."

"Are you sure they'll help?" Sarah asked. "Jackson is Abner's father."

"He's also an outlaw with a price on his head. I didn't want to say anything before, but I heard Jackson killed a man in a bank robbery in Wyoming shortly before robbing the Dry Gulch bank. The army has an obligation to protect the people in the territory. They don't recognize vigilante law. There are few regular lawmen in the territory, it's the army's job to protect the citizens. I'll send someone to the fort with you."

Sarah nodded agreement. To argue with Ryan was pointless. He didn't need aggravation added to the pain he was suffering. Besides, it made sense to have a cowboy accompany her as far as Fort Ellis.

Two hours later, Sarah and a young hand named Brock Murray left the Delaney ranch and headed to Fort Ellis. The doctor had arrived before she left and set Ryan's leg. Cookie had been put to bed and told to rest a day or two before resuming his duties.

Fort Ellis was a long day's ride, but Sarah didn't want to wait till morning to leave. Jackson already had a five- or six-hour head start. Sarah and Brock rode until darkness threatened their safety, then they made a makeshift camp and ate food Sarah had taken from the Delaney kitchen. Brock proved to be a taciturn young man, but that was fine with Sarah. She was far too worried to engage in pointless conversation.

Sleep was elusive, but Sarah managed to doze off and on during the uncomfortable night. She was up at first light, eager to reach the fort and get the help she so desperately needed. When the stockade came into view, Sarah entertained hope for the first time since Abner had been abducted. She paused before the open gate.

"You can return to the ranch now, Brock. I'll be safe here."

"Are you sure, ma'am?"

"Very sure. Ryan is going to need every available hand while he's laid up. Thank you for your escort."

"You're welcome, ma'am. Good luck finding your boy. We're all right fond of him." He tipped his hat and rode off. It was the most words he'd strung together since they'd started out yesterday.

Sarah waved him off, then rode through the gate.

Chapter 16

Sarah faced Major Dalton across his littered desk and explained her problem to the best of her ability. She'd thought her need was justifiable and was shocked by Dalton's reply.

"I'm sorry, ma'am. I'd like to help, but I just can't spare the men right now. A group of renegade Indians have left the reservation and are preying on the ranchers. Chiefs Cunning Wolf, Yellow Dog, and Snake have been running amok, stealing cattle and chickens and just about anything they can lay their hands on. It's going to take every able-bodied man at my disposal to round them up and drive them back to their reservations."

Sarah stared at the major in disbelief. "A little boy's life is at stake, Major. Freddie Jackson is a dangerous outlaw. It's your duty to bring him to justice."

Impatience colored the major's words. "Granted, ma'am, but my first consideration is protecting the ranchers from Indians. Once the renegades are back where they belong, I'll give your request every consideration."

Sarah fumed in impotent rage. How could Major

Dalton deny her? She was living a nightmare. "I can't wait that long, Major. Jackson is taking my son to Mexico. If you won't help me, I'll just have to help myself."

Major Dalton had already dismissed Sarah from his mind as he turned his regard to more pressing matters. "Ask my clerk to find you a billet on the way out," he said absently. "I'll make your request my first priority when I return."

Sarah's chin stiffened. "That won't be necessary. I'm leaving immediately. Good day, Major."

"Miss Temple, I strongly advise . . ."

Sarah never learned what he advised as she stormed out of the office. The unthinkable had happened. The army had refused to help her. Before she left home, Ryan had begged her to wait for Chad, or at least wait until he could summon Pierce. But Sarah had been adamant. There had been no time to lose. She had taken a handgun, a shotgun, supplies to last several days, and left immediately. Unfortunately she was no better off now than she was before. There was the remote possibility that she would run into Chad, but it wasn't something she could count on.

Chad spent several days searching for Jackson before he began to wish he had followed his gut instead of his common sense. Apparently Jackson had acted contrary to what everyone believed, and Chad was now inclined to believe that Jackson was still hanging around Dry Gulch. There had to be only one reason Jackson would stick around with a posse on his tail instead of hightailing it out of town. Jackson wanted Abner and was waiting for the opportunity to seize the boy.

Chad felt reasonably certain Jackson wouldn't succeed. Not with Ryan, Cookie, and the hands protecting Abner. Still, a nagging fear formed in the pit of his stomach and grew with each passing minute. Then Chad ran into Riley Reed and learned that the vigilantes hadn't crossed Jackson's trail either. That was the day he decided to look closer to home for the outlaw.

Sarah knew nothing about tracking. All she could do was head south and keep going. The mild weather turned nasty after she left the fort, but she blundered on. That night she found shelter in a crevice beneath a ledge and passed a miserable night. When snow began to accumulate at an alarming rate, she bravely plowed forward. But when the wind turned the drifting snow into a blizzard, she knew she had to find a more substantial place to take refuge or risk death from exposure.

Shortly after dark Sarah stumbled upon a ranch. Her relief was sharp and vivid as she made her way through the snowdrifts to the front door. A dog barked from somewhere within the depths of the barn, but didn't venture out into the cold to investigate. Sarah's frantic pounding on the door was answered by an elderly man carrying a shotgun.

"Who are you?" he asked, squinting through the darkness at the slight figure huddled on his doorstep.

"My name is Sarah Temple. I mean you no harm. I'm cold and need a place to spend the night."

"Is that a woman I hear, Curtis?" a voice called from inside the house. Sarah felt warmth seeping through the open door and was tantalized by it.

"It surely is, Martha. Says her name is Sarah Temple."

"Well, land sakes, come on in, child," Martha said, appearing in the doorway beside her husband. "You must be nearly frozen to death."

Curtis held the door open and Sarah stepped inside. "Is there someplace I can shelter my horse?"

"I'll take care of him," Curtis offered, grabbing his jacket from a hook by the door.

"Come sit by the fire," Martha invited after her husband departed. "We're the Darrows, Martha and Curtis. What in tarnation brought you out on a night like this?" The rotund little woman's keen blue eyes were bright with curiosity as she took Sarah's coat and led her to a bench before the fireplace.

"It's a long story," Sarah said as she stretched her hands toward the warmth.

"I'll bet you're hungry. There's some stew left over from supper, and hot coffee sitting on a back burner. You can talk after you eat, if you've a mind to. We don't get much company out this way."

Curtis Darrow came into the house, stomping snow from his boots. "Your horse is all taken care of, Mrs. Temple," he said. "I see Ma fixed you up with some grub. Eat hearty, now, Ma's a mighty fine cook."

Martha Darrow blushed like a young girl. "Go on with you, Pa."

Sarah smiled at the comfortable camaraderie between the Darrows, wondering how it would feel to have the same kind of closeness with Chad.

"Food's on the table, Mrs. Temple," Ma Darrow said as she placed a slice of fresh bread beside the bowl of stew. "Eat your fill. There's more where that came from."

Sarah ate until she thought she would burst. The food was delicious. Then Ma Darrow placed a slice of dried apple pie in front of her, and she thought she'd died and gone to heaven.

"I can't recall when I've had a better meal," Sarah said, patting her full stomach. "Don't know what I'd have done if I hadn't stumbled upon your place."

"Froze to death, most likely," Pa Darrow said dryly. "You must have a good reason for being out in weather like this, Mrs. Temple."

"Please call me Sarah. And I do have a good reason. My son was kidnapped by an outlaw. I have to catch up with him before he reaches Mexico."

"Oh my," Ma said, her eyes round with concern. "You poor thing. How old is your son?"

"He'll be six soon."

"What about your husband? What must he be thinking to let you go off on your own?"

"I'm not married," Sarah admitted. She held her breath, waiting for their disapproving frowns. When none were forthcoming, she let her breath out slowly.

"What about relatives? Is there no one who can help you?"

"The only person who can help me is presently unavailable, and I couldn't wait for him to return."

"You're very brave, dear," Martha said, patting Sarah's shoulder in motherly concern.

"But foolish," Curtis added pragmatically. "Indians are raiding again. They hit my ranch just three days ago and made off with some of my stock."

"I know," Sarah said with a sigh. "I stopped off at Fort Ellis to ask for help and was told I'd have to wait until the renegades were rounded up and sent back to their reservation."

" 'Pears to me that the Indians are raiding because they're starving. What with corrupt agents and all, the poor creatures haven't enough to hold body and soul together."

"Now, Martha, you don't know that," Curtis chided. "I'm just trying to impress upon Sarah here the danger of continuing her mission. Best you should go back home, Sarah, and wait until the army can help you."

Sarah's voice was taut with resolve. "I can't. Abner is all I have in this world."

Tears sprang to Martha's eyes and spilled down her chubby cheeks. "I'd do just as you're doing," she said fiercely. "Pa and I had a son once. He died many years ago of fever. I would have done anything to save him. We have a spare room you can use. Things will look brighter after a good night's sleep."

"You're very kind," Sarah said. "Thank you. I'll be happy to accept your hospitality."

Though the bed was comfortable, Sarah couldn't sleep. She worried about Abner being exposed to the raging elements. He was so little, so young and innocent. How could he survive against such odds? Was Freddie looking out for him? Was he warm enough? Did he have enough to eat?

Concern for Chad added to her misery. The same questions she entertained about Abner could just as well apply to Chad. He was braving the harsh elements for her sake. Chad was such a kind and compassionate man, she found it difficult to believe no one else thought so.

Oblivion finally came. Sarah slept dreamlessly, awaking hours later to a dirty gray dawn. The snow had tapered off sometime during the night and Sarah took it as a sign that she should continue on her mission. She left the Darrows' house after a satisfying breakfast.

During the following two days Sarah had cause to wish she'd stayed with the Darrows. The snow had turned to slush and then to mud. She was so exhausted that when she stopped at a town to buy feed for her horse, she decided to spend the night at a hotel. She was in desperate need of a hot bath and a good meal. The questions she asked about two men traveling with a young boy were met with negative replies. No one had seen strangers in town bearing the descriptions she gave. But gossip abounded about Indian raiders who were scaring the devil out of ranchers and townspeople alike.

The following day snow and cold returned with a vengeance. Nevertheless Sarah took to the road, disheartened because she'd seen nothing to indicate that Jackson was ahead of her on the trail. Toward late afternoon a raging wind whipped the snow into a blizzard. Sarah began to look for shelter. She grew alarmed when she realized she was no longer on a marked trail, that somehow she had become disoriented and lost her way. Without the sun to guide her, she could be traveling in any direction.

Suddenly a group of horsemen appeared through a curtain of blinding snow. They appeared almost ghostlike, and utterly frightening as they surrounded her. Her relief at seeing other humans turned to panic.

Indians!

They were close enough now for Sarah to see their dark faces. Wearing buckskins and wrapped in threadbare blankets, Sarah thought them fierce harbingers of doom. She'd seen very few Indians in her life, and those she had seen were pitiful creatures compared to these savage warriors.

"What do you want?" Sarah cried as they closed around her in a tight circle. They appeared not to understand so she asked again, more slowly this time. "What do you want? I mean you no harm."

One warrior grabbed her reins from her hands, while another slapped her horse's rear. Sarah clung to the pommel as the warriors took off through the trees, forcing Sarah's horse along with them. They continued tirelessly, until Sarah feared she'd fall off her horse from sheer exhaustion. The passage of time was a blur. It could have been an hour, or five hours, before they reached an Indian camp situated at the edge of a spruce forest. The dozen or so tipis were partially obscured by swirling white masses of snow and tall trees.

The Indians dismounted. Pulled roughly from the saddle, Sarah landed hard. Her knees buckled and she fell on her rump. She picked herself up, expecting the worst. This couldn't be happening, she silently lamented. Indians were no longer the threat they once were. For the most part, they lived peacefully on reservations. Something drastic must have happened to make them take up raiding again.

Sarah's eyes burned, her cheeks were chafed raw from the wind, and she wished something would happen soon. And then it did. The crowd parted to allow an older man and a young woman to approach Sarah. The woman raised her head. Sarah gasped when she realized she knew the woman.

Spotted Deer!

Spotted Deer stared at Sarah, her eyes flaring with recognition. She turned abruptly to whisper something to the older man standing beside her. Sarah couldn't stand the suspense. Her courage returned as she blurted out, "Am I a prisoner?"

"How did you find us?" Spotted Deer asked.

"I wasn't looking for you. I'm looking for Abner. Freddie Jackson kidnapped him. Have you seen them?"

Spotted Deer conferred with her companion. They spoke at length in a guttural language Sarah didn't understand. The Indian woman translated. "We have seen Fred-die."

Incredible joy surged through Sarah. If Spotted Deer saw Jackson, then surely she'd seen Abner. "Was Abner with him?"

Sarah chafed impatiently as Spotted Deer spoke once again to the old man before addressing her question.

"You will remain here as Cunning Wolf's guest."

"What about my son? Please tell me about Abner."

Spotted Deer's expression softened. "The boy is well."

Relief shuddered through Sarah. "Thank you for your kind offer, but I can't stay here. I have to find Abner. I strayed from the trail and got lost, but if you'll just point me in the right direction, I'll be on my way."

"The choice is not yours to make. My father is

taking you hostage. He will trade you for cows to feed our people. And for warm blankets. Corrupt agents have taken what belongs to us. Father was forced to join other tribes who left the reservation to raid and forage for food. Soon our people will travel north to Canada, where we will be free to hunt where we choose."

"I sympathize with your plight, but I have problems of my own. I may never see my son again."

Gathering her courage, Sarah attempted to mount her horse. A harsh word from Cunning Wolf sent two warriors rushing forward. One forcibly prevented her from mounting while the other led her horse off to join those already being held in a makeshift corral.

"You can't do this!" Sarah cried, struggling to escape her captors.

Suddenly a small boy burst out of a tipi, charging full tilt toward her. Sarah feared she was hallucinating when she heard the child call her Mama. Then he plowed into her, nearly tumbling her to the frozen ground. His little arms held her tightly, as if afraid she would disappear if he let her go.

"Mama, you're here!" the little boy sobbed. "I knew you would come for me. Is Chad with you?"

"Abner? Oh my God! Abner! It is you. How? Why? I don't understand any of this. How did you get here?"

"The Indians made us come with them," Abner explained.

"Are Jackson and Sanchez here with you?"

"Fred-die is my prisoner," Spotted Deer said smugly. "He awaits punishment for his harsh treatment of me."

"What are you going to do to him?"

"It hasn't been decided. Cunning Wolf wants to kill him quickly, before the army finds us and demands his return. But I wish him to die slowly and painfully."

Sarah shuddered. "Your argument is with Freddie, not me or Abner. We were his prisoners, if you recall. Let us go. We've done your people no harm."

"No. Cunning Wolf wants to make an exchange with the army, you for cows. You will not be harmed. A messenger will be sent to the fort with our demands for your release. Come, the weather worsens. I will take you to shelter."

Grasping Abner's hand, Sarah followed Spotted Deer. The Indian woman stopped before a tipi and held the flap open. Sarah ducked inside, finding the warmth a welcome relief from the biting cold. She gazed around in awe, never having seen or been inside an Indian dwelling before. She found it surprisingly warm and comfortable, and roomier than one would expect.

"You will stay here," Spotted Deer said. "Abner will share my lodge."

"No!" Sarah protested. "Why must you separate us?"

"You are less likely to escape without your son," Spotted Deer said.

"Just let him stay with me a little while. I won't try to escape, I promise."

"Let me stay with Mama," Abner begged, clinging to Sarah's hand.

Spotted Deer crumbled beneath Abner's pitiful plea. "You may stay for a little while. I will return for you later."

A blast of cold air marked her departure as she

lifted the tent flap and stepped outside. Having won that round, Sarah hugged Abner tightly, reluctant to let him go even for a minute.

"Have they treated you well?" Sarah wanted to know. If Abner had been hurt by either Jackson or the Indians, she'd find a way to make them suffer.

"Mr. Jackson wanted me to call him papa, but I wouldn't," Abner said belligerently. "He said he'd spank me if I didn't mind him. I don't like him, Mama. Neither do the Indians. They keep him and Mr. Sanchez tied up all the time. They know he's a bad man. Are you sure he's my real papa?"

"Oh, honey, I'd give anything if I could tell you he's not your papa, but I can't. The only good thing to come of my association with Freddie Jackson is you. You don't have to like him. Lord knows, I don't. Did the Indians hurt you?"

Abner shook his head. "They like me. Spotted Deer said Indians love children. Can we go home now, Mama? I miss Chad."

"That's not possible just yet. I'm not even sure I can find my way back to Dry Gulch without a guide. I became hopelessly lost in the storm."

Suddenly the tent flap was thrust aside and Spotted Deer entered. She carried a bowl of steaming food, which she placed before Sarah and Abner. "Eat," she said, indicating the bowl. "Food is scarce, if the hunters return empty-handed this will be the only meal today." Then she departed in another blast of cold air.

Sarah stared at the unidentifiable mess in the bowl, wondering if she dared to eat it. Abner had no such qualms as he dug in, using two fingers to scoop the solid pieces into his mouth. Sarah gingerly retrieved a morsel that looked like meat and popped it into her mouth. She chewed slowly and swallowed, finding it not unpleasant but definitely not something she'd eaten before. Nevertheless, she and Abner managed to clean the bowl.

Darkness came early. Spotted Deer returned for Abner before Sarah was ready for him to leave. No amount of pleading could change the Indian woman's mind as she dragged Abner away. Miserable and alone, Sarah fed sticks to the small fire, then she lay down on the pallet she found rolled up in a corner and tried to sleep. She had no idea how this would all end and prayed for intervention, divine or otherwise. And she longed for Chad. Hugging herself tightly, she imagined Chad's arms around her, holding her, Chad offering her comfort. She fell asleep pretending that Chad loved her.

The next morning Sarah awoke feeling queasy and upset. She barely made it outside, where she lost the meager contents of her stomach in a clump of bushes. She blamed it on the food she had eaten the previous night and hoped Abner hadn't been afflicted with the same malady. Making her way back to the tipi, she lay down again and lapsed into an uneasy sleep.

During the fiercest part of the blizzard, Chad blundered into the army bivouac area. He'd been headed back home, eager to see Sarah again, and concerned that Jackson was too close to the Delaney ranch for comfort. Chad was more worried about Sarah and Abner than he cared to admit.

Sarah.

God, he missed her. He'd done a lot of thinking since leaving the ranch. After much soul-searching, he decided to accept his shortcomings and stop blaming himself for events he'd had no control over. Sarah had taught him that some women were worthy of love and trust.

Unfairly labeled a whore and ostracized, Sarah had made the best of an intolerable situation and persevered, raising her son alone and doing a damn fine job of it. Sarah had suffered disgrace, lived with a stigma she hadn't earned, and became a stronger person for it. He could do no less than follow her example by accepting the good things in his life instead of dwelling on the bad.

Sarah. She was one of the good things.

He ached to hold her in his arms. To make love to her. To mold her responsive body to his and receive the incredible gift of her pleasure. Love was wonderful with the right woman, and that's exactly what he was going to tell Sarah when he returned to the ranch.

Chad was taken to Major Dalton's tent immediately after dismounting and voicing his request to speak to the commanding officer. He was eager to learn how long the patrol had been in the area, and if they had seen Jackson and Sanchez.

Chad introduced himself immediately. Major Dalton supplied his own name and greeted Chad with a mixture of wariness and curiosity. "What brings you out in this blizzard, Mr. Delaney?"

"I'm a bounty hunter, Major. I'm tracking Freddie Jackson, and a man named Sanchez. Both are notorious bank robbers. Have you crossed their path?"

Dalton rubbed his chin as he considered Chad's question. "Funny you should ask about those men."

Chad's attention sharpened. "Why do you say that?"

"A woman turned up at the fort the day before we rode out. She wanted help to find her son. Seems the boy was abducted by a man named Freddie Jackson."

Chad went still. "Was the woman's name Sarah Temple?" When Dalton nodded, Chad's worst fears were realized. "How could that have happened? My brother and ten armed men were on hand to protect the boy."

Dalton's brows rose sharply upward. "You know the woman?"

"I know her. She's my . . . I'm going to marry her. What happened? Did you assign soldiers to help her? Have you any idea where they are?"

"I couldn't spare the men. The fort is down to bare bones now. I told her to wait until we returned and I'd consider her request for help."

"You what?" Chad shouted. "Jackson is a dangerous man. How could you *not* help Sarah?"

"Now see here, Delaney, I'm doing my best for the people who depend upon the army for protection. A group of renegade Indians left the reservation and are raiding ranches in the area. They may even be heading for Canada. My first priority is to stop the raids and send the renegades back where they belong."

"And to hell with a small child who needs your help," Chad spat with disgust.

Dalton shrugged. "As I said, first things first. We would have gotten around to him eventually."

Chad struggled to rein in his temper. Losing it now wouldn't help Sarah. "Did Sarah return home?" Though he knew the answer, he still had to ask the question.

"Damn stubborn woman," Dalton said, shaking his head. "She said she was going to continue on alone. I warned her against it, but she wouldn't listen."

Not for an instant had Chad doubted Sarah's decision. "Have you succeeded in your mission? Have you rounded up the renegades and sent them back to the reservation?"

"Not all of them. We've managed to intercept Yellow Dog and send him back, but Cunning Wolf and Snake are still out there somewhere. So far no one has been killed or hurt, but the longer they remain on the loose, the greater the danger that it will happen."

His words sent fear racing through Chad. Sarah was out there somewhere in this raging blizzard, and so were renegade Indians looking for trouble. Dear God! The thought of losing Sarah when he had finally found the courage to acknowledge his love was unbearable.

"The Indians wouldn't have left the reservation if the government hadn't reneged on their promises," Chad charged. "The poor wretches are probably starving and were forced to leave the reservation to hunt for food."

"Indian agents I spoke with swore that the government cows and blankets had been delivered. I have no choice but to believe them. Don't worry, we'll have the Indians back where they belong soon. As for your fiancée, she's a very foolish young woman. However, we'll keep an eye out for her. Feel free to share our meal and shelter," Dalton said in dismissal.

"Thanks for nothing," Chad muttered as he took his leave. Hospitality wasn't what he wanted. Nor could he afford to waste precious time warming himself over a campfire while Sarah was wandering around in a raging blizzard and Abner was missing. He had a gut feeling that Sarah was close. This time he was going to follow his gut.

Two days later, Chad stumbled into Cunning Wolf's camp. Dusk had already turned the sky to murky gray as he rode boldly into the cluster of tents, displaying no fear. He was quickly surrounded, pulled from the saddle, and brought before the chief.

Roughly, Chad was pushed down beside the small fire in the center of the chief's tipi. The heat felt good and Chad held his hands out to the blaze. When the warmth finally began to thaw his bones, he took note of his surroundings. The chief sat across from him, smoking and studying Chad through hooded eyes. A woman sat beside him, staring openly at Chad. It took a moment for Chad to realize that he'd seen the woman before.

Spotted Deer. He spoke her name aloud and she bowed her head in acknowledgement.

"I know you, white eyes, but not your name."

"My name is Chad Delaney."

"Why are you here, Chad De-laney?"

"I'm looking for my woman. Her name is Sarah Temple. Have you seen her?"

Spotted Deer continued to stare at Chad. Chad could almost see the wheels turning in her brain. Then she turned to her father, speaking rapidly in the Shoshone tongue. After what seemed like an eternity, Spotted Deer smiled and nodded in acknowledgement of her father's wisdom.

"Your woman is with us, De-laney."

Chad leaped to his feet. "Sarah is here? Thank God. Is she all right?"

"Sarah and Abner are our hostages. Father intends to trade them for cows and warm blankets."

Chad reeled in confusion. "Abner is here, too? I don't understand. Where are Jackson and Sanchez?"

The smile Spotted Deer gave Chad was not a pretty one. "They are my prisoners. They await public torture and death before the entire camp. Fred-die will suffer for his insult to me."

"I will take my woman and her son and leave," Chad said, not waiting for permission.

He was stopped in his tracks by Spotted Deer's reply. "They cannot leave. Our people are starving. The army will give us cows for their return."

"The army is camped not far from here. I left them not two days ago. When they find you, you'll be driven back to the reservation. It will go easier on you if you release Sarah and her son to me now."

Spotted Deer turned to confer with Cunning Wolf. "Cunning Wolf does not think the army will find us."

"I found you," Chad reminded her.

"We let you find us. Our warriors saw you coming. They let you pass because you were alone. Had you been the army, you would not have found us so easily."

Chad realized he was getting nowhere with Cunning Wolf and his daughter and racked his brain for a solution. Suddenly the answer came to him. He was amazed at how simple it was.

"There are many cows on my ranch. I will give you cows in exchange for your hostages. Release Sarah and Abner and I will bring the cows to you myself."

Chapter 17

"You will give us cows?" Spotted Deer asked, skeptical of Chad's offer.

"In exchange for your hostages," Chad bargained.

"How do we know you do not speak with a forked tongue? Promises come easy, keeping them is more difficult. White eyes have broken countless treaties with the people. They forced us from our lands, promised us food and blankets, and gave us nothing."

"I am not the government," Chad said. "My word is my honor. I will bring the cows to you personally."

"I will confer with Cunning Wolf. He will decide."

Spotted Deer spoke with Cunning Wolf at length while Chad chafed impatiently, unable to contain his anxiety. He didn't see how Cunning Wolf could refuse his generosity but there was no knowing the savage mind. Finally Spotted Deer was ready to announce her father's decision.

"Cunning Wolf accepts your offer."

Chad felt like leaping for joy, but forced himself

to harness his exuberance. He had a feeling there were conditions, so he composed himself and waited for Spotted Deer to continue.

"The hostages will be released when you return with the cows and blankets, but Fred-die and Sanchez are ours to keep. Fred-die is a wicked man and must be punished."

Chad did some swift calculations in his head and didn't like the answer. "It will be at least a fortnight before I can get back here with the cows and blankets. The distance isn't great, but winter is a bad time to drive cattle anywhere. What you're asking is impossible. I can't leave Sarah and Abner here. You have to let them leave with me. Isn't my word good enough for you?"

"Promises have been made and broken before," Spotted Deer said. "Your woman will be safe with us until you return. But if you break your word . . ." Her sentence fell off, leaving an ominous threat hanging in the air.

"Tell your father I will hold him personally responsible for Sarah and Abner's well-being. If they are harmed, I will hunt him down like a dog. I could bring the army if I was of a mind to. They are camped not far from here."

Spotted Deer translated swiftly. Cunning Wolf's reply did nothing to relieve Chad's mind. "We are desperate people. We have nothing to lose by killing the woman and boy. Without food, our people will starve before spring. Bringing the army here will gain you nothing except the deaths of your loved ones."

Frustration sat heavily upon Chad. These Indians were desperate for food and blankets. Had they enough to eat they would never have left the reservation. They saw Sarah and Abner as a means to an end, a way to obtain relief. He couldn't blame Cunning Wolf for wanting to save his people.

"You will have everything you requested," Chad said. "First, I wish to see my woman and Abner. I won't leave until I know they are well."

Spotted Deer conferred briefly with her father. The conversation was quite heated before an agreement of sorts was reached.

"I will take you to your woman," she told Chad. "The hour grows late. Tonight you will share her meal and her mat. You will be escorted from our camp at first light. We will look for you to return with the cows and blankets at the end of a fortnight. If you bring the army, you will see your loved ones in the spirit world. Come, I will take you to Sarah."

Spotted Deer couldn't have made it any clearer. If the army showed up before the cows, Sarah's life wouldn't be worth a plug nickel. And yet, he couldn't help feeling compassion for these downtrodden people. Starvation led people to act rashly and without conscience. He knew he could get the cows back here in the allotted fourteen days, but he wasn't so sure the army wouldn't find Cunning Wolf first. He had to make sure that wouldn't happen.

Huddled before the meager fire inside the tipi, Sarah felt miserable. Little of what she'd eaten had stayed with her since that first morning she had awakened and rushed outside to empty her stomach. She had her suspicions about what was wrong but she was still in a state of denial. She couldn't be pregnant. Not now. She wasn't even sure she and Chad had a future together.

Earlier that morning Spotted Deer had informed her that Abner had accompanied an ancient Indian brave into the forest to check traps, and Sarah had felt too wretched to protest. Abner was a big hit among the tribe members. He was spoiled outrageously, and it worried Sarah. What if the Indians wanted to keep him? Neither she nor Abner had been mistreated in any way, but she didn't fool herself into thinking their good will would continue if the army refused to ransom her.

When the tent flap was thrust open Sarah didn't bother to look up. Had it been Abner she would have heard his exuberant cries of greeting. And there was no other person she cared to acknowledge in this place. The first signal that her visitor wasn't an Indian was the scrape of boots upon the ground. Indians didn't wear boots. Slowly she raised her eyes, gliding past buckskin-clad legs and sheepskin jacket, over a broad chest and impressive shoulders, to vivid hazel eyes set in the ruggedly handsome face she knew better than her own.

She stared at him, closed her eyes, then opened them quickly. When he didn't go away, she rose slowly to her feet and stepped into his arms. A sob was wrenched from her throat as his arms closed around her.

Chad hugged Sarah tightly, feeling as if he held the whole world in his arms. The moisture that gathered in his eyes was so foreign to him that he blinked in dismay. Chad couldn't recall when he'd last shed tears. Perhaps when his mother had left, but he wasn't sure it had happened even then. He felt Sarah brush away the moisture with the tips of her fingers and he no longer cared that it wasn't considered manly to cry.

"How did you find me?" Sarah asked, stunned at the sight of a grown man shedding tears.

"Pure luck," Chad replied, swallowing past the lump in his throat. "I ran into Major Dalton from the fort. He told me you'd been there asking for help. I couldn't believe it. How did Jackson get by Ryan? Something must have happened. What?

Sarah trembled against him.

Noting the fragile condition of her composure, Chad swept her up into his arms, lowered himself to the pallet, and cradled her in his lap.

"That's better," he said, kissing her forehead. "Now you can tell me how Jackson got to Abner."

"Ryan stuck close to the ranch like he promised," she explained. "He didn't leave until he learned that some calves were trapped in a gully. I could tell Ryan was itching to help the men. The only reason he declined was because of his promise to you. Both Cookie and I urged him to go. Everyone assumed Jackson had already left the area."

"Jackson was just waiting for the right time," Chad muttered. "He found it when Ryan left. Damn Ryan! I told him not to leave for any reason."

"Don't blame Ryan. We all became too complacent."

Chad shrugged away her excuse with a wave of his hand. "I'll never forgive Ryan for allowing you to go off on your own."

"There was an accident. Ryan broke a leg. He wanted to send for Pierce but I couldn't wait. I had to catch up with Jackson and Abner before it was too late. I wouldn't have stopped at the fort if Ryan hadn't insisted."

"What about the hands? Ryan could have spared someone to accompany you."

"He did. Brock Murray went with me, but I sent him back to the ranch when I reached the fort. No one expected Major Dalton to refuse my request for help. You don't understand. I had no recourse but to continue on alone. A few days ago I became lost in a blizzard and wandered close to Cunning Wolf's camp. I was surrounded and brought here."

"Was Abner here when you arrived?"

"Yes. Jackson blundered into the camp a few days before I did. He and Sanchez are prisoners, but Abner fared much better. Indians love children, so he's been treated very well. But he's anxious to go home."

Chad tightened his hold on her. "I feared I'd lost you after I spoke with Major Dalton. I envisioned you lying in a snowdrift, injured or dead. I was in agony when I learned there were renegade Indians in the area. Any number of things could have happened. I don't think I could have borne it if you or Abner had come to harm."

Sarah stared at him, drawn into the mesmerizing intensity of his glittering gaze. His eyes were still moist with tears and tenderness welled up inside her. This incredible man had ridden blindly through heinous weather searching for her. How could she not love him? She raised her chin for his kiss.

Chad cupped the smooth curve of her cheek, and she lifted her face as he licked the soft fullness of her lips. She parted them, welcoming the bold thrust of his tongue as he tasted her fully.

She moaned with pleasure. Her arms circled his neck, pressing closer to the heat of his body. This was the man she loved. The only man she would ever love. And whether he said the words or not, she knew he loved her too.

"I love you, Sarah," he whispered against her lips.

Sarah's eyes grew misty and her heart nearly burst with happiness. "I think I've always loved you, Chad. You're the kindest, the most compassionate man I have ever known."

"Only for you, love, only for you."

She wanted Chad to kiss her again, and they probably wouldn't have stopped with mere kisses had Abner and Spotted Deer not entered the tipi just then.

"Chad!" Abner cried, leaping into Chad's lap. Sarah quickly moved to make room for him. "You're here! Can we go home now?"

"Oh, yes," Sarah agreed with alacrity. "Can we go home?"

"I bring food," Spotted Deer said as she sat a pot of something edible beside them. "Eat. I will return later for the boy."

"Can't I stay with you and Chad tonight, Mama?" Abner asked, pouting.

"Abner will stay with Spotted Deer," the Indian woman said, forestalling Sarah's reply. Turning abruptly, she ducked through the tent flap.

"Let's eat," Chad said. "I'm starving. Afterward, I'll tell you about my discussion with Cunning Wolf."

Chad and Abner dipped their fingers into the pot and began eating the disgusting mess. When Chad tried to feed a morsel to Sarah, she gagged and turned away; the smell made her stomach roil sickeningly.

"Eat something, sweetheart," Chad urged. "It isn't too bad. Abner seems to enjoy it."

Sarah buried her face in Chad's chest. "I can't. I haven't been able to hold anything in my stomach since arriving here. It could be the vile-tasting food they bring me. Even water makes me queasy."

Chad searched her pale face. In some ways Sarah was fragile, but she wasn't a weak or sickly woman. Her puzzling illness worried him. He wouldn't rest until Sarah and Abner were back home where they belonged.

Spotted Deer returned for Abner a short time later. No amount of pleading moved the woman as she took Abner away.

"Spotted Deer won't let Abner sleep in my tent," Sarah explained, once the Indian woman left with Abner in tow. "It's a ploy to prevent me from escaping. She knows I wouldn't leave without Abner." She gazed at Chad, her concern obvious. "Are you a hostage, too? How are we ever going to get out of this? Will the army ransom all three of us?"

Chad didn't want to alarm Sarah, but neither did he wish to lie to her. He had shed his heavy sheepskin coat and they were sitting side by side on the pallet now. With a deft movement, he brought her back onto his lap.

"I'm not a hostage, sweetheart. As much as I hate it, I'm going to have to leave you and Abner with Cunning Wolf a while longer."

Sarah stiffened. "You're leaving us?"

"Only for a little while. I don't trust the army to ransom you, so I offered to do it myself. Cunning

Wolf agreed, but I have to leave you and Abner here while I get the cows and return. A fortnight, Sarah. I'll be back in fourteen days; less, if the weather holds. Cunning Wolf promised that no harm will come to you and Abner in my absence."

Sarah mulled over Chad's words, not completely convinced that fourteen days was enough time for all Chad had to do. "What will happen to us if you don't return in the allotted time?"

"Don't even think about it. I *will* return in time."

"What if Major Dalton finds Cunning Wolf's camp first?" Sarah asked.

Chad thought her too astute for her own good. "Although he's camped not far from here, I intend to stop just long enough to make sure he doesn't find Cunning Wolf. Leave it to me, love. I'll do everything humanly possible to keep my future wife and son safe."

"Your . . . your wife? You want to marry me?"

"Of course I want to marry you. You restored my sanity and gave me back my life. How could I not love you?"

"I never actually believed I was lovable," Sarah whispered. "Everyone considered me the town whore. Even my parents found me offensive."

"I hadn't known you ten minutes before I knew you weren't the kind of woman people described. It took me a great deal longer to realize I loved you and wanted you and Abner in my life forever. You will marry me, won't you?"

"If that's what you truly want," Sarah said, breathless with wonder. She hadn't believed there was a man worthy of love until she met Chad.

"That's not all I want," he replied in a voice that was seductively low and husky. "I want to love you tonight. When dawn arrives, I want to be sated with the taste and scent of you. I want to fill you with myself and feel my love flow from me into you. Oh God, love, I never would have believed there was this much wanting in the world."

Sarah flushed with pleasure. His words were more potent than the headiest wine. She could feel herself swell and dampen in anticipation of his loving. She realized suddenly that lust and wanting were all part of love. One couldn't exist without the other. She wanted both . . . she wanted it all.

"I want the same things you want, Chad," she said on a sigh. "I need you."

He claimed her lips with an urgency that left her breathless and as needy as he. His kisses sent her stomach into a wild swirl, and she returned his kiss with reckless abandon. She had loved him for so long it was difficult to believe he returned her love, but she could taste it on his mouth. The proof was in the desperate yearning of his kiss, the way he held her and caressed her. His body proclaimed it with every breath he took.

With a tenderness that belied his need, Chad removed her clothing, piece by piece, nuzzling and caressing each portion of skin he uncovered. Then she helped him to undress, baring his muscular flesh to her searching lips. She kissed and caressed him just as he had done her, delighting in the hair-roughened skin stretched over rippling muscles.

"Your body is so different from mine," she whispered against the warm hollow of his throat.

"Thank God," Chad muttered fervently. She was so delicate, so exquisitely made, he feared he would break her. Yet, he knew she was stronger than she looked, that her passion matched his in intensity, and that her strength of character was invincible. God, he loved her!

The fierceness of her response to his caresses, the tantalizing thrust of her lower body against his, were almost more than Chad could stand. His tenuous hold on his control snapped as his hands tightened fiercely around her hips and jerked her hard against him.

He felt Sarah arch up into him and her fingers clench in his hair as he brought his mouth down to meet hers. Buffeted by potent emotions, he kissed her with almost savage urgency, his tongue surging boldly into her mouth. He was mindless and wanting . . . and impatient.

He bent forward, flicking his tongue against the sweet fullness of her breast, then took a nipple into his mouth and suckled her. Sarah went wild beneath him, arching and bucking, moaning softly as he licked and sucked hungrily.

"Chad, please . . ." She reached for his staff; it slid smoothly into her hand. He gave a violent shudder and went still.

"Soon, love, soon," he murmured against the lush ripeness of her nipple. Reluctantly, he removed her hand from his member. "Behave yourself. Tonight I'm going to take my time loving you."

His hands brushed between her legs. He heard her breath quicken and when he lightly cupped her there, she gave a muffled groan. But Chad wasn't finished. He caressed her soft folds, parting her with his fingers, then slipping them inside, savoring the powerful sensations overwhelming him. His swollen, wet member slid smoothly back and forth against her belly and he wanted it inside her, filling her with himself.

"Open your legs," Chad urged hoarsely.

She opened immediately. "What are you... oh..."

Her words ended on a ragged sigh as Chad's head dipped between her legs and he tasted her. She cried out softly as his tongue parted her and slipped inside her moist passage. A great shudder shook her body as a delicious agony seized her.

"Don't hold back, love," Chad murmured as he lifted his head and smiled at her. "Come to me now." Then he returned to his magical caresses and took her over the edge. Violent tremors created havoc within her as rapture mounted, carrying her into a churning sea of pleasure.

Trembling with the force of his passion, Chad slid up her body and went deeply inside her, thrusting repeatedly in and out of her welcoming warmth. Incredible pleasure surged through him. His mind and body were overwhelmed by the exquisite softness of her flesh, the sweetness of her kisses, her tightness, the slick heat of her body. The sexy sounds that came from her throat as he buried himself in her silky passage increased his own exhilaration and nourished his hungry need to attain rapture.

Sarah found that lofty place first. A startled cry escaped her. Her body went rigid as wave after wave of unspeakable pleasure swept through her body. The utter delight, the sheer sweetness of it, left her dazed as she lay beneath his thrusting body.

Chad felt the vibrations charging through her body, and something untamed inside him took over. His thrusting grew frantic, each incredible sensation that cascaded through him more potent than the last. It was pure magic, created by the love that flowed between them, a magic he'd never felt before with any other woman.

Sarah slowly floated down from a place only lovers dared to venture, into the arms of the man she loved. Chad was waiting for her. He gathered her close and held her tightly as she drifted off to sleep. Several hours later she awakened to the arousing touch of Chad's mouth on her sensitive breasts. She opened her eyes and smiled at him.

"I love you," she said.

"Don't ever stop loving me," Chad replied. "How do you suppose Abner will react to our wedding plans?"

"He'll be ecstatic. He's crazy about you, Chad."

"I feel the same about him." He kissed her eyelids and brushed her lips with his. "I couldn't sleep. I hope you don't mind being awakened."

Her arms came around his neck. "That depends. What did you have in mind?"

"I'd rather show you."

Sarah squealed with surprise as Chad lifted her and set her atop him. He rubbed his sex against her stomach and she was surprised to find him already swollen and slick.

"You're insatiable," she said, laughing.

"Only with you, love, only with you. Take me inside you."

She grasped his stem with both hands, raised her hips, and slid down onto him. She gave a little sigh, loving the way he filled her. He fulfilled her every desire, then brought them both to shattering climax. She remained atop him, resting her head on his chest until he softened and slipped from her body. Then she stretched out beside him and joined him in slumber.

The next time Sarah awakened she was alone on the pallet. Chad was standing beside her, pulling on his clothing. "Is it time?" she asked.

"The sooner I start the sooner I can return," Chad said. "I want to say goodbye to Abner before I leave. Don't give up hope, sweetheart, I'll be back before you know it."

She pulled a blanket around her and stood to help Chad with his jacket. Suddenly she clutched her stomach and moaned. "Oh God, it's happening again and I didn't even eat anything last night." She sent Chad a helpless look. "I'm going to be sick."

Chad reacted with incredible haste. He swept her into his arms and carried her outside, supporting her while she retched in the bushes. When she finished he carried her back inside and handed her the waterbag he found hanging from a lodgepole. Sarah rinsed her mouth and spat into the firepit.

"I can't leave you here," Chad said with concern. "You're sick. Are others in the camp ill?"

"I don't know," Sarah said miserably. She didn't think it was the right time to tell him what she suspected about her condition.

"I'm going to speak with Spotted Deer. Rest until I return."

Chad charged out of the tipi. He found Spotted Deer cooking over a communal firepit at the center of the camp.

"Where is Abner?"

"With Cunning Wolf. Will you eat before you leave?"

"Is there illness in the camp?" Chad asked abruptly.

Spotted Deer stopped stirring the contents in the pot and stared at him. "There is no sickness. Why do you ask?"

"Sarah is ill. She vomited this morning. She said it wasn't the first time. If there is a serious ailment in camp, I want to know."

"There is nothing. We are hungry, not sick."

"How do you explain Sarah's illness?"

Spotted Deer sent him an inscrutable look. "I suspect it is a passing thing. I will prepare an herbal remedy to soothe her stomach."

"I want to take Sarah and Abner with me. My word is good. You'll have your cows."

"Wait here," Spotted Deer said as she turned abruptly and went to her father's lodge. She returned several minutes later. "You can take the woman, but the boy stays until you have fulfilled your promise."

Chad's fists clenched at his sides. He knew Sarah would never agree to that arrangement. "Is that the best you can offer?"

"Cunning Wolf has spoken."

"Very well. I'll speak to Sarah."

First Chad went to find Abner. He saw the boy sitting beside Cunning Wolf, sharing his breakfast. Chad beckoned to him, he came immediately.

"What is it, Chad? Are we leaving now?"

Chad hunkered down beside him. "Your mother is sick. Cunning Wolf has agreed to let your mother leave with me, but he wants you to stay until I return with the cows I promised him."

Abner chewed over Chad's words. "If you and Mama leave, I'll be alone again."

"I have Spotted Deer's word that you'll be safe here. It will only be for a few days, son. I'll come back for you, you have my word on it. Then the three of us are going to live on the ranch and be a family. Would you like that?"

Abner's small face lit with happiness. "You, me, and Mama? Will you be my papa?"

"Darn tootin', I will."

Abner launched himself into Chad's arms. "I like that just fine. Are you sure you'll come back for me?"

"I'd defy heaven and hell to come back to you," Chad said solemnly.

"I don't want Mama to be sick. Take her with you, Chad. I'll wait here for you." He sent Chad a wobbly smile. "Don't be too long."

Chad hugged the little body tightly. He loved the boy as fiercely as if he were his own flesh and blood. It nearly broke his heart to leave him, but he had to think of Sarah's fragile state of health. If she was seriously ill, she needed a doctor.

Chad was returning to Sarah's lodge when he saw Jackson and Sanchez being prodded and pulled none too gently toward a clump of bushes. Their hands were lashed together and they were being dragged along by ropes tied around their necks. Jackson spied Chad and yelled out to him.

"Delaney! I heard you were here. Do something, man. Get me out of this mess. These damn savages are gonna kill me. I ain't done nothing to deserve that."

Chad barely gave Jackson a passing glance. "I've got my own problems, Jackson. You brought this on yourself, now get yourself out of it."

A twinge of conscience smote Chad. He knew

what was going to happen to Jackson, but there was nothing he could do about it. Whether or not Jackson was turned over to the law for the bounty, the outlaw would face the hangman for his crimes. The man would die one way or another. It was the torture Chad didn't condone. Nevertheless, Jackson was no longer his concern. He no longer needed the bounty.

Sarah had dressed but was still pale when Chad entered the lodge. She could tell by his frown that things hadn't gone as he wished with Spotted Deer and Cunning Wolf.

"Gather your things, sweetheart, I'm taking you with me," Chad said without preamble.

Sarah's face lit up. "Thank God! I'll go get Abner."

Chad stopped her with a hand on her arm. "Sarah, listen to me. You're free to leave with me, but Abner has to stay here until I return with the cows. You're ill. You need a doctor."

Sarah collapsed against his chest. She said nothing for several long minutes. Then she lifted her head and glared at him. "You know I won't leave without Abner. If he stays, so do I. Besides, my illness isn't serious. It will pass soon." In about seven months, if she wasn't mistaken. "Hurry back, Chad, please hurry back."

Frustration stabbed at Chad. Sarah was ill, she needed to return home so she could receive proper care. There had to be some way to convince her to leave. Her pallor and gauntness were even more apparent in the light of day than they had been last night. What would fourteen days of cold and exposure do to her state of health? he wondered. The answer frightened him.

"The Indians won't hurt Abner," Chad argued. "You saw how they dote on him. I've already explained the situation to Abner and he's willing. He's a brave little boy."

"No, Chad, I can't leave Abner. We'll both wait for you."

Chad seized her shoulders, giving her a little shake. "I love Abner. He's as dear to me as he is to you. I'm convinced he'll be fine during our absence."

His words were for his own sake as much as for Sarah's peace of mind. He was fairly positive that Abner would fare well with the Indians but unforeseen things could always happen. The boy could sicken and die, he could be attacked by a wolf or bear, he could be caught in a confrontation between Cunning Wolf and the army.

"Forget it, Chad," Sarah said. Her firm little chin jutted out stubbornly. "I'm not going anywhere without Abner."

Chad's response came from his fear for Sarah and a spontaneous reaction to that fear. He gave Sarah a sad smile, said, "Forgive me, sweetheart," then clipped her on the jaw. Not hard enough to do her permanent damage, but solid enough to render her unconscious.

Chapter 18

The Indians had saddled horses for both Chad and Sarah. One parfleche filled with trail food and another with water were tied to Chad's saddle. Bedrolls had also been provided. Spotted Deer didn't seem surprised when Chad ducked out of the tipi carrying Sarah. She was still unconscious. He had pulled on her coat and wrapped her in a blanket to protect her from the cold.

"It was the only way," Chad shrugged, sensing Spotted Deer's curiosity. "Sarah is a stubborn woman. But heed me well, Spotted Deer. If any harm comes to Abner, there will be hell to pay. I expect you to persuade your father to cease raiding in my absence. I'll do my part. I'll try to convince Major Dalton that I saw your people returning to the reservation. I want the camp safe from attack while I'm gone."

"It will be as you say," Spotted Deer agreed. "Take this and go before your woman awakens," she said, handing him a small pouch. "It's an herbal remedy for Sarah's sickness. Brew a small amount of the herb in boiling water and feed it to her."

Chad nodded his thanks as Spotted Deer stepped back to allow a warrior to take Sarah from his arms so he could mount. Then Chad took Sarah up before him, settling her across his thighs as the warrior tied the leading reins of Sarah's horse to Chad's saddle.

Chad was relieved that Abner hadn't witnessed his departure. It wasn't exactly the kind of leave-taking Chad had planned, but he was determined to take Sarah with him and this was the only way she would go. In fourteen days, less if he could manage it, he'd have Abner, too. God, he hated to leave the lad. It nearly tore him apart. But he felt secure in the knowledge that the Indians loved the boy and wouldn't harm him.

Jackson and Sanchez were another matter altogether. If they were still alive when he returned, he intended to convince Cunning Wolf to release them so he could turn them over to the law. Chad didn't know much about Indians and their customs, except that they followed their own laws and doled out punishment according to the crime. He didn't envy Freddie Jackson.

Sarah began showing signs of regaining consciousness about an hour later. She moaned softly and her eyes fluttered open. It took but a few moments for her to realize where she was and what had happened.

"You hit me!" she charged, glaring at him.

"It was for your own good."

"Where are we?"

"Several miles from Cunning Wolf's camp. You've been out for over an hour."

"Damn you! You know I would never have left Abner behind. What kind of a man are you?"

"One who loves you. I love Abner, too."

"You could have fooled me," Sarah shot back. "Stop! I'm going back."

"Be reasonable, love. Fresh snow has covered our tracks and you'll never find your way back. Besides, I need you to help me convince Major Dalton that Cunning Wolf has returned to the reservation. It's vital for Abner's safety that the army discontinue their search for Cunning Wolf. If they find him, Abner could be hurt in the melee."

"I hate you," Sarah hissed.

Chad winced. He couldn't blame her for feeling as she did, but she could at least give him credit for doing what he felt was best for everyone.

"Hate me all you want, Sarah, but you're still not going back. I haven't the time to take you back now. Abner really will be in trouble if I don't get those cows to Cunning Wolf in the allotted two weeks."

"Bastard!" Sarah blurted out, obviously distraught. "You don't love me and you don't love Abner. I'll never forgive you for this. Abner needs me. He probably thinks we both abandoned him."

"I spoke with the boy, sweetheart. He understands, even if you don't. How do you feel?" he asked, deftly changing the subject.

"Like hell, and it's all your fault." She struggled against him. "Let me down. I'll find my way back without you."

"Stop fighting, Sarah. You're slowing us down and time is against us. You can ride your own horse if you settle down and accept that I'm not going to let you return. I asked you a question. How do you feel?"

"I answered your question. Like hell. My stomach is doing somersaults and I feel lightheaded. Does that satisfy you?"

"It's little wonder. You haven't eaten anything this morning. When we stop to rest the horses I'll brew some tea from the herbs Spotted Deer gave me. She said they'd relieve your symptoms. I wish to hell I knew what was wrong with you."

"I'm pregnant!" Sarah shouted angrily.

Chad reined in sharply. The expression he wore was a mixture of shock and pleasure. "You're having my baby? That's what's wrong with you?"

Sarah didn't bother to reply.

"Dammit, Sarah, this is serious. Thank God I took you away from Cunning Wolf's camp when I did. Did you know you were pregnant when you left the ranch?"

Sarah shook her head. "Even if I did, it wouldn't have mattered."

"In other words, my child doesn't mean anything to you."

"That's not what I said and you know it. I'd never do anything to harm my unborn child. I don't even know if you want this baby."

"You're going to be my wife. Of course I want our child. I promised Abner that we're going to be a family and I meant it."

"I'm not so sure marrying you would be a good thing," Sarah said. "I can't trust you, Chad. You aren't the man I thought you were."

"I'm glad I brought you away with me. I'd do it again, knowing what I do now. You need rest, good food, and the services of a doctor. You'll have them at the ranch. I want us to have a healthy baby, love."

"I'm no longer sure there's going to be an *us!*"

Sarah fumed in silent rage. She wanted to rant at Chad but he seemed disinclined to argue.

"I want to ride my own horse," Sarah said.

"Very well, but only if you promise not to bolt back to Cunning Wolf's camp. We need to get home as soon as possible."

Sarah realized the wisdom of Chad's words, but they didn't make her any less resentful. She wanted to withhold her promise, but knew Chad wouldn't hesitate to follow her if she took off on her own. Ultimately her rashness could hurt Abner. She feared for Abner's life should Chad fail to return with the cows in the allotted time.

"I promise," Sarah said, glaring at Chad.

Chad dismounted, then helped Sarah from his horse and onto hers. "We have to make up for lost time," he told her. "I'll set the pace. If you can't keep up or feel ill, be sure and let me know."

Sarah nodded grimly as Chad kneed Flint forward. They rode for several hours. By the time Chad called a halt to rest the horses, Sarah was reeling in the saddle. She was pale as death. Had she food in her stomach, she would have lost it long ago.

Chad retrieved his bedroll and placed it on the ground for Sarah to sit on. Her pallor frightened him and he remembered the sack of herbs Spotted Deer gave him. In minutes he had gathered a handful of dry twigs and started a fire in a pit he'd scraped out of the snow. He heated snow in the beat up coffeepot he carried with his supplies and added a pinch of dried herbs to the boiling water. He let it steep a few minutes, then poured it into a battered mug and handed it to Sarah.

"Here, drink this. If it settles your stomach, you

can try a piece of Indian bread and some jerky later. Later I'll hunt for fresh meat for our supper."

Sarah stared at the dark liquid with aversion. "How do I know Spotted Deer isn't trying to poison me?"

"You don't. But I think she realized you were pregnant and was trying to help. Indians have been using remedies like this since before whites came to America. I don't think she'd poison you. If she did, she'd have me to deal with."

He offered her the cup and Sarah took it between her palms. The warmth was comforting. She held it a moment before lifting it to her lips and drinking deeply.

"Let me know when you feel like you can eat something," Chad said. "You're as thin as a rail."

He settled down beside her, placing his arms around her in an attempt to shield her from the wind. She stiffened against him and pulled away. She was still too angry with him to suffer his touch. Continuing to sip the tea, Sarah was amazed that it actually did seem to settle her stomach. By the time the cup was drained, she was ready to attempt the bread and jerky. She really *was* hungry. For the past few days she'd been afraid to eat food she didn't recognize.

"I think I can eat something now," she told Chad.

Chad gave her a grin and a hug and handed her a stick of jerky and a piece of bread. She bit off a tiny hunk of bread, gnawed at the jerky, swallowed, and waited for her stomach to rebel. When it didn't, she finished off every morsel Chad had placed in her hands.

"Do you want more?" Chad asked. "It looks to

be bringing some color into your cheeks."

"Not now."

"Then I reckon we'd best be on our way. I hope Major Dalton hasn't moved his camp."

He helped Sarah to mount, jumped astride his own horse, and broke a trail through the snow. Sarah followed close behind. They continued on until dusk, then Chad found shelter beneath a protected ledge and placed their bedrolls side by side in front of the fire he had built for warmth. Then he wandered off, returning a short time later with two plump rabbits. That night they dined on roasted rabbit, washing it down with strong coffee. When Sarah offered to clean up, Chad declined. He finished up quickly and joined Sarah, who was already half-asleep.

Chad rolled over to take her into his arms, frowning when she resisted. When he persisted, she pushed him away. "I don't want you to touch me, Chad. I don't even like you anymore."

"You don't mean that, sweetheart. You're angry right now, but that will change when Abner is back with us again. It won't be long, you'll see."

"No, Chad, I don't see. All I know is that you took me away from my son."

"An Indian camp is no place for a pregnant woman. You're no strapping Indian squaw who can drop a baby and walk ten miles in the same day. You're delicate and more fragile than you think."

Now Sarah really was angry. "I'm not at all delicate. I'm strong. How do you think I survived all these years?" She didn't appreciate Chad's assumption that she was weak simply because she was a woman.

"Why can't you understand my concern for you? I love you, for God's sake! Your pregnancy makes you doubly precious to me. I'd die if anything happened to you or to our child." When he withdrew his arms from around her, she suddenly felt cold.

"Your judgment is flawed," Sarah charged.

"Very well, Sarah, if that's the way you want it. But I'm not going to let you pull away from me. Go to sleep. Tomorrow promises to be a long day. Pray that it doesn't snow."

Chad arose before Sarah, brewed her tea, and made her drink it before she was fully awake. A few minutes later her stomach was settled enough to accept a hunk of dry bread.

"I hope Major Dalton is still camped nearby," Chad said as he helped Sarah to mount.

"Maybe he has taken his men back to the fort," Sarah replied hopefully.

"We'll find out soon enough."

As it turned out, they found out sooner than expected. They met Major Dalton's column late that afternoon, heading in the direction of Cunning Wolf's camp. Dalton halted his troops and waited for Chad and Sarah to approach.

"Delaney," Dalton greeted, "we meet again. And I see you found your fiancée. I must admit, I had my doubts. I'm sorry about the boy. By now he's probably out of my jurisdiction. I'll wire authorities to be on the lookout for him when I return to Fort Ellis. They might be able to intercept Jackson."

"Much obliged, Major," Chad said evenly. He didn't want to let on that he knew where Abner was. A confrontation between Cunning Wolf and the army could end in disaster for the boy. Sarah would never forgive him if that were to happen.

"Has your mission been successful?" Chad asked.

"Almost. We found Yellow Dog a few days ago and convinced him to return to the reservation. We located Snake just yesterday. He was a little harder to convince, but he finally saw it our way. It won't be long before we track down Cunning Wolf and send him back where he belongs."

Chad sent Sarah a silent warning when she made a strangled sound deep in her throat. "That won't be necessary, Major. We ran into Cunning Wolf and his people yesterday. They appeared to be headed back to the reservation. We hid behind some rocks until they passed so they wouldn't see us."

"Are you sure?" Dalton asked sharply.

"As sure as I can be. There appeared to be sickness within their tribe. Perhaps they were going back to seek medical help from the reservation doctor or from their own medicine man."

"Sickness? Could it be smallpox?" The men behind him stirred uneasily. "The disease has been spreading like wildfire among the Indians. Few of my men have had smallpox themselves and are scared to death of it. Are you sure of what you saw?"

"I know what I saw," Chad lied. It seemed as if he'd hit a raw nerve when he'd mentioned illness.

"Did you see the same thing, Miss Temple? Was Cunning Wolf heading back to the reservation with his sick?"

Sarah wasn't very good at lying. She always stuttered when she did. "I . . . yes, I mean, it appeared th-that way."

Dalton appeared not to notice her hesitation as he mulled over the information he'd just been given.

"If what you say is true, I think we can safely assume that Cunning Wolf will cause us no more trouble. Smallpox is a terrible disease, it could decimate his entire tribe. I think I'm justified in taking my men back to the fort. I don't want to expose them unnecessarily to disease. Can we assist you and your fiancée in any way, Delaney?"

"Much obliged, Major, but we'll be home in a day or two, providing the weather cooperates."

"Good luck to you," Dalton said. "I hope you find your son, Miss Temple." Reining his horse around, he returned to the head of his patrol.

Sarah nearly collapsed with relief. "At least we don't have to worry about a clash between Dalton's troops and Cunning Wolf."

"No, but we have something else to worry about," Chad said, glancing up at the lowering sky.

Sarah followed Chad's gaze, gasping in dismay when she saw ominous dark clouds gathering below towering snow-capped mountain peaks. New snowfall could slow them down, preventing Chad from meeting the deadline set by Cunning Wolf.

That night they slept in a cavelike opening carved out between two boulders. This time Sarah didn't protest when Chad took her into his arms. She was so cold she didn't think she'd ever be warm again. Although she was grateful for the fire Chad had built, and the shelter he had found, she still found it difficult to forgive him. Oh, she knew his motivation, but that still didn't make it right. Chad might think she was going to marry him but Sarah was no longer sure it was what she wanted.

It had taken her a long time to learn to trust Chad and he had damaged their tenuous relationship, perhaps irrevocably.

The world around them was clothed in white when they awakened the next morning. Sarah gazed around her in wonder. The earth appeared new and pristine, almost like a rebirth. How could anything so beautiful be so treacherous?

Chad stirred up the fire and asked if Sarah wanted a cup of Spotted Deer's remedy. Sarah sat up, felt bile rise in her throat, and nodded. The water in the coffeepot was already boiling as Chad dropped in a pinch of herbs to steep. A few minutes later he brought Sarah a mug filled with the fragrant liquid and watched as she drank it.

"Can you go on?" Chad asked with concern. "Dammit, Sarah, I get mad whenever I think about you taking off after Jackson by yourself. That's my baby you're carrying."

Sarah closed her eyes and let the hot liquid soothe her. When she opened them again she felt better able to cope with Chad's anger. "Hashing over this is getting us nowhere. What's done is done. I'm here, I'm pregnant, and I'm not going to lose this child. Besides," she added, glaring at him, "it's my child. I'm the one who will nurture him for nine months. I can raise him alone, just as I did Abner."

"By taking in laundry?" he asked sarcastically.

She saw the rapid pulsebeat at his throat, and the quick darkening of his eyes, and she knew he was angry. Her chin lifted to a stubborn angle. "If I have to."

"Like hell! You're going to marry me. We'll raise our child together and that's the end of it. Are you ready to go on? I want to reach home by tomorrow."

Sarah wondered how she could have thought she was in love with Chad. He was overbearing, domineering, and arrogant. And he felt no remorse over striking her. Her jaw still bore the imprint of his fist.

"What are you thinking, sweetheart?" Chad asked when Sarah continued to brood in silent rage.

"You don't want to know. Is there any rabbit left from last night?"

"Getting our appetite back, are we?" Chad teased as he handed her a piece of stale bread and a hunk of meat he'd warmed over the fire.

Sarah disregarded his question as she bit into the meat. She'd ignore him altogether, if she could. But without Chad she had virtually no hope of getting Abner back. For now she needed him, but that didn't necessarily mean she'd always need him. He'd have to earn her trust once more, and the way she felt now, it wasn't going to be easy for him.

Snow continued to fall intermittently throughout the day. It was light and fluffy and without substance, which thankfully didn't impede their progress. The wind remained calm until shortly before dusk, when it began to bluster. They had waded through several drifts when Chad calmly informed her that they were on Delaney land. Sarah wanted to collapse on the spot, but she continued on through sheer grit and determination.

Sarah spied the lights from the house through the blowing snow. The welcome sight brought tears to her eyes. She knew she couldn't have gone on much further and thanked God for bringing her this far without mishap. They rode into the barn. Sarah dismounted and leaned against a stall while Chad unsaddled their weary horses. She started out of the barn and was suddenly overcome by a terrible weakness. The space around her began to spin and her knees buckled beneath her. She started a slow spiral to the ground and knew nothing more as blackness closed around her.

From the corner of his eye, Chad saw Sarah stagger and begin to fall. He reached for her, handily catching her before she touched the ground. Charging out of the barn, he carried her through the swirling snow to the back door and kicked it with his foot until Cookie came to open it.

"Chad! You've brought Sarah back. Praise the Lord. We heard that the soldiers from the fort were out chasing renegade Indians who had left the reservation to raid ranches and steal cattle. When Sarah didn't return home, Ryan figured she must have gone on alone, knowing the army would be of no help to her until the renegades were rounded up. We were worried sick. Ryan blames himself for what happened."

Cookie's mouth was going so fast it took a moment for him to realize that Sarah lay unmoving in Chad's arms. He peered at her anxiously. "Is she all right?" Then he noticed that Abner wasn't with them and his eyes grew misty. "I reckon you didn't find Abner. Poor little lad."

"I'll tell you all about it later. Sarah's exhausted. I'm taking her up to bed. We both need something nourishing in our stomachs. Can you rustle up something for us?"

"Darn tootin', I can."

"Fix Sarah something light. Her stomach is too fragile for regular fare. Indian food didn't agree with her."

"Indians! Well, if that don't beat all. Get Sarah to bed, Chad. I'll be waitin' anxiously for that explanation."

Chad headed for the stairs. Ryan met him at the top, leaning heavily upon crutches. "Chad! I thought I heard your voice." His gaze settled on Sarah's lifeless form. "Is Sarah all right? We've been worried sick about her. Where did you find her? Is Abner with you?"

"Later, Ryan."

Ryan moved aside as Chad hurried past him, then followed his brother into Sarah's room. "What's wrong with Sarah?"

"I'll explain later. I want to get her into bed. If you can negotiate the stairs, meet me in the kitchen. After I've settled her, I'll tell you and Cookie everything."

"Is she going to be all right?" Ryan asked anxiously.

"I certainly hope so." Carefully he placed Sarah on the bed and removed her coat and shoes. When he began unbuttoning her dress, Ryan beat a hasty retreat.

Chad worked swiftly. In minutes he had Sarah naked and into her flannel nightgown. She barely stirred as he pulled the covers over her and tucked her in. A moment later Cookie stuck his head in the door. "Grub is ready. Do ya want it up here?"

"I think Sarah needs rest more than food right now. I'll eat in the kitchen. Maybe later she'll take some broth or something more substantial."

Ryan was waiting for Chad in the kitchen. He

twitched impatiently as Chad tore into thick slices of roast beef left over from supper, biscuits, gravy, and several cups of hot coffee. When Chad indicated he was full, Cookie produced a huge piece of chocolate cake and he dug in with gusto.

"I've never seen anyone eat so much," Ryan said, staring at Chad's empty plate.

"Trail food gets pretty monotonous."

"Tell us about the Indians," Cookie urged as he pulled out a chair and joined the brothers at the table. "We heard that renegades were wandering the area. Did Sarah run into savages?" He sobered suddenly, his face screwed up as if he wanted to cry. "Sarah must be devastated about the boy. Damn shame."

"Chad, about Abner," Ryan began. "I don't know what to say. I'm entirely to blame for his abduction. I should never have left the ranch."

"I'll admit I was damn upset with you when I learned about Abner's abduction. What's done is done, Ryan. The important thing now is to return with the ransom in time to rescue Abner."

"Ransom?" Ryan asked, bewildered. "I don't understand. Is Jackson asking ransom for Abner's safe return?"

"I'd better start at the beginning," Chad said. "I was returning to the ranch when I ran into a patrol from the fort. Major Dalton told me that Sarah had been to see him, and that he had been unable to supply men to help find Abner because Indian trouble in the area required all his troops. He said that Sarah ignored his warning and went on alone, despite the danger and recklessness of her venture."

"I would expect nothing less from Sarah," Ryan

intoned dryly. "She'd do anything for her son. What happened next?"

Chad launched into the tale of how he had found both Sarah and Abner at Cunning Wolf's camp, and backtracked to when he'd first met the chief's daughter.

"Cunning Wolf plans to remain at his camp until the cows arrive, then he's going to take his people to Canada. They're in desperate need of food and warm blankets to last through the worst of the winter. He intended to ransom Sarah and Abner to the army for cows and blankets. I feared a confrontation and offered to pay the ransom myself."

"How did you manage to get them to release Sarah?" Ryan asked.

"Sarah's been ill. Cunning Wolf let her leave, but he demanded that Abner remain behind until I return with the ransom."

"I'm surprised Sarah would leave her son behind."

"Leaving Abner behind wasn't my idea. Chad knocked me out and carried me away against my will."

Three pairs of eyes shifted to the doorway, where Sarah, clad in nightgown and robe, leaned against the doorjamb. She looked ghastly. Chad jumped up to steady her as she lurched into the kitchen. He pulled out a chair and eased her into it.

"What are you doing out of bed?"

She stared deliberately at his empty plate. "I smelled food. I'm hungry."

Cookie leaped to his feet. "How about a bowl of chicken soup, Miz Sarah? Made it specially for you."

"Sounds wonderful, Cookie."

Sarah devoured two bowls of soup and a cup of tea before she sat back, seemingly sated.

"Feel better?" Chad asked with concern. Sarah had survived an ordeal that would have defeated most women. Her pregnancy hadn't made things easy for her.

"Yes, thank you," she said coldly. Deliberately she turned away from him. "Have you heard about Abner?" she asked Ryan.

"Chad told us. Did my brother really hit you?"

Sarah turned her face so he could see the fading bruise. She opened her mouth to speak, but Chad forestalled her.

"I did it for her own good. I wouldn't hurt Sarah for the world. She refused to leave without Abner, and you can see for yourself that she's been ill. I was desperate to get her home. We'll have Abner back with us in no time."

"What can we do to help?" Ryan asked. "Damn, I wish I could go with you, but my leg won't be out of this cast for several more weeks. Take as many men as you need."

"I'm sending a man to town tomorrow to purchase every blanket he can get his hands on. The others can help me cut ten cows from the herd. I want everything ready the day after tomorrow. I'll take two men with me to drive the cattle and another to drive the wagon containing the blankets, supplies, and feed for the cows. They might not be able to forage beneath the snow for grass. I have nine days in which to meet Cunning Wolf's deadline."

No one asked what would happen should Chad fail, but Chad could tell from their grave expressions that they understood the situation. Cunning Wolf might not kill Abner, but he'd take the boy away and they'd never see him again.

"I'll be ready to leave when you are," Sarah said, fixing Chad with a look that defied him to deny her.

"Like hell!" Chad shouted. "You're not stepping foot outside this house until I return with Abner."

Chapter 19

"Cookie and I will leave you two to hash this out," Ryan said as he adjusted his crutches and rose clumsily to his feet.

Cookie leaped up to help him and they left the kitchen together. Neither Sarah nor Chad seemed to notice as they continued to glare at one another.

"You're staying here, Sarah, that's my final word," Chad bellowed. "I won't have you chasing around the countryside in the dead of winter in your condition."

"Leave my condition out of this, Chad. We're talking about my son. Abner needs me. I want to be there for him."

"You're going to be *here* for him and that's final."

Sarah's protest ended in a squawk when Chad rose abruptly, scooped her up from the chair, and carried her out of the kitchen, through the parlor, and up the stairs.

"Damn you! What do you think you're doing?"

"You belong in bed. You've been living under harsh conditions for two weeks and you're exhausted. I won't let you expose yourself to danger again. There's no way, Sarah, no way you're going to leave this house until I say so."

Chad kicked open the bedroom door, carried her inside and placed her on the bed. Then he backed away, sending her a look that begged for her understanding.

"What are you going to do?" Sarah asked, glaring up at him.

"Make damn sure you stay in bed where you belong."

On his way out, he slipped the key from the lock and put it in his pocket. He didn't lock her in yet, but he would when the time came. She'd left him no recourse. It was the only way he could be assured that Sarah wouldn't follow. Despite her bravado, Sarah wasn't strong enough to undertake another journey in the dead of winter.

"Have you and Sarah settled things between you?" Ryan asked when Chad joined his brother and Cookie in the parlor.

"Not yet," Chad said grimly. "She's determined to return with me to Cunning Wolf's camp. The little hellion is too damn stubborn for her own good. A woman in her condition should be coddled. She shouldn't be exposing herself to danger or running around in weather fit for neither man nor beast."

"Exactly what 'condition' are you referring to, brother?"

Dropping into a chair, Chad, so weary he could have fallen asleep then and there, closed his eyes. "You may as well know. Sarah is expecting our child."

"Damn!" Ryan swore. "Had I known, I would never have left the ranch that day. No wonder she's ill. I won't let you down this time, brother."

"Neither will I," Cookie promised. "Are you sure Jackson is no longer a threat to Sarah?"

"As sure as I can be. I told you that he and Sanchez are Cunning Wolf's prisoners. Spotted Deer didn't strike me as a forgiving woman. She won't forget what he did to her. Now if you'll both excuse me, I'm going to bed." He heaved himself to his feet.

"What are you going to do about Sarah, brother?" Ryan wanted to know. "She's having your baby."

"I know, and I'm going to fix things as soon as I return. I've asked Sarah to be my wife."

"She didn't look none too happy with you tonight."

"I can't blame her," Chad said as he headed for the stairs. "She objected to leaving Abner with the Indians. I've never seen her so angry. She'll come around once Abner is back home where he belongs."

Chad climbed the stairs slowly. He paused before Sarah's closed door, then opened it quickly and stepped inside. Glowing embers in the hearth provided ample light as Chad settled his gaze on Sarah's face. He saw that her eyes were open and he stepped into the room, closing the door behind him. "Are you all right?"

"I could be better," Sarah said sullenly. "What do you want?"

Chad crossed to the bed and sat down beside her. "Don't be angry, sweetheart. Not when I've finally buried my demons and realized how much I love you."

"You have an odd way of showing love, Chad

Delaney. I'll never forgive you for taking me away from Abner."

Chad sighed tiredly as he pulled off his boots and dropped them one by one to the floor. His stockings followed.

Sarah stared at him, alarmed. "What are you doing?"

"Getting ready for bed. We're both tired. This bed is going to feel mighty good after sleeping on the cold ground for so long." He stood abruptly, shed his shirt and trousers, and pulled back the blankets. "Scoot over, love."

Sarah opened her mouth to protest, realized it would do her no good, and moved to the opposite edge of the bed. "I don't want to sleep with you. I don't even like you anymore."

Chad paid her scant heed as he climbed into bed and pulled the covers over him. "I want to be near you. Don't worry, all I'm going to do is hold you in my arms. I wouldn't dream of disturbing you tonight, not after everything you've been through." His voice lowered to a husky whisper. "I can't bear the thought of sleeping apart from you. After we're married . . ."

"We're not going to be married," Sarah said, swallowing past the lump in her throat.

She turned her back on him, stiffening her spine against the powerful seduction of his words. She had no willpower where Chad was concerned. When his arms closed around her, she made a weak effort to escape the comfort he offered, but he wouldn't allow it. Sarah sighed in reluctant surrender. The knowledge that she didn't want to escape made submission all the more galling.

"Go to sleep," Chad whispered into her ear.

Sleep proved elusive for Sarah. She was too worried about Abner and too angry at Chad to relax. What if Cunning Wolf had taken his people elsewhere and Chad couldn't find him? So many things could happen to her son before Chad's return to Cunning Wolf's camp. Just considering the consequences should Chad fail to reach the camp within the allotted time was frightening.

Thoughts of Abner's plight sent tears flowing down her cheeks as she sobbed quietly into her pillow. She should be with him, comforting him as only a mother can. Chad had prevented her from protecting her son and she couldn't forgive him for that. After all the disappointments she'd suffered in life, she thought she'd finally found a man worthy of her love. But her future no longer looked promising. Trusting Chad had been a mistake. Loving him a tragedy.

Chad was gone the next morning when Sarah awoke. When she dressed and went downstairs, Cookie told her that Chad and the hands had gone to round up the cows he had promised Cunning Wolf. She was pushing her breakfast around the plate with her fork when Ryan hobbled into the kitchen.

"Did you and Chad patch up your differences?" he asked, lowering himself into a chair.

"What Chad did was unforgivable," Sarah said, laying her fork down and frowning at Ryan. "And then he's going to make it worse when he leaves in the morning."

"I reckon it's for your own good, Sarah. He'll take good care of Abner."

"Abner's a little boy. He needs his mother."

"Traveling in wintertime is dangerous. You've another child to consider now."

Streaks of red colored Sarah's cheeks. "Chad told you about the baby?"

Ryan had the grace to flush too. "There is little Chad and I don't share. It was the same with Pierce before he married. You have to admit that having a baby is a serious undertaking for both you and Chad. That's one reason I'll never marry," Ryan contended. "I don't want the responsibility of a wife and family. Playing the field is more my style."

Sarah barely listened as Ryan rambled on. She was still seething at the callous way Chad had revealed her secret to his brother. The least he could have done was ask her permission to divulge her secret. She hoped Ryan didn't expect her to marry Chad. She'd already had one child out of wedlock. She supposed that having another couldn't do any further damage to her reputation.

Suddenly Sarah turned a peculiar shade of green as the same vile morning sickness she'd been experiencing the past couple of weeks returned with a vengeance. Bile rose in her throat and she swallowed convulsively.

"Would you be needin' this, Miz Sarah?" Cookie asked, noting her sudden pallor. "Chad asked me to brew up some of them herbs he gave me yesterday in case you needed them this morning." He handed her a cup.

"Thank you," Sarah said as she took a sip of the soothing tea. "It does seem to help."

"Now you know why Chad wants you to stay home," Ryan contended. "You can't travel while heaving your guts out every morning."

"Your concern is gratifying," Sarah said sarcastically. Ryan made her sound weak and incompetent. She'd managed fairly well on her own until Chad came along and disrupted her life. "Pregnancy is a natural condition, the sickness will pass in a few weeks."

"But until it does, you're better off at home where we can take care of you."

"Excuse me," Sarah said, pushing up from the table. "I think I'll return to my room. The tea seemed to work wonders."

"That's one stubborn woman," Ryan remarked after Sarah left. "We're going to have our hands full trying to keep her from following Chad. Cookie, if I ever get notions about taking a wife, just remind me of the problems Pierce and Chad had with their women."

"Why do you think I never got hitched?" Cookie said, slapping his knee and chuckling. "It's gonna be kinda nice havin' a little one around, though. Can't wait to spoil the tyke."

Sarah didn't see Chad again until he returned late that night and let himself into her room. She would have locked the door on him but couldn't find the key. He looked so tired, though, she almost forgot how shabbily he had treated her.

"Everything is ready. We're heading out at first light tomorrow," Chad said as he sat heavily upon the bed.

"I'm going with you," Sarah insisted.

"You're staying here." Chad's tone brooked no argument. "It's bitter cold outside. The snow isn't deep right now, but that could change tomorrow, or the next day. Montana winters are unpredictable."

Sarah thought it best not to argue. She didn't want to rouse his suspicion. She knew what she was going to do and no one was going to stop her.

Chad undressed quickly and climbed into bed. Before Sarah could move away, Chad captured her in his arms and brought her against him. "You feel so good," he whispered as he nuzzled her cheek. "And you smell good, too. I never believed it possible to want a woman the way I want you."

"It's too late, Chad," Sarah said, trying to push him away. "I don't want you." To Sarah's disgust, her body didn't agree with her mind and she knew Chad sensed it.

"I want to love you, Sarah."

"I don't think that's a good idea. It's not what I want."

"I think it is," he said. Suddenly he frowned and placed a splayed hand over her stomach. "Will it hurt the baby? If I recall, Pierce and Zoey had a rather active love life while she was increasing."

"It won't hurt the baby, but that doesn't mean . . ." Her sentence ended in a gurgle of surprise as Chad's mouth converged on hers.

He kissed her ravenously, showing her without words how much he loved her, how sorry he was to have hurt her, and how desperately he needed her right now.

His kisses were potent reminders of Sarah's attraction for Chad. His roving hands and soft lips made it difficult to resist the need pounding through her. She tried, truly she did. But the clamoring of her blood and furious beating of her heart destroyed her will, making her even more resentful of Chad and the effect he had upon her. He had besotted her mind until she fancied herself in love with him. Now her mind refused to believe she no longer loved or wanted him.

"Let me," Chad said as he raised her nightgown and kissed a trail of fire to the sensitive crests of her breasts.

Sarah forgot to breathe as his lips closed around an aroused peak and he suckled her. She made one last effort to defy his seduction, and when that failed, she gave a small cry of surrender and arched up against him.

"Sarah . . . Sarah . . ." He sighed her name as he spread her legs and thrust into her.

Sarah tried to deny her love for this exasperating man, attempted to control her response, but failed miserably. Chad was touching her in places, both inside and out, that made her body sing and her blood boil. She felt her soul leaving her body; she was a mass of tingling nerve endings and skin so sensitive Chad's merest touch set her to trembling. Then she shattered, crying out from the sheer beauty of it.

Chad held onto his control by sheer dint of will. He was so near to the edge he could feel his seed rushing toward final culmination. When Sarah went to pieces beneath him, he set himself free, grasping her thighs and raising them to his shoulders, opening her to his furious stroking. Then he was there, crying out her name as his seed filled her.

Sarah knew that no other man could ever affect her like Chad. He had but to touch her and she was his to do with as he pleased. Freddie Jackson had hurt her in the worst possible way, but Chad had driven all the pain from her mind and heart. She wasn't a sinner like her parents claimed. She was a mother who loved her son intensely. And she would love this child just as fiercely. Deep in her heart, she knew she loved Chad, too.

Chad watched the play of emotions on Sarah's face. She was so transparent he could almost read her thoughts. He prudently refrained from intruding upon her silence as he held her in his arms, content with the knowledge that she would be safe when he left tomorrow. Then he felt Sarah relax against him and knew she had finally fallen asleep. Only then did he seek his own rest.

Sarah awoke with a start, dismayed to find that Chad had already left her. She glanced out the window at the hazy gray dawn and realized she had overslept. She wasn't too worried. She'd have no trouble catching up with Chad and the slow-moving cows. She rose swiftly and dressed in her warmest clothing. Then she reached for the doorknob, stunned when the door refused to budge. She spit out an unladylike oath, enraged at Chad's devious methods to control her.

He had locked her in! How dare he.

Sarah pounded on the door until her knuckles bled. No one responded. She cried and cursed, to no avail. She should have known Chad would do something despicable like this. He'd been deaf to her pleas, ignoring her need to be with her son. And to think she'd actually been softening toward Chad. No one, absolutely no one, was going to keep her from her son.

Cookie unlocked the door to bring her breakfast a short time later. Sarah sent him a venomous look and turned away. "Take the tray away. I'll eat downstairs in the kitchen."

Cookie gave her a soulful look. "Sorry, Miz Sarah, Chad's orders. You can take supper downstairs with Ryan this evening. But you're to be locked in your room again tonight. Chad ain't takin' no chances this time. He don't want to worry about you tryin' to follow him. You'd best eat somethin'. I brewed you some tea, drink that first."

He left before Sarah's scathing reply left her mouth. She heard the key turn in the lock and felt the uncontrollable urge to pick up the tray of food and toss it at the closed door. Clenching her fists, she forced a calm she didn't feel. Whether she liked it or not, she was stuck in this room, and when she was finally released it would be too late to catch up with Chad. She should have anticipated that he'd try something like this and been prepared to deal with it. There was nothing for her now but to sit home and pray that Chad reached Abner in time, and that he found the boy in good health.

Chad found travel agonizingly slow. Driving cows, even a small number of them, during winter was time-consuming and difficult. Chad was kept busy digging them out of the drifts and prodding them to maintain a steady pace. Fortunately the weather held. Though no new snow had fallen, the wind at times whipped what snow there was into a fine froth, while the temperatures were manageable, but barely. Still, Chad kept to his pace.

Despite his efforts to remain focused on the trail, Chad couldn't help but wonder about Sarah. He regretted having to lock her in her bedroom, and feared it would adversely affect their faltering relationship. He had wanted to keep her safe and would do it again if he had to. Still, he couldn't help glancing behind him, fearing that Sarah would somehow outsmart her brother and Cookie and follow him. When three days passed with no sign of Sarah, Chad allowed himself to breathe easily again. If nothing drastic happened in the next several days, he would reach Cunning Wolf's camp with time to spare.

"The camp is just beyond those trees up ahead," Chad told Murray as they herded the cows along a narrow trail. Suddenly several braves burst from the trees, surrounding them on all sides. Chad greeted them calmly but warily.

Chad hissed a warning when Murray and Clem shifted nervously in their saddles and looked as if they wanted to bolt. "Don't be frightened. All they want are the cows." Then he spied Spotted Deer and rode forward to meet her.

"Come no further," Spotted Deer said, raising her hand to stop them.

"What is it?" Chad asked in alarm. "Where is Abner?"

"There is sickness in the camp. It came on suddenly. One of our people must have caught the spotted sickness before we left the reservation and told no one for fear of being left behind. It spread swiftly. Many have died."

Chad paled. "Smallpox. What about Abner? Is he . . . Has he . . ." He couldn't say the word, let alone think it.

"Abner is sick, but he still lives. I have been treating him with herbs and ancient remedies. He is strong; he will not die."

"What about Sarah? Could she still fall ill from the disease?"

"I believe Sarah is safe. She did not mingle with us like Abner did."

Chad allowed himself to breathe again. "Are you sure Abner will recover?" If anything happened to Abner, Sarah would never forgive him.

"I have done everything in my power to save him. I will bring him to you."

"That won't be necessary. I've already had smallpox. I will get him myself."

Spotted Deer nodded and trotted off.

"Wait here," Chad told his companions. "I'm going to get Abner." He took off through the trees after Spotted Deer as the Indians took charge of the cows and wagon.

Few people were in sight as Chad entered the camp. The ill were unable to move from their beds, and those who were well nursed the sick. Chad found Abner lying on a pallet in Spotted Deer's tipi. He dropped to his knees and brushed damp strands of hair from Abner's forehead. His pale face was covered with tiny eruptions and he moved restlessly upon his pallet. Abner opened his eyes when Chad lifted him into his arm.

"You're here," Abner said weakly. "I've been waiting. Where's Mama?"

"Waiting for you at home. I'm taking you away from here, son. We'll be home in no time."

"I'm sick, Chad. Am I gonna die?"

Chad forced a smile. "No, you're not going to die. I won't let you."

"The wagon has been unloaded and fitted with a pallet for Abner," Spotted Deer said.

"A wagon will slow us down. You keep it. I need to get Abner home as quickly as possible." He ducked outside and handed Abner to Spotted Deer.

After he mounted, he held out his arms for the boy. "What about Jackson and Sanchez?" he asked as he settled Abner on his thighs. "I'd like to turn them over to the law."

Spotted Deer's expression hardened. "Fred-die cheated me of my revenge. He was one of the first to die of the spotted sickness. I wanted to peel the skin from him strip by strip, but it was denied me. Sanchez died yesterday. They are beyond the law now."

"It's just as well," Chad said, feeling no remorse over their deaths. Jackson had put Sarah and Abner through hell. "What will you and your people do now?"

"When our sick recover, we will journey to Canada, where we can live free. The cows will feed us until we reach our new hunting grounds, and the blankets will keep us warm."

"May your journey lead you to peace," Chad said, eager to be off as he nudged his horse into motion. With luck and good weather on his side, he would reach home soon. He prayed that Abner would survive the trip.

"He's back!" Cookie cried, rushing into the kitchen to inform Sarah and Ryan. "He just rode into the yard."

"Is Abner with him?" Sarah asked, leaping to her feet.

"He sure is," Cookie grinned. "Come see for yourself."

Sarah grabbed a wrap and ran out the door. Ryan followed more slowly, hindered by his crutches. She skidded to a halt when she saw Chad dismount with Abner in his arms. Abner was so still Sarah knew immediately that something was wrong, dreadfully wrong. She ran out to meet them.

"Stop her!" Chad shouted. "Don't let her come any closer."

His words stunned Sarah. She faltered, inadvertently allowing Ryan to catch up with her.

"What is it?" Ryan asked. He was having trouble restraining Sarah and motioned for Cookie to help.

"Smallpox," Chad said grimly. "I know you've had smallpox, Ryan, but I don't know about Sarah or Cookie."

Sarah tried to break free, but failed. "I've not had smallpox, but . . ."

"Then you can't come near," Chad warned. "What about you, Cookie?"

"Not that I know of, Chad."

"Then Ryan and I will be the only ones allowed in Abner's room until he's fully recovered."

Sarah couldn't believe her ears. It wasn't enough that Chad had separated her from Abner, now he wanted to keep her away from her son's sickbed. "You can't do that!" she all but screamed at him.

"Be reasonable, Sarah," Chad pleaded as he carried Abner into the house. "You've a responsibility to your unborn child. If you catch smallpox, you'd harm an innocent child. Think about it."

Ryan held Sarah securely as Chad disappeared inside the house. Sarah was wild with worry. Her child was sick and needed her. If she didn't already hate Chad, she would now. Garnering her strength, she twisted out of Ryan's grasp and rushed after Chad. She arrived too late. Chad had already reached Abner's room and closed the door to her. Undaunted, Sarah grasped the doorknob, fully intending to disobey Chad's orders and care for her son herself. Her intentions were thwarted when she found the door locked against her.

"Damn you, Chad Delaney! You can't keep me away from Abner. Let me in!"

"I sent Murray to town for the doctor," Chad called through the door. "Don't worry, love, I won't let anything happen to Abner."

When it became apparent that Chad wasn't going to let her inside the sickroom, Sarah slid down the length of the door to the floor. She wasn't going to move until Chad let her in. Ryan stayed with her but didn't try to move her. Two hours later, Doctor Adams arrived and found her huddled against the door with Ryan sitting beside her.

"This is Doc Adams, Sarah," Ryan said, helping her to her feet. "He's going to take care of Abner. Move away so he can go inside."

"Thank God you're here," Sarah said on a sob. "I'm Sarah Temple. Abner is my son. Chad won't let me in the room."

The rotund doctor gazed at Sarah with compassion. "Let me go in first, Sarah. If I think it's safe for you to go inside, you'll be allowed in immediately. Am I right to assume you've never had smallpox?"

"Yes, but . . ."

"Ryan said you're pregnant."

Sarah slid Ryan a reproachful glance. "That's true, but . . ."

"Let me be the judge of matters pertaining to health," the doctor said kindly.

Chad must have heard voices in the hallway, for he appeared in the open doorway and motioned the doctor inside. Before Sarah could follow, the door closed in her face and the key turned in the lock. "Damn you, Chad," she muttered darkly.

"Cookie has a pot of coffee going, why don't you go down to the kitchen and wait. You're not accomplishing anything up here," Ryan said.

"I can't accomplish anything down there, either," Sarah said crossly. "I want to see Abner. I'm his mother, Ryan. Why can't anyone see that he needs me? This wouldn't have happened if Chad hadn't taken me away from Abner against my will."

"Now that's downright stupid," Ryan chided. "You could have done nothing to prevent this. Besides, you might have fallen ill yourself. Think of the consequences, Sarah. Chad did the right thing."

Sarah turned away, refusing to bandy words with Ryan. Chad and his brother were cut from the same fabric; she expected them to stick together.

As the minutes ticked by, Ryan was unable to coax Sarah from the hallway outside Abner's closed door. She paced restlessly, hardly noticing when Ryan gave up and returned downstairs. A good hour passed before the door opened and Doctor Adams stepped into the hallway to speak to Sarah.

"How is he, Doctor? Can I go inside now?"

"Abner is holding his own, Sarah. He's young and healthy. I expect him to make a full recovery. Chad is doing a fine job of caring for him."

"Chad isn't his mother. I want to see Abner."

"I'm afraid that's impossible. Abner is still contagious. I've left medicine and instructions for its use. And I've instructed Chad to bathe the lad with a baking soda mixture to ease the itching. We don't want Abner to carry scars the rest of his life, do we?"

"How long are you going to keep me from my son?" Sarah asked, refusing to be humored.

Suddenly the door opened and Chad stepped into the hallway. Sarah ignored him.

"Until Abner's no longer contagious," the doctor said. "Two weeks, perhaps longer, depending on Abner's progress. There's nothing more I can do right now, so I'll leave Abner in Chad's capable hands. Send someone to town for me if the lad takes a turn for the worse," he called over his shoulder.

That's all Sarah had to hear. She made a mad dash for the bedroom. Chad stepped in front of her. "For once in your life follow orders, Sarah. I don't know what I'd do if anything happened to you or our child. Smallpox is a serious illness. You're going to have to trust me to take care of Abner."

"Trust you!" Sarah spat. "I don't even like you, Chad Delaney. Unfortunately I have no choice in the matter. You're all I have right now. Until Abner is out of danger, I'm going to park myself outside this door, so get used to it."

"You'll make yourself sick," Chad warned. "Dammit, Sarah, I love you. You're carrying my child. I'd do anything to protect you and our children. Once we marry, Abner will be as much mine as the new baby you carry. I've gone through hell to work through my demons. I wouldn't have succeeded without you. I'm not going to lose you no matter how difficult you make this for me. However," he warned, "if you try to get into Abner's room, I won't hesitate to have you forcibly restrained."

"You can't . . ."

He stopped her complaint with a kiss. He kissed her until her head spun and her blood thickened. Until she melted against him, forgetting everything but the heat and hardness of his body, until she forgot exactly why she was angry with him.

Chapter 20

Sarah broke off the kiss while she could still recall her own name. She had been seduced by Chad's intoxicating kisses before and knew how fatal they were. She didn't want to fall in love with him all over again. She couldn't bear the pain of loving him.

"Sarah," Chad murmured when Sarah pushed away from him. "Don't do this to us."

Sarah sighed and gave him her back. Her words were crisp and to the point. "I'm going downstairs to see about getting some broth for Abner. He needs plenty of nourishing liquids to strengthen him until he can take solid food."

Chad watched her walk away, sick at heart and unable to do anything about it. If he had to play the villain in order to keep Sarah from catching smallpox, then so be it.

Sarah was pleased to learn that Cookie already had a pot of chicken broth simmering on the back of the stove. She sat down to wait for it while Cookie bustled about the kitchen preparing supper for the family.

"You missed lunch, Miz Sarah. Would you like a sandwich to hold you over till supper?"

"I couldn't eat a thing, Cookie. Perhaps later. Do you suppose the broth is finished yet? I'd like to take it up to Abner now."

"You can take it to the door and no further," Cookie warned.

"I know," Sarah said, disheartened. She had finally resigned herself to the fact that she wasn't going to see her son until he was no longer contagious.

Sarah languished in profound anxiety during the following days. She knew Abner was feeling better when the sound of his voice drifted to her through the closed door. Doc Adams returned twice. The second time he had pronounced Abner out of danger and praised Chad and Ryan for taking such good care of the lad. Abner continued to be contagious, however, and Sarah was still barred from his room. Though she talked to him through the door, it wasn't the same as seeing his dear little face.

Sarah saw little of Chad during the days and nights he spent nursing Abner. Chad and Ryan had taken turns sleeping on a cot in Abner's room. On the rare occassions she encountered Chad, she thought he appeared drawn and exhausted.

Sarah had no complaints about the care Abner was receiving. She couldn't have done better herself. But it was galling to have to depend on others to do things she should be doing herself. She still believed a mother's care was the best medicine, and she fumed ceaselessly at being denied access to his room. But more importantly, she should have been with Abner when he had first fallen ill. She was still upset with Chad for forcing her to desert her son. True, she might have become ill herself, but she'd been willing to risk exposure to the disease for Abner's sake.

One evening Chad joined her for supper. He was freshly shaven; his hair had been trimmed and was wet from a dunking. He looked tired but happy as he took a seat at the table.

"I hope you cooked a lot, Cookie," Chad said, eyeing the pot roast sitting on the stove. "I could eat a good-sized steer tonight."

"I didn't cook the whole steer, but I don't think you'll go away hungry," Cookie said with a twinkle. He set the dish on the table with a flourish, revealing a succulent cut of beef surrounded by potatoes, turnips, and onions.

Chad's mouth watered as he sliced the beef into man-sized slices. "You've outdone yourself, Cookie." He placed a slab of beef, along with a portion of potatoes and turnips on Sarah's plate, then served himself.

"I'll take something up to Ryan," Cookie said as he filled a plate and departed.

"Is Ryan with Abner?" Sarah asked, toying with the food on her plate.

"It's Ryan's turn to stay with the boy tonight," Chad said. "Actually, Abner is well enough to get up now. He's made a remarkable recovery. We're all pleased with his progress."

Sarah leaped from her chair, her face suffused with joy. "Does that mean I can see him now?"

"I suspect it does, but the final word has to come from the doctor. He'll be out tomorrow. I know how anxious you are, sweetheart, but one more day isn't too much to ask, is it?"

"One minute is too much!" Sarah exclaimed. "I'm going up there now."

"Ryan won't let you in. Sit down and enjoy your supper. You're eating for two, remember?"

"How could I forget?" Sarah said bitterly. "If I wasn't carrying this child, I wouldn't have been denied my son." She touched her stomach. "This baby has brought me nothing but grief."

Chad's face contorted with anguish and his eyes went cold. Sarah saw and wanted to call back her words. She'd been overwrought and worried and hadn't been aware of what she was saying. Her words had tumbled out before she realized what she'd said. She wanted this baby. She loved it already, and she'd be as fiercely protective of it as she was of Abner.

"I'm sorry my baby is such a burden to you," Chad said with cool disdain. "After it's born, you may leave it with me and go wherever you please. I'd prefer to keep Abner, too, but unfortunately I have no say in his future."

Leave her baby? Sarah shuddered at the thought. "No one is taking my children from me," she said fiercely.

"We'll see. Finish your supper. I know you don't care for my child, but I intend for you to deliver a healthy babe." His expression hardened and he turned away.

Sarah knew exactly what he was thinking and it frightened her. She couldn't let Chad revisit the past, to succumb to those terrible demons that had plagued him for so long. He'd fought a fierce battle to banish them and she prayed that her careless words wouldn't return him to his former state of self-loathing.

Sarah managed to consume enough food to satisfy Chad. From the corner of her eye she watched him chew and swallow his own dinner, his fork moving mechanically from his plate to his mouth. Sarah wondered if he tasted anything as he stared off into space.

"Chad, I didn't mean what I said about the baby. I've been upset, you know that."

Finally he looked at her, but Sarah wished he hadn't. His eyes were dark with pain and shadowed with disillusionment. She hadn't seen that particular look in a long time. Not since the day they had visited the Doolittle house and made love on Cora Lee's bed.

"You hate me, don't you, Sarah? And you hate my child. I made you leave Abner with the Indians and kept you away from him during his illness for a very good reason. Why can't you understand that? I should have learned my lesson where women are concerned. Trying to do what is right never pays off. I listened to my heart instead of my head. Love is for fools, and I'm the biggest fool of all." He pushed his chair away from the table.

"Chad, wait! I don't hate you. I could never hate you. Pregnant women often say things they don't mean."

Chad sent her an inscrutable look, then turned away. "Good night, Sarah."

Speechless, Sarah watched Chad stride from the room. She was stunned at the change in him. It was true that Chad had taken her from her son and kept her away during his illness, but she realized now that he had been right to do so. God, what had she done to him? How could he believe she hated him when she was crazy in love with him? No other man would have nursed Abner back to health as tirelessly and with as much compassion as Chad. Only a stupid woman would become upset with a man who had done so much for her. He'd dragged her from the depths of poverty and despair, even though he was fighting a battle of his own at the time.

Cookie walked into the kitchen, took one look at Sarah, and poured her a fresh cup of coffee. "Are you all right, Miz Sarah?"

Sarah shook her head. "I'm afraid not, Cookie. I've been stubborn and foolish and realize now that I said things I didn't mean. I don't think Chad will ever forgive me."

"I thought Chad looked a mite green around the gills when I passed him in the hallway just now. You can always make things right."

"I might have gone too far this time," Sarah said on a sad little sigh. "I owe Chad so much."

"He don't want your gratitude. I can't tell you what to do, Miz Sarah, but I sure would hate to see Chad lose all the ground he's gained since he returned to Dry Gulch."

"Thanks, Cookie," Sarah said as she scraped her chair back and rose. "I'm going to try to undo the harm I've done. I hope it's not too late."

Sarah remained thoughtful as she climbed the stairs to her room. She undressed by lamplight, donned a nightgown, shoved her bare feet into slippers, and sat down in the windowseat to contemplate her next move. She'd acted hatefully toward a man to whom she owed her very existence. She'd flung words at him she regretted and didn't know how to make amends. Chad deserved her gratitude, not the sharp edge of her tongue. She wouldn't blame him if he wanted nothing more to do with her.

This tension between them couldn't go on, Sarah decided as she opened her door and stepped into the hallway. Their problems would only grow worse with each passing day, widening the gap between them until it was too large to mend. She searched her heart and discovered that her love for Chad was secure, that it had never really been in jeopardy. She prayed they still had a future together, and hoped her careless words hadn't destroyed Chad's love for her.

Chad lay in bed, arms folded behind his head, recalling every word Sarah had spoken in anger. Sarah didn't want their child. She hated him. She had flung those words at him too many times for him to disbelieve them. He'd been crazy to think his life had changed for the better, that he'd found a woman he could trust . . . one he could love, one who'd love him in return.

Of one thing Chad was certain. Sarah wasn't going to take his baby with her if she left. No child of his was going to be called a bastard. He'd force her to marry him for the child's sake. Then, if she wanted to leave without her child, he wouldn't stop her.

Chad's ruminations were so distracting he didn't hear the metallic click as the door opened and closed, or the soft footsteps approaching. He sensed Sarah's presence before he heard or saw her. His head turned toward the door, peering through the darkness to find her.

Sarah stepped into the pool of moonlight spilling through the window. "Are you awake?"

Chad sat up, his gaze riveted on the slender figure poised in a beam of golden moonlight. "What are you doing here?"

"I . . . I want to talk."

"I'm listening."

"You're not going to make this easy for me, are you? About tonight . . ." She shivered and hugged her arms across her breasts. "I didn't mean what I said."

Exasperated, Chad heaved a sigh and held up a corner of the blanket. "You'd better get under the covers if you intend to make this a lengthy visit."

He moved over and she slid beneath the blanket, pulling it to her chin. "I'm still listening," Chad said coolly. "To what do I owe the pleasure of this visit? If you're going to tell me you hate me, don't bother. I've heard it countless times in the past few days."

"I've been a fool."

Chad's eyebrows spiked upward. "Like hell! I thought I was the fool."

"Maybe we've both been a little foolish. You've been my salvation and my rock. I don't know what would have become of Abner and me if you hadn't walked into our lives."

Chad snorted in derision. "You wouldn't have an unwanted baby in your belly if I hadn't walked into your life."

Sarah found his hand and placed it over her stomach. It was still so flat he found it difficult to believe a new life was growing inside her.

"We made this baby together, Chad. I don't regret it. I believe it was conceived that day we made love in Cora Lee's bed. The day you banished your demons for good."

Chad reached over to the nightstand and struck a match to the kerosene lamp. Light flared, and he searched her face in the revealing glow. "What is it you're trying to tell me, Sarah?"

"I love you, Chad. Nothing will ever change that. I tried to hate you, but when I searched my heart I found nothing but love for the caring, compassionate man that you are. I don't want you to go back into your shell because of words spoken in anger." She touched his face in a gentle caress. "You're the best thing that ever happened to me and Abner. I'd be a fool to leave you."

"I wasn't going to let you leave me," Chad confessed. "No matter how much you professed to hate me. You're carrying my baby. Even if you couldn't love it, I was prepared to love it enough for both of us.

"I don't regret taking you away from Cunning Wolf's camp. You could have caught smallpox and died." That horrifying thought made him shudder. "I could have lost you."

"You're never going to lose me. You promised Abner a complete family. I can't wait to see him. Do you think the doctor will allow me inside his room now that he's nearly recovered?"

"I'm certain he will. I'm sorry for the anguish I caused you."

"You have nothing to apologize for, not after the way you took care of Abner in the sickroom. I couldn't have done better."

A heady sigh rushed past Chad's lips. "I was so afraid you'd leave me, sweetheart. I feared I'd never hold you in my arms again, or make love to you."

Chad's arms came around her, cuddling her against his chest, reveling in the sweet warmth of her pliant body. He groaned as she moved sinuously against him, molding them together, breast to breast, thigh to thigh. Shifting to make a space between them, he trailed his fingertips across her stomach, moving lower, delving into the fine curling hairs between her legs. He traced the outer edge of the triangle, then slid into the moist folds of her female flesh.

"Oh Chad, yes," Sarah said on a sigh. "Love me. Please love me."

"Let's get rid of this first." Deftly, he pulled off her nightgown and tossed it aside. Then he simply stared at her, his heated gaze slowly traveling the length of her body. He rubbed his knuckles against her tender nipples, then he began to knead her breasts, pulling and lifting them to his hungry mouth.

Sarah whimpered in delight as he drew a nipple between his lips and suckled her. She touched a kiss to his chest, then slid her hand down to stroke his hardening manhood. He retaliated by caressing the aching flesh of her ribs, belly, hips, and thighs. He stroked every inch of her he could reach as she pleasured him with her hands. Her titillating rhythm kept him on the sharp edge of passion as he panted and groaned in an effort to control the savage instinct to spew forth his seed.

His eyes reflected his erotic agony as he lifted his head from her breasts and fastened his mouth on hers, his tongue delving deeply into her sweet warmth. He shifted between her legs and her thighs opened wide in loving welcome. He could feel the throbbing of her body as he probed against her wet entrance. Then he drove inside, jerking her hips against him. He nearly lost it as she arched up sharply, drawing him deeper into her hot center. Buffeted by elemental emotions ripping through him, his movements grew fierce, uncontrolled. Then she cried out, clenching him as if trying to absorb all of him into her body.

The wildness of her response, the bold thrust of her loins against his, were almost more than Chad could bear. His hands tightened fiercely around her hips as he plunged in and out, the violent friction of their joining sending him toward mindless oblivion. He was painfully swollen, ready to burst, and he hung on through sheer dint of will.

Sarah was nearly insensate with pleasure. Her body thrummed, her heart pounded, and her skin burned. Her blood thickened and pooled in the place where they were joined. The violent roar of pleasure reverberated like thunder in her ears. Then she was soaring upward, reaching blindly for the most incredible rapture she'd ever experienced. When she reached that lofty paradise, she hung on for dear life and waited for Chad to join her.

"I'm coming!" he cried as he raced to catch up. He held her tightly as his own release tore through his body.

They rested briefly. The next time they loved, Sarah was the aggressor. She kissed him all over, teasing him unmercifully, her hands, lips, and mouth moving over him in loving exploration. When she closed her lips over the rounded tip of his staff, he arched up violently, nearly toppling her off the bed. With a fierce growl, he carefully removed her and settled her atop him. She opened her thighs and he slid inside. Once again they found that place where only lovers dared to venture.

Chad awoke with a smile on his face and was smiling as he quietly dressed and went downstairs to join Ryan and Cookie in the kitchen the next morning. Cookie poured him a cup of coffee. Chad sipped the scalding brew, unable to wipe the smile from his face.

"You seem in good spirits this morning," Ryan remarked. "Did you and Sarah make up?"

"You could say that. How was Abner's night?"

"The boy is well enough to leave his bed," Ryan said. "He's asking for his mother. I came down to get his breakfast. He's suddenly found his appetite."

"Doc Adams will be here today. He'll probably give Abner a clean bill of health and free rein to do as he pleases within reason. Sarah is anxious to see him and I can't blame her."

"When is the weddin'?" Cookie asked out of the blue.

"As soon as Abner is well enough to attend. I'd like Pierce and Zoey to be there too, if it's at all possible."

"You might have to wait till spring if you want Pierce to come," Ryan said. "Winter's not over by a long shot. There's more to come."

Chad frowned. "If the weather won't cooperate, I reckon we'll do it without Pierce. I don't want to wait till spring."

Ryan shook his head in mock disgust. "I never thought you'd marry, Chad. Pierce's marriage came as a surprise but yours is a shock, considering your aversion to the state of wedlock. No woman is going to hogtie me," he vowed. "I can get all the loving I want from a woman without putting a ring on her finger."

Chad tried to hide his amusement. Ryan had no idea what love did to a man. "When you fall, brother, you're going to fall hard. Mark my words. I pity the woman who sets her sights on Rogue Ryan."

"So do I," Ryan smirked. "It's not going to do her a damn bit of good. I'm not as gullible as you or Pierce, though I'll be the first to admit you've both found good women. Probably the only two left in the world."

"Say, ain't that Doc's buggy comin' down the lane?" Cookie said, glancing out the window. "He's makin' his rounds early today."

Doc Adams entered the house in a blast of frigid air. "It's damn cold outside," he said as he shed his coat. "How's my patient today?"

"Hungry as a bear and eager to leave his bed," Chad said. "And he wants to see his mother. I can't hold Sarah off much longer."

Doc chuckled. "Thought that might be the case. Well, let's have a look at him."

Sarah awoke to the sound of voices in the hallway. She cracked open her bedroom door and saw Doc Adams and Chad entering Abner's room. She washed and dressed and left Chad's room in a rush. Skidding to a halt at Abner's door, she was somewhat reluctant to enter without an invitation. She was more than a little surprised to see the way opened to her.

Abner saw her standing in the doorway and his face lit up. He called out to her. The sound of his voice released her feet and she flew across the room, scooping him up into her arms and hugging him fiercely.

"Too tight, Mama," Abner said when her hugs became too exuberant. "I'm not sick anymore. Doctor Adams said I'm not 'tagious, either."

Sarah searched Abner's face. A few scabs remained where the pustules had been, and he appeared to have lost some weight, but otherwise he looked wonderful. "I've missed you so much."

Doc Adams stepped forward, smiling at the poignant sight of mother and son reunited. "Abner is no longer contagious," he said. "The lad can leave his bed, but I suggest he take it easy for awhile. Feed him whatever appeals to him."

"Thank you, Doctor," Sarah said tearfully.

"Thank Chad, here, he's the one who nursed the boy through the rough parts."

Chad gave her a cheeky grin. "She already did thank me. I hope you won't mind taking a look at Sarah before you leave, Doc. I want to make sure everything is all right with the baby."

"I'd be happy to. Show me your room, Sarah, we'll conduct the examination there." He turned to Chad. "You *will* invite me to the wedding, won't you?"

"You can count on it. I was just waiting for Abner to recover to fetch the preacher out here."

"You're gonna be my papa," Abner said proudly.

"You bet, son. I meant it when I said we'd be a family."

* * *

Sarah received a clean bill of health from the doctor. Assured of Chad's love and with Abner well beyond his illness, she'd never been happier. She thought briefly of her parents. Had there been no estrangement, her joy would have been complete. Since she couldn't make her parents love her, she contented herself with the knowledge that she had Chad's love in abundance.

During the following days Chad gave no indication of allowing his demons back into his life, which eased Sarah's mind considerably. Only one jarring note marred her joy. Chad hadn't mentioned marriage again. She hoped he wasn't having second thoughts about making her a permanent part of his life.

One gray morning about a month later, Chad went to town for supplies. He kissed Sarah goodbye, hitched the horses to the buckboard, and left immediately after breakfast. Doc Adams was due out that day to take the cast off Ryan's leg and Sarah couldn't imagine what was so important in town that couldn't wait until tomorrow. Chad was acting so mysterious about his errand that she spent the rest of the morning wondering at his strange behavior.

Doc Adams arrived later that day. He removed Ryan's cast and pronounced his leg strong enough to bear his weight. For some strange reason he seemed in no hurry to leave as he chatted with Ryan over coffee. Delicious aromas were wafting from the kitchen and Sarah was surprised to find Cookie dexterously engaged in a frenzy of baking. Abner was sitting on a stool at the table, stirring frosting. Neither gave her a second glance when she looked in on them, so she retreated back to the parlor.

A short time later the entire Zigler family converged upon them for a visit. Things really got hectic when Pierce, Zoey, and Robbie arrived unexpectedly.

Sarah was beginning to suspect something was afoot when Chad blew into the house on a cold wind, accompanied by a man he introduced as Parson Higgens. Bewildered, Sarah glanced around the crowded room. Abner was jumping up and down with excitement and she suddenly realized she was the only one unaware that this was to be her wedding day. She sent Chad a fulminating look, but apparently it did little to dampen his high spirits.

Then Zoey grasped her hand and dragged her upstairs to her room. Sarah let out a gasp of dismay when she saw a lovely cream silk creation that was to be her wedding dress spread out on her bed.

"How . . . ? When . . . ?" Sarah's eyes misted. She had never seen anything so lovely.

"I brought it," Zoey said. "I never had a wedding dress myself and wanted you to have one. I purchased it for you as soon as Chad sent word about the wedding. I hope you like it."

"It's beautiful. You're all wonderful. Why didn't Chad tell me?"

"He wanted it to be a surprise. He wasn't sure we'd make it, but the mild winter we're having made it possible for us to be here. We owe you so much, Sarah. We all feared Chad was lost to us after that tragedy. It broke our hearts when he left. You and Abner gave him his life back. He had another surprise planned, but I guess it didn't work out the way he hoped. Never mind," Zoey said brightly. "We're your family now, never forget it."

Zoey and the Zigler girls helped her into her dress and fixed her hair. When they finished, they stood back to admire their handiwork.

"You're beautiful," Zoey said wistfully, recalling her own hasty wedding. "I would have been married in denims and plaid shirt if Pierce hadn't insisted I wear a dress. I'll go down and tell them you're ready."

Chad and Abner were waiting for her at the foot of the stairs. Chad's eyes were warm with love as he watched her descend.

"Are you surprised, Mama?" Abner asked gleefully. "Chad told me not to say anything."

"You keep a secret well, son," Chad said, giving Abner's narrow shoulder a squeeze. "Take your mother's other arm, the parson is waiting for us."

The parlor was packed with smiling faces. While she was upstairs dressing more people had arrived, including the family who had purchased the Rocking D.

"Are you happy?" Chad whispered as they approached the parson.

"Ecstatic," Sarah said, giving him a blinding smile. "If only . . ." A shadow darkened her eyes, then quickly vanished. "Forget it," she said cheerily. "Your family is all I need."

When they had reached the parson, Chad squeezed her hand. "Shall we begin, Parson?"

The parson opened his Holy Book, but before he could begin, a late wedding guest arrived. Ryan opened the door. The woman standing on the doorstep appeared ready to turn and run. Then she spied Sarah. With a muffled sob, she rushed forward.

Rendered speechless, Sarah's shock was such that she could do little more than stare at the woman. Chad gave her a hug of encouragement and her ability to speak returned.

"Mama!"

"I didn't know if she'd come," Chad said. "I wanted to give you a day you'd remember forever. I hope you're pleased."

"I love you, Chad Delaney."

Sarah and her mother shared a brief hug and the promise for a longer visit, then the parson began the ceremony. A short time later she was Chad's wife, and so happy she couldn't stop smiling. The rest of the day passed in a blur. Through it all, Chad remained her rock. He was with her when Hazel Temple explained how Chad had sent one of the hands to fetch her for her daughter's wedding, along with a letter from Chad explaining things she'd never known before.

"Your father wouldn't come," Hazel said with a sad little shrug. "He's too inflexible in his beliefs and too proud to admit he misjudged you. I pray he'll come around one day," Hazel said hopefully. "Can you forgive me, daughter? Your father put you through hell and I was afraid to speak up in your defense. It wasn't until you left town that I realized what I had lost."

"I forgive you, Mama. I hope you can stay awhile to get to know your grandson."

"I'll start right now," Hazel said brightly. "Where is the little scamp?"

When Hazel went off in search of Abner, Chad grasped Sarah's hand and pulled her away from the crowd. "Let's get away from here," he said, giving her a smile filled with wicked promise. "I told Ryan to leave our meals outside our door for the next week."

Sweeping her into his arms, he took the stairs two at a time. He carried her into their room and slammed the door shut behind him with a resounding bang.

"I love you," he whispered seconds before his mouth covered hers. "Let the honeymoon begin."

Epilogue

Summer 1883

Sarah pulled the row of diapers off the clothesline and stuffed them into the basket. Before she carried them into the house, she cast about for a glimpse of Abner and saw him playing with the puppy Chad had bought him a few days after their daughter Amanda was born. Chad hadn't wanted Abner to feel left out by the attention given to the new baby and had surprised the boy with the playful pet.

With the passage of time Sarah was learning more and more about the caring man she had married. He could deny his compassionate nature all he wanted but nothing would change the fact that he was kind and thoughtful, a man who put the happiness of others before his own.

Sarah hummed to herself as she carried the basket into the house and began folding Amanda's diapers. Life was wonderful. With the addition of her tiny daughter, their family was perfect. Of course she wouldn't mind having another child or two sometime in the future.

"What are you thinking about?" Chad asked as he walked into the room and gave her a quick hug. "You look like a kitten that just swallowed a bowl of cream."

"I'm happy," Sarah said. "I keep pinching myself to see if I'm dreaming."

Chad grinned at her. "I'm living a dream every time I wake up with you in my arms."

Sarah gave a wistful sigh. "I wish Ryan could find the kind of happiness we have. There are times when he looks so lonely my heart goes out to him."

Chad snorted in derision. "Rogue Ryan lonely? Every eligible and not so eligible woman in town has her cap set for him. He has his pick of any female he wants."

"It's not the same," Sarah contended. "Everyone needs a 'special someone' in their life. By the way, where *is* Ryan?"

"Gone to town for the mail. He should be back soon. I just came to tell you I'll be mending fences in the north pasture the rest of the day. Tell Ryan he can join me when he returns."

"You can tell me yourself," Ryan said, ambling into the room.

"You're home. Good," Chad said. "We can pick up something from the kitchen for lunch and leave right away. Any mail?"

"There's a letter from Sarah's mother." He handed Sarah the missive and she sat down to read it. "And this one is addressed to Pa. It's from Bert Lowry, remember him?"

Chad's brows puckered, trying to recall the name. Apparently Bert Lowry didn't know their father had died several years ago. "He's that old army buddy of Pa's, isn't he?"

"The very same," Ryan returned. "I reckon no one told him about Pa. He owns a ranch near Tucson. Here, read the letter yourself."

Chad pulled the letter from the envelope and perused it slowly. "Well I'll be damned. Bert is searching for his long-lost daughter and wants to know if Pa can spare one of his sons to help find her."

"Bert says he's dying and wants to see the girl before he leaves this world," Ryan added. "There's a lot Bert left out, but I reckon I'll find out when I see him in person."

"You're going to Tucson?" Chad said, surprise coloring his words. "Why not just write and tell him Pa is dead and none of us can be spared?"

"I want to go, Chad. You and your family can use some time alone, and the women in Dry Gulch are starting to bore me." He gave Chad a cheeky grin. "Thought I'd find out for myself if Arizona women are any different from Montana women."

"What about the ranch?"

"What about it? I ran it alone for the two years you were gone, now it's your turn. We've got a good crew of experienced hands; the ranch can almost run itself. I'll find Bert's little girl, try out the women between here and Arizona, and return when I've had enough. Maybe I'll appreciate the ranch better after a vacation."

Chad was aware that Ryan had been restless of late, but until now hadn't realized just how restless. Ryan wasn't consumed with ranching like Chad and Pierce, and Chad couldn't fault Ryan for wanting to experience more of life than what the ranch had to offer.

"You're no detective, Ryan. Bert said he'd already hired a detective, and the man learned little beyond what Bert already knew."

Ryan shrugged. "I'd like to give it a shot. What can I lose?"

Sarah had finished reading her mother's letter in time to get the crux of the conversation. She was saddened by Ryan's intention to leave, but not surprised. She, too, had sensed a restlessness in Ryan, that's why she'd been eager for him to find a special woman to love.

"We'll miss you, Ryan," she said with feeling. "It won't be the same here without you."

"I doubt you'll miss me too much," Ryan said with a twinkle. "You two have eyes for no one but each other. It's downright sickening."

"When are you leaving?" Chad asked.

"In a day or two. I'll need to make arrangements with the bank to have funds available to me during my absence. I'm thinking of riding down to Cheyenne and taking the train to Tucson."

"Be careful," Sarah said.

"It's a rough world out there, Ryan," Chad warned. "Take my word for it. The two years I spent drifting from town to town, chasing outlaws and collecting rewards for their capture, were enlightening in the extreme. Ranching is tame compared to what you're likely to find."

"Don't worry about me, Chad," Ryan said jauntily. "I can take care of myself."

His words hung in the air like a heavy layer of smoke as he strode from the room.

"I've got a bad feeling about this," Chad mused, frowning.

"Ryan's only a year younger than you, Chad,

he'll be fine. It's the women between here and Arizona I pity," Sarah teased.

"I reckon a man's got to spread his wings," Chad allowed. "I did, and look what I found. A woman who cared enough about me to overlook all my faults. You captured my heart so thoroughly I thank God every day for bringing us together and giving me a son and daughter dearer to me than my own life."

"I love you, Chad Delaney. I wish there was some way I could show you how much I appreciate you."

Chad's smile held a wealth of promise. "You can, sweetheart. Instead of mending fences, let's you and I go upstairs."

"Abner . . ."

"I saw him go off to the stables with Murray."

"Amanda . . ."

"Is sleeping. Any other excuses?"

"I never did have any willpower where you're concerned." She lifted to her tiptoes and kissed him full on the mouth.

It was all the permission Chad needed. Scooping her into his arms, he raced up the stairs.

Author's Note

I hope you enjoyed *To Tame a Renegade,* the second book of the Delaney trilogy. The town of Carbon, Wyoming, no longer exists. At the time my story took place, the town was just as I described it. Around the turn of the century the mines played out and eventually Carbon disappeared from the map.

If you enjoyed *To Love a Stranger* and *To Tame a Renegade,* watch for *To Tempt a Rogue,* due on shelves fall 1999. *To Tempt a Rogue* is Ryan Delaney's story. Rogue Ryan lives up to his nickname as he travels the West in his search for the daughter of his father's old friend. But he meets his match in Kitty Jackson. You'll have to read the book to learn exactly how Kitty tempts Ryan into doing something he's vowed to avoid at all costs. Can it be marriage?

I enjoy hearing from readers. For a bookmark and newsletter, write to me in care of Avon Books at the address on the copyright page. Please enclose a #10, self-addressed, stamped envelope.

All My Romantic Best,

Connie Mason

Author's Note

Dear Reader,

Next month, there are so many exciting books coming from Avon romance that I wish I had two or three pages to talk about them all! But I only get one page, so I'll get right to it.

October's Avon Romantic Treasure is *A Rake's Vow,* the next in Stephanie Laurens' scintillating series about the wickedly handsome Cynster family. Vane Cynster has vowed to never marry, no matter that his cousin Devil has just tied the knot. But once he meets the very tempting, delectable Patience Debbington he decides that some vows are meant to be broken.

Kathleen Harrington's *Enchanted by You* is for anyone—like me—who loves a sexy Scottish hero! When dashing Lyon MacLyon is saved by Julie Elkheart he can't help but tell her how much he wants her—in Gaelic. But pretty Julie understands every scandalous word of love that this sexy lord says...

What if you could shed your past and take another's identity? In Linda O'Brien's *Promised to a Stranger* Maddie Beecher does just that, and discovers she's "engaged" to a man she's never met. Trouble is, she falls hard...for her "fiancé's" brother—enigmatic Blaine Knight. And when Maddie's past catches up with her, she must decide if she should tell Blaine the whole truth.

And if you're looking for a sexy hero to sweep you off your feet—and fix your life—then don't miss Elizabeth Bevarly's delicious Contemporary romance *My Man Pendleton.* When a madcap heiress runs off to Florida, her rich father sends Pendleton after her...but he never thinks his wayward daughter will fall in love.

Until next month, enjoy!

Lucia Macro
Lucia Macro
Senior Editor

AEL 0998